Praise for KRON⬛ ⬛⬛⬛⬛ ⬛GUE

KRONOS RISING: PLAG⬛ ⬛⬛⬛ *⬛r (horror category)*

—AUTHORSdb

"The entire horror universe now has a new writer . . . a delightful edge-of-your-seater, guaranteed to leave readers wanting to keep the lights on."

—YeahStub.com

"Max spins another harrowing, action-packed monster tale, painstakingly researched, and rich in scenic and historic detail, while delivering the same true-to-form, page-turning intensity as always."

—The Crypto Crew

Praise for KRONOS RISING: DIABLO

"Kronos Rising: Diablo, one of 2016's Top Ten Books!"

—AUTHORSdb

". . . the story retains Max Hawthorne's uncanny ability to make his monsters feel like characters in their own right, as well as his innate aptitude when it comes to invoking a sense of awe and wonder in the reader."

—Geek Ireland

"A riveting offshoot of the wonderful Max Hawthorne books, *Kronos Rising* and *Kraken*! Keeps the excitement and momentum of those stories going strong! More, more, more!!"

—Kevin Sasaki, Media Representative

Praise for KRONOS RISING: KRAKEN (vol. 1)

"It's *Jurassic World* on steroids . . . a fun, fast read even if you have to take the kids to the ball game and mow the lawn."

–Kevin J. Coolidge, From My Shelf Books

"*KRONOS RISING: KRAKEN* (vol. 1): 2016's People's Choice Award Winner & Book of the Year!"

–Geek Ireland

"Hawthorne's writing evokes a sense of awe and terror, tapping into a deeply-rooted and primal fear of the unknown. The Kraken possesses an otherworldly aura which is hard to describe, but it really makes your skin crawl."

–Sean Markey, DinoGuy

"While most authors would have played it safe and stuck to a formula emulating the successful elements of the first novel (think the "Meg" series), Hawthorne's vision is cast on a larger canvas. KRAKEN jumps ahead 30 years into the future, depicting a worldwide ecological shift in earth's oceans as a consequence of the events in the first novel. Hawthorne certainly knows how to tell and pace a fine adventure tale, in the tradition of Robert E. Howard."

–Richard Reagan, Cryptomundo

Praise for KRONOS RISING

". . . a master class in the suspension of disbelief. Kronos Rising is reminiscent of the work of Michael Crichton (Jurassic Park, Congo) in that it weaves together an exciting and gripping yarn which, despite depicting fantastical subject matter, doesn't insult the reader's intelligence by appealing to the lowest common denominator."

–Krank.ie

"*KRONOS RISING* by Max Hathorne; 2014's PIX Book of the Year!"

–Prehistoric Times Magazine

"Batten down the hatches and brace yourself . . . Hawthorne delivers suspense at a breakneck pace in his terrifying debut."

–Ryan Lockwood, Author of *Below*

"A word to the wise: if you bite your nails, you'd better wear oven mitts when reading *Kronos Rising*. It will drag you down to the depths of fear and take you back for a breath of air as fast as you can turn the pages. Readers beware: a new Master of Marine terror is in your bookstore, and his name is Max Hawthorne!"

–Stan Pottinger, NY Times Bestselling author of *THE BOSS*

"Kronos Rising takes readers on a roller coaster ride of gigantic scale. We're talking prehistoric big."

–Toledo Free Press

". . . a great addition to this genre, worthy of sitting on the shelf next to Peter Benchley's *Jaws*."

–Publisher's Weekly/Book Life

". . . a fabulous debut by Max Hawthorne. Simply put, it's got teeth. Big ones!"

–Chris Parker, screenwriter
(*Vampire in Brooklyn, Battle of the Year, Heaven is for Real*)

"What a ride! An adrenaline pumping, non-stop descent into terror, *Kronos Rising* will do for this generation what "JAWS" did for the last one. Forget going *into* the water; I'm not going <u>near</u> it!"

–Mara Corday, sci-fi classic star of *Tarantula, The Black Scorpion*, and *The Giant Claw*

Praise for MEMOIRS OF A GYM RAT

"Max Hawthorne's raunchy, revealing memoir is certain to induce bouts of calorie-burning laughter, embarrassed grins, and reconsiderations of one's gym membership. A smutty and enjoyable exposé of life behind health club doors, *Memoirs of a Gym Rat* is both a scandalizing and edifying read."

–Foreword Clarion Reviews

Kronos Rising:

KRAKEN

(VOLUME 2)

A Novel

Max Hawthorne

FAR FROM THE TREE PRESS

Kronos Rising: KRAKEN (Volume 2) is a work of fiction. Names, characters, places, and incidents are either the products of the author's imagination or are used fictitiously. Any resemblance to actual persons, living or dead, events or locales, is entirely coincidental.

Copyright: © 2005 (original) © 2017 by Max Hawthorne (extended and revised)

ISBN-13: 9781732378513
ISBN-10: 1732378517

All rights reserved. No part of this book may be used or reproduced in any manner whatsoever without written permission, except in the case of brief quotations embodied in critical articles or reviews. For information contact: *Far From the Tree Press, LLC.*

Published in the United States by: *Far From the Tree Press, LLC.*

Visit *Far From the Tree Press, LLC* online at: www.farfromthetreepress.com

Manufactured in the United States of America

First Edition

Sale of this book without a front cover may be unauthorized. If this book is coverless, it may have been reported to the publisher as "lost and destroyed" and neither the author nor the publisher may have received payment for it.

For Ava, my light in the darkness "when all other lights go out."
Daddy loves you, Peanut.

"Whoever fights monsters should see to it that, in the process, he does not become a monster. And when you look long into an abyss, the abyss also looks into you."
–Friedrich Nietzsche
Beyond Good and Evil

ACKNOWLEDGMENTS

It is with tremendous pride and humility that I acknowledge the following individuals for their support and/or contributions to this book.

Before anyone else (and this is something I should have done years ago), I wish to express my gratitude to the indefatigable Kenneth "Ken" Atchity: author, producer, and founder of *The Writer's Lifeline*. Interacting with the editor Ken assigned to me for my book, *Memoirs of a Gym Rat*, shone a bright light on the assorted "holes" in my writing style – holes which I quickly shored up. I became a far more formidable writer as a result. Thank you very much, Ken. If you were Dr. Frankenstein, I would definitely be one of your "monsters".

As always, my heartfelt appreciation to my intrepid publishers over at *Far From the Tree Press*. As an indie author, it's great to have free rein to let my imagination run wild; the size and scope of my stories are all the better for it.

I'd also like to give a big shout-out to the following *Blog Talk Radio* hosts, whose shows I've had the privilege of appearing on. This includes the incomparable Holly Stephey, over at *Red Velvet Media*; my peeps, Scott Mardis and Julie Rench, at *Monster X Radio*; Shannon "The Voice" LeGro over at *Into the Fray Radio*; and cryptozoologists Mike Richburg and Adam Davies, from *Undiscovered Beasts and Strange Phenomena*. I'm especially appreciative of the team over at ICRA, for giving me the opportunity to host my own show. It's a privilege, and I'm sure *Max Hawthorne's Marine Mysteries* is going to rock the boat – literally.

I'd be remiss if I didn't express my thankfulness to graphics artist/animator Matt LaFreniere, who not only did the animation for my plesiosaur locomotion study, but also took my roughed-out cover design for *Kronos Rising: Kraken 2* and polished it to perfection (no easy task, with me cracking my perfectionist's whip).

Also, all my best to Jason Pearce and his tireless team over at Newgen. Thanks for doing such a professional job, both on the cover and interior for *Kronos Rising: Kraken 2*. I look forward to working with you in the future. I'd also like to express my gratitude to my Grammar Nazi-slaying editor, Willis Beyer, for taking the time to review the book. Thank you very much for contributing some much-needed input, and for giving my manuscript that last bit of spit-and-polish – something that *every* novel should have (wink wink).

Last, but certainly not least, to my incredibly supportive family, my everlasting devotion. And to my readers, including the eternally enthusiastic (but not always patient) *"LEGIONS OF KRONOS,"* thank you for your ongoing patronage. You have my ongoing promise to always do my best to keep you entertained.

–*Max Hawthorne*
"Prince of Paleofiction"

ONE

'*Today is a good day to die.*'

As he stood facing the darkened observation portal that comprised much of USS *Gryphon*'s armored bow, his booted feet planted shoulder-width apart and big hands clasped behind his back, Garm "The Gate" Braddock pondered the familiar 19th century quote.

His dad had taught it to him a lifetime ago, back when he was nine.

According to Jake Braddock, it originated with Tasunka Witco, AKA "Crazy Horse", the Teton Sioux chieftain who, with his band of Lakota warriors, slaughtered General George Armstrong Custer and 267 soldiers of the 7th Cavalry on June 25, 1876, during the Battle of the Little Big Horn. Garm had always admired Crazy Horse's combat style; he was fierce and brave and rode into battle half-naked, with hailstones painted on his chest and a lightning bolt on his face.

Garm nodded grimly. Like his father who, thirty years prior, proved his valor against a host of enemies aboard the commandeered research vessel *Harbinger*, Crazy Horse had been an untamable bastard. But neither man's fearlessness had saved them from a sorry death. Jake met his end strapped to a hospital bed, shrieking his lungs out from the agonies of Cretaceous cancer, while the proud Sioux warrior took a fatal bayonet through the back, while under a flag of truce.

Garm's lip curled up in disgust. He planned to do everything in his power to ensure that, when his own demise came, it was far more . . . *worthy*.

The big sub commander's pale eyes contracted, as the red-rimmed darkness of Tartarus's "Tube" was shattered by golden beams of light that pierced the aquamarine waters around Rock Key like celestial spears. In an instant, *Gryphon*'s transparent titanium prow was transformed from an opaque, twenty-foot barrier into a portal looking in on the world's largest aquarium. Fish of every size and color fled before their bow's powerful pressure wave – a kaleidoscope of frightened marine life.

Seconds later, the heavily-armed vessel was past the curtains of kelp and seaweed that warded the Tube's gaping entrance, and heading for the nearby trench. Garm glanced at a rear-facing monitor and chuckled. Entering the submarine tunnel's craggy opening, with its beard-like blind of plants, always reminded him of ramming his 435-ton warship down Poseidon's throat. Which meant coming out was the equivalent of being vomited into the surrounding sea.

Not an altogether inappropriate metaphor for him and his crew . . .

"Captain, we're approaching Jörmungandr," Ensign Brown announced.

Garm blinked at the unexpected baritone, and the subsequent realization he had forgotten he'd assigned his secondary bridge crew duty. He was, admittedly, far more used to helmswoman Connie Ho's feminine tones.

Not that there was anything wrong with Akio Brown. The half-black, half-Japanese military brat was alert, intelligent, and a talented navigator. His only "flaw" was his ongoing attempts to bond with his captain over their shared Nipponese heritage. Garm had no problem with his own background; far from it. During his formative years, his mother made it a point to teach him everything she could about his assorted ancestors – Irish, Norwegian, and Okinawan – and he took pride in them all. He just didn't think his genetic makeup ultimately mattered. He was what he was: a six-foot-four, 245-pound, former heavyweight boxing contender, who had killed one man in the ring and crippled another, and who now hunted sea monsters for a living.

Garm didn't have his brother Dirk's dizzying intellect, nor his knack for learning and absorbing other languages. Most of all, however, he didn't give a rat's ass that Akio translated to "glorious hero" or some such nonsense.

Having your name associated with heroism wasn't like being assigned a driver's license. You had to earn it. And glory often came with a hefty price tag.

"Very well, ensign," Garm said over his shoulder. Ahead, the opening for the winding, seven-mile trough named after the mythological Norse "World Serpent" awaited them, its hundred-foot depths gouged deep into the coral and surrounding seabed. Jörmungandr gave Coastal Defense Force submarines like *Gryphon* the required clearance to traverse the Keys' notoriously shallow waters. Of equal import, it kept their comings and goings free from prying eyes.

"It's dawn and there's already traffic up there. Let's try and be unobtrusive, people. Make your depth thirty feet," Garm instructed, mentally accounting for the height of the 132-foot sub's armored sail. He thought for a moment, then added, "Speed, eight knots."

"Aye, sir," Brown said, one hand gripping the yoke while the other made quick adjustments.

Garm turned from the mixed school of Atlantic tarpon and Jack Crevalle that darted away from the ORION Class AB-Submarine and surveyed the balance of his secondary bridge crew. Ensign Juanita Alvarez was poised over Adolfo Ramirez's station, *make that sonar*, he self-corrected. The slim, 27-year-old Puerto Rican with the close-cropped coif was perky and astute, with intense eyes that never left her scopes. The fly in her five-foot-six-inch ointment was a well-earned reputation for promiscuity. That, and the fact that she was openly and overtly bisexual.

Garm had no problem with Alvarez's lifestyle choices. Indeed, from a decidedly "male" perspective, he considered them pluses. But last month, the sonar tech's decision to enter Ensign Connie Ho's shower uninvited had proven problematic. The two women quickly came to blows, and Garm had had no choice but to pull a naked and thoroughly enraged Ensign Ho off her bloodied opponent – fortunately, before the diminutive cage fighter did any real damage.

Luckily for the two women, their commanding officer preferred to handle such matters in-house. After he'd given Alvarez the bitching out of a lifetime, coupled with a 15% pay dock, the incident was redacted from *Gryphon*'s official log.

On fire control was Lieutenant Brody Blair. The hulking six-foot-two red-haired Scot was a champion powerlifter, and his 280-pound frame literally overflowed what was normally CSO Kyle Cunningham's seat. Blair certainly took up a lot of space, Garm lamented. Worse, he suffered from occasional and intense bouts of flatulence – a major problem within the cramped quarters of any submarine. On the brighter side, unlike Brown and Alvarez, he was soft-spoken and kept to himself. Unless otherwise directed, his lightly-freckled face and blue-gray eyes stayed glued to his targeting systems.

Gryphon's captain suppressed a snicker. If it wasn't for the guy's dreaded gassiness, Blair would've been the ideal Combat Systems Officer. Of course, he could never tell Cunningham that.

As his almond-shaped eyes swept communications, Garm experienced an uncharacteristic moment of trepidation. With their backup communications officer, Merle Atkins, laid up with a bad case of food poisoning, Ensign Heather Rush was stuck pulling double duty. Garm surreptitiously studied the willowy blonde as she monitored a barrage of local boat communications. Rush had followed him from command to command and, her presumed interest notwithstanding, was a dogged worker. His concern wasn't a question of skill or dependability. It was how long it would take Atkins to recover, and whether fatigue would become a factor before then. The last thing he needed was one of his primaries screwing up under combat conditions.

Garm shrugged. At least it was only communications, and not navigation or weapons. It was one of the downsides of the ORION class. As automated as *Gryphon* was, compartmental space was at a minimum. As a result, she got by with a minimal crew – her current complement was seventeen. The loss or incapacitation of even one crew member subjected the rest to undue pressure. And as any submariner would tell you, pressure was your ultimate nemesis.

"Sonar, distance to the Gate," Garm inquired.

"Two-point-six miles, sir," Alvarez replied. "We've got moderate boat traffic, bearing two-eight-eight, distance one mile. Designate: recreational vessels."

Garm nodded. "Helm, maintain speed and depth." He squashed the grin that tugged at the corners of his mouth. Often, when leaving Tartarus, he enjoyed torturing local boaters with his obnoxious "Apocalypse Now" routine: blasting music from *Gryphon*'s underwater hydrophone array, and causing unsuspecting charter captains to freak out, as something huge and melodious passed directly underneath them.

He was in that kind of mood now. In fact, *"The Sound of Silence"* by *Disturbed* would have been perfect, he lamented, but not with his less-familiar secondaries at the helm. And certainly not with his by-the-book first officer lurking directly behind him.

Garm didn't have to avert his eyes from the sea outside to know Jayla Morgan's were on him. He could feel her scrutiny. The athletic South African with the dark skin and darker disposition would be where she always was whenever they both occupied the bridge: standing beside *Gryphon*'s captain's chair in a formal "at ease" pose.

Jayla made it a point to never occupy her commanding officer's seat while he was on the bridge. Even if he took up position by the bow, as he was wont to do. She considered it a "breach of protocol". Not to mention rude.

"Sonar, give me status on *Antrodemus*," Garm ordered.

Alvarez cricked her slim neck as she spoke. "*Antrodemus* is on our six, 500 yards back, captain. She's mirroring our course and speed."

"Communications, any update on their repairs?"

Rush removed her headset and spun in her seat. Judging by her smile, she was happy for the chance to contribute. "They're still beaming messages through their *Remora*, sir. Damage to their sail's outer casing was completed before we left port but, per Captain Dragunova's last update, repairs to their photonics mast remain incomplete."

Garm nodded. USS *Antrodemus* was *Gryphon*'s sister ship – the second of the vaunted ORION Class of Anti-Biologic submarines. They were the brainchildren of Grayson Defense Technologies; built from the keel up to combat the pliosaur menace. *Antrodemus* was commanded by his peer and clandestine "fuck-buddy", Captain Natalya Dragunova. Despite a series of modifications completed during their last overhaul, the two vessels were practically clones. That was, if you discounted *Antrodemus*'s traditional battleship-gray colors having been replaced by a thick layer of dark-red ceramic.

At least it isn't brown, he thought with a chuckle. *Come to think of it, do I even have a pair of brown pants?*

"Sir, I have a communique from Captain Dragunova," Rush announced.

"Uh . . . read it."

"To Captain Braddock, Commander USS *Gryphon*. We shall split with you after we pass the Gate. Per mission directive, we shall run on the surface as opportunity permits, with intent to effect repairs to photonics assembly en route. Updates to follow. Captain Dragunova, Commander USS *Antrodemus*, out."

"Well, that was succinct," Garm said with a grin. He eased out a sigh of relief. Nat was too intelligent to have included any mention of their pending mission. Or rather, *hers*. As far as his crew, and even Commander Morgan knew, officially, both *Gryphon* and *Antrodemus* were engaged in a hunt for the giant bull pliosaur designated *Typhon*. *Typhon* was the one that had damaged *Antrodemus* during their last encounter, but not before they ID'd him. Only Garm, Natalya, and, of course, his brother Dirk, back in Tartarus, were privy to the fact that Dragunova's ship would break off the chase at the Gate. From there, she would commence a top-secret and incredibly time-sensitive mission to Diablo Caldera, in the hopes of exploring the volcanic island.

Lying twelve miles off the coast of Cuba, Diablo's isolated saltwater lake was believed to be the source of the man-eating pliosaurs that currently plagued almost all the oceans of the world. After decades of waiting, and with political strife currently wracking the tiny island nation, this could be the best, possibly *only* opportunity Dr. Derek Braddock would have to send people to explore the caldera's hidden depths.

It was an opportunity Garm's twin wasn't about to miss. Even if it meant betraying his mentor to do so.

"Communications, give me full frontal on *Antrodemus*," Garm ordered. "Put it on the main."

"Full frontal." Rush cleared her throat. "Yes, sir."

There was a hum and shimmer as *Gryphon*'s transparent bow turned opaque. A moment later, a shot of the red sub's menacing bow filled the screen. As he admired her lines, Garm felt a pang of regret that Nat wouldn't be joining him for the hunt. Not that he needed her help. He just relished the notion of them prowling the deep blue together, their paired vessels like a pair of colossal wolves, tracking their monstrous quarry.

He snorted in amusement and shook his head. Somewhere along the way he'd picked up his dad's habit of watching too many nature documentaries . . .

"Off screen," he said.

There was a moment of static as the sub's rearview optronics disconnected. Then the green and azure seas before them once more occupied the bridge's view.

Closing his eyes, Garm inhaled slowly through his nostrils, then exhaled through his mouth. Like ripples spreading across a pond, his senses extended from his skin and hair and the soles of his feet, filling the bridge as they traveled outward.

In unscientific terms, he was gathering the *feel* of his vessel. Like many ship and submarine commanders, Garm had an almost personal relationship with *Gryphon*. He could sense her speed and depth, taste the quality of her recycled air, and feel the thrum of her eight Mako M69 pump jet MHD Propulsors. He found the immense energy her AMS-424 High Yield Nuclear Reactor generated as it rippled through her armored hull particularly intoxicating – like hot blood, coursing through the veins of some impossibly huge creature.

She feels good, Garm acknowledged. *Like an apex predator on the hunt.*

And what a hunt it will be.

He breathed out a final lungful and opened his eyes. Turning from the bow, he weaved his way around sonar and headed toward his elevated chair. His first officer's eyes sharpened as he drew near and she sprang to attention.

"Orders, captain?" Morgan inquired.

"Yes, commander," Garm said. "Per mission mandate, we're to investigate the seas around the yacht that issued yesterday's distress call, inspect said vessel, if feasible, and interview whoever made the call." He handed her a digital clipboard. "According to satellite reports, she's still at anchor. *Gryphon*'s course is preset and, barring outside interference, you are to maintain speed and depth. I'm retiring to my quarters. Kindly notify me once we've reached the prescribed coordinates."

The frown lines at the corners of Morgan's dark eyes deepened as she perused the notebook-sized screen. "Uh . . . a question, captain?"

"Of course."

"At our current speed, it will take us hours to get there."

Garm nodded. "That is correct. And, barring an emergency, you are to maintain course and heading."

As his second's eyebrows lowered, he readied himself.

"But, what if we encounter a rogue *Kronosaurus* en route? For example, one on our list. Do standard rules of engagement still apply?"

He shrugged. "If you ID a suspect biologic, your first course of action should be to cloak the ship, as opposed to engaging."

"And if the cloak is penetrated and we're attacked?"

Garm tapped the bottom of the screen with a callused fingertip. "Tie the LADON turret directly into ANCILE's acoustic intercept, and OMNI ADCAP's active search and attack sonar. If no other alternative presents itself, engage and blow it to hell."

As she continued reading, Morgan's head snapped back on toned neck muscles. "Wait, we're also running with acoustics full-out?"

"Yes. I want all systems, active and passive, running at the highest possible frequencies, and SVALINN Active Sonar Suppression powered up and on standby. Any and all contacts are to be recorded. If a seal passes gas, five miles out, I want to know about it."

Garm pretended not to notice as Blair shifted uncomfortably in his seat.

Morgan gave a vigorous headshake, in an effort to dispel her confusion. "With our projectors emitting that much noise, any echolocator within ten miles is going to know we're there, long before we get within range, and make tracks."

"That's the idea, commander – conserving ammunition."

"B-but, how are we supposed to make any money if--"

"Ah, you're forgetting Grayson's generous offer," he interjected. "If we succeed in bringing *Typhon* back alive, each crewmember earns approximately--"

"A hundred and twenty-five thousand dollars." Morgan finished.

"That's right," Garm said, cocking an eyebrow. He leaned close and gentled his tone. "Of course, as first officer you get a double share, so I think you'll be okay."

"I could . . . pay off my mortgage."

"There you go," Garm encouraged, clapping her good-naturedly on a surprisingly firm shoulder. "Eyes on the prize, commander." He turned to go, then looked back and added with an exaggerated buccaneer's brogue, "And a big fish to fry, it be."

As Morgan stood there, licking her lips, Garm swung open the bridge's heavy hatch and stepped sideways into the narrow corridor beyond. As he glanced back, he felt a twinge of remorse. It wasn't as if he'd technically lied to Jayla, or to the rest of his crew, for that matter. Everything he'd said was one hundred percent true. Eric Grayson had offered a fortune for *Typhon*'s capture.

And why wouldn't he?

With luck, Tartarus's captive *Kronosaurus imperator* queen *Tiamat* would accept the battle-scarred old bull as her mate and give Grayson Defense Technology's eccentric CEO what he wanted most: a new breed of super-pliosaurs that dwarfed their primeval brethren. Such creatures would have the mass and power to sink vessels the size of naval destroyers. Of course, if allowed to escape and multiply, with time they could also tip the ecology of the oceans in their favor.

Not that his brother's mentor would allow that to happen.

Grayson planned on keeping *Tiamat* and *Typhon* captive, and turning their progeny into the deadliest bio-weapons the world had ever seen. As if his current billion-dollar collection of marine monsters wasn't lethal enough.

Therein lay the source of Garm's guilt. Despite his mandate, the promise he'd made Eric Grayson, and even the needs of his loyal and dependable crew, he planned to do what he and Dirk agreed must be done. He would track down *Typhon*. But he had no intention of capturing the wily son of a bitch.

He was going to blow him out of the water.

———

So many pieces on the board . . . I feel like I'm playing three-dimensional chess, except each piece represents dozens of lives. I wonder how Vulcans handle this kind of pressure?

Exhaling hard to mitigate his mounting stress, Dr. Derek "Dirk" Braddock rubbed his aching temples with one hand. With the other, he reached for what was rapidly becoming his best friend these days – his coffee cup. He brought it to his mouth and took a careful sip, grateful for the self-heating mug that kept his overly-sweetened Kona at near-scalding temperature, then glanced up at the wall clock.

Five AM . . . Dirk groaned. He'd been up since three, having snuck over to his work station while his paramour still slumbered.

He peeked around the edge of his five-foot-wide monitor, just in time to see Dr. Stacy Daniels, Tartarus's head of neural surgery, shift soundlessly in her sleep. She was wearing one of Dirk's t-shirts, and as the bountiful curve of an exposed buttock peeked into view, his pearl-white incisors couldn't help but dig into his lower lip. Despite both the intensity and duration of their late-night lovemaking, he could feel the inevitable male horniness trying to reassert itself. He allowed himself only a possessive grin, before focusing once more on the task at hand.

Make that *tasks*.

Dirk's mind was a windstorm of concerns, most of which were reflected in the assorted windows he had open on the shimmering curved screen he and Stacy had installed, earlier that evening. As his nimble fingers experimented with adjusting the assorted images – opening, closing, expanding, and contracting them, the young scientist had to admit he was impressed.

Touch-screen technology that worked a foot or more from the expensive monitor's shimmering surface not only expedited things, it allowed for complex layering and all but eliminated cleanup.

Shifting the camera screens that looked in on several of the facility's captive pliosaurs off to one side, Dirk brought up a global satellite map and punched in some coordinates. Once he was close, he split the image in two, then zoomed in again until he found exactly what he was looking for: a pair of pulsing red symbols – the transponders for Grayson Defense Technologies' ORION-class anti-biologic submarines *Gryphon* and *Antrodemus*.

Dirk noted the two warships' positions, as well as their respective courses and speeds. His brother Garm's boat, *Gryphon*, was approaching that mysterious luxury yacht they'd been sent to investigate. Captain Natalya Dragunova, on the other hand, was some seventy miles off the coast of Cuba, slipping stealthily toward the dormant volcanic island known as Diablo Caldera. Dirk checked his watch; *Antrodemus* was making good time. She should reach her primary launch point in less than three hours.

As less professional thoughts of the anti-biologic sub's captain wormed their way into his brain, a wave of remorse suddenly inundated him. At its crest was him having committed to what was effectively a "bootie-call" relationship with Stacy. Technically, he wasn't guilty of anything; it was his ex who'd initiated things, even after he'd been brutally honest with her. To his bemusement, the headstrong paleo-surgeon had expressed absolutely no regrets about how things stood between them, even going so far as to make light of his "painfully apparent" obsession with Dragunova.

Despite Stacy's reassurances, however, Dirk was far from comfortable. Based on his, admittedly limited, experience in such matters, the whole "friends with benefits" thing usually ended up with either or both parties developing strong feelings for one another.

Things only got worse from there.

The young scientist gritted his teeth, reaffirming his commitment to simply enjoy things while they lasted. He had enough weighing on him, without having to worry about whether Stacy might get attached. He was up to his eyeballs in deceit, and his relationship with the headstrong Jamaican girl was pretty much the only honesty he had going for him.

Dirk shook his head as he did a quick mental tally of his crimes; He'd betrayed his mentor, Eric Grayson, by sending his brother off to destroy the rogue bull pliosaur designated *Typhon*, instead of fulfilling their mandate to capture it.

It was a decision he'd not taken lightly; Grayson was counting on adding the bull's genetics to his existing stable, to improve the quality of his brood stock. Without it, the aging CEO stood to lose a fortune.

And if that wasn't enough, Dirk had sent Dragunova and her team off to explore Diablo Caldera, without his mentor's approval, or even knowledge. The subterfuge had proven expensive; to gain access to the volcanic island, he'd spent ten million dollars of his own money, in bribes alone.

He eyed a news channel that was documenting the ongoing ground war in Cuba. The current footage was spectacular: burning buildings, piles of bodies, and a smoldering tank. At least the shooting had stopped temporarily. He inhaled deeply and let it out slow. If his prayers were answered, and the Cuban rebels managed to hold the line, *and* if they honored his arrangement with them, he'd have a research team on the ground in Diablo Caldera within hours.

Dirk licked his lips. The thought of pressing the first human footprints in the history of the world into the sands of the Cretaceous-era volcanic island was titillating. He'd have given just about anything to be there.

But he couldn't.

Playing his role of "the man behind the curtain" was for the best. *Someone* had to be at the helm, and there was a lot riding on the outcome, most notably the lives of people he cared about. To be sure, under normal circumstances Garm and Dragunova could take care of themselves. But *Typhon* was far from normal; he was the deadliest pliosaur they'd ever encountered – an experienced submarine-killer – and *Gryphon* would be facing him alone.

And as for Dragunova, Lord-only-knew what prehistoric horrors awaited *Antrodemus*'s landing team, once they found themselves within the confines of Diablo's towering ramparts. The depths of its saltwater lake could be home to monstrous marine predators, the likes of which the world had never known.

Of course, Dirk chuckled almost maniacally, things could go wrong with the Cubans, as well. They could just change their minds and revoke his access and keep the funds he'd transferred to their accounts. What would he do then? It wasn't like he could file a federal complaint for monies intended to fund a covert operation, in complete violation of the tiny island country's sovereignty...

At that point, he might as well have flushed ten million bucks down the toilet.

He took another sip of Kona, wondering how Grayson would respond once he discovered what his second-in-command had done. Assuming the old man didn't suffer a stroke, some damage control would undoubtedly be in order. If Garm managed to find and dispatch *Typhon*, that part was readily explained – self-defense, and all that.

The fact that he had gone behind his employer's back when it came to Diablo, however, was another thing. Still, he couldn't see it amounting to much. They'd discussed it dozens of times, and Grayson himself had said he'd been dying to explore the place for the better part of a decade; they'd just never had the opportunity.

Dirk scoffed. If anything, he should be excited about his protégé's accomplishment, if not his initiative.

That was, assuming they got in and found something.

He was sure they would. Based on extant food webs, he believed Diablo contained life far beyond the handful of marine species that escaped into the Atlantic, some thirty years prior. In addition to undiscovered fauna, it was likely to house undocumented plants and bacteria. The possibility of developing new vaccines from their finds loomed large. It could open a whole new era for Grayson Defense Technology's beleaguered pharmaceutical division.

Dirk nodded confidently. *No need to worry. Everything will be fine.*

He glanced one last time at the two subs' GPS coordinates, before suspending his cursor over the desktop icon that contained his mother's death video. He hesitated, his finger trembling. Then he hit the play button. Muting it, he leaned sideways in his chair to make sure Stacy was still asleep, then fast-forwarded to the last thirty seconds.

It was just past the point where *Tiamat*, Tartarus's captive pliosaur queen, had murdered his mother, and consisted of nothing but boring, ground-level security camera footage. All you could see was water, a maintenance ledge, and a nearby security door. Amara had been swimming toward the ledge when she'd been swallowed.

There was something about that particular scene that called to Dirk, despite the fact he'd watched it dozens of times. It was more than just the wet concrete, the dimmed amphitheater lighting, and the overheads glistening off the water. It was something else. He didn't know what, exactly. Maybe—

"You're up early, stud-muffin."

"Jesus!" Dirk nearly jumped out of his skin as Stacy's smiling face popped up around the monitor's edge. "You scared the shit out of me!"

"Really?" Stacy replied. Her dyed blonde curls jiggled as she made a show of sniffing the air. "I don't smell anything..."

He frowned at her jocularity, then reached for his mouse, reordering his screen as she made her way around the corner of his desk.

"Whatcha doing?" Stacy asked, wrapping her arms around his shoulders as she settled playfully into his lap. The smell of jasmine and musk inundated Dirk, and he swallowed despite himself.

"Actually, I've been reviewing that study I ordered on the absorptive qualities of *Proteus*'s scales, and it's absolutely fascinating." As he spoke, he enlarged the link to the camera looking in on their chameleon-like pliosaur, nearly invisible as she hovered near the bottom of her tank.

"How so?" Stacy asked, eying the monitor.

Out of reflex, Dirk went into demo-mode. "Well, in addition to her epidermal iridophores which, as we know, allow her to change hue and pattern, it appears that the ridged edges and surfaces of her scales have evolved to absorb echolocation clicks, reflecting them back at odd angles."

He indicated a quick computer simulation he'd thrown together the day before. "At close range, and blanketed with heavy sonar from, say, another pliosaur or a sperm whale, it wouldn't be effective. But at a distance, her scales cause sonar waves to break apart, giving her a reading that appears like a school of small bait fish, as opposed to a seventy-ton predator."

Stacy nodded, shifting in his lap. "Sounds like a sensible mutation, especially for a hatchling or sub-adult. In Diablo, it would've helped her avoid her larger, cannibalistic brethren."

"Or, as an adult, to draw predators that feed on baitfish right to her."

Stacy's eyes opened wide and she gave him a weird smile. "Good cover."

"What do you mean?"

"Wanna know a secret?" she asked.

"Uh, sure."

Stacy leaned in close, putting her lips next to his ear. "Whenever your response to a question starts with 'actually', you're either hiding something or lying."

Dirk's head jerked back. "Really?"

"Oh, yes, it's one of your many tells." Stacy reached for the mouse, eyeing his expression as she did and, without asking for permission, started exploring the minimized windows on his monitor.

"Let's see . . ." she continued clicking, amused by his obvious discomfiture. She paused, studying the news program that followed the Cuban conflict. "I notice you've been watching a lot of this, lately. Anything going on there?"

"Just what you see."

"Indeed," Stacy's tight curls brushed his face as she turned back toward the monitor. "What else do we have here . . . pliosaur tanks . . . an update on *Goliath*'s post-surgical status . . . and--"

She gave a tiny gasp as she opened the old footage from *Tiamat*'s tank.

Dirk blinked as her head whipped back toward him. Her eyes dug into his, searching for and finding the pain she knew would be there.

"Oh, honey . . . why do you keep doing this to yourself?"

He cleared his throat. "It's nothing. Actually, I . . . *damn*."

Stacy gave him a sad-but-supportive smile. Then her head cocked to one side and she focused on what looked like an electronics-covered bicycle helmet, sitting on one of the shelves, overlooking his desk.

"Is that what I think it is?"

Dirk nodded. "The very first prototype cortical controller for our upgraded cybernetic implants. Grayson had it in his desk drawer. He said I could have it."

"May I?" Stacy asked. At his nod, she reached for the bulky helmet and hoisted it from the shelf. "Wow, it's heavy."

"Most prototypes are."

"Does it still work?"

Dirk shrugged in his seat. "I don't know, probably. Why?"

Stacy blew the dust from the helmet, before running her fingers over its crudely-constructed exterior. She turned it this way and that, then flipped it over and inspected its worn padding and chinstrap. "I, uh . . . I was just thinking it would've been great if someone had known about your mother's fall. If they had, then one of us could've used this to--"

"Yeah," Dirk sighed. "Even with the first-gen implants the helmet would have allowed some basic control. Could've been a life saver."

"Sorry, I didn't mean to compound your grief."

"Is it that obvious?" As she nodded, his frown deepened. "So, what other 'tells' do I have?"

Stacy grinned, "Oh, I'm not *telling* . . ."

"What do you mean?"

"You think I'm going to give up my advantage?"

"Advantage?" Dirk shook his head. "What is this, a chess match?"

"Chess?" A mischievous look crept across Stacy's heart-shaped face, and he felt her warmth through his boxers as she swayed playfully in his lap. Eyes twinkling, she reached for his nearby collection of marine predator teeth and started stroking his huge *Livyatan* tooth. She smiled sinfully. "Well, you certainly 'mated' me a few times last night."

Dirk swallowed nervously.

"So, what do you say, 'big boy' . . . a little 'hair of the dog' that bit you?" She chuckled as she touched a finger to her lips. "Or was it a cat?"

"What hair? You're, uh . . . waxed."

Sensing his hesitation, Stacy leaned in, bringing her glistening lips so close to his he swore he could taste them. "C'mon, baby, I won't bite . . ." Then she added hotly, right in his ear. "*Hard.*"

Dirk felt his arousal kick in but somehow managed to clamp down on it. "Um, actually, I mean, it's still the middle of the night, and we *both* need sleep. Big things happening tomorrow."

"Oh, really?" Stacy asked mirthfully, her amber eyes running down the front of his undershirt. "How big?"

"Seriously," he said on a swallow. He felt a trickle of sweat run down his back and glanced at his quarters' climate control console, wondering if something had gone wrong with his air-conditioning. "You go on. I'll turn in shortly."

Stacy got up off his lap. "Are you sure?"

He cleared his throat. "Uh, yeah. I've got some research to do and--"

"Suit yourself," Stacy said, reaching down and stripping off the t-shirt he'd given her in one smooth motion.

Dirk's eyes were the size of hen's eggs as they took in her nakedness. With her flat stomach, full breasts, and heavenly hips, all coated with soft, sweet-smelling skin the color of caramel, he could stare at her forever. "Uh, what are you doing?"

"Oh, nothing," Stacy said, sauntering toward the bed, her hips swaying provocatively. "I'm not really that sleepy, so I'm going to do a little exercise to help me nod off."

"Exercise?" Dirk echoed as she climbed atop his expensive mattress. "What kind of exercise?"

"Yoga," she replied, flashing him that gleaming smile. "Now, don't you worry about little ol' me, I know you've got important work to do."

"Uh, yeah, I . . ."

Stacy sat back on her haunches, her exposed nipples jutting invitingly outward. Suddenly, a mock look of confusion came over her. "Gosh, what position shall I start with?" She gave Dirk a sideways glance to make sure he was watching, then turned her back to him. "Ah, I know . . . my 'extended puppy' pose. It's one of my favorites."

As Stacy moved into an all-fours position, Dirk's heart started pounding in his temples. Still watching him out of the corner of one eye, she lowered her chest down onto the bed, her arms extended in front of her, until her naked ass was propped up in what was, in his opinion, the most incredible doggy-style position he'd ever seen.

"So, what do you think?" she giggled. "Oh, I'm sorry. I forgot. You go on with your 'research.'"

The growl Dirk emitted as he tossed his keyboard into a nearby wastebasket sounded more like a pliosaur than a man. "Research?" he muttered as he stalked toward her. "Oh, I got your 'research' right here, woman . . ."

"That's it, Garm . . . stick heem hard. Steef jab, right on nose. Break nose if you can. Now left, right, sleep punch, duck, then come up. Now . . . strike! Strike again! Da, perfect keel shot. Absolyutnyy!"

As a shirtless Garm Braddock weaved ghostlike around the heavy bag he'd constructed in the middle of his quarters, he unleashed a blistering barrage of hooks, uppercuts, and over-hand rights, any one of which would have staggered an ox. Ignoring the annoying rivulets of sweat that stung his eyes, the one-time heavyweight contender's mind waged a tug-of war through time, alternating between memories of one of his earliest boxing trainers, and his present-day concerns about his brother, Dirk.

As trainers went, Oleg Petrikov had been an enigma to the then seventeen-year-old boxing phenom. A former Soviet Union Olympic boxing medalist and friend of his father's, the aged Georgian prizefighter had just completed his third prison stint – this time for assault and battery – when Jake Braddock hired him to train his son. Garm took to the old man immediately. The combination of knife scars decorating his leathery fists and forearms, and the leonine ferocity he exhibited when it came to both training and life, had a profound impact on the still-undisciplined teen. But it was Oleg's attempts at harnessing the young Braddock's killer instincts that really struck home.

His chest heaving, Garm paused to recalibrate, his wolf's eyes burning bright. He remembered their first heavy bag workout as if it was yesterday. The retired pugilist had started by giving him his street-smart version of an anatomy lesson on the human head: basically, pointing out its most vulnerable spots. *"Here . . . keel. Here . . . keel."* Oleg repeated as he indicated weak points on the jaw, temple, and directly below the nose. Everything was "Kill, kill, kill," with the steely-eyed curmudgeon, Garm reminisced with a sad smile. Unfortunately, less than a year later, the old Soviet warhorse was gone: downed by two bullets to the heart, following a fistfight in some seedy Miami hangout.

A sudden burning sensation caused Garm to stop. He examined his callused knuckles, his lips dipping into an all-too-familiar frown. He'd reopened the gash he'd gotten on his hand the other day, while engaging Tartarus's now-suspended security chief Angus Dwyer in a vicious bare-knuckles brawl in the facility's gym.

The fight had been over Dirk.

Despite outweighing his fraternal twin by nearly a hundred pounds, the hulking ex-convict had been trying to goad the young scientist into a lopsided sparring match when he showed up. The ORION-class sub commander's lips pulled back into a predatory snarl. What ensued had been vicious, but brief. And if Eric Grayson hadn't ended up intervening, he probably would've left Dwyer in a coma.

Or, better yet, dead.

Garm scoffed at the dark thoughts he harbored. Still, despite the inevitable complications such a thing would bring, the latter was decidedly more appealing. The anthropoid-like head of Tartarus's private security had some sort of perverse vendetta against his little brother. He could tell. And, if that wasn't bad enough, the guy was patently psychotic: he could see it in his eyes. Why Grayson couldn't, remained a mystery.

Peeling off the blood-dotted hand wrap, Garm checked his injury. He exhaled his annoyance. The wraps hadn't helped, and there was no point in continuing. Any additional pounding on the gravel-filled makiwara bags he'd duct-taped together around the steel column in the center of his quarters would only make things messier.

So much for bagwork, he grumbled. He was in the middle of stripping off his remaining wrap, when there was a familiar rapping on his door.

"Enter," he commanded, not bothering to look down as Jayla Morgan invaded his quarters. At five-foot-nine, his first officer was a good seven inches shorter than him. Still, with her military air, athletic frame, and innate aggressiveness, she had no difficulties making her presence known.

"Captain Braddock," Jayla began, standing at attention. Garm finished his unwinding and hung the pair of wraps on a hook to air out.

"What is it, commander?" he asked, then added with a perfunctory hand motion, "At ease, please."

Jayla relaxed – meaning she became less stiff – then glanced at Garm's bleeding knuckle. "Are you alright, sir?"

"It's nothing," he replied, holding up his injured mitt. He suppressed a smirk, as his normally outspoken first mate made it a point to avoid focusing on his sweat-soaked chest and abs. "Just opened a cut I got in the gym last night." He managed to catch her gaze. "By the way, thanks for coming to find me. I owe you one."

"No problem, sir," she acknowledged. "You'd have done the same for me, or any member of the crew."

"Absolutely. If some miscreant twice your size threatened you, I'd knock his head clean off his shoulders. Or Ensign Ho might beat me to it and scale him like a siege tower." He winked at her. "But, then, you already know that."

Jayla allowed herself a furtive glance at Garm's chiseled torso before averting her eyes once more. "It's, uh . . . common knowledge, sir."

Garm grabbed a nearby towel and draped it over his shoulders, covering up as best he could. As he did, he gave his second-in-command a quick up-and-down in turn. With her full lips, and an innate buxomness that no uniform could conceal, Jayla had a provocative aura about her. And there was some mutual attraction. Once, while *Gryphon*'s crew was doing shots in a Key West bar, she'd loosened up and broached the topic of them "hooking up". He'd politely declined. It would've been a bad career move. Not to mention, if Nat found out, one or both of them would have ended up in the infirmary.

"Look, Jayla. I know you well enough to recognize when you've got something on your mind, so out with it."

She cleared her throat. "You asked to be notified when we were within thirty minutes of the last reported position of that 'mystery yacht'. We're approaching those coordinates now. The vessel appears intact, but remains radio silent and at anchor. According to satellite scans, their coordinates haven't changed since the distress call."

"Is that all?" Garm asked. "You could've told me that over the comm."

Jayla licked her lips. "You also requested *Gryphon*'s primary bridge crew take over at this point. My team has only had the con for four hours and . . ."

"And?"

Even without the overt side-eye Jayla was giving her captain, her bunched jaw muscles were an obvious tell. "Is there a problem with our performance? Because if--"

Garm chuckled. "I love how that South African accent of yours comes out whenever you get riled."

The irritable snort that spewed from Jayla's flared nostrils spoke volumes.

"Relax, commander," he appeased. "There's absolutely nothing wrong with you, or your people. You're all tops, as far as I'm concerned. But, you *were* at the briefing, yes?"

"Of course."

"And you saw what we're up against?"

"Yes, sir. But I thought that--"

"Commander, we are hunting *Typhon*, the most powerful, craftiest *Kronosaurus imperator* we've ever faced. By mass alone, he's as big as the biggest blue whale that's ever lived."

Jayla wore a confused look. "But, we're only supposed to tag him in prep for capture, right?"

Garm hesitated. "Yes . . . and then hold off until *Antrodemus* rejoins us for the actual hunt. But, tell me, commander. Have you faced this particular pliosaur in combat, like I and the primary bridge crew have?"

"Obviously not, sir."

"Do you expect him to just lay there like some lap dog in a veterinarian's arms while we hit him with a tracker?"

"You're patronizing me, sir," Jayla replied evenly.

"Fair enough. I apologize," Garm said with a nod. "You're a capable officer – one of the best in the CDF – and your record speaks for itself." He drew a breath, his deep voice taking on a tone more appropriate for a eulogy. "But this is not some ordinary pliosaur we're pursuing. He's centuries old and an experienced sub-killer. He disabled *Antrodemus* while taking fire, and a few years before that destroyed *Titan*. Lord knows how many other fish he's sent to the bottom. Hell, for all we know, he could've been responsible for both the *Dakar* and *Minerve*, and you can bet the Russians lost a few boomers to him that we'll never know about."

"So, you think I'm not up to the task."

Garm's pale eyes bored a hole in *Gryphon*'s non-slip deck. As much as he was tempted, he couldn't risk telling Morgan their real mission. "Look, it's very simple; this creature is extremely dangerous and, if we're in an area where we're likely to run into him, I prefer to have the only crew that's faced him and lived running point." He looked up. "I'm sorry, but that's my decision. If you feel slighted, feel free to document it in your log. Or, you may file a formal complaint when we return to port."

Jayla shook her head. "Put that way, your decision makes perfect sense. Besides, one thing I've picked up during our time together: however unorthodox your primaries are at times, they're a team. And that's what we all are, a team. Any problems or issues we have should be handled in-house, yes?"

"Very good," Garm said, nodding approvingly. He inclined his head toward his bathroom. "I've got to get cleaned up. Kindly deal with the shift change. I'll be up in twenty. Until then, you have the con."

Jayla's lips parted. "Wait, you mean I have twenty un-interrupted minutes to run roughshod over Lieutenant Cunningham?"

Garm smirked at the thought of *Gryphon*'s verbose Combat Systems Officer feeling the lash of Commander Morgan's by-the-book command style, especially without his captain and friend there to shield him.

"You know, I think that's a *wonderful* idea."

"Full system's check on all armaments?" Jayla pressed.

"Why not?" he half-chuckled. "Hell, I'd even do a detailed accounting on the LADON Gun System. You know . . . make sure all ten thousand of those new supercavitating penetrator rounds are fully accounted for."

Jayla's brown eyes brightened. "That sounds *wonderful*, sir."

"Then make it happen. I'll see you in twenty."

"Yes, sir!" Jayla barked, saluting him sharply and closing his quarters' door behind her.

As he turned on the water and waited for it to warm up, Garm began to shake with uncontrollable laughter. This was going to be the longest shower of Kyle Cunningham's life.

Two

As his stomach grumbled for the third time in less than twenty minutes, Martin O'Dare threw a glance at his truck's stereo system clock. The look was tailgated by bunched eyebrows and one of his characteristic scowls.

And, yes, it's suppertime, ladies and gentlemen. Looks like it's gonna be another grab-n-go tonight. Damn local roads . . .

Recoiling as a huge dragonfly exploded into paste a few feet from his face, Martin checked the outside temperature gauge and whistled. It was in the upper nineties – still a scorcher, even this late in the day. Add on the region's innate mugginess, and the damn bugs were just lining up to plaster your windshield with their fast-drying remains.

Florida summers sucked.

Emitting a grumble that mirrored the one emanating from his gut, Martin reached down and cranked the AC up a notch. *Better make that two.*

"Thank God for you, Matilda."

The stocky, 43-year-old truck driver extended a freckled hand and gave the dash of the old Peterbilt 579 an affectionate pet. "Matilda" was the love of his life these days. He'd bought her at auction, four years earlier, and spent the next two pulling the mammoth six-by-four tractor unit out of mothballs and restoring her to her former glory. Initially, he'd anticipated reselling her for a hefty profit. As semis went, she had been quite an outlay, and her restoration even more of an ordeal – one that resulted in him spending most of his nights working in the barn, while the rest of the family slept.

In the end, however, what started as an investment opportunity became a labor of love. When that last layer of clearcoat finally dried, Matilda had it all, from her brand new, 40,000-pound-rated, tandem drive axels, to her refurbished satellite system, to the beast of a Paccar MX-13 engine he'd rebuilt and transplanted into her with his own two hands. With over five hundred horsepower and 1,850-foot-pounds of torque, the aged truck had the strength to haul a mastodon.

Literally. Which was ironic, he realized. Because today, she was going to.

Martin reached down, grabbed a tepid cup of roadside coffee from one of the tractor's assorted cup holders, and chugged down what remained. He blanched, then a moment later, decided it was too quiet and flipped on his favorite country station.

Much better.

With Matilda's aerodynamic fairings, skirts, and closeout, there was so little road noise, it was all-too-easy to fall asleep behind the wheel. Martin whistled an exhale and glanced over his shoulder. His reddened eyes perked up as he caught a glimpse of the Peterbilt's spacious sleeping compartment, situated directly behind him. He'd really missed sacking out last night, but he had no choice. His current run had required it.

Martin gave a nod of acquiescence and turned front once more. It would be worth the fatigue. Once the package was delivered, he'd find a good rest stop, pig out, get shit-faced, and then crash for twenty-four hours straight. He couldn't wait. *Screw wasting hard-earned bread on fucking motels. Who needs them?* With her queen-size mattress, swivel flat screen, fridge, and mini-head, and an assortment of other amenities, Matilda's aluminum-framed cocoon was literally a home away from home.

Or, in his case, home *period*, these days.

That's okay. We'll be addressing that shortly . . .

Martin's face brightened as he passed a sign indicating he'd just entered Highlands County. According to the map, the farm he was headed for was just a few miles outside of a quiet little town named Lake Placid. He grinned, remembering an old horror movie that bore the name, back when he was a kid. A monstrous crocodile on the loose in some New England lake, if memory served. A scary beast, to be sure, the trucker admitted. But it was nothing compared to the real-life reptiles that prowled their oceans nowadays, and occasionally made their way up some of the country's larger rivers.

Martin glanced at his navigation, checked and rechecked his speed, and then nodded. Less than twenty miles to go, and not a state trooper in sight. He glanced up at himself in an overhead mirror and made a face. He looked pale and haggard, and two days of reddish-brown stubble pricking up from his chin like the hairs on an angry hedgehog wasn't helping any. He considered pulling over to search for his electric razor, but then scoffed and shook his head. No fucking way. He was doing these people a huge favor already. They'd just have to accept him as he was.

Besides, he had a schedule to keep.

He had to make the pickup and get to the dock by 2 AM or he'd miss his ride. If that happened, he and his cargo would be left standing there staring at one another. And that was *not* about to happen.

Grabbing the outdated flip-phone he'd tossed on the next seat, Marty pressed autodial and held the phone to his ear. A woman answered, but not the one he was expecting. She sounded younger. And more competent.

"Hello?"

Martin swallowed nervously. "Uh, hi. Who's this?"

Whoever it was sounded put off. "This is Janet. Who's this?"

"This is Marvin O'Hare. I'm scheduled to pick up Nero? I've been dealing with Mrs. Dalworth and I--"

"Oh, shoot . . . hi! So sorry about that," the woman said, suddenly chipper. "Yes, absolutely. I'm Janet, her daughter. I'm here lending a hand. How far away are you?"

Martin relaxed as the suspicion disappeared from Janet's voice. "I'm about thirty minutes out. Listen, I don't mean to be a pain, but I'm on a tight schedule. Is the lowboy ready and everything prepped?"

"Yes, and as much as it can be."

"Okay, great. Thanks, Janet. I'll see you in a bit."

"Great, see ya!"

Martin smiled, realizing he'd enjoyed their brief conversation. Sure, he was trapped in the truck most of the time, so human conversation of any kind was a plus, but Janet sounded very pleasant. He wondered how old she was and if she was attractive . . .

A headshake that was borderline injurious disrupted Martin's musings. He had no time for socializing, not to mention, with his occupation it could be downright dangerous. Plus, given his "personal" situation, the only romantic encounters he experienced these days were with strippers or hookers from roadside bars. Strictly a "pay for play" kind of affair. He chuckled mischievously. That was another advantage to the Peterbilt's spacious – and surprisingly soundproof – sleeping compartment.

Martin's eyes shone then narrowed. Yes. He was long overdue for some female companionship. Someone he'd never have to see again afterward, of course. Maybe after he'd made the drop-off and gotten paid . . .

The trucker's lecherous grin vanished, when the smartphone he had affixed to the dash rang. He glanced at it, his expression morphing from curiosity to bitterness as he mouthed the name on the screen.

Meghan O'Dare.

Martin hit the speakerphone button, the feed emanating from the truck's internal speaker system.

"Hello."

"Martin?"

"Yes."

"What do you mean, 'yes'? Is that all you have to say to me?"

As his ex-wife's ubiquitous nagging started, Martin could feel his temper start to flare. He began taking calming breaths and glanced ahead at the assorted road signs, making a mental tally of each one he saw in an effort to waylay his growing fury.

"What's on your mind?" he intoned.

"What's on *my* mind? Gee, I don't know!" Meghan remarked. "How about the nearly six thousand dollars of child support you owe me? Oh, and let's not forget the mortgage on the property, which is over two months in the red! Who the hell do you--"

Screw the signs.

Martin's voice became a veritable snarl. "Go fuck yourself, Meg."

The near-choking sound that preceded his ex's reply was priceless.

"W-what the fuck did you just say to me?"

"You heard me, you skank-ass bitch," Martin continued. He could feel the adrenaline rushing through him. He'd been hoping to give her both barrels in person, but this would have to suffice. "You're a fucking user and a whore, and you're going to get exactly what's coming to you."

"A 'whore?' You're starting with the accusations again, you fucking loser?" Meg's nasally voice lashed out of the truck's speakers like a bullwhip. "The judge wasn't buying that crap before, and she--"

"Oh, but she is now, *whore*." Martin emphasized. "It took a while, but I finally found the email I was looking for. You know me, never throwing things away . . ."

"What email?"

"The one your doctor's office sent me late last year, after they called the house looking for you," Martin gloated. "Would you like to know what it said?"

"You're full of shit," Meg shot back. She was doing her best to sound imperious, but he could hear the uncertainty in her voice.

"I can't read it because I'm driving, but there was something about 'gonorrhea of the rectum.'" He said, chortling. "Really? How the fuck does one get the clap in their ass? I mean, I know how *you* obviously got it, but since you never did anal with me and, since my bloodwork shows no history of contracting anything, the judge was willing to reopen the case."

"You fucking piece of shit!" Meg screamed. "Those were my private records! I'm gonna--"

"You're going to do exactly what the judge says," Martin said tauntingly. He popped open a nearby compartment, eyeballing a letter he had stashed inside. "And according to the pricey lawyer I just hired, that includes submitting to a paternity test – both you and little Johnny. You know, I always said that kid was a bit dark to be 100% Irish."

"You go to hell, Stumpy!" Meg shrieked. "You're gonna get yours, you dickless bastard! You'll see!"

Stumpy. Martin's face darkened and his voice turned chill. "You're right, and I intend to. Do you know the legal definition of *fraud*, my dear? Because if you don't, you're about to learn it."

The click that came out of the truck's speakers as his ex slammed the phone down was so loud, he was sure she'd shattered both the handset and the base. He paused to take stock of his feelings, as his therapist had instructed, then realized he felt light-headed. He let out the breath he'd been holding.

It felt good to get it all out. Better yet, *he* felt good. And things were only about to get better.

Stumpy.

The stocky trucker shook his head ruefully. Like the saying went, *you can take the trash out of the gutter, but you can't take the gutter out of the trash.* Leave it to Meg to go for the cheapest shot imaginable.

As the familiar ache in his groin invariably reasserted itself, Martin's mind rewound itself to a day, thirty years prior. It was the moment that changed his life.

Make that ruined it.

He was fourteen and playing "cowboys and Indians" with a few friends in the field beyond his parent's property. They had their usual toy guns and bows, but he had something special. He'd gotten his hands on the key to his dad's gun case and "borrowed" his Colt Walker replica pistol.

Martin half-smiled at the memory. The Walker was a beast of a gun, the largest and most powerful repeating black powder pistol ever made, in fact. It weighed nearly five pounds – heavier than a Smith & Wesson .44 Magnum – and fired a .454 caliber, conical round. His friends were astonished when he showed up with it, its polished hickory handle sticking out of his pants like a pirate's pistol. He'd made quite the show of waving it around and, although he couldn't get the trigger to pull for some reason, just hefting it and yelling "boom" over and over made him feel like a modern-day "Josey Wales".

As their play wore on, Martin finally figured out how to work the big, single-action weapon. By cocking the heavy hammer back and then pulling the trigger, it produced a loud and satisfying snapping sound. Of course, the teen had no idea there was a full powder charge and ball in one chamber. That was, until he'd cocked the hammer back for the sixth time and cockily shoved the pistol's nine-inch barrel back inside the front of this trousers.

The sound of it going off was, to this day, the loudest thing he'd ever heard.

Louder than the ambulance's sirens. Or his screams.

The pain had been astonishing and increased by the minute. The doctors rushed him into emergency surgery and, after two hours on the operating table, Martin was saved. Most of him, that is. His penis had taken the worst of the blast, and the bloody scraps of skin that made up the corona and part of the glans had to be amputated. Thankfully, his testicles were spared and, after a series of painful and humiliating operations, the surgeons proudly announced that, not only could he urinate normally, with pills he'd be able to get at least a partial erection *and* would most likely be able to father children one day.

'Father children'? As if any woman would be interested in the scarred-up, four-inch piece of bratwurst he'd end up showing them ...

Martin's life turned to shit after that. His ego and sense of self-worth had been blown away, along with his manhood. His friends vanished, and his social life went with them; girls wanted nothing to do with him – not that he tried. Of course, the next three years of high school were the obligatory hell, with the older boys relentlessly tormenting and beating on him, all the while calling him names like "Stumpy" and "Stubby" or braying Meat Loaf's old love song, "Two Out of Three Ain't bad."

Stumpy.

By the time he'd met Meghan, Martin was in his late thirties. She'd seemed a godsend to the withdrawn trucker back then: attractive, busty, and very outgoing. To his surprise, it was she who asked him out. He figured, with them being the same age, maybe she was feeling the pressure and decided it was time to settle down. Maybe she just felt sorry for him. Regardless, he wasn't about to pass on the opportunity. After a quick courtship, they'd run off to Vegas.

Next thing he knew, Meg was pregnant.

Things fell apart shortly after that. His wife never seemed to be satisfied about anything, and between her constant complaining about his job, and her occasional, not-too-subtle digs about his "shortcomings" in the bedroom, he knew it was just a matter of time before she'd cut and run.

The adultery, however, had been a surprise. He'd often suspected things were going on while he was away, and Meg's explanation that their son's dark hair and permanent tan was the result of her Sicilian grandmother's genes, just didn't sit right. Still, he'd never had any proof.

Not until after the divorce, that is. That was when he'd come across the email. It was from his now ex-wife's gynecologist. When they'd called with details about some bloodwork, he'd told them to just email him the test results, not asking or caring what they were, nor even remembering to tell her about it.

But *now* . . .

Martin relaxed back into Matilda's bosoming driver's seat and sighed. That forgotten old email had turned out to be the ticket to a lot of things. It had inspired him to buy a paternity test, and the last time he'd been alone with his son – the last time he *was* his son – he'd tricked the poor kid into letting him "check his teeth".

He'd never let on that he was collecting a DNA sample.

A few weeks later, the results and the truth reared their misshapen heads. Johnny was not his, and his estranged wife was confirmed as the disease-ridden skank his friends had always warned him about. All that was left now was to settle things.

Martin tabbed a button to open his driver's side window and spat into the wind. That would be up to the lawyers, of course. But if the new firm he'd just taken on were correct, Meg was in for it. Forget future child support payments. He was going to sue for reimbursement of all the money he'd already been bled for, and a good portion of the house as well.

Then, of course, there was the possibility of pressing charges for fraud. From what he understood, that was a felony in Florida . . .

Martin smirked evilly at the thought of Meg's condescending mother being forced to take care of her bastard son while she served time.

Yep, payback is indeed a bitch. And I know a bitch who's got a semi-load coming her way.

True to his word, twenty-two minutes later, Garm arrived, freshly showered and feeling refreshed. *Gryphon*'s primary bridge crew did a collective head turn, as the helm's entry hatch swung open and their captain entered, closing and securing it behind him.

"Captain on the bridge!" Commander Morgan called out, instantly snapping to attention.

"At ease, commander," Garm said as he stepped forward. "Status?"

"We're cruising at eight knots, sir," Morgan responded. "Depth is two hundred feet, distance to target one-point-four miles."

"Good," Garm said. As he moved to stand beside Ensigns Ramirez and Ho, manning sonar and helm, he noticed the bow shield was still down. "Sonar, any contacts?"

Ramirez cleared his throat. "Beyond the pod of bottlenose dolphins passing over us, and the school of *Xiphactinus* following them, nothing of any consequence, sir." He glanced up at Garm. "Per orders, both active and passive sonar systems are running at highest frequency, and ANCILE is emitting active pinging."

Garm nodded and turned to his first officer. "Target status?"

"No change, sir," Morgan said, then hastily added, "Oh, and before you ask, weather topside is a balmy eighty-two degrees, with wind from the southwest at two to four miles per hour. Seas are lake-calm."

Garm grinned. "Very good. And the bridge crew?"

"Functioning at peak efficiency."

I bet, he thought as he took in Kyle Cunningham's uncharacteristic rigidity. "Good work, commander. I've got it from here."

"Very well, sir," Morgan replied. She turned to go, surprising him with a wink, once no one could see, then let herself out.

Behind her, the bridge remained crypt-silent as the heavy hatch door closed. There was the expected thump, followed by a low hiss, indicating the pressure seal was in place.

Whistling to himself, Garm sauntered over and dropped down into his oversized chair, its pneumatic shocks creaking as they absorbed his weight. He leaned back, his fingers interlocked behind his head, relishing the unspoken air of expectancy.

"Okay, guys . . ." he drawled. "Let it out."

"Blücher!" Cunningham spouted through a makeshift sneeze.

An instant later, a chorus of incredibly loud horse whinnies erupted from just about everyone on the bridge. Even the normally reserved Ensign Rush got in on the action, her willowy frame shaking with laughter.

"You guys are awful," Garm said, shaking his head as the guffawing gradually died down. "She's not that bad."

Helmswoman Connie Ho wore an incredulous look. "Who's not that bad – Attila the Huntress?" she scoffed. "Do you know what--"

"It was only twenty minutes."

A collective gasp filled the bridge.

"Wait a minute . . ." Cunningham said from his station. "Are you telling me I just counted the serial numbers on one thousand, two-hundred and forty-two shells, and you *knew* about it?"

"Would you like to count the remaining eight thousand, seven-hundred and fifty-eight?" Garm countered.

"Uh . . . no," Cunningham replied, looking up as he crunched the numbers in his head, to see if his captain was correct.

"Okay, people, enough fun and games," Garm said, rising. "Let's--"

He hesitated as Rush's hand went to her earpiece. "Captain, I have a communication from Captain Dragunova aboard the *Antrodemus*."

"Read it."

"No, sir. It's not a patch from their Remora. It's a direct feed," Rush said.

One of Garm's eyebrows did the Spock thing. The notion that Dragunova's team had been able to reinstall their photonics assembly in barely four hours – while underway, no less – was borderline incomprehensible.

"On the main."

The freckle-faced blonde touched a pair of keys. In an instant, the interior of *Gryphon*'s twenty-foot bow window turned opaque, then shimmered. A second later, Captain Natalya Dragunova appeared from the waist up. She was in full uniform and seated in her captain's chair, her hair tied tightly back. With her storm-cloud eyes, strong jaw, and angular features, the imposing Russian reminded Garm of a Viking goddess, poised atop her throne.

"Captain Dragunova, it's good to see you . . . have your communications fixed," he said, clamping down hard on the lust he experienced, whenever he locked gazes with his fiery paramour.

"Actually, we have . . . repaired short . . . so far," Dragunova replied. Her image crackled and shimmered, causing half of what she said to be lost.

"Still, my compliments to your engineer," Garm replied, wondering how much of what he said was getting through.

Dragunova nodded. "We are about . . . submerge and . . . our target at flank speed. We weel run silent until . . . meeshun is complete. I wanted to weesh you and . . . crew good luck."

"Good luck to you, too, captain."

She gave him a knowing smile. "Happy hunting. And--"

There was a sudden burst of static and the screen went blank.

"Sorry, captain," Rush said. "I lost them."

Ensign Ho cleared her throat. "Permission to speak freely, captain?"

"Granted."

The feisty helmswoman shook her head. "I don't say this about many women, or *men* for that matter, but that is one bitch I would not want to tangle with."

"Duly noted," Garm said with a smirk.

A moment later, he dropped back down into his seat. "Okay, people. Let's look alive. Helm, raise shield. Sonar, distance to target?"

"Half a mile," Ramirez said. "Shall I continue banging away? Because anything out there is gonna hear us from a long way off and make tracks if we keep going like this."

"Negative," Garm replied. "That was just to ensure our second-stringers didn't encounter *Typhon* while I was in the head."

He paused as the super-slick, foot-thick ceramic-steel composite barrier that reinforced *Gryphon*'s clear titanium bow slid smoothly up, exposing the oncoming seas. It was a gurgling world of swirling blues and greens, complete with fish and squid of every color and description. No matter how many times he saw it, it always took his breath away.

Garm took a breath. "Helm, reduce speed to five knots."

"Aye, sir." Ho replied.

"Sonar, disable ANCILE," he continued. "I don't want it giving away our position. Give me OMNI ADCAP at medium frequency, with active search and attack. And reinforce that with passive fathometer readings."

"Aye, sir," Ramirez said, flipping switches. The glittering gold screen he shared with Ho brightened, as the sub's arrays absorbed ambient sounds and converted them, creating a 3D hologram of the surrounding sea. "POSEIDON passive sonar active, sir. OMNI ADCAP is up and running."

"Good. Helm, when we get to the 500-yard mark, reduce speed to three knots and make our depth one hundred. Then take us straight in."

"Aye, sir," Ho acknowledged. "Are we going in cloaked?"

Garm nodded, his eyes focused on the onrushing seas. Suddenly, a horde of two-dozen chrome-colored *Xiphactinus* swarmed past, their toothy jaws opening and closing as they cast about for prey to feast upon.

"They're amazing predators, aren't they, captain?" Ensign Rush offered.

"Not my favorite fish," Garm said dryly. His mind wandered to poor Sam Mot, stuck sitting in the galley, and he made a note to go hang with him after they'd checked out the distress signal.

"I mean they've adapted so well to our oceans. Their bodies, their fins . . ."

The big sub captain rubbed his scarred thigh absentmindedly. "As Darwin put it, 'It is not the strongest species which survives, nor the most intelligent, but the one most responsive to change'"

"Guess that's why we're inundated with pliosaurs," Cunningham muttered.

"That's okay," Garm replied, resting his big hands on the backs of Ramirez and Ho's chairs. "We just need to give them changes they can't respond to."

"Sir," Ho interjected as she eyed the butterfly bandages on his hand, "What happened?"

"Hmm? Oh, bagwork . . ."

Cunningham chuckled. "Don't you think it's a little bizarre, sir, that you're traveling in a titanium-steel tube, beneath hundreds of feet of hostile seas, the pressure of which could, given the chance, squash us all to jelly, and you're standing there in that tiny box of air you call your quarters, pounding away on a canvas-covered pole?"

"What can I say? I'm an island unto myself," Garm remarked. "Besides, 'pounding on that pole', as you put it, is how I let off steam. Otherwise," he spun his seat toward his CSO, his glittering eyes narrowed for effect, "I'd end up taking my frustrations out on *you*. You know, like Commander Morgan does."

"Then, by all means, pound away, sir!" Cunningham said, clicking his tongue. "Pound away!"

"That's what she said," Ramirez snickered.

"For all the good it did . . ." Ho muttered amidst all the chuckling.

———

It was nearly six PM, as Martin approached the entrance to the Dalworth's ranch. He slowed Matilda to a crawl as he drove noisily under the towering gateway arch, his rig kicking up stones as he went. To his surprise, there was no security guard. There was, however, a security camera. He tabbed open his driver's side window and stuck his head out, blanching and spitting out a misting of harsh road dust that a hot breeze instantly deposited in his open mouth.

"Woof!"

A pungent aroma struck Martin in the face like a fist and he recoiled. The place definitely smelled like a zoo, and not a very clean one, either. Easing forward, he glanced up, eyeballing the stone-and-wrought-iron entrance as he went. A heavy exhale slipped from the tired trucker's mouth, and he nodded, relieved that there would be no height issues on his way out.

At least something's going my way. As the ranch's carved wooden sign caught his eye, Martin chuckled. *Paradise Falls.*

Hardly original, but a fitting name for the place, he mused. Originally, the Dalworth's impressive eleven-hundred-acre spread had been part of a much larger forty-thousand-acre orange grove. But, after miraculously surviving their cabin cruiser being rammed and torn out from under them by the *Kronosaurus imperator* that attacked Harcourt Marina, some thirty years earlier, Mister and Misses Dalworth had wisely decided that the sea wasn't for them.

They sold all their property in Paradise Cove, as well as the bulk of their real estate bordering Lake Placid, and invested the hundreds of millions they made wisely. They kept the acreage surrounding their twelve-thousand-square-foot ranch home, and converted it into an animal sanctuary of sorts. Rather than traveling the globe like many wealthy couples their age did, they decided to bring the globe to them. They spent their days taking in all sorts of used and abused exotic animals – the more endangered the better – rehabbing and releasing them if they could, and giving them a comfortable place to live out their days if not.

Guiding the massive Peterbilt tractor unit up along the crunchy gravel road that led toward the main house, Martin espied dozens of animals lounging around in their respective enclosures. The place had literally miles of fencing, but was set up in such a way as to mirror the African savannah. That was, except for the much lusher foliage, and the omnipresent palm trees.

Many of the herbivores were permitted to mingle, he noted. Within eyeshot, he could make out a dozen zebras, four or five obviously well-fed giant elands, and a pair of giraffes, moseying their way along toward what, at first glance, looked like a treehouse built into a towering black oak. As the pair of eighteen-foot ungulates shoved their faces inside an open wooden platform on one side of the structure and started chewing, however, he realized it was a built-in feeding station, cleverly rigged to accommodate the browsing requirements of the world's tallest living land animals.

A sudden flurry of black and white bodies moving quickly past his window gave Martin a start. It was a group of ostriches, a full score from the looks of things, stretching their legs as they sprinted across an open field. As he watched the eight-foot, three-hundred-pound birds thudding along at over thirty miles an hour, the trucker grinned. It reminded him of a scene from that old movie *"Jurassic Park"*, where a herd of similar-sized theropod dinosaurs were running for their lives, only to be ambushed by a prowling *Tyrannosaurus rex*.

Martin cast his anticipating eyes around like a trawler's net.

Nope, no dinosaurs these days. At least, not on land . . .

As an unusually acrid whiff of manure burned its way along his nasal passages, Martin grimaced. Muttering irritably, he jabbed the tab closing off Matilda's air vents from the outside. A glance out his passenger-side window confirmed the source of the unpleasant aroma – a breeding pair of Northern white rhinoceros, as well as a strapping yearling calf.

Judging from the cow's bulging sides, she was pregnant again, which meant she'd soon be driving off her current calf. Martin's lips compressed into a tight line. He'd learned that on his way here, along with sixteen hours of other useless information, absorbed from the assorted audio files he'd programmed for the trip. It wouldn't do to have his customers doubting his expertise. He liked to think of it as cramming for an exam. And he'd always been a quick study.

Martin's eyes narrowed as he approached the main house and a series of paddocks to his right. These enclosures were more limited in size and scope and, judging from the heavier-gauge fences and built in security measures, he imagined they were meant to house less amiable guests.

As a huge, black-maned lion went bounding past, its gleaming yellow eyes fixed on him, pacing the noisy tractor-unit as it rumbled by, his suspicions were confirmed. There were five adult lions sharing the enclosure, the big male and four females, as well as a handful of cubs.

The following cage housed a massive Siberian tiger, content to lounge in the evening sun, yawning, and the one after that a scarred old bear that looked like a mainland grizzly.

Cool. I thought they were extinct, Martin noted, nodding.

Spotting a small group of people waiting outside a heavily-barred paddock that was separated from the other enclosures by a small grove of willow trees, he pulled up close. He threw Matilda into park, left the engine running, and climbed down.

A woman stepped away from the rest and sauntered purposefully toward him, a welcoming smile on her face. She had on well-worn jeans, hiking boots, and a long-sleeved white t-shirt, rolled up to the elbows. She was curvy, with bright blue eyes and a mane of blondish-brown hair that reminded him strongly of the lion he'd just passed.

Martin stepped toward her, smiling back and extending his hand.

This must be—

"Janet Dalworth," she opened warmly. "You must be Marvin O'Hare."

"That's what they tell me," he replied. She was pretty, he noted, and had the grip of someone who's worked hard all their life and is happy to show it.

"Thanks so much for doing this," Janet said. She looked over his shoulder, her eyes rounding as she took in the old Peterbilt. "Wow, he is a *big*-boy! You weren't kidding when you said you had the right tool for the job."

"Big *girl*," Martin corrected with a smile. "This is Matilda, my one and only."

"Even better." Janet smiled amiably as she fell in beside him, leading them toward a trio of farmhands who stood waiting in one of the willows' shadows. "I know you're on a tight schedule, so let me introduce you to the guys and we can get things moving."

"Sounds good."

Janet turned to the three teens. "Boys, this is Marvin. He's with SARS, the South African Rescue Society, and he's here to help save Nero." She indicated the three tanned teens, "Marvin, this is Mikey, Johnny, and Stevie. They're at your service."

Nodding at the trio, Martin moved a step closer to Janet and lowered his voice. "Um, is your mom here? I just . . . well, we spoke a few times on the phone, and I know how distraught she was after your father's death and I wanted to extend my condolences."

Janet's eyes shone as she smiled sadly. "That's very sweet of you. I'll be sure to relay your message, but my dad's funeral was only yesterday and she's resting. Out of sorts, if you will . . ."

"I understand," Martin said, sighing knowingly. "Please accept my condolences on your loss."

"Thank you." Janet's smile dipped. "If you'd come last week, I suppose things would've ended up differently."

"Yeah . . ." He licked his lips and looked furtively around. "So, should we get started, then?"

"Surely. I know you've got a boat to catch."

"Absolutely. If we don't make it, the deal's off. Customs and what not . . ."

"Of course," Janet nodded, signaling to the farmhands. "Come on, I'll ride with you around back and the boys will meet us there."

"Works for me." Martin looked around as he walked to the passenger side of the Peterbilt and opened the door for her. "Were there any problems with the lowboy?" he asked, giving her a hand up.

"Not at all," Janet said, smiling at the burst of cool air that greeted her as she settled into Matilda's near-virgin passenger seat. She looked around, studying the layout of the big semi, and casting an amused glance over her shoulder at the sleeping compartment as Martin climbed in. "After they dropped it off, we used a tractor to get it into position, up against the paddock, like you requested, but that's as far as we got. Nero's antsy and refuses to go near it, so how you're going to get him inside is anyone's guess."

"Now, don't you go worrying your pretty head none," Martin said, incorporating his best Walter Brennan accent. "You don't get to be a man of my advanced years without having a trick or two up your sleeve!"

Janet's eyes danced with merriment. "'Advanced years', eh? I'd say we were about the same age, wouldn't you?"

"You know, you college co-eds are mighty kind in these parts," Martin continued, putting Matilda into gear.

"I like your style, Marvin," Janet said, relaxing back and smiling.

As they rumbled around the corner of the oversized paddock she'd directed him toward, Martin spotted the GDT lowboy. They had it backed up against the paddock door, just like he'd asked. An enormous flatbed semi-trailer that was originally designed to haul construction equipment, with its detachable gooseneck and powerful hydraulics system, the lowboy was perfect for his needs. Its spring-ride and mill-rolled beams weren't his first choice by far, but it had a fifty-ton load capacity that, combined with Matilda's workhorse of an engine, meant there was almost nothing he couldn't haul.

At least by weight. It was the willingness of his cargo that occasionally proved problematic.

Pulling smoothly in front of the flatbed, Martin paused to gauge his approach, then backed up carefully, his eyes on the video screen that switched over from his navigation system the moment he shifted into reverse.

Janet cleared her throat. "So, I was--"

"One second," he said, shushing her.

A moment later, there was a beep and a series of lights atop the LCD display turned green. He threw Matilda into park and put the parking brakes on.

"Sorry about that," he said, turning to Janet. "She's a bit touchy where her kingpin is concerned, and if you don't hit the turntable hitch just right, coupling can be a real bitch."

Janet stared off into the distance and grinned hugely. "Yeah, it can be."

Martin blinked, then reached for the flip-phone he had sitting nearby. He pushed a button and turned the tiny screen toward her. "I brought some videos to show your mom, some of the past rescues we've done to show the kind of home Nero will have. Would you like to see?"

Janet glanced at the footage of an Indian elephant and her calf frolicking in a waterhole and grinned. "It's fine, I've already seen your website." She popped open the passenger door, a blast of hot air filling the compartment and causing her hair to billow up as she prepared to step down. "Honestly, I would've been fine with him being put down."

Martin hurried down from his side and came around, his hands deftly connecting the hydraulic connectors between the lowboy and Matilda. Out of the corner of his eye, he could see one of the farmhands, Mikey, he believed, peeking through the bars of the nearby paddock. His two friends, he noted, kept a respectable distance. A moment later, the shirtless teen backed hurriedly away and joined them.

"You mean you *wanted* him destroyed?" he asked, keeping his voice down. He could feel pools of sweat beginning to collect in his armpits from the heat and exertion and worked hurriedly, suddenly wanting things over and done.

Janet turned to face him. "He killed my dad, Marvin. And my mom watched him do it. How would you feel?"

Martin nodded. "I . . . understand."

She nodded, her taut lips a seam whose stitches had been over-tightened. "My mother could never do it. Don't get me wrong, I respect her more than anyone. She does great work, especially with her rhino breeding program, but she's a bleeding heart who sees nothing but the best in everyone. She just can't accept the fact that Nero is evil, pure and simple."

"But isn't he just an animal?"

Janet folded her arms across her chest as if cold. "Yes. An intelligent and mistreated one. When we rescued him from that bullshit circus, after he killed one of his handlers and maimed another, we felt the same way. It's 'our' fault, mom said, as if *we* were the ones that abused him. But the bottom line is that Nero is like one of those grandiose movie villains. And, as we all know, the greatest of them always have a heartbreaking backstory."

"Yes," Martin said, contemplating himself. "I suppose they do."

"But that doesn't make them any less villainous," Janet continued. She shook her head vehemently, her tawny hair flagging back and forth. "Nor does it ease the suffering of their victims, or the ones left behind."

Martin finished his work and wiped his hands on a small rag. He looked at her, took a deep breath and let it out in a rush. "I'm sorry. I understand how you feel. Do you want me to *not* take him, so the sheriffs can come and . . .?"

Janet looked down and kicked in frustration at the dirt at her feet. "No, my mother would be devastated." She sighed. "Let's just do what you came to do."

Nodding, Martin walked with her along the length of the lowboy's imposing steel frame, heading toward the point where it pressed snugly against the paddock's reinforced gate. Atop the lowboy, and ratcheted to its frame with a series of chains reminiscent of the shackles from "King Kong", was what he affectionately called "The Box". It was a rectangular container formed of half-inch-thick layers of corrugated steel, and welded to a framework of foot-thick I-beams. Topping out at over fifteen tons, the Box measured twelve feet in width, fifteen feet in height, and twenty-five feet in length.

Besides a yard-wide window on each side that provided circulation, as well as a means to check on its contents, the Box had only one entrance: a hydraulically-powered, sliding door measuring ten feet in width and fourteen feet in height. The door was reinforced steel and, according to the engineer that designed it, strong enough to stop a tank.

We'll see about that, Martin thought, scoffing. *Seeing as how I'm about to transport one.*

"So, how exactly do you expect to get him in here" Janet asked, running her fingers along the Box's corrugated flanks. She stopped a good ten feet from the paddock gate. "We powered it up and left the gate up like you said, to see if he'd go inside to explore. Even tried baiting it with bananas, but he's had too much experience with human trickery. He knows something's amiss."

"Don't worry," Martin assured. He patted his shirt pocket and winked at her. "I've got it covered."

"Good. So, do you want to see your passenger now?"

He nodded and glanced up, warily eying the three-inch-thick iron bars that comprised a good portion of the walls of the darkened, fifteen-foot-high by one-hundred-foot-wide paddock. The bars were securely anchored, he noted, top and bottom, in buttresses of steel-reinforced concrete. Combined with the ten-foot-thick, stone block and cement towers that helped support the weight of the enclosure's roof, they formed an imposing barrier.

"Helluva cage," he said, taking a step closer. He paused in mid-step and did a doubletake as he noticed the bars were bent or pushed outward in several locations.

"Be careful," Janet cautioned. Martin noticed that, although she was accompanying him, she kept two paces back. "Big as he is, he's ninja-quiet when he wants to be. That's how he got my dad, by stealing up on him. Before we knew what was happening, he'd reached through the bars and yanked him inside."

"Jesus," Martin mouthed, swallowing the fast-growing lump in his throat. He shielded his eyes with one hand, trying to block the setting sun's blinding red orb. "I can't see him; where is he?"

"Hold on." Janet reached into her pants pocket and came up with a portable tracker. She glanced at it, the tip of her tongue running over her teeth, and pointed. "He's near the far South wall, about thirty yards that way. It's okay, just be ready to haul ass if he rushes us."

Martin cleared his throat and moved closer, until he was resting one forearm against the bars. The skin of his forearm registered the surprisingly coolness of the metal and he felt gooseflesh prick up all over his body. Still not seeing anything, he leaned in, his middle-aged eyes straining. There were no lights inside, at least none he could make out, and between the angle of the sun and the surrounding trees, it was a lightless cave within. The mercenary side of him began to worry he'd come all this way for nothing.

"I don't see anything. Are you sure he's in there?"

"He's in there," Janet reassured. She licked dry lips as she moved to stand beside him. "He's in musth right now, so we keep the lights off to keep him calm."

Martin recalled reading about musth, the elevated hormonal condition sexually mature male elephants experienced at certain times, but his recollection of the biology lesson did little to curb his growing exasperation. "That's commendable, but it would really help if I could actually *see* what I'm transporting."

"Just say something."

"*Say* something?"

"Yes," Janet confirmed. "Just call him. He'll come."

Martin wasn't sure if Janet's stepping back a few more yards was done for effect or not, but he screwed up his courage and stuck his head between the bars. "Hey, Jumbo! Get your sorry ass over here!"

He heard a surprisingly loud inhalation come from a far corner of the paddock, as if a giant had sucked in a breath. There was a series of loud thuds, like a telephone pole was being rammed against the side of a hill, accompanied by vibrations that penetrated the soles of his feet, before shimmying up his spine.

A moment later, Nero emerged ghostlike from the shadows. "There you . . . *Holy sh-mmf!*"

Martin almost had a heart attack as Janet crept up behind him and clamped a hand over his mouth.

"No yelling," she whispered, hauling him out of trunk range with impressive strength. "I don't know if the bars can withstand him ramming them again."

"And if he . . . *did* get out?"

She swallowed nervously at the thought. "He'd kill us all."

THREE

"Sonar, distance to target," Garm said, shifting for the umpteenth time in his oversized captain's chair. He'd had his primaries on high alert for the last hour, their vessel's acoustics on full and weapons systems at the ready, as they guided *Gryphon* soundlessly toward her target.

The strain was beginning to show.

"Three hundred yards, captain," Ensign Connie Ho replied. Her angular jaw set, the petite helmswoman's tired eyes moved like windshield wipers as they alternated sweeping her screens and the sub's twenty-foot bow window. "Maintain course and speed?"

"What's our depth?"

"Holding steady at three hundred feet, sir," Ho said.

"Max depth?"

"One thousand, sir," she replied over one shoulder. "We're steady at eight knots, estimated time to--."

"Reduce speed to six and maintain depth," Garm said, sitting up straight. His height, coupled with his elevated seat, enabled him to oversee the ORION-class submarine's entire bridge crew, but right now, his eyes weren't on them. They were focused forward, past the foot-thick, clear titanium barrier that formed the upper half of the anti-biologic sub's armored prow and peering into the clouded waters up ahead.

Something about the sea seemed off. But he couldn't put his finger on what.

Garm exhaled slowly. In the distance, he could just make out the hull of the mystery yacht they'd come to investigate – the one his brother and Eric Grayson believed had been attacked by *Typhon*.

He had his doubts. Plus, even if they were right, with the entire Gulf of Mexico as his playground, not to mention access to the always prey-rich waters of the Atlantic, the odds of their rogue pliosaur still being in the area were about the same as hitting the lottery.

Except, the latter didn't include your winning ticket trying to eat you.

"Bring us to within two hundred yards and set course to two-one-zero," Garm ordered. "Sonar, let's do a quick hull scan and check for damage."

"Aye, sir."

He swiveled to the right, until he was facing communications. "Ensign Rush, any response to our hails?"

Her back turned, the willowy blonde paused to free one ear from her headset before responding. "Nothing, sir. Not in any language or frequency." She turned partly toward him and shook her head. "No engine noise, music, ambient noise . . . nothing. She seems dead."

Garm's head swung toward Ramirez. "Sonar, can you confirm?"

Ramirez stopped stroking his mustache, his eyes, with their 20/10 vision, intense as he studied his instruments. Chief among them was the glittering 3D hologram their POSEIDON passive sonar system projected, mid-point between his station and that of Ensign Ho.

"Confirmed," Ramirez replied. "Their engines appear to be offline. I'm reading a few systems functioning, but on battery power only."

Garm nodded. A moment later, he felt *Gryphon*'s sturdy deck shift as Ho guided the 132-foot attack sub into a tight turn and prepared to circle the anchored luxury yacht. "What's going on with the water clarity? Based on the weather, it seems, I don't know . . . off."

"Aye, sir," Ramirez answered. "I'm reading high quantities of silt and detritus, and a boatload of coral polyps." His sharp eyes creased at the corners as he checked one sonar screen. "A big swath of the seabed directly underneath us has been badly ripped up, like what happens when two alpha male Kodiak bears get into a slugfest in the middle of your rose garden."

"Oh, yeah . . . well, of course. We've all had *that* happen," Garm remarked with a chuckle. "Still no biologics?"

"None, sir."

"Nothing at all?"

"Not within a four-hundred-yard radius, at least." Ramirez said. Garm watched him do an involuntary headshake. "No large life forms whatsoever, almost no small fish . . . I've got a below-normal count of crustaceans and anemones, but that's about it."

"Helm, prepare to--"

"Sir, there's something else," Ramirez interjected, his lips pursing as Ho threw him a side-eye.

"Let's hear it," Garm said, his ears pricking up.

"I'm picking up a small vessel on the bottom, three hundred yards to starboard, bearing three-four-four. It's not on any of my charts. Looks like a recent addition."

Garm nodded. He felt a yawn coming on and fought down the urge to reach for the steel coffee mug he had sitting in his left armrest. "Helm, plot an intercept course. Make your depth eight hundred feet."

Ho nodded. "Aye, sir."

"Communications," he continued, his opalescent eyes dead ahead, watching intently as they sank below the sea's sunlit phototropic zone and the region's green-gray waters faded to dark. "Go to infrared and give me eyes on the wreck, maximum resolution, and transmit it to the main."

"Yes, sir," Rush said, her fingers moving across her assorted touch screens like a concert pianist's. "Target sighted, zooming in . . . now."

Garm exhaled slowly, his head cocking from side to side as he studied the remains of an obviously expensive civilian vessel. It was lying smack dab in the middle of what had once been a healthy coral reef, now demolished beyond recognition or recovery.

"Sonar, what've we got?"

"Checking registry now," Ramirez replied. He ran his index finger down one of his screens. "Vessel is, make that *was* a 46-foot cigarette boat. A Rough Rider, christened *Scion of the Times.*"

Well, it certainly ended up being an apropos name, Garm mused. Pushing off his armrests, he rose and took two steps toward *Gryphon*'s bow. His expression intensified as Rush zoomed in on the wreck, its white hull and gunnels appearing in dull shades of bluish gray, as the submarine's advanced infrared optronics swept back and forth across its length.

"Let's throw some light on the subject."

"Aye, sir," Rush replied, hitting a tab.

Garm's pupils contracted into pinpricks, as *Gryphon*'s potent searchlights lanced through the murky water like tractor beams, zeroing *Scion of the Times.*

"Jesus," Cunningham muttered from fire control.

"Her back's been broken," Garm observed. He took another step closer, one of his eyebrows creeping upwards as the sub's viewer revealed the full damage to the ruined Rough Rider. Her keel had been completely shattered, to the point it looked like a sea serpent of old had wrapped itself around the fiberglass vessel from bow to stern, and then crushed it like an egg.

He turned back to Ramirez. "She's too clean – can't have been here long. Was a distress call made?"

"Nothing in my files, sir."

"Still no biologics?"

"No, sir."

"What about the yacht?" Garm asked, motioning toward the surface, some eight hundred feet above them. "Is *its* hull intact?"

"From what I can see, yes."

He blew out a breath of bewilderment. "Okay, helm . . . take us to periscope depth, extend photonics mast, and circle the ship. Rush, I want a complete visual, complete with satellite overview."

He turned to Ramirez, and then to Cunningham. "Sonar, I want ANCILE's acoustic intercept running full out, and OMNI ADCAP set for active search and attack, maximum range. Feed any incoming biologic larger than a dolphin straight to Fire Control. CSO, I want LADON on standby. Anything tries sneaking up on us, you're cleared to engage."

As both men set about their tasks, Garm headed back to his chair and settled in. He felt that familiar pressure buildup in his bowels, as Ho used *Gryphon*'s powerful maneuvering thrusters to propel the sleek sub straight up like a high-speed, 435-ton elevator. Outside, the water column beyond their bow grew progressively brighter, and he forced himself to relax. His gut still told him something was out of place, but based on the available data, a pliosaur attack seemed unlikely.

A collision of some kind, perhaps? Maybe the cigarette boat somehow ended up sandwiched between two steel-hulled ships and got all twisted up?

Nah, it would've been reported . . .

Annoyed now, Garm shook his head. The second-hand distress call they'd been forwarded – a text message, of all things – had seemed ridiculous at the time. Everyone assumed it was the work of some shitfaced partygoer, playing an adolescent prank. But now, with the huge yacht above them seemingly derelict, and a crushed racing boat laying on the bottom nearby, something was definitely amiss.

A moment later, *Gryphon*'s captain's thoughts were waylaid, as the big pliosaur hunter broke through to the surface. Her thick gray hull streamed torrents of seawater, while a welcome burst of sunshine flooded the bridge. Less than two hundred yards away, their mystery yacht lay directly in their sights.

Garm's jawline tightened, and he studied the nearby ship with a practiced eye, his callused knuckles emitting loud popping noises as he cracked them one by one.

Enough foreplay. It was time to get down to business.

Martin O'Dare's jaw ratcheted its way down his chest as the elephant padded toward the paddock bars. It was the biggest thing he'd ever seen, a moving cottage of gray-colored concrete at least twelve feet at the shoulder. It had ears the size of a patio door set, that undulated to keep the flies at bay, and its curved tusks made a gong-like noise as one of them brushed against the thick iron bars.

The steely columns of ivory would have made a poacher's day. They were enormous, at least eight feet in length and nearly two hundred pounds each, and ended in well-worn, rust-colored points.

It was Nero's eyes, however, that really threw Martin for a loop. Deep-set and red-rimmed, they glared down at him with undisguised animosity. There was an intelligence behind those eyes, too. That, and a healthy dose of hatred. He felt like a baby springbok, gazing up in awe at an approaching lion, too terrified to move.

"So, what do you think?" Janet mouthed in his ear, obviously amused.

Martin was too stunned to think as his mind tried to wrap itself around the sheer size of the bull *Loxodonta africana*. Based on his tapes, he'd been expecting something in the six-to-seven-ton range, but *this* . . .

A second later, Nero raised his anaconda-like trunk and emitted a deep-throated rumble that nearly caused the astonished trucker to piss his pants.

"W-what do I think?" he sputtered. "He's fucking huge!"

"Thirteen feet at the shoulder and just under twelve tons," Janet stated with undisguised pride. "Just an inch and a few hundred pounds shy of the world record for the species."

Martin shook his head, wondering if the immense bull would even *fit* in the Box.

"Still think you can find a home for him?"

He let go of the breath he'd been holding. In his head, he was trying to calculate exactly how much money he was going to make off this deal. "Oh, yeah. Are you kidding? I've got the perfect place for him, no worries!"

At the sound of a human voice, Nero uttered a deafening bellow and turned at a forty-five-degree angle, pressing one shoulder against the thick bars. He began to exude a low, pulsating rumble that shook the loose dirt around his paddock. As Martin continued to stare, he noticed the elephant's nearest eye was narrowed and focused directly on him. He also spotted the thick, tar-like secretions oozing from the bull's temporal glands – a dead giveaway that the huge beast was, indeed, in musth.

Just then, the wind shifted and Martin's head snapped back. The elephant's odor was like a hard slap across the face, reminiscent of the group of white rhinos he'd passed on the way in, only even more pungent. Nero reeked of dung, urine, and testosterone, and something else he couldn't put his finger on. It reminded him of the smell emanating from the piles of rust he's sanded off Matilda's frame, over the course of her rebirth.

As he studied the elephant's red-tinged tusks, he realized it was blood.

Dried, human blood.

As if reading his thoughts, Nero's huge, fan-like ears stopped flapping. He uttered a thunderous bellow and shook his head from side to side, rattling the bars and displaying his enormous tusks to full effect.

Janet said, "So, how exactly do you plan on getting him into the lowboy?"

Martin blinked and cleared his throat, grateful for the distraction. "Uh, the same way you catch any big fish."

"And that is?"

"We're going to lure him in with bait."

Janet did a double-take. "Bait?" Her head whipped around on her shoulders, scanning the box's interior. "Wait, you're not thinking of climbing in there and trying to get him to come after you. Because trust me, you'll never make--"

"Are you insane?" Martin asked, trying his best to ignore the malevolent looks the monstrous pachyderm continued to throw his way. "Listen, I may not be the sharpest tool in the shed, but I am *far* from the dullest!"

"Oh, thank God," Janet said on an exhale.

"First, we've gotta get prepped."

Without a word, Martin moved to a locked hatch on one of Matilda's side panels, directly above the gas tank, and inserted a key he had clipped to his belt. Reaching inside, he extracted a folded-up and obviously well-used, black-colored drop cloth. As Janet watched, he clambered nimbly up onto the rear of the big tractor, squeezing carefully past the hydraulics, and began working his way up a series of steel rungs that were welded onto the side of the box. A moment later, he was standing atop the roof of the colossal steel container, with a spectacular view of the setting sun.

Whistling to himself, Martin unfolded and began spreading out the thirty-by-twenty-foot drop cloth, fluffing it as needed, until draped over the Box's sides like oil-stained curtains, with only the entrance remaining uncovered. This accomplished, he dropped down on one knee, peering over each side in turn and tugging with both hands, until he was satisfied with the tarp's position. Still whistling, he climbed back down and stood next to Janet, grinning as he admired his own handiwork.

"Well, what do you think?"

"It's fine," she said confusedly. "And, also, dark and uninviting. So, what's the bait? Because, frankly, I don't think that's going--"

"Oh, wait, I forgot something!"

"Okay . . ."

Rushing back to the semi's still-open compartment, Martin returned with a four-foot-long contraption that looked like a section of thick dock rope, wrapped with multiple layers of gray-colored duct tape. There was a curved piece of metal at one end, and at the other, what looked like a straw broom's head, painted black.

"A little added enticement," he said, smirking.

"What the hell is that supposed to be?"

"It's the tail of an elephant cow," Martin replied. He held it at arm's length and wiggled it back and forth. "See? I made it myself. Doesn't it look enticing?"

Janet's headshake said things she would not. "Marvin, you don't actually think Nero is going to be fooled by that, do you? I mean, no offense, but it's not exactly convincing."

"Not by itself," he said with a nod of acknowledgment. "But when we add my special sauce to it . . ."

"What 'special sauce'?"

"This stuff, right here," he replied, removing a small cologne bottle from his shirt pocket and holding it between his thumb and index finger.

"And that is . . ."

"Concentrated African bush elephant estrus hormones," Martin announced with a shit-eating grin. He pulled the cap off the tiny spray bottle and sniffed the atomizer nozzle. "Ah, pure heaven." He replaced the cap and gave her a wink. "Six hundred dollars of pure ecstasy. Personally, I think it stinks like a rotting cow's cunt. But, hey, if *he* likes it . . ."

"Such *language*," Janet chided. She gave him an inscrutable look.

"Oh, geez, I'm so sorry," he stammered. "I forgot myself,"

"Just kidding. I hear far worse around here, trust me."

"Uh, okay." Climbing back up onto the rear of the tractor, Martin raised the edge of the drop-cloth enough that he could access the rear window of the box. Peeking to make sure it was safe, he hung the fake elephant's tail down over the edge and secured it in place. He glanced down at it and, satisfied that it looked inviting enough, lowered the cloth back into place and hopped back down. He contemplated the nearby ranch hands, then gave Janet an appraising look before clearing his throat and indicating the GDT lowboy.

"Are you okay with working the gate hydraulics?" he asked. "I need to get on the bed behind the box, and with the limited visibility, it would be a big help."

"I suppose so," Janet said. "What do I do?"

"One second." Hightailing it to Matilda's driver's side door, Martin hopped in and turned the ignition key. After checking his gauges, he climbed down, leaving the big rig running, and moved around to where Janet waited. He indicated a panel he'd jury-rigged to the front of the lowboy, directly adjacent to its removable gooseneck, and indicated its gauges. "Okay, the hydraulics are at full power, and the gate is already primed."

"Okay . . ."

"When I give the word, all you have to do is flip this lever from green to red and step back."

Janet cocked an eyebrow. "That's it?"

Martin chuckled. "Yep. Not exactly neural surgery."

"Okay. But, one question, before we begin?"

"Go ahead, shoot," he said, climbing onto the lowboy's expansive bed and positioning himself back by the rear of the Box, facing its tarp-covered window.

"I saw how long it took to raise the gate on your cage," she began. "A good ten seconds. I hope it comes down faster than that, because if Nero realizes what's up, he could back up and get caught under it."

Martin shook his head. "The drop is gravity-assisted and much faster, like two seconds at most. It'll be fine."

At least, I think it will.

He watched as Janet glanced back at Nero's enclosure. The huge bull was still lurking near the bars, but with them having moved a fair distance away, appeared to be losing interest. Soon, the trucker realized, he'd go back to lurking in the shadows.

"We should hurry this up," Janet stated.

Martin stuck his index finger in his mouth, then held it up to the breeze.

Perfect.

He smiled, then glanced back toward the nearby paddock gate. "I'm ready when you are."

"Let's do it."

Ducking under the dark-colored drop cloth, Martin gripped the edge of the heavy-gauge corrugated steel that framed the Box's rear window, and peered into the near-darkness of its interior. He could just make out Nero's hindquarters and swishing tail, off to the left.

It was time.

Removing the cap from the spray bottle of elephant estrogen, he inserted his right arm into the window and gave it three quick pumps. The pheromones quickly filled the Box's interior, their scent so strong he had to breathe through his mouth.

Man, that stuff stinks!

To his bemusement, however, Nero appeared oblivious.

Glancing left and right, Martin realized, with some consternation, that the tarp he'd used to darken the interior of his enormous live animal trap was also blocking the breeze. He nodded and, with a chuckle, reached into his other shirt pocket and came up with a small, battery-powered fan.

Oh, no, you don't, Dumbo. You're not costing me my big payday!

Pushing the tiny fan's switch forward, Martin held it into the box's window with one hand, then, with his other, positioned the bottle of pheromones directly in front of it. A few quick pumps into the artificial breeze, and the scent of randy lady elephant began to swirl around the Box's interior like a genie, frantic to get out of its bottle, and headed straight toward the open end.

To his surprise, the results were faster than he anticipated. Nero uttered an ear-splitting rumble of excitement and his huge body began to seesaw back and forth. A moment later, he spun completely around, the tip of his wrinkled trunk exploring the Box's open end as he tasted the air like a hungry python, tracking its quarry.

Ducking down fast, as the dominant bull's gigantic head unexpectedly filled the Box's entrance, Martin stayed stock-still, afraid to move. He heard a substantial creaking sound, coupled with a shuddering breath from the elephant, and realized Nero had taken his first step inside. Then, as the lowboy shifted on its springs, and its shocks emitted a metallic groan, he knew the aroused pachyderm had, at least partially, entered the trap. Martin's chest swelled with anticipation, and he stuck his head out from the drop cloth, prepared to signal Janet.

Then Nero stopped.

He could hear the huge bull's excited breath, followed by a series of rumbling groans that signaled his imminent excitement, but he appeared disinclined to proceed further into the Box.

Shit, what the hell's it going to take? What does this fucker need, a goddamn lap dance to get his ass in . . . ?

Inspiration, backed by flashbacks from his last strip club visit, sparked in Martin's avaricious mind. He reached up, grabbed the exposed, topmost portion of his makeshift elephant's tail, and gave it a twist. Gritting his teeth and ignoring the complaints his wrist gave off, he began torqueing the heavy contraption clockwise, then counter-clockwise. Within seconds, he had it swishing back and forth and so smoothly he had to stifle a chuckle; to poor, hard-up Nero, it must've looked like the cow elephant's version of twerking.

A loud bellow shook the interior of the box, coupled with a series of thunderous footsteps that would've done Godzilla proud. From the way the lowboy was dipping from side to side, Martin could tell his target was in the strike zone. He emerged out from underneath the drop cloth and signaled to Janet. At the same time, he mouthed the words:

NOW!

Janet reached over and pulled the release lever. As the door slid smoothly down and locked into place with a loud *ker-chak*, Martin uttered a sigh of relief. His estimate had been spot-on. The elephant was—

There was a loud "ping" sound, as the fake cow's tail was ripped loose and pulled inside. Then--

REEEEEAAAAAAAAARRRRR!

Like an enormous tentacle, Nero's trunk exploded out of the box's rear window and began feeling about. A jolt of panic shot straight up Martin's spine and he dove for it, the eight-foot mass of rock-hard muscle just missing his head. He grunted as he landed hard in the dirt next to the lowboy and crawled for it.

Infuriated at the deception, Nero's muscular trunk lashed to and fro like an angry serpent. Wrapping around a section of the drop cloth, he yanked it free and dragged it inside, shredding it like parchment as his thunderous bellows threatened to deafen everyone within a hundred yards.

"I think he's a wee bit pissed!" Janet yelled, covering her ears and indicating the big steel Box, which creaked violently back and forth on the lowboy's spring-loaded frame.

"Ya think?" Martin shouted back, climbing to his feet and dusting himself off. There was a sudden booming sound, and he did a double-take as the Box vibrated like a tank getting hit by a Bazooka.

"He's trying to break free!" Janet yelled, watching with fear-inundated eyes as the box shook again and again. "Will it hold?"

"It should!" Martin yelled back, his voice drowned out by the oversexed elephant's bellows. His eyes fell on the box's corrugated steel walls and the chains that held it in place, as they continued to shake and rattle. Behind him, he heard the alarmed cries of the nearby ranch hands, who looked ready to bolt.

"You better do something!" Janet said. Spotting his indecision, she reached for her cell phone. "I'm going to call the sheriffs to put him down! If he gets out he'll kill you, me, and anything else that moves, and level half the ranch while he's at it!"

Martin felt cold fury settle over his tensed shoulders and he shook his head hard. "No, don't. I got this."

Rushing to Matilda's passenger-side door, he swung it open and lunged inside, emerging with a plastic case, two feet in length. He popped it open, extracting the high-powered dart gun he'd brought along, and hurriedly inserted one of the pricey projectiles he'd prepped before leaving. Pulling the weapon's charger handle back to engage the CO2 cartridge, he strode toward the wildly-swaying lowboy, an intense look on his face.

"What's that?" Martin saw, rather than heard, Janet exclaim.

Nero's bellows were coming non-stop now, their bass trumpets only interrupted by periodic crashes of thunder as he rammed his head and tusks against the rear and side walls of the Box.

"It's ten milligrams of Carfentanil!" he shouted, moving cautiously forward. His eyes were glued to the elephant's hair-dotted trunk, as it thrust itself out of the box's rear window once more, feeling around for something to destroy.

"Isn't that illegal?"

"I won't tell if you won't!"

Eyes wide, Janet shook her exasperated head. "Just fucking do it!"

Martin took aim at Nero's exposed trunk, but a look of doubt creased his countenance, and he changed his mind. He had only three darts and couldn't afford to miss. Moving down the lowboy's flank, he stopped at the box's midpoint section and peered in the side window. The thick-skinned wall of concrete that greeted him was exactly what he needed. Nero was too big to turn around, which meant his captor couldn't miss.

Martin aimed and fired the dart gun into the opening in one continuous movement. The .50 caliber aluminum dart, with its four-inch steel hypodermic syringe, flew true, burying itself in the giant bull's exposed flank, and injecting its contents on impact. Nero uttered a scream of rage as he felt the jab of the needle and shifted from side to side, the dart's tufted, bright-red tailpiece giving the appearance of an open wound in his side.

Whether the effects of the synthetic opioid were instantaneous, or Nero just knew what was coming from experience, the twelve-ton pachyderm stopped attacking the walls of the Box. Within seconds, his furious trumpets ceased and were replaced by low rumbles of discontent. He stopped shifting back and forth in his cage, and his body movements became less and less noticeable, until, finally, he was frozen in place and swaying gently from side to side.

Moving closer to the box's side window, Martin peeked inside and uttered a heavy sigh. "Well, that worked."

"Thank God," Janet said, gnawing her lower lip.

"Sorry about all that," he began lamely, then indicated the dart gun. "The opioid, I mean."

She turned thoughtful, then licked her lips. "It's okay. You've got a dangerous road ahead of you. I don't envy you it, that's for sure."

Martin sighed again and checked his weapon. "Well, if you're okay with things, then I should get moving. That stuff makes morphine look like baby aspirin. It should slow his breathing for a while, but he's a lot bigger than I expected." He indicated the Box. "Don't want him coming out of it and trying to rip Matilda's hydraulics apart while I'm stuck in rush hour traffic." His expression turned thoughtful. "In fact . . ."

Climbing quietly back up onto the rear of the tractor, Martin approached the open window at the rear of the Box. With a caution that bordered on reverence, he peeked in to make sure, then reached for the steel window cover that hung beneath it on thick hinges. Hoisting it up, he swung its giant hook-and-eye over and snapped it into place, securing the portal for the up-coming drive.

"Will that hold if he comes to?" Janet asked, eyeing the window guard nervously as Martin hopped back down.

"I think so. But, to be honest, I'm hoping to not have to find out."

"I hear that."

He gave her a forced smile. "I'm, uh . . . sorry again about your dad. And all the drama."

Janet's smile was equally strained. "No worries. I'm just glad to have Nero out of here. We've been living in fear ever since, well, you know."

"Yeah . . ."

"I'll tell my mother you gave her your regards, okay?"

"Thanks," Martin replied. He felt a strong urge to reach over and give her a hug, but his subconscious recoiled against the idea. "You take care."

Janet stepped back, her ranch hands still loitering nervously in the background, and gave him an appraising look as he climbed up into Matilda's driver's side, closed the door, and put the old Peterbilt in gear. She smiled as he rolled down the passenger side window.

"Wish me luck!" he said.

"Good luck, Marvin O'Hare," she yelled. "And, if you're in these parts again, don't be a stranger!"

Martin nodded and smiled, easing Matilda forward and closing the open window. He felt the air-conditioning's cool breeze strike his damp skin and shivered in response.

"*Don't be a stranger,*" he repeated, watching Janet watch him through his side mirrors as he drove slowly away. Behind him, Nero's empty paddock and its protective palisade of trees gradually vanished in the distance.

"*A stranger . . .*" he muttered morosely, running one hand up through his damp hair, until he ended up massaging cramped neck muscles.

If she only knew.

———

Twelve miles and twenty minutes later, Martin pulled Matilda over on a deserted stretch of road, lined with shrubs and bordered by a seemingly endless forest of pine and palm trees. It was pitch black, with no streetlights as far as his middle-aged eyes could see and, as he clicked off the vintage tractor's headlights, he felt confident he'd spot any approaching vehicle long before they saw him.

With a sturdy manila envelope tucked under one arm, his flip-phone and a screwdriver in one hand, and a military-style flashlight in the other, Martin got out. He made his way cautiously along the edge of the GDT lowboy, tiptoeing past the Box's chained-down length. A mild breeze carried with it the night's moist scent, and other than the sounds of a few bugs and the crunch of mossy gravel beneath his boots, it was eerily quiet. That was, except for the rhythmic rumbling coming from inside the Box.

Martin gave a hearty exhale. From the look of things, Nero was still in a state of induced catatonia from the dart, and would hopefully remain that way for the remainder of the trip. The animal trafficker's requisite research had taught him that elephants typically slept on their feet and he was praying he wouldn't have to dose the aggressive bull again. The last thing he needed was the huge pachyderm passing out before he made his drop and ending up wedged inside. He'd have to give up the Box as part of the deal, and Lord knew those surly bastards wouldn't reimburse him for it.

As he reached the end of the lowboy, Martin set his flashlight down, its adjustable light trained on the rear bumper and illuminating the trailer's well-worn Mansfield bar. He dialed a number on his smartphone and left it on speaker, tucking it in his shirt pocket to free up his hands, while he dropped down on one knee. He was already working away with the screwdriver, when a gruff and unfamiliar voice answered.

"Identify," the voice commanded.

"This is O'Dare," Martin replied. His teeth gritted as he increased the pressure on the screwdriver, trying to loosen a rusty screw without stripping it.

"Identify," the voice repeated, this time with a hint of annoyance.

"This is O'Dare, number 34629," he replied with a sigh. *All this damn secrecy bullshit. These guys watch too many James Bond movies.*

"Hello, Martin," the voice said after a moment. "What have you got for us today? Not another Chianina, I hope. Don't get me wrong, at 3,000-plus pounds, that last bull was entertaining, but we've got plenty of beef here already."

"No, no more cattle. I've got something far more imposing," the trucker said, blowing out a breath. He spat out a bug, wiped the sweat from his brow with the back of one hand, then glanced over his shoulder at the night, out of sheer paranoia. "Where's Dwyer, I'd like to speak with him."

"Sorry, Martin. He's on vacation."

"Vacation? Who's this?"

"This is Sergeant Wurmer. You'll be dealing with me today."

As the screwdriver slipped, Martin started to curse, but he settled for a sigh. "Fine. How much does an elephant go for?"

"An . . . elephant? Hmm, how did you manage that?"

"Let's just say I'm always on the lookout for any endangered species that need relocating."

"I see." There was a moment's silence. "African or Asian?"

"African," Martin replied, a smile creasing his perspiration-soaked features as the last screw finally gave up the ghost. "And we're not talking some namby-pamby forest elephant, either. I've got a bush elephant bull, and a damn big one."

". . . that's a serious payday," Wurmer said, the clacking sounds of a keyboard being worked evident in the background.

"The rate is half-again what we paid you for the hippo, so six bucks a pound."

Six bucks a pound . . . Martin's brain started doing cartwheels as he mentally crunched the numbers.

"And that's cash, as usual?"

"Of course. Approximate weight of the animal?"

"Almost eleven tons."

"Holy fucking shit."

Martin chuckled. His buyers were usually robotic when it came to these kind of transactions, and it felt good to be able to get a rise out of one of them.

Wurmer cleared his throat. "You'll be looking at somewhere in the $130,000.00 range."

"Sounds fair," he said, trying his best to sound unruffled.

"You bet your pasty ass it is," Wurmer remarked. "Time check is half-past-eight. I'm emailing the necessary permits and paperwork to your account as we speak. Be at the secondary dock in Islamorada by 1:40 AM. The ferry leaves at 2 AM sharp. If you're late, you're fucked."

"I know the drill," Martin remarked.

"Good. Come get your cash."

"Oh, you can bet--" There was a painfully loud click, as Wurmer hung up in his face.

Rude bastard.

Hoisting himself erect, Martin gnawed on his lower lip as he took stock of his situation. *130K . . . cash!* That bitch Meg would never know about his score – not that it mattered. He was through being bled by that unfettered skank, and now he had enough bread to bury her *and* her lawyers.

"Stumpy . . ." he muttered through his teeth as he ripped open the manila envelope and started screwing again. She was about to see what the word "stumpy" really meant. Especially when it came to her bank accounts.

Martin's grin dipped as Janet Dalworth's face suddenly popped into his head. He could've been wrong, but he had the distinct impression she'd given him an open invitation, earlier. She was nice, kind of sexy, too. And wealthy. Maybe once the legalities were all settled he'd--

Shit, what the fuck am I thinking?

Smacking himself on the forehead with his palm heel, Martin shook his head hard. A pissed-off look came over him, and he dropped the flip-phone on the ground, stomping it with his work boot until he'd reduced the dated device to nothing but shards of broken plastic and wires.

With an exhale, he checked his shirt pocket for his smart-phone. Screwdriver in hand, and with his trusty flashlight lighting the way, he tiptoed past a soundly slumbering Nero and climbed back inside Matilda. He checked his mirrors for cars one last time, then flipped on the semi's powerful headlights and eased his way forward, taking care to avoid jostling the doped-up elephant as best he could.

On the side of the road behind him lay what remained of his flip-phone, a torn-up manila envelope, and an abandoned license plate.

FOUR

"**M**ierda, look at all the damage!" Ensign Adolfo Ramirez sputtered. He flushed pink as helmswoman Connie Ho shot him a chastising look. A moment later, his gaze ran like spring frost down *Gryphon*'s huge bow window, ending up back on one of his assorted sonar screens.

Ignoring the slip of protocol, Garm shifted forward in his captain's chair. His eyes were intense, his pugilist's hands gripping its reinforced armrests. He had *Gryphon* at periscope depth, photonics mast extended. Twenty-five feet from his booted feet, the source of their distress call lay displayed in full color, a live feed, streaming across the inside of the ORION-class sub's transparent nose.

With the mystery yacht sitting motionless, dead in their sights, a warped thought suddenly wormed its way into Garm's mind. He found himself wondering what it would be like to be a WWII submarine captain, in command of *Gryphon*. He could see her now, his armored attack sub, loaded with advanced stealth capabilities, slipping ghostlike beneath the waves, ready to surface at a moment's notice.

Garm checked himself. Technically, the CDF sub wouldn't need to surface to unleash its rocket-propelled NAEGLING torpedoes into the fragile hulls of unsuspecting merchant ships. The poor bastards would never see it coming.

Like lambs to the slaughter . . .

"Communications, what am I looking at?" he asked, wondering when he was due for his next psych-eval.

71

"Coming up now," Rush replied. Her lithe fingers reached up, brushing wisps of strawberry-blonde hair away from her lightly-freckled face, before she started reciting. "Vessel is a 2038 steel-hulled, Triton Tri-deck yacht . . . twin Caterpillar diesels, each generating 2,400 HP . . . maximum speed eighteen knots. LOA is 156 feet, beam twenty-eight feet . . . 526 gross tons." She craned her neck, glancing from her screens to the bow window image, and then touched a key. Instantly, a smaller file photo of the ship at dock appeared in the lower right corner of the main for comparison.

Rush licked her lips. "Her name is the *Pride of Arabia.*"

"Doesn't look very proud to me," Cunningham remarked from his station. Beside him, Rush's eyebrows lowered as she continued perusing on-screen readouts.

Garm silenced Cunningham with a look, but his gabby CSO was right. Despite their initial scans, which indicated *Pride of Arabia*'s hull was intact below the waterline, above it, the once glamorous vessel was a wreck. Both her radomes and photonics assemblies were gone – snatched right off the superstructure – and her sturdy bridge was flattened, like a house had come down on top of it.

The yacht's ornate white railings, visible in the file photo, were also stripped away, and any sections of deck that had fiberglass gunnels had enormous gouges in them, some almost to the waterline. To the untrained eye, it looked like Paul Bunyan had gone apeshit on the pricey vessel, with his own, personal Louisville Slugger.

Topping off all the other damage were a series of carbon trails, running willy-nilly all over the ship. It looked like a horde of giant fire snakes had been dumped along its length and then ran rampant. There was no pattern to the strange marks, with many decorating the sides of the hull, and a few even vanishing into the water.

Garm scratched his head. From the weird burns, it was beginning to look like there'd been a fire of some kind. But even taking arson into consideration, he'd never seen flames do that peculiar kind of damage.

"Still no answer to our hails?" he asked.

"No, sir," Rush said. "Continuing to broadcast on all international frequencies, as well as topside audio transmissions via LRAD. They *could* simply be ignoring us."

"Sonar, assessment," Garm said, stroking his chin thoughtfully. "Could a fire have left scorch marks like that? An intentional one?"

Ramirez shook his head. "Doubtful, sir. I'm not picking up any trace of accelerants. Plus, the superstructure shows no evidence of charring."

"Military ordnance?"

"No, sir. Via satellite overview, I *am* detecting lots of spent shell casings littering what's left of her decks, but it seems to be from small arms. And there's no damage to her hull to indicate the ship was actually *taking* fire."

"A lotta brass, eh?" Garm arched an eyebrow. "Well, now, *that* is interesting. Okay, next step, we--"

Rush made it a point to noisily clear her throat before interrupting. "I'm sorry, sir, but . . ."

"Go on, ensign. Anything may be useful."

"Records indicate the ship underwent a full refitting in 2042, before being purchased by her current owner, Sirdar Abdullah."

Ensign Ho twisted around in her seat, a surprised look on her face. "Wait, Sirdar Abdullah, as in the creepy 'coma diet' guy?"

"Looks like it," Rush replied.

"Oh, *really* . . ." Garm smirked. He remembered the media circus from a few months back. Sirdar Abdullah, youngest son of a Saudi Arabian real estate magnate. He'd come to the US to "make his own fortune". Using his family's money, naturally, he'd set up secured facilities in both New York and California, and started doing infomercials, peddling his infamous "coma diet" to the rich and famous.

Obnoxious TV promos or no, on the surface, his business model appeared ingenious. For an outrageous sum of money, he'd take an overweight actress, supermodel, CEO, or superstar athlete, and put them in a doctor-overseen, chemically-induced coma, for anywhere from a week to six months. During that period, the "patient" was limited to a low-calorie, high-nutrient liquid diet, fed intravenously, with the goal of them losing pounds and inches in their sleep.

To maximize calorie burning, and to ensure clients looked fit and trim when revived, Abdullah incorporated a series of high-tech electro-stimulation pads, attached directly to the host. Depending on current fitness level, desired results, and, of course, dollars invested, a full-body "exercise routine" was implemented on them, ranging from as little as fifteen minutes to as much as several hours per day.

Innate human laziness was the secret to Abdullah's success. After a few highly-publicized transformations, Hollywood's elite were lining up in droves for his so-called miracle procedure.

Garm sneered at the elitist mindset. Why worry about what you ate or drank, when you could go to sleep a fat slob and wake up a god or goddess? Price was certainly no object; not when results could be obtained without work, and clients happily shelled out tens or even hundreds of thousands of dollars to look good for that next part or party. The coma diet spread like wildfire, and for Abdullah's seemingly endless parade of overindulgent clients, their weight loss dreams had come true.

That was, until the nightmares started.

The prime suspect was the "special sauce" Abdullah's carefully screened physicians pumped down people's throats. Not even the FDA knew what was in it, and problems started popping up only a few months into the initial rollout. They were minor at first – the kind easily overlooked by prominent members of the media, many of whom were clients. They included PTSD-style dreams of drowning, being buried alive, or molested in one's sleep. But the nightmares were often tailgated by other, far more serious consequences. Among them was an alarming increase in the number of clients who, for whatever reason, could not be revived from their drug-induced hibernation.

Garm ground his molars. He remembered the networks seizing upon the story of a hapless young actress, who had fallen victim to this particular side effect. "Saudi 'Witch Doctor' creates real-life 'Sleeping Beauty'", the headlines had screamed.

A few suicides later, topped off by two clients flatlining under his care, and Abdullah's plans to "sleep his way to the top" were finished. Both of the eccentric CEO's facilities were shut down, and a warrant was issued for his arrest. The wealthy Saudi must've been tipped off, however, because he cleaned out his accounts and hopped on his private plane before the long arm of the law got its hands on him.

And now, he's here, just outside the twelve-mile limit.

"Rush, what's the status of our attempts to extradite Mr. Abdullah from his home country?" Garm asked.

"Mired in bureaucracy, sir."

"Is there still a warrant pending for his arrest?"

Rush's rounded eyes contrasted with her angular face, as she spun in his direction. "Yes, sir."

Garm permitted himself a smile. It wasn't often he got to deal with human villains. His monsters were usually the oversized, scaly kind. This would be a welcome changeup. His smile broadened, and he hit his padded armrest's intercom tab.

"Attention, this is the captain. Commander Morgan, please report to the bridge." He took his hand off the button and surveyed the ravaged *Pride of Arabia* once more. His gaze hardened and he hit the intercom again. "Lieutenant Blair, Ensigns Akio and Alvarez, meet me in the sail in ten minutes. Bring a medical kit and arm for a level-A1 boarding party."

As Garm rose, he could feel every pair of eyes on the bridge. He knew they all wanted to go, but nobody, not even Cunningham, would risk appearing to question his judgment by asking.

Beee-ooo!

As the galley's familiar boatswain's whistle sang out of the overheads, Garm shook his head. *I stand corrected.*

"Go on, Rush," he instructed as she touched her earpiece. "Put him on speaker."

"Uh, sure thing. You're connected, sir."

"Go ahead, Mr. Mot," Garm announced. "That *has* to be you."

"Damn straight it's me, I've been--"

"Before you continue," he cut in. "Let me point out that you're on speaker, and you are addressing me in front of my crew. Please conduct yourself accordingly, and make it brief."

"Uh, right, your high . . . I mean, right, sir. I, uh, heard you're going to a party, and--"

"A *boarding* party, Mr. Mot. Aboard a foreign vessel. There will be no dancing, and the only shots involved, if any, will involve bullets. That means we'll be carrying guns."

"Come on, Gar—I mean, captain." Sam's voice took on that whiney tone he used when he knew he wasn't getting his way. "I'm going stir-crazy down here! Seriously, how many episodes of 'Kraken Quest' do you think I can stomach? Besides, if it's danger you're worried about, I've got--"

"The Talos suit is not appropriate for this type of operation," Garm advised, his jaw muscles beginning to tighten. "We're boarding a yacht. Even if our gangplanks were rated for the Mark VII's weight – which they're not – the ship's deck would never hold up. Forget it."

"B-but, maybe--"

"Be patient, Sam. You'll get your chance. Bridge out."

"Yes, sir . . . thank you, captain."

Garm winced as he heard the sorrowful tone that preceded the line being cut. He felt terrible that his crippled friend was trapped down there in the galley, with nobody but Yeoman Perkins and a tiny television for company. But there weren't many options. Sam's bulky bionic wheelchair was a major hindrance in *Gryphon*'s cramped quarters. Hell, it wouldn't even *fit* through most of the sub's narrow corridors.

Garm uttered a grumble of regret, then pushed the problem out of his mind. It was an issue he'd address upon his return.

"Helm, plot course two-nine-five," he commanded, plopping back down into his chair so heavily, its shock absorbers creaked. "Bring us alongside, at the point on her portside where the decks are most intact, maneuvering thrusters only." He paused, drew in a breath. "Once we're in position, extend docking ramps five and six and lock on."

"Aye, sir," Ensign Ho replied, laying in their course with one hand, while working the yoke with the other. "Speed is three knots, steady as she goes."

Garm turned his attention to Ramirez. "Sonar, still no biologics?"

"No, sir. I picked up a small school of X-fish, but they turned off about 400 yards out and headed due east. A pod of dolphins did the same thing, fifteen minutes earlier."

"Your thoughts?"

Ramirez stroked his Don Juan mustache as he considered. "I'm not sure, captain. It could be all the racket our sonar projectors are putting out. Might account for the cetaceans, at least."

Garm nodded. "Okay, but stay frosty. I want ANCILE running full out, with both acoustic intercept and intruder alarms. We're at our most vulnerable while docking, and if *Typhon*'s nearby, I don't want to get blindsided."

"Aye, sir."

Ensign Ho spoke up. "I've got us portside-parallel to *Pride of Arabia*. Distance, 30 yards. We've got some light chop on the water with wind from the southwest, at nine mph. Compensating with maneuvering thrusters and preparing to dock."

Garm turned to communications. "Rush, maintain real-time visual on the main. Any updates, sing out."

"Yes, captain."

His keen wolf's eyes zeroed the bow viewer, watching intently as the battered hulk of the Triton tri-deck drew steadily closer. "Fire Control, activate Ladon gun system."

Cunningham cleared his throat before flipping the switch. "Uh, activated, sir. What's the target?"

"Train her on *Pride of Arabia*'s decks and prep for auto-engage."

"Um, what exactly are we targeting?"

Garm knew from experience that Kyle was averse to firing on human beings and swiveled to face his long-time friend. "Anyone shooting at us, CSO. We already know there was one hell of a firefight onboard. We don't know what kind of reception is waiting for us, or what weapons they may have. If the boarding party or boat are fired upon, your orders are to engage. That means you cut any and all enemy combatants in half."

Cunningham licked his lips as he gripped Ladon's joystick. "Captain, we're packing 30mm, armor-piercing, depleted uranium penetrator rounds. A full burst from this girl will cut that *ship* in two, never mind people."

"Then keep your bursts short, lieutenant."

"Aye, sir."

On the bow viewer, the damage to the huge yacht's steel hull became ever more telling, as the space between them decreased.

Ho cleared her throat. "Distance to target, twenty yards. Extending docking ramps five and six."

There were a series of muffled clunks, followed by a sustained thrumming sound. On the viewer, two of *Gryphon*'s yard-wide, titanium-steel ramps slid smoothly out. On the bow viewer, they looked like the investigatory antennae of a colossal mantis, straining to explore the battered white branch that was just out of reach.

"Mating commencing . . . *now*," Ho announced.

There was a pair of low thumps, audible even through the submarine's acoustic cladding, and a vibration that shimmied through the hull. A moment later, the bridge began to sway sickeningly up and down in response to *Pride of Arabia's* movements.

"We're locked on, captain," Ho said, her eyes sweeping her board. She hit a few quick tabs. "Initiating auto-hover to compensate for the chop."

Garm exhaled as things began to stabilize. A sudden whooshing sound drew his attention to the rear of the bridge, as his first officer drew open the hatch and then closed it loudly behind her.

"Commander Jayla Morgan, reporting as ordered, sir," she said, taking up position beside his chair and saluting smartly.

"At ease, commander," Garm drawled.

"Situation, sir?"

"We're locked onto the source of yesterday's mysterious distress call, an apparent derelict luxury yacht, christened the *Pride of Arabia*," he said, indicating the high-resolution image of the ravaged ship. "There's been no answer to hails and, as they're well within our EEZ, and a wanted fugitive may be aboard, we're commencing boarding procedures."

"And you want me to lead the--"

"You have the conn, commander," Garm advised, rising. He took a moment to straighten up and smooth down the front of his uniform. "I'm leading the boarding party."

Morgan's already dark face darkened even further, but she nodded. "Very good, sir. Any orders?"

"Yes. I don't like being hamstrung, latched onto that thing," he said, indicating the wreck. "Based on an absence of life signs, I don't think we'll need it, but I've got Ladon primed and ready, just in case. Assuming we don't encounter an unpleasant welcoming committee, once we're aboard, you're to disengage at once and return to periscope depth. I want all hands on deck, tubes one and four flooded, and acoustics at maximum. You're to keep one eye on *Pride of Arabia*, and the other on the lookout for incoming transients. Monitor our progress via satellite and multiband."

"Very good, sir."

Garm stepped to the exit hatch. Opening it, he glanced back and, once he knew no one was watching, gave Jayla a grin.

"Oh, one more thing, commander?" he said, loud enough for all to hear.

"Yes, captain?"

"This should be quick. Try not to hurt anyone while I'm gone."

Morgan tried and failed to keep her own grin in check.

"I'll do my best, sir," she replied, throwing a wry look in a noticeably tense Cunningham's direction. "But no promises."

"Your SR, sir," Ensign Akio Brown announced, literally bowing as he offered his captain the service rifle he'd brought up from *Gryphon*'s armory, as if it were a samurai sword.

Garm regarded his backup helmsman with calculating eyes, before nodding approvingly and accepting the GDT M18-DT carbine. He gave the M18's serial number a cursory glance, confirming it was his, then gave the weighty weapon a onceover.

Although he was partial to the .50 caliber S&W he wore like a wedding band, the big pistol didn't pack anywhere near the punch of the military's replacement for the rugged and reliable M4 rifle.

The M18-DT was one of the brainchildren of Eric Grayson, a sleek weapon's design that had enabled him to all but monopolize service rifle contracts for every branch of the US Armed Forces. Rather than discarding the M4's design altogether – itself based on the venerable M16 – GDT's weapons designers had engineered a carbine that enabled the incorporation of many existing parts, including preexisting stores of magazines and ammunition.

After checking his rifle's foregrip, stock, and optics, Garm ejected its double-wide magazine, made sure it was fully loaded, then slapped it back in hard. Pulling the center-core charging handle partially back, he checked its chambers and safety, before propping the evil-looking weapon against a nearby bulkhead.

The "DT" designation in the M18's moniker was Garm's favorite; it stood for "double-tap". At least, unofficially. The rifle was a dual-barreled design that incorporated matched chambers – mirrored versions of the same modified gas-operated, rotating-bolt actions. Its twin barrels were fed from specially-engineered, side-by-side magazines, but in a pinch, it could also accept a pair of traditional thirty-round box mags instead. Ejector ports were, like the matched barrels, bilateral, and selective fire was semi-automatic or full-auto. With both barrels firing even on semi-automatic settings, the weapon packed twice the stopping power of the traditional M4, while conserving ammunition versus a three-round burst. On full auto, the rifle was a fire-spitting demon, even utilizing the rather archaic .223 caliber, rimless FMJ ammunition that was stockpiled in most US arsenals.

Some people didn't like the M18, Garm acknowledged. At twelve pounds fully loaded, it was on the hefty side; double-mags meant double the weight. But it was steady and reliable, with jams practically unheard of. Best of all, the former pugilist noted with a grin, it had something he gravitated to – knockout power. Especially when loaded with the expensive, tungsten-core, expanding copper slugs Grayson provided to all CDF operatives.

Garm's acknowledging lips compressed inward. Say what he might about GDT's eccentric CEO, the SOB spared no expense when it came to his agents' ammunition. The high-speed, polymer-tipped .223 rounds made the older style 5.56 NATO slugs look like they were wearing a dress. At close range, the M18s his people carried could punch through just about any body armor on the market, and on full-auto, could chew their way through half-inch-thick armor plate.

Gazing around the cramped interior of *Gryphon*'s sail, Garm watched as the rest of his boarding party completed their preparations. Always striving to be the first to finish, Ensign Akio Brown was already geared-up. He had his pack on, rifle slung over one shoulder, and was standing in an at-ease pose, shifting his weight impatiently from one booted foot to the other. With his regulation haircut, at six-foot-one and a lean buck-ninety, Brown had the appearance of a battle-ready marine. It was obvious to his commanding officer, however, that the former military brat was a wee bit too anxious to get into the thick of it.

Garm had a momentary flashback of an instructor in the academy telling him one of Murphy's Laws of Combat Operations: *'Never share a foxhole with someone braver than you.'*

Hopefully, Akio Brown's exuberance would end in disappointment today. The last thing he needed was a crew casualty this early in the game.

The entire mission could end up getting scrubbed . . .

To Brown's left, red-haired Lieutenant Brody Blair was trying to squeeze into his body armor. At a rock-solid two-eighty-five, the six-foot-two powerlifter may have been two inches shorter than his towering captain, but he was a full forty pounds heavier. He had a tough time fitting into even the biggest standard-issue military gear.

Still, for Blair and the rest of them, it was worth the effort. With the exception of the pricey rounds their M18s were packing, the graphene vests they'd been issued were not only ultra-lightweight, they were ten times stronger than steel. Backed by ceramic chest and spinal plates, in a firefight, they could mean the difference between life and death.

Personally, Garm despised body armor. He felt it slowed him down and made him psychologically dependent. He preferred to rely on his mind and catlike reflexes to get him out of harm's way, as opposed to walking directly in its path, with the foolhardy notion he was indestructible. Besides, he thought, suppressing a chuckle as he watched red-faced Blair force his beefy arms through his vest and begin to grapple with its overlapping fasteners, if the shit really hit the fan, his backup combat systems officer would make one hell of a shield.

Smirking now, Garm threw a quick glance in Juanita Alvarez's direction. *Gryphon's* backup sonar tech had her weapons and armor ready and was down on one knee, looking over the oversized first-aid kit they'd brought along. With any luck, it would see a lot more action than the guns they were toting.

Time will tell.

Garm straightened up and sucked in a breath. As he surveyed his team's final preparations, he felt a sudden rush of anticipation. As gratifying as it was to hunt down man-eating marine menaces all day, the thrill of watching a NAEGLING torpedo cut a bull pliosaur in two just didn't pack the punch of pummeling some bipedal asshole who oh-so-desperately deserved it.

Like that walking manure sack, Dwyer, he mused, his hand traveling to the mottled bruise that graced his temple from the cheap shot he'd received. There was a serious debt still outstanding between him and *Tartarus's* sadistic security chief, and he had every intention of collecting on it.

In the meantime, maybe the "coma king" will resist arrest.

Garm's lips curled up into a sinister smile. "Okay, people," he said, his deep voice resounding within the cramped confines of the fortified sail. "Listen close. We're going to split into--"

"Captain Braddock," Jayla Morgan's voice interrupted from a nearby intercom. "Before you initiate boarding procedures, we have something of note."

"Go ahead, commander," Garm responded, holding and then releasing the intercom link.

"We've detected radiation readings emanating from *Pride of Arabia.*"

"What kind of radiation?" Garm asked, his opalescent eyes narrowing. Around him, there was a marked inhalation, as the boarding party sucked in a collective breath.

"The system is showing indications of uranium-235, sir."

"Uran-- are you *shitting* me?"

"Uh, no sir. It's--"

"Forgive the interruption, commander," Garm cut in. "But are you telling me that *Pride of Arabia* is carrying nuclear material, as in a *weapon* of some kind?"

"No, sir," Morgan stated. "This is LEU – low-enriched stuff, basically reactor-grade. We're picking up trace elements only, but the readings are definitely higher than normal."

Garm studied his understandably nervous team before responding. "How high?"

"Sensors indicate a radiation dose of approximately . . . thirty millisieverts per hour of unprotected exposure."

"*English*, commander."

"Sorry, sir." Morgan cleared her throat. "That's about the equivalent of a full body CT scan every twenty minutes."

"Dangerous?" Garm asked, suddenly mindful that there was only one radiation suit onboard *Gryphon*, and that was reserved solely for the reactor room.

"No, sir. I mean, I wouldn't recommend spending the night there, but a brief exposure shouldn't result in any long-term effects."

Easy for you to say, he thought. *Your eggs aren't at risk of getting fried.*

"Noted, commander. Thank you."

"Yes, sir. Bridge out."

Garm smacked his lips, then turned to gauge the boarding party's resolve. "Okay, people. As you've heard, we now have added motivation to make our visit a quick one. Anyone having second thoughts about coming? Lieutenant Blair?"

The beefy CSO appeared less enthused than before, but shook his head.

"Ensign Brown?"

Akio Brown scoffed as he snapped to attention. "No, sir. You can count on me, sir."

Garm nodded, then turned toward his backup sonar tech. "How about you, ensign?"

Juanita Alvarez looked up from checking her optics. "I'm good, sir," she said, then threw him a wink. "Besides, I wasn't planning on having kids anyway."

Garm's eyes widened a bit. "*Okay*, then . . ." He stepped nimbly around the room-sized stainless-steel column that housed both *Gryphon*'s optronics mast and the LADON turret's ammunition stores, then smacked the release lever that depressurized the sail's vault-like, titanium-steel exit door. As he watched the LEDs above the sealed portal transition from red to orange to green, he had a flashback of escorting Dr. Kimberly Bane through that same door, two days prior.

He wondered how she was doing. After what she'd been put through – his own antics, included – she'd had a rough first day.

"We'll form two teams," he said, grunting as he gave the two-foot-thick door a shove that cause it to swivel outward on humongous hydraulic hinges. A blast of wind-backed sunlight and salt spray practically blinded him, and he reached for his goggles. "Blair and Brown, take ramp five. Alvarez, with me on six."

Holding the weighty door open for them as his team exited, Garm met and held each of their eyes in turn.

"Stay on your toes and make this quick." He paused, raising his eyebrows and sucking on his teeth for effect. "I don't know about the rest of you, but I'd prefer to avoid hard-boiling my nuts in whatever nuclear microwave they've got cooking up over there."

Their snickers helped to dispel any lingering nervousness, as the boarding party eyed their pending target. Less than thirty feet from the submerged edge of *Gryphon*'s hull, the wrecked *Pride of Arabia* swayed slowly up and down. Overhead, a trio of seabirds soared like circling buzzards, their keen eyes scanning the interlocked vessels.

Taking up position at the base of the nearest ramp, with Alvarez at his six, Garm crouched down like a defensive tackle. The exposed fingertips of his gloved right hand came into contact with the foot-thick ceramic armor-plating that formed the outermost layer of the ORION-class sub's near-frictionless hull, and he glanced down.

The skin of the big pliosaur-killer was silky-smooth and surprisingly warm; not hot, as one might expect from a warship basting in the Florida sun. It was more like the skin of some slumbering behemoth.

And it was appropriate.

Regaining his feet, Garm gripped his M18 in one hand. He pulled the carbine's charging handle back, feeling its action kick in, and directed its double-barrels at the nearby yacht's debris-dotted upper deck. All the while, using his peripherals, he watched Blair and Brown as they worked their way carefully down the submarine's sloped hull, passing one of its shielded sonar arrays, until they reached the tread-coated surface of ramp five.

A sudden humming sound, coupled with a passing shadow, drew Garm's eye. He craned his neck just in time to see the LADON system's turret sweeping slowly back and forth, twenty-five-feet above their heads. As ordered, his CSO was scanning *Pride of* Arabia's decks with all the attack-sub's myriad high-tech sensors, ready to neutralize any possible threat.

The big submariner's chest swelled with pride as LADON's imposing eight barrels continued to track like a targeting tank turret. He drew a briny breeze through flared nostrils and let it out slowly. Named for the hundred-headed dragon of Greek mythology, the GDT Gatling cannon was originally designed as a tank-buster for the Air Force's new C-88 Hedgehog. To some of its designers, adding LADON to the ORION-class sub's list of already formidable armaments had seemed like overkill – the equivalent of a nightshade berry sitting atop a cyanide sundae; yet there it was.

Whatever the case, Garm thought, as reassuring as it was to have one of the notorious bunker busters watching his back, with LADON spitting fifty 30mm supercavitating penetrator rounds per second, *Gryphon*'s captain had no desire to be anywhere near it when it started firing.

Especially not with those discarding sabots flying all over the place . . .

Garm glanced across the ramp, up at the latched-on Triton tri-deck. With his bullet-resistant combat goggles already in place, the yacht's beat-up hull appeared in various shades of crimson, black, and white. He swiveled his head slowly, allowing the oval-shaped, tinted titanium lenses, with their built-in motion detectors, to scan for signs of life. A moment later, he reached up and tapped the goggle's integrated earpiece, keying its secured-channel mic to life.

"Beta team, begin approach. On your toes, people," he whispered, then quickly added, "Standard rules of engagement. Do not fire unless faced with an imminent threat or fired upon."

"Check that," Blair replied.

"Alvarez, stay on my six," Garm said over his shoulder. "I'll cover middeck, you sweep the stern."

"Yes, sir."

Moving forward like a SEAL team approaching a target, the four-person boarding party moved as one up the slope of the gently swaying docking ramps. Three yards beneath their booted feet, the churning sea dropped a thousand feet into darkness. Within seconds, they reached the derelict yacht's upper deck and were in position.

What greeted them was like something out of a horror film.

"Holy shit!" Blair blurted out, only to be silenced by a curt hand signal from his captain.

Garm signaled for Blair and Brown to join them. As they drew near, he dropped down on one knee with Alvarez at his three, his carbine sweeping the twenty-eight-foot-wide deck.

Although a quick sideways glance in *Gryphon*'s direction showed the two vessels were approximately the same size, there was a marked difference between the predatory sleekness of the gray-colored ORION-class anti-biologic submarine and the pearl-white Triton tri-deck. *Pride of Arabia* was far removed from the sumptuous, thirty-million-dollar luxury yacht whose photos they'd just seen.

She looked more like a battlefield.

One glance confirmed what *Gryphon*'s satellite overview had shown; the ship's spacious bridge looked like a Titan had stomped on it, and the expensive teak decks that ran the length of the vessel were torn up as if someone had taken a backhoe to them. Across the shattered decks, dozens of heavy-molded chairs, along with a series of custom-made, white fiberglass tables with matching illuminated umbrellas, were upended and smashed. The scene reminded Garm of an enraged child's playthings, following the world's worst temper tantrum.

His eyes narrowed. Several of the pricey tables and chairs appeared to be somehow . . . *wilted*, as if a great heat had been applied to them and then removed, melting and molding their once sturdy frames into bizarre and unnatural shapes.

As far as he could tell, the destruction continued all the way to the bow. And there was not a passenger or crewmember in sight. He stood up and took a step, then stopped as a familiar crunching sound caused him to look down. He was standing on a veritable sea of spent cartridges. There were hundreds, possibly thousands of brass casings, littering the white yacht's tarnished decks like golden sprinkles on a singed wedding cake.

"Well?" Garm asked, watching as Akio Brown bent down and scooped up a handful in one gloved fist.

"Mostly 9mm with some 5.56 NATO thrown in, sir."

"Small caliber . . ." Garm mused. He spotted a handful of submachine guns, mixed in with the debris. They were the kind typically carried by private security forces. Nothing sizable, mostly HK-MP5's and a few others. Several of them were bent and a few were melted – especially the barrels and fore-stocks. He reached down and examined an intact-but-empty UZI that lay discarded nearby. It was sticky with blood and some sort of clear goop. He sniffed it, made a face, then discarded it, before checking the dispersal patterns of the nearest clusters of spent cartridges.

"The fire definitely seems directed outward," he stated. "So, any inter-ship conflict appears unlikely." He took several steps, expended casings and fragments of fiberglass grinding under his boots, before stopping and shaking his head in exasperation. "There was obviously a firefight. But what the hell were they shooting at? And why aren't there any bodies?"

"I don't know about any bodies, but we've got a serious blood trail here, captain," a tiptoeing Brody Blair announced from thirty feet away. "Or make that a smear, sir."

"Here, too," Alvarez said, pointing to a nearby bulkhead. "And there, and there . . . Jesus, it's everywhere."

She was right, Garm realized. He took a deep sniff and grimaced. All around the decks were rust-colored trails of human blood, baking in the midday sun. There weren't many actual spatters – a few here and there, caused by the spray of what must have been horrifying arterial wounds – but rather, a series of long, winding drag marks. Many looked as if someone had gotten wedged under a combat vehicle, with only a few inches of ground clearance, and then dragged across a long stretch of cement.

Except, of course, there was no concrete to be found. Nor were there any vehicles of any kind.

No, not a battlefield. This is more like a slaughterhouse.

Garm's eyes shifted seaward, as the familiar thump of *Gryphon's* loading ramps retracting filled his ears. In moments, his mighty mistress would submerge from sight and take up position nearby, an indestructible sentinel, waiting and watching.

"Okay, people, I'm transmitting the vessel's blueprints to your goggles," he announced, touching a series of buttons on his forearm transmitter. "Assuming their last modifications didn't stray from the norm, you should be good. Blair and Brown, take the lower levels. Alvarez and I will sweep the upper decks. Search for survivors and call in anything of note."

"Yes, sir," Brown said, stepping forward. He had a light sheen of perspiration on his bronze-colored face and gripped his carbine tightly, "Captain Braddock, I just want to say, it's an honor finally going into combat with you, sir."

Garm suppressed a chuckle. "Technically, there hasn't been any combat yet, ensign, but I appreciate the sentiment. Now, get to work."

"Yes, sir," Blair said from a few yards away. He turned on his heel, signaling Brown to follow.

Watching them go, Garm hoped his gung-ho backup helmsman didn't end up getting trigger happy and blow away some innocent survivor by mistake. That would be wonderful, an international incident sitting in his lap.

Man, I bet Grayson would love that.

"Okay, Alvarez," he said, stepping carefully around a congealed pool of blood nearly three feet across. "Let's start with what's left of the bridge, see if there's any record of what went down."

"Yes, captain," the slim sonar tech replied. She hefted her heavy carbine with surprising ease. "Since you're not wearing a vest, would you like me to take point?"

Garm chortled, then winked at her. "Maybe next time."

As they worked their way along the Triton's upper deck, pausing once to spring over a yard-wide, ten-foot rent that exposed the deck below, the seasoned sea captain wondered at the extent of the violence they'd missed. Everywhere they looked there were streaks of dried blood, urine, and even feces, and the same, strange charred marks that coated much of the hull. He noted that several of the burn trails – some four or five feet in width – led to similar-sized, gaping holes in the ship's gunnels, with the glittering sea visible through the ragged-edged openings.

The warrior in him sensed a bizarre uneasiness creeping up. It was a feeling that continued to build as he listened to Blair and Brown's cabin-by-cabin updates. No bodies, no survivors, and even the lower decks were trashed.

Whoever had done this had been astonishingly thorough. Everything on *Pride of Arabia* except them was dead. Could the boat's private security have been responsible? Or maybe some elite paramilitary outfit? He wasn't writing anything off. The "coma king" must have made some powerful enemies.

Alvarez cleared her throat. "Bridge is a complete no-go, sir," she said, then indicated a once-colorful banner that covered much of a now-defunct hot tub. A sudden commotion caused her to stagger back, and a trio of black-backed seagulls, concealed behind the tub, took flight in a shower of feathers.

"Fucking birds!" she said with a chuckle.

"Vultures of the seas," Garm muttered. He looked up, watching the scolding gulls arc overhead.

"Jacuzzi's got a lot of blood in it," Alvarez resumed, shrugging and hoisting the end of the banner with her carbine's twin barrels. "Jesus, what a mess. Someone definitely met their maker in here. What do you . . . *fuck!*"

Garm saw her pale up and sprang to her side, his M18 primed and ready. He followed her wide-eyed gaze and did a double-take.

Bobbing up and down in the hot tub's crimson-brown water was a leg – a woman's from the look of it – severed from where it had joined the torso. It was bloated and pale and, judging by the ragged hunks of thigh tissue, appeared to have been wrenched from the socket. It reminded him of a rotisserie chicken leg someone had torn off, when they were too impatient to wait for a knife.

"Ugh," Alvarez managed, blanching.

"Walk it off, ensign," Garm said, giving her a reassuring pat on the rump. He pulled the banner back in place, covering the orphaned limb.

"Who the fuck would do something like that? Pirates? Drug dealers?"

"Whoever it was, if they're still here, they've got a nasty surprise coming," he said through his teeth. He indicated the sprawling debris field ahead. "On my four, but keep your finger off the trigger."

Weapons at the ready, they worked their way from stern to bow, finding nothing but rubble and death. They were about to head below decks, when Blair's voice burst into Garm's ear.

"Captain, we've got a survivor!" the CSO shouted.

His muscles tensed. "Location."

"Ship's galley, deck three! I'm pinging it!"

"On our way."

Working their way down a curved stairwell, the steps of which had been fused into a slippery mass of aluminum and fiberglass, Garm made for the yacht's galley. His heavy footsteps reverberated off the burnt and bloodied walls of unfamiliar corridors and bulkheads, but he never slowed. The ship's map and locator on the inside of his optics grew steadily brighter, the closer he got.

Lips curling in disgust, he sprang over a mess of intestines that reminded him of the recent death scene he'd seen on the docks in *Tartarus*, and kept going. Behind him, he could hear Alvarez cry out, curse, and continue on, huffing and puffing under the weight of their medical kit as she struggled to keep pace.

A moment later, he banked left to find Blair and Brown standing outside what remained of *Pride of Arabia*'s galley. Catching sight of his captain's intense expression, Blair took a step toward him, his hands extended out in a gesture for caution.

"What've we got?" Garm asked. He peeked over the hulking powerlifter's shoulder into the galley. It was a shambles, with once-shiny pots and pans and shattered china and wine bottles forming blood-spattered mounds, atop which rested a pair of warped stainless-steel fridge-freezers.

"She's over there, in *that* . . ." Blair advised, indicating a massive, cast-iron oven, topped with what looked to be sixteen burners.

"What?" Garm shook his head in incredulity and took his goggles off before peeking in the galley. A heatwave immediately assailed his eyes, and he realized all the burners on the expensive range were on and running full blast. He turned back to Blair and Brown. "Is she alive?"

"Yeah," Brown said. He tapped his goggles. "Picked up her heartbeat and breathing, but when we opened the oven door, she freaked the fuck out. Got herself way in the back and she won't come out." He glanced back inside and licked his lips. "She's terrified, captain. Scared shitless."

Garm glanced at Blair, who gave him an affirming nod. "What the *hell* is she doing in the oven? Did she hear you coming?"

Blair cleared his throat. "I don't know, but she's in bad shape, sir. We need to get her out of there, ASAP."

"Okay, you two, stay here," Garm ordered. He considered the situation, then turned to his sonar tech. "Alvarez, you're running point on this. Go talk to her."

"Yes, sir," she replied, gripping her M18.

Garm stopped her in midstep. "Alvarez . . ."

"Yes, sir?"

"She's already scared. Lose the gun."

"Oh, shit," she said with an embarrassed grin. She handed him her rifle. "Sorry, sir, I should've known."

Hanging back, Garm watched as she moved quietly toward the oversized oven. Its black, five-foot, cast-iron door was still hanging open, and from the look of things, you could've roasted a good-sized pig in there. Obviously, the heating elements inside weren't on, or the girl would already be dead. But with the burners all going like that, the inside of that thing must've been a steel sauna. Why anyone would want to hide inside it was beyond him.

"Hey, how's it going?" Alvarez prompted, dropping down on one knee.

"Stay away!" a shrill voice screamed out. "Shut the fucking door and get out of here!"

"Look, we're here to--"

"I said, get away!"

Garm signaled Alvarez to back off. His eyes tightened and he ground his molars in frustration.

'Shut the door?' What does she have, a death wish? Has she been in there for two days, and with the door closed the entire time? Impossible. She would be dead already from dehy . . .

A half-dozen empty one-gallon water bottles, scattered around the garbage-strewn floor outside the oven, caught his eye. He shook his head, then signaled Alvarez and handed her his carbine.

"Let me try," he said. He looked around, plucked a one-liter bottle of water off the only intact shelf in the place, and approached the oven on puppy's paws. Still a good five feet away, he sat down on his haunches and glanced inside. Even from that distance, he could feel the heat.

He could see the girl; she was in a fetal position, and had wedged herself under one of its shelves, and as far back inside the cavernous range as space would allow. She appeared to be Caucasian, a once-pretty brunette in her mid-twenties, he estimated.

She saw him and opened her mouth to shriek again. "Who the fuck--"

She did the deer-in-headlights thing when Garm leaned his head back, showing off his strong jawline and pale-blue eyes to full effect, followed by giving her his most winsome smile.

"How *you* doin'?" he said, doing the "Joey Tribbiani" thing as he held out the bottle of H2O. "Can I buy you a drink?"

The girl froze, with the exception of her expression, which morphed from hysteria to astonishment. "I . . . I . . ."

"Here, let me open it for you," Garm said, one of his big hands grabbing the plastic bottle top and peeling its transparent safety-lock off. He placed the bottle gingerly on the steel floor of the oven, and then rolled it toward her.

Speechless, the girl hesitated only seconds before snatching the bottle up and pulling its nipple out. A moment later, she was suckling water like a starving infant at its mother's teat. He could see the dried skin of her throat convulsing as she drained two-thirds of the bottle. Her thirst momentarily quenched, she paused to catch her breath and studied him. Her soot-stained face began to wage a tug-of-war of expressions, going back and forth from guarded to what might have been attraction.

He had no alternative but to bank on the latter.

"Hi, I'm Garm Braddock," he opened up, giving her the same easy smile he'd used to psyche out opponents in the ring, after they'd caught him with a good, clean shot. He placed one hand on the blood-stained floor and eased himself down as best he could, ending up in a lotus position with his muscular forearms resting on his thighs for added effect. "You got a name? Or should I just call you 'hot stuff'," he said, indicating her position and blinking.

The girl's head gave a confused twitch. A moment later, she started to smile, but then caught herself. "Y-you should go," she said, her eyes turning feral as she looked nervously behind him. "It may come back."

It.

"We'll be leaving shortly," Garm said, nodding in agreement. "But I'm the leader of an elite military rescue team, and it wouldn't be right for me to just abandon a damsel in distress. Especially such a pretty one. Can I convince you to come with me?"

She shook her head vehemently. "No! It's not safe! It's going to get us!" She paused to suck in air. "*Please*, you need to leave . . . leave . . . now."

Garm became alarmed. He could see the girl was getting woozy, undoubtedly suffering from heatstroke. Information be damned; he had to get her out of there; she'd die if he didn't.

"Exactly, what is it you're afraid of?" he gently pressed. "You're safe with us, believe me."

"Not safe," she asserted, trying to squirm further inside what would end up being her cast-iron coffin. "You can't stop it. Guns don't hurt it. *Please* . . . I don't want to see you die, too!"

Garm nodded. Pistol rounds were useless against a big pliosaur. Maybe *Typhon* was responsible for the ship's condition, after all. Maybe they'd had a flamethrower on board, or even some sort of advanced plasma torch like the *Talos* suit was packing, and tried using it to fight him off. He'd never seen a plasma weapon in action, but that might explain all the weird burn trails.

"We have something much bigger and better than guns," he said, trying to exude charm and confidence. "If I prove to you that I can keep you safe, will you come out?"

"W-what?" the girl's lips continued moving after she stopped speaking, and he wondered how much of her mind was still intact. "Who-who are you?"

"I told you, I'm Garm Braddock," he said. He pointed a thick index finger at the insignia on his shoulders and lapels. "I'm captain of an ORION-class anti-biologic submarine . . . the *Gryphon*."

The girl licked her cracked lips and struggled to swallow. "Is that like a . . . nuclear submarine?"

"Yes, but we're faster and tougher than the kind you're thinking of. We hunt down and kill sea monsters."

"Sea monsters?" she licked her lips again. "You mean like--?"

"Like the *Kronosaurus imperator* that attacked your ship."

Her headshake was a spasmodic jerk. "Not . . . one of them . . ."

Garm leaned toward her, unmasked concern etched across his chiseled features. "What's your name, girl?"

"It's . . . Amber."

"Look, Amber, if you stay in there much longer, you'll die," he announced with eerie calmness. "But we can protect you. *I* can protect you. Please, come with me."

Amber's dry eyes ping-ponged from his face to his extended hand, trying to gauge his genuineness. He hoped she'd cooperate – for her sake. If not, their only recourse would be to drag her out of her makeshift sarcophagus – something he was praying to avoid. Her sanity hung in the balance, but at the same time, he wasn't about to leave her there to turn into a desiccated corpse.

"Does your submarine . . ."

"*Gryphon*."

"Does *Gryphon* have weapons?"

Garm smiled rakishly. "Are you kidding? She's a high-speed killing machine, with everything from rocket-propelled torpedoes to a rail gun that could reduce what's left of this yacht to cordwood." He leaned forward and extended his arm further, once more offering her his hand. 'Please, let *me* protect you."

Amber regarded him through the eyes of a traumatized child, found hiding under its bed after suffering the mother of all nightmares. He watched as she gnawed her cracked lower lip. Then, to his surprise, with those same, haunted eyes never leaving his, she began to creep forward. It was a painful and laborious process, dragging her blistered skin across the hot metal of the stove's blackened interior. As she reached the opening, she looked up and blinked at the bright sunlight streaming thorough a nearby porthole. Once a foot across, the tiny window was now a blown-out opening over four feet wide.

Garm saw her fixate on the gaping hole and her terror begin to build. "Easy," he cooed, his big hand palm-up and less than a foot from hers. "Don't look at that. Just look at me, okay?"

Amber turned to him once more. He could feel the weight of her stare, as if she was trying to draw out some of the confidence that he exuded. Then, her eyes flitted to Alvarez and the rest of the boarding party, some ten feet to her left. Finally, she swallowed her fear and, as if making sure he was real, she touched his palm.

A moment later, she took his hand.

Garm heard Alvarez shift and froze her with a gesture. With small words of encouragement – never grabbing or pulling – he allowed Amber to climb carefully back out of the hotbox she'd called home for the better part of two days. Gripping his callused palm as much for support as for reassurance, she struggled to her feet.

His nose crinkled up as he caught a whiff of her. She was pale, bruised, and gaunt, and the undersides of her forearms and legs were covered with blisters, but she was alive.

Garm cleared his throat. "Okay, Amber, we're going to bring *Gryphon* back alongside and do a quick check for   *oof*!"

The impact as the girl threw herself at him caught him off guard.

"Please, get me out of here," she whispered, gripping him tightly around the waist.

Considering her condition, she was surprisingly strong. Garm took the deepest breath he could manage and then exhaled. "You got it."

He angled his head toward the remainder of the boarding party. "You three, split up and sweep any part of the ship that's been missed. Keep in radio contact at all times."

"Yes, sir," came the united response as the group spun on their heels.

"*Gryphon*, this is Captain Braddock," he said into his commlink. "I presume you've been monitoring our transmissions?"

"Yes, captain," Morgan radioed back immediately. "Orders, sir?"

Garm felt himself beginning to sway slightly back and forth and realized, to his bemusement, that Amber had started slow dancing with him. As he looked around, a wave of surrealism crested over him. Standing amid a graveyard of smashed appliances and blood-spattered kitchenware, with him garbed for battle and her wearing a party dress that looked like it had come from a landfill, the two were like a prom date from hell.

"Bring her about and recommence boarding procedures," he ordered. "Keep the sub on full combat alert and be ready for an emergency dive at any time, including during our boarding."

"During boarding, sir?"

"You heard me. If I give the word, I don't care if you have to dump us in the drink."

"Uh . . . yes, sir. Understood, sir."

Garm hesitated, as he realized Amber had begun humming to herself. It was Henry Mancini's *"Moon River"*, if he wasn't mistaken. He craned his neck to one side and checked to see whether her eyes were closed.

They were.

His lips compressed inward, and he shook his head sadly. The poor thing's mental state was worse than he'd thought. Not that he could blame her. He didn't know who, or what, had put her in her hellish prison, but hiding in a broiler for two days would drive anyone to the brink of insanity.

If not over it.

"Have the medical officer stand ready to treat survivors," he said, then added, "And get the Coast Guard on the horn. We've got at least one survivor we'll need medevacked, stat."

"Roger that, sir."

Barely cognizant of the sharp click that indicated his conversation with Commander Morgan had been severed, as well as subsequent transmissions from the boarding party as they continued their fruitless search, Garm remained where he was. With her body practically melded to his, and her arms bear-hugging him so tightly it hurt to breathe, he allowed Amber's bizarre dance to continue. Her contented humming gradually increased in volume, its melody filling the ruined galley, backed by the rhythmic crackle of shards of china, shattering beneath their shoes.

Fifteen feet to his left, Garm's gaze fell out the ragged, four-foot hole where the galley's porthole had been.

And the fathomless seas beyond.

FIVE

"Ya look tense, O'Dare," a gruff voice remarked over Martin's shoulder. "Ya oughtta try and relax more." There was a pause, followed by a nasal chuckle. "I mean, look around . . . sun's up and it's a beautiful day!"

"Right," the stocky trucker drawled. Still resting his forearms on the archaic ferry's flat wooden railing, he didn't bother turning around. He had little desire to exchange pleasantries with Bryan Wurmer – make that *Sergeant* Bryan Wurmer – at least according to his black uniform's insignia. As traveling companions went, the muscular, six-foot-one military thug was hardly Martin's type. Despite being in his early fifties, he was nosey, uncouth, and literally radiated menace – on a level that went far beyond the myriad scars tattooing his scalp, face, and forearms.

Of course, for all his surliness, Wurmer was right about one thing; it had been a glorious sunrise. Moreover, with a light breeze wafting in off the water, and nary a boat in sight, it was shaping up to be one hell of a day. Especially when Martin contemplated the mountain of cash that would soon be his. But, after being up all night, almost four hours of which were spent on what was, effectively, a slow-boat-to-China, and with nobody for company but a foul-tempered ex-marine, he'd pretty much stomached all the chit-chat he could take.

There was a sudden squawk of static as Wurmer spoke in low tones into his walkie-talkie. "This is Sergeant Bryan Wurmer,

101

ID 4247, approaching loading dock. Kindly have the weigh station prepped, and a crew ready for debark."

"Roger that," an unfamiliar voice monotoned.

"How's our passenger?" Wurmer asked, turning toward Martin. He adjusted the ferry's trim smoothly with one hand, while sipping a cold cup of coffee with the other. "Quite the score for ya, eh?"

Shrugging, Martin wandered over to the end of the giant steel box they had chained to the bed of the forty-foot barge. A deafening rumble, coupled with a loud scraping sound, caused him to step hurriedly back, to his escort's considerable amusement.

"Boy, he's a piece of work, ain't he?" Wurmer said, sniggering. "Don't worry, we'll take the fight outta him."

Martin shook his head as he surveyed Nero's current prison. The people from Rock Key were taking no chances. The riveted steel container they'd transferred the giant pachyderm into back in Islamorada made the animal trafficker's corrugated metal "Box" look like thin carboard by comparison. It was of similar size, but the new container's walls looked to be enamel-coated steel plate, some two inches thick, with steel I-beams reinforcing all stress points.

He gave a self-assuring nod. As enraged as the musth-fueled African elephant was – and the use of heavy-duty cattle prods to "motivate" him into his vault-like home had added to Nero's already intense fury – he was confident he and Wurmer were safe. A charging *Triceratops* couldn't have penetrated the walls of the ferry-borne box.

As the familiar outline of an enormous, boulder-shaped island formed in the distance, Martin felt an anticipatory sense of relief well up. He glanced at Wurmer, now humming to himself as he guided the unwieldy vessel toward their destination. For the last few hours, the tired trucker had been forced to listen to the vet-turned-mercenary's assorted "war stories"; how he'd run a Cuban refugee camp outside of Miami, and a laundry list of the illicit activities he'd engaged in to line his pockets.

Assault, gambling, underground fight clubs where prisoners were forced to beat one another to bloodied pulps, prostitution, even *child* prostitution – and all of it on Uncle Sam's dime.

It was no wonder he'd done some serious time.

He needs to do more.

Martin surreptitiously studied the powerfully-built merc. With his carved countenance, cruel features, and well-groomed, salt-and-pepper mustache, he looked like some aged-but-still-dangerous Gestapo officer. Especially with that all-black uniform he wore, and those nasty-looking combat boots.

He found himself wondering if he could take him in a fight.

"Something on your mind?" Wurmer said, turning around so unexpectedly he caused the surprised trucker to jump.

"Uh, no," Martin replied lamely. He suppressed a shudder. Up close, the guy's red-rimmed eyes were downright scary, like he was on hardcore opiates or something. "Just wondering, how long is this gonna take? I don't like leaving my truck for long periods like this."

"Yeah, I got jealous when I saw that rig of yours. She is a thing of beauty."

"Thanks," Martin replied, watching as the intimidating mountain known as Rock Key grew ever larger. Soon, its granite dome towered hundreds of feet over their heads, like the bleached skull of some murdered titan, left by the Gods of Olympus to spoil pristine seas.

He felt a sudden pressure in his bowels and realized Wurmer had turned hard to port. A moment later, the mustached merc increased speed and began circling the mile-wide island. Fifty yards ahead, a flock of yellow-eyed gulls, floating serenely atop the swells, took wing as the big ferry bore down on them.

Watching the scolding birds gain altitude, Martin felt a pang of jealousy. He longed to be free; not just of this transaction, but of all of it. Maybe, once he'd dealt with his whorish ex and gotten his finances in order, he'd give up the whole "exotic animal relocation" gig. Maybe it was time to find something more sedate and legit to occupy his time. He'd certainly have enough cash to make a go of things. There *was* that little lakeside bait shop/diner he used to go to. He'd heard the owner was getting along in years and was looking to sell . . .

Martin's ponderings were interrupted as Wurmer pointed to the sharp chasm that split a goodly portion of Rock Key's northern face, starting midpoint in the mountainous rock, and expanding steadily as it worked its way to the waterline. At the base of the cleft was the facility's all-too-familiar loading dock, already peppered with an orange-clad dock crew, standing around waiting for them.

"Won't be long now," Wurmer yelled over the sounds of the engine.

"Good. Let's get him weighed and me paid, then laid."

"I hear that."

As the old ferry chugged steadily closer, Martin scrutinized "the Rock's" towering walls. He'd heard about the devastation inflicted on the island during assorted military tests, nuclear and otherwise. Despite all the stories, from where he stood, the curved surfaces of its natural stone ramparts seemed remarkably smooth. It would make for a tough climb, that was for sure.

Clocking a sudden disturbance in the water, his heart skipped a beat. He remembered the heavy-gauge pliosaur nets that protected the region, however, and relaxed a bit. There *was* something amiss in the water – a billowing disruption that started from deep down, along the submerged walls of the island, and then extending out across an area fifty feet across and a hundred feet in length.

As he took in the swirling swath of sea, Martin realized there was more than one. In fact, there were many such disturbances, all emanating from far underwater, and of similar size and shape. Whatever their cause, the marine disruptions seemed to take place at the same time and at regular intervals.

Definitely man-made . . . no doubt about it. Probably some sort of overgrown coolant or filtration system.

His face a mask of curiosity, he turned back toward the bow. As he watched, Wurmer slowed their approach, then threw it into reverse. They were less than a hundred feet from their pending anchorage now, and on a perfect approach.

"So, tell me, what do you use the animals for?" Martin asked, inclining his head toward the caged elephant.

"You know better than to ask questions like that," Wurmer said, his brow beetling up as he worked the wheel. "What did Dwyer tell you?"

"He said you guys do cosmetic testing on them, like beauty products."

Wurmer turned toward him, his eyes wide with amusement. "Yeah, that's right . . . cosmetics. That bull of yours is definitely going to experience real beauty!"

Martin's annoyance at the patronizing response was sidelined by a loud thud, as the barge-like ferry bumped up against the reinforced concrete dock. He looked up, noting for the first time how the two-hundred-foot crevasse the tiny mooring station was nestled in completely concealed it from overflies. It was like a high-arched cathedral, a magnificent byproduct of erosion in the granite. Although narrow at its peak, at the waterline the cleft was well over a hundred feet across – a tranquil grotto of swirling turquoise waters that housed not only the dock, but a trio of twenty-foot skiffs with rugged outboard motors.

As he took in the tied-off boats, partially obscured from view by both the dock and the ferry, a half-dozen waiting workers sprang aboard. Like foraging ants, they swarmed over the vintage vessel, tossing thick dock ropes around its thigh-sized cleats, and pulling back hard to secure it in place.

Wurmer turned to him then and tossed him a weighty skeleton key. "Here ya go, trucker. Make yourself useful and help me undo the anchor chains, so we can get this bad boy unloaded."

Amid the hustle and bustle of workers inspecting their cargo and talking into hand-held radios, Martin worked his way around the base of the imposing steel container. Ignoring Nero's rage-filled trumpets, he inserted the skeleton key into each of the fist-sized padlocks, before undoing the associated ratcheting mechanism that pulled each chain tight. Within minutes, the container was free from the ferry's reinforced deck and ready to be moved.

Wurmer directed Martin to accompany him onto the adjacent dock, then paused to wipe a sheen of sweat from his mustache with a callused palm, before speaking into his walkie-talkie.

"Okay, lower away," he ordered.

His eyes drawn by the rumble of its powerful diesel engine, Martin glanced up at the discharge ship loader. A heavy-duty, albeit compact, version of the cranes he'd seen unloading containers from incoming cargo ships, the metal monstrosity was built right into the side of the island. With its battleship-gray, riveted exterior, and its hundred-foot arm, gears, and counterweight system protruding from a towering wall of solid stone, it looked like some sort of gargantuan steampunk shore battery, waiting to unleash its exotic payload on any unsuspecting trespasser or passersby.

"Stand clear," Wurmer warned as he signaled to the crane operator, now visible inside the machine's reinforced cab.

Within moments, the harbor crane's four-inch-thick woven steel wire cable, terminating in a gigantic, four-legged wire rope sling, each leg formed of three-inch-thick cable stretching thirty feet in length and ending in a massive drop-forged latched hook, was lowered into position. Suspended a few feet above the ferried container, it held position, its swaying in the stiff breeze almost imperceptible. There was a quick toot from the crane's claxon, and four dock workers instantly went to work.

Grasping a series of steel rungs, welded directly into the box-shaped container's flanks, they scaled it like tangerine-colored monkeys. Martin's heart skipped a beat as Nero, suddenly aware of their presence, abruptly rammed the reinforced sides of his enclosure. To their mutual surprise, other than a deep, gong-like sound, punctuated by a rumbling bellow of rage from the frustrated pachyderm, the great bull's assault was ineffectual.

It was confirmed. Having pitted his titanic strength against the armored walls that surrounded him, Nero had finally met his match.

Thirty seconds later, the connectors were in place and the workers had retreated back to the safety of the dock. Wurmer did a quick walk-around, checking the positions of the cables, then turned and signaled to the cargo loader's operator. Like a pack of black mambas slithering upward, the oiled cables instantly tightened. Hard on their heels, the sound of the big crane's caterpillar engine straining filled the cleft and echoed across the surrounding water.

As he eyed the spectacle, Martin felt a sudden pang of panic. Nero weighed nearly twelve tons, and Lord-only-knew how heavy his bank-vault-of-a-prison was. If either the cables or crane motor weren't up to the task, his precious prize would end up in the drink.

A moment later, a wheeze of relief escaped Martin's chest. With its powerful engine revving, the harbor loader's huge gears and column-like hydraulics picked up the container and its infuriated occupant like they were a child's playset. Continuing upward, until the rust-stained bottom of the steel box was suspended ten feet above everyone's heads, the experienced operator directed the load slowly inward, the crane's mighty arm swiveling atop its base like one of the *Yamato*'s main gun batteries.

"Okay, hold her steady," Wurmer radioed. "Let's get a weight."

Already slowing, once it cleared the ferry, the crane ceased moving altogether and held position. To Martin's surprise, their unwilling passenger remained stock-still and didn't make a sound. In fact, other than the huge bull's heavy breathing, and the metallic groan of the crane's cables creaking in the wind, it was eerily quiet.

Nero was cooperating.

Smart. He knows he's high enough up that, if dropped, he'll get hurt.

"Okay, let's hear it," Wurmer radioed, his eyes focused on the crane cab's operator.

"Sans container, you're looking at 23,724 pounds," the operator radioed back. "That's a facility record."

"Very good," Wurmer replied. "Get it on the flatbed, call receiving, and let's finish up here."

Martin glanced up as the black-clad sergeant turned away from the loading process. Over Wurmer's shoulder, he watched as the crane's arm resumed its inward arc. Swinging smoothly inward, it stopped once more, this time with the imprisoned elephant positioned directly above a waiting flatbed rail car.

Martin was familiar with the oak-topped flatbed. Built on a larger-than-normal six-foot gauge track, it was enormous – designed to transport heavy equipment – and self-propelled by a built-in 1,200 horsepower diesel engine that allowed it to move in and out of the mountain.

Of course, what was *inside* the mountain remained a never-ending mystery.

"Okay, O'Dare," Wurmer said, his thick index finger jabbing the buttons of the calculator he'd extracted from his uniform's shirt pocket so hard, it was a miracle he didn't punch holes in it. "It appears we owe you $142,344.00."

"Holy shit."

"Fuck, yeah. And if you drop the money case overboard on your way back, I guarantee that'll be the nicest thing to come out of your piehole."

A resonating thump, and the resultant dust cloud that accompanied it, drew Martin's attention back to the nearby flatbed. It was practically inundated with dock workers, working quickly and efficiently to ensure the elephant and its mobile prison were secured for transport. Within minutes, the "Mankiller of Mozambique" would permanently vanish into the mouth-like darkness of the rail tunnel, as every other so-called rescue he'd brought there had.

"Uh, maybe I should ride along?" he offered. "You know, to make sure he settles in properly."

Wurmer's smirk seemed to exude both amusement and malice. "Ya know full well civilians ain't allowed inside. Besides, you and me both know, give him the chance, that tusk-fucker will stomp you to jelly."

"Um . . ."

"Relax, O'Dare 32649," Wurmer said, resting a gnarled hand on his shoulder. "Ya should know by now, we're not going to cheat ya. So, just cop a squat and chill. I'll be back out with your hundred-and-forty-two large in a few minutes."

"Make it one-forty even," Martin decided.

"Come again?"

"A modest gratuity, for all your help."

For the first time, one of Wurmer's smiles appeared genuine. "I like the way ya do business," he said with an approving nod. He indicated the trio of nearby skiffs. "In fact, for that, I'll let ya zip back on one of our runabouts, instead of wasting the rest of your morning being driven back on that slug's-ass old rust bucket."

"That'll work. Thank you."

Casually leaning against the docked ferry's gunnels, Martin folded his arms across his chest and watched the merc strut away. Ten yards ahead of Wurmer, a dockworker keyed an access code into a concealed wall pad, at the point where the trestles the flatbed railcar rested upon appeared to disappear into solid rock.

There was a grindy grumble, and the cement under Martin's feet began to tremble. As he watched, a steel wall, overlaid with texturing that made it blend in with the surrounding rock, slid noisily upward, exposing a railway shaft some thirty feet wide. At Wurmer's signal, the flatbed's driver cranked up his engine and began to chug, slowly but steadily, into the dimly-lit tunnel.

Following the train car on foot, Wurmer started forward. Behind him, a procession of one-dozen dock workers, their orange uniforms reminiscent of prison attire, trudged wearily behind him.

As Martin watched the last of the workers disappear into the maw-like opening, he tensed. He felt a strong and sudden urge to follow them but knew better. He'd been warned once already. Still, curiosity was a real bitch . . .

He'd always wondered what deviltries went on inside Rock Key. He'd asked around, but nobody seemed to know. In fact, most people had no idea the place was even in use, let alone occupied by some sort of paramilitary task force. At least, that was what they said. Officially, the island was listed as abandoned and off-limits.

Nobody went there. At least, not without an invitation.

Of course, Martin had an invitation. He'd had many, in fact. Yet, in all his visits, he'd never gotten past the dock. He'd politely inquired several times, but his entreaties had always been rebuffed. And he wasn't about to risk souring his relationship with these people. At least, not before he'd gotten his money.

And speaking of money, how long is this gonna take?

The minutes continued to tick by. Five . . . then ten. Patience had never been Martin's forte and, after he'd been pacing and twiddling his thumbs for the better part of twenty minutes, paranoia began to get the better of him. Worrying made no sense, of course. He'd brought these guys plenty of cargo before. The croc, the giraffes, the hippo . . . they'd always played it straight and anted up.

Still, Nero represented his biggest score by far. A veritable bonanza.

Hell, you could buy a small house with that kind of bread.

Martin had just about reached the end of his anchor rope, when he heard the familiar sound of Wurmer's size-12 combat boots, crunching the gravel that served as ballast for the tracks.

Seconds later, the mustached merc emerged from the darkness of the railway tunnel.

Martin smiled. He was carrying an attaché case. The kind with combination locks, and an attached shackle.

"Okay, O'Dare, here ya go," Wurmer announced. Stepping carefully over the slick rails, he moved to a nearby fillet station and placed the case atop the slick, stainless-steel table. "All non-sequential c-notes, as per SOP."

Although he did his best to appear calm and composed, it was all Martin could do to contain his burgeoning excitement. He licked his lips, then rested his thick palms on the knurled aluminum case and hit the thumb latches.

Snap.

Finally, ever-conscious of the light breeze filtering through his suddenly damp hair, he raised the lid and peeked inside. His Cheshire cat smile said it all. It was a Ben Franklin Christmas morning, with row after row of neatly stacked greenbacks, all bound in tight bundles, and bearing the calm countenance of the famed founding father, staring amiably back at him.

"Now, there's something ya don't see every day," Wurmer said, standing beside him and sharing the view.

Martin ended the moment by slamming the attaché case shut. "The combination?"

"Already set," Wurmer replied. "Last three digits of your ID code." Then, as if an afterthought, he fished inside his pants pocket and came up with a key. "For the cuff."

Martin accepted it but frowned. "I doubt I'll need this."

The silver-haired sergeant pursed his lips. "Six miles back to your truck, buddy-boy. It can get pretty choppy out there, not to mention the occasional bulldog. Ya never know . . ."

"Good point," the animal trafficker agreed. He hefted the case by its handle and grinned as he felt its weight. A contemplative look came over him, and he reached down and snapped the shackle around his left wrist, before dropping the key inside his back pocket.

"Pick your poison," Wurmer said.

"Come again?"

"The skiffs," the big merc replied, indicating the trio of nearby boats. "And don't sweat it. They're small but nimble, and very seaworthy."

"Works for me," Martin said, eyeing the nearest runabout. He was comfortable with tillers, and figured to be back in time for lunch. "What should I do with the boat when I get there?"

"Just tie it off."

"That's it? Aren't you worried someone will make off with it?"

Wurmer's snicker reminded him of a hunting hyena's chuckle. "It's got a built-in tracker. And besides, nobody in these parts would be stupid enough to steal from us."

Martin nodded, then extended his hand. A look of surprise came over him as Wurmer pulled him in for an unexpected hug, one of those the chest-to-chest ones that guys gave one another in bars.

"Good work, O'Dare."

"Yeah. Well, uh . . . thanks for everything," Martin mumbled, feeling awkward. "And, uh, please tell Chief Dwyer I hope he enjoyed his vacation."

"Ya got it. I'm sure he'll look forward to your next delivery."

Without another word, Wurmer spun on his heel and made strides back to the railway passage entrance. Opening the keypad's plastic cover, he punched in a quick code and stepped inside. Thirty seconds later, the rock-textured wall rumbled slowly back down, until it settled into place with a testicle-rattling "whump".

As the noise from the door closing echoed around the cleft's walls, then gradually faded, Martin stood motionless. For whatever reason, his senses began to soar. He could hear slack tide waves lapping gently against the edges of the dock, and smell the saltiness left behind, as their spray dried atop its sunlit sections.

He took a deep breath, then shook the attaché case up and down, as if reassuring himself that it was real. It was. He couldn't believe he'd done it; he'd actually pulled it off. He had all the money he needed to deal with his problems. He could teach his slutbag ex how using people could come back to bite you, and then start a new life for himself.

Yeah, *Stumpy* was through taking shit. He was done with it – with *all* of it.

This was it for him, his last--

My last time here.

As the realization hit that, in all likelihood, this was the last time he'd ever set foot on Rock Key, Martin frowned. An unsettled feeling came over him. It wasn't that he enjoyed coming there – the exact opposite in fact – the place literally reeked of danger, and he never knew if he'd get out alive. It was that he was dying to know what went on inside. The possibilities were endless. The base (and he was certain that it was, indeed, a base of some kind) could be anything from an exotic dogfood plant, to a top-secret chemical weapons testing facility, to a CIA spook training center.

As he caught his eyeballs doing the pendulum thing, ricocheting from the closed gate, to the nearby skiff, and then back again, Martin realized something.

He wanted to know. More than that, he *needed* to.

He couldn't just walk away without finding out. He knew himself. He'd end up waking up every night, in the middle of the night, for the next two or three years, frustrated because he hadn't discovered what mysteries awaited behind that monstrous barrier. It would drive him nuts. Especially, since *now* he had a chance to find out.

He grinned, amused that scary Sergeant Wurmer wasn't as smooth as he thought he was. A moment ago, he'd made the foolish mistake of not covering the entrance keypad properly, when he keyed in his access code. And Martin had clocked it. It was 0-4-2-4.

He also knew, per his previous visits, that there were no external security cameras around the debarking dock. True, when activated, the railway gate was frightfully noisy, but based on the size of the tunnel, the place had to be huge. If nobody was nearby when he opened it, he could hop in, take a quick stroll around, and he back out and gone before anybody knew what was up.

Martin stiffened suddenly.

But wait, what if he got caught? Would he be arrested? Would Wurmer and his thug friends put him in a body cast? Or, worse, would they confiscate his hard-earned score? He shook his head. No, no . . . that was impossible. If they tried, he'd squeal like a pig to the authorities.

His lips a tight line, Martin shifted his weight from foot to foot. His freckled face contracted, and he started sucking in breaths, Lamaze-style. He could feel the weight of all his tension, sitting like a cinderblock in the base of his belly. Finally, a look of steely determination came over him and his tired eyes narrowed. With his jaw set, and his gaze focused on the big stone gate's reinforced archway, he spat into the wind.

Fuck it.

He was going for it. Whatever it was that waited behind that intimidating steel door, he planned on seeing it.

"So, we have a new enemy, then?" Garm said, sitting back in the sturdy desk chair that, combined with his fold-down writing desk and bunk, comprised the only real furniture in the confines of his captain's quarters.

Discounting his makeshift heavy bag, of course.

"Apparently so," Dirk replied from the nearby wall monitor.

Garm shook his head, suppressing a growl of frustration. Less than two yards away, the ragged panel of polished aluminum he'd directed his boarding party to remove from a downed freezer in

Pride of Arabia's wrecked galley, stood propped up against a nearby bulkhead. Gracing its once-shiny surface were four . . . make that nearly five pairs of circles, ranging from four to six inches in diameter. They ran parallel to one another, forming an almost a straight line that swept across the four-foot piece of metal.

"I don't know, little brother," he said, swiveling in his chair so he could see Dirk's face. "Seems hard to believe we've got yet another marine monster on our hands."

"Given the world we live in, I think we both know better than to play the doubting Thomas when it comes to such things," his brother said, sipping coffee from his favorite mug.

Garm's snort came out more like a scoff. "I hear that." He leaned forward, his big palms resting on his thighs. "So, where exactly did this thing come from? Do you think it's another Diablo escapee?"

The creases of his twin's increasingly familiar frown were more pronounced than usual, on the wide HD monitor. "I doubt it. There've been legends of monster octopi around for centuries, long before the caldera unleashed the 'Legions of Kronos' on us. Supposedly, they inhabit the deepest ocean abysses. And they probably do. Mom certainly believed they did."

"She did?"

"Oh, yes. She was never convinced that all the classical low-frequency 'Bloop' sounds that were detected by NOAA and SOSUS were made by pliosaurs. Many were so deep down and of such long duration . . . no air-breather could stay submerged that long."

Garm sat rigidly upright, his curiosity piqued as much by uncovering something new about their mother, as discovering a species of mythical creature that, as the evidence apparently indicated, was frighteningly real.

"Did she investigate?"

Dirk shrugged. "A bit. I remember her interviewing a retired sonar tech, a real old-timer who'd worked on one of the old *Los Angeles*-class subs."

"Wow, the 688s?"

"Yes. He claimed to have picked up a large, organic life form on sonar that went super-deep once it sensed the sub's approach."

It was Garm's turn to shrug. "That's it?"

"No," Dirk said, grinning. "He claimed the sonar image indicated something huge – at least one hundred feet in length – and that it 'jetted away' at a speed of over sixty miles an hour. Using active search-and-attack, he tracked it to the sea floor, some twelve-thousand feet down, but then lost it."

"And mom suspected it was one of these octopuses?"

"Or a monstrous squid of some kind."

"Well, at least we know now that the yacht's survivor was telling the truth."

Dirk's expression changed, becoming noticeably compassionate. "Speaking of the girl, how is she?"

Garm's eyebrows hiked up. "As well as can be expected. The Coast Guard medevacked her out about an hour ago. It was pretty unpleasant, let me tell you. Ever since I carried her off *Pride of Arabia*, she was on me like Velcro. She wouldn't let go for anything. In the end, my IDC had to sedate her."

"Not the first time you've left women in such a state . . ."

"Ha-ha," Garm replied, shaking his head at the uncharacteristic lack of consideration, but still grinning. "Seriously, she went through quite an ordeal, hiding out in what was effectively an overgrown crucible."

"It saved her life," Dirk asserted, disappearing off-screen for a moment, and then returning. "The animal must've been using its arms to explore every inch of the boat, and anything edible was dragged overboard and devoured. She was smart; turning on the burners like that kept it from feeling its way inside the oven entrance. Otherwise . . ."

"Yeah."

Dirk's dark-colored eyes grew as he leaned closer to the camera. "Was there anything else in her story that might prove useful?"

"Not really. She and her girlfriend got invited to a party on the boat. They were wannabe models, both with a nudie magazine spread under their belt. They went, hoping for a break through the rich-shit who owned the yacht." Garm shook his head. "They got more than they intended. The coma guy turned out to be a real piece of shit. And, in true, stereotypical dirtbag fashion, he offered them money for sex – twenty grand cash and a Rolex, each, if memory serves."

"Are you serious?"

"Yep."

"They said no, I assume."

Garm got up, his thick arms folded across his chest. "The friend said yes, believe it or not, but our girl refused. She wanted off the boat, but the asshole refused to let her leave until the party was over. When she made a stink, the guards gave her a choice: the galley, the meat locker, or swim for it."

"What class. Well, we know how that worked out for *them*."

"Yep. Who would've thought Karma had eight arms?"

Dirk cleared his throat. "Actually, a 'party' like that explains why the security cameras were deactivated. Too bad. It would've told us both the species and size of the cephalopod we're dealing with."

Garm indicated the sheet of polished aluminum. "Well, it can't be *that* big. I mean, these suction-cup marks are smaller than my hand."

"Big brother, those marks are from the suckers near the very *tip* of the tentacle. They start out tiny and get progressively larger."

"Oh," Garm said, making a show of stroking his chin. "So, how big of an animal are we talking about?"

Dirk glanced sideways on the wall monitor, his eyes focused on one of his screens as he tapped away on his keyboard. "Well, going off the pictures you sent me . . . and the satellite overview of what must be the offending cephalopod's tentacle tracks all over the hull . . . and the diameter of the hole that formed around the galley's ruptured porthole . . ."

"Can I get the Cliff's notes version of this?" Garm said with a chuckle.

"Yeah, yeah, yeah . . . Very funny."

Dirk's gaze intensified as he studied hidden figures. "Humph. Well, it's hard to be precise, but I'd say that old sonar tech's estimate was more-or-less accurate."

"So, you're telling me we've got a blue-whale-size, man-eating pile of calamari running around, attacking boats and eating the occupants?"

"Looks that way."

"Fuck . . . Wait, what the hell's it doing here in the first place?" Garm said, genuinely annoyed. After the incident with the girl, the last thing he needed was another delay or distraction. "You said they're deepwater hunters, so why's it attacking surface ships?"

"Well, if--"

"And when I say ships, I'm assuming this thing was responsible for the attack on that schooner, and not *Typhon*, as we originally figured."

"Most likely," Dirk said with obvious patience. "You know better than anyone that our oceans are, as mom put it, 'all fucked up'. If these things *do* live in the abyss, making a living off the occasional errant sperm whale, then it's distinctly possible that recent alterations in cetacean behavior have . . ."

"They've run out of food," Garm finished, his lips pursing. "And we've been tacked onto the menu as a substitute."

Dirk nodded. "Based on the damage to *Pride of* Arabia, it looks that way. The animal's attack pattern indicates a deliberate and methodical search of the vessel. It started at the topmost decks and worked its way down. Moreover, it knew exactly what it was looking for, meaning human beings, and it actively sought them out. Like how you or I would behave if, say, we were digging for the seeds of a pomegranate."

Garm paused, his wolf's eyes studying his reflection in the marred sheet of polished aluminum, as well as the foot-wide line of sucker marks that appeared to cut him in two. He squinted at the disc-shaped impressions in the metal, then dropped down on one knee and ran his fingers over one of the larger ones. The sheet had come from the fridge's roof and, based on the pattern, he figured the tentacle had slapped down on top of it, scarring it before it toppled.

He peered more closely at the metal, then pressed down on it. The sucker marks weren't just surface blemishes like one would expect. They were deeply indented in the metal, but not crisp, like you'd get if you used a power tool of some kind. Rather, they were smooth and had an amorphous, almost bubbly quality to them.

Strange.

Garm exhaled, low and long, before standing back up and straightening his uniform. "So, tell me, Dirk . . . do I have to kill this thing?"

His brother cocked an eyebrow. "You mean, does the hunt for *Typhon* have to be postponed, in favor of tracking down and neutralizing this creature?"

Garm turned back toward the monitor, meeting his brother's gaze.

"Gotcha," Dirk nodded knowingly. "Let me run a full security and media sweep and see what I can find. I'll get back to you in twenty."

"Okay. I'll be waiting."

———

Like a monstrous marine gargoyle, the male *Octopus giganteus* sat perched on the very edge of the deepwater drop-off, his gleaming eyes gazing broodingly down into its unfathomed depths, his back turned toward the bothersome daylight. Except for occasionally champing his razor-edged beak in frustration, he remained stock-still, ignoring the schools of tiny fish that explored his craggy skin, and the painful hunger pangs that wracked his massive body at regular intervals.

A hundred yards behind the male, draped across the bluff like some impossibly large whale carcass, lay the remains of the ancient iron vessel, within which his monstrous mate had constructed their midden. At over a hundred yards in length, it dwarfed even the giant female.

Like some amorphous demon, she had emerged the moment he returned, spilling through the forty-foot rent that split the barnacle-tinged submarine's flank, and sending a nearby school of bluefish scurrying for their lives. Now, she was in full feeding mode. The billowing of her bulbous mantle was reminiscent of a partially-inflated hot air balloon and, splayed out beneath it, her massive tentacles, lined with manhole-sized suckers, swarmed like a frenzied pack of pythons.

The male gazed pensively back, before paling and averting his eyes. Despite the poor water clarity – more and more impeded by the growing cloud of skin and flesh particles that surrounded the female – he could see her clearly. She was gorging herself on the banquet he'd provided.

The male octopus was confused. Despite the fact that she'd recently birthed their latest brood, nearly 200,000 eggs, which hung suspended within their nursery like clusters of foot-long grapes, his mate's appetite had not stabilized or decreased.

In fact, if anything, it had grown.

He hunkered down, the chromatophores in his bark-like skin changing color and helping him blend in with the seaweed-tufted edge of the drop-off. Through his sensitive suckers, he could hear, feel, and even *taste* the impacts of the female's five-foot beak, as she attacked the oozing gray whale carcass; each snap sheared away over three hundred pounds of meat, blubber, and bone.

Although his stomach was literally cramping with hunger, the male feigned indifference. With the female's temper growing fouler by the hour, he knew better than to risk trying to claim a portion of the kill. The cetacean he'd successfully stalked was large for its kind – nearly fifty feet in length and over forty tons – but at the rate she was tearing into it, it was evident there would soon be nothing left.

Peering down from the ragged summit upon which their lair was situated, the male gazed longingly into the blackness of the abyss. From where he sat, it was over a thousand feet to the bottom – a sheer drop down crumbly, anemone-dotted walls, back to the welcoming frigidity from whence they'd come.

As he contemplated the inviting darkness, a series of finger-like ridges extended from the wrinkly skin on his twenty-four-foot mantle and swept back and forth across it in waves. The ridges were the result of thousands of projection-like papillae. They were like the gooseflesh that adorned the skin of the tiny bipeds the two of them hunted, but with one important difference; his epidermis changed texture based not only on mood, but at his command. He could mimic sand, stone – even coral. And all in the blink of an eye.

His papillae suddenly went flat, and the male's temperament with them. Starvation began to breed desperation. Perhaps he would try hunting the deep once more. With the female already engaged, perhaps he could find something upon which to sustain himself. Something large enough that--

A sudden shift in pressure displaced both the octopus's thoughts and tens of thousands of gallons of seawater. Like a barrage balloon lifting off, his mate unexpectedly arose from the gray whale's savaged remains and settled down directly behind it. A deep, bloop-like rumble emanated from her cavernous mantle, and her glittering yellow eyes sought and found her mate's, irrespective of his attempt to conceal himself.

The male tensed. The meaning portrayed via the repeated undulations of the female's colossal arms was obvious. It was a summons.

She wanted him to come closer.

A shudder passed through the male's 134-ton body; if his copper-rich blood hadn't already run cold, it would have. A powerful fight-or-flight impulse permeated his enormous brain, but he suppressed it. With her appetite at least partially satiated, and him having done nothing to provoke her, he reasoned the odds of her attempting to devour him were slim.

Still, as he rose from the drop-off's rim in a cloud of silt and sand, the male remained alert and adrenalized. He began to draw copious amounts of seawater into his muscular siphon, preparing to jet away at the first sign of aggression.

As he came within striking distance, the female's tentacles lashed out, wrapping around the gnawed remains of the gray whale. With a powerful shove, she pushed the stripped mass of bones, ligaments, and tendons in his direction, then indicated the rusticle-draped hole that served as their lair's entrance.

Her meaning was obvious. He was to play brood-mother once more to their clutch, while she prowled the surrounding seas.

Shrinking down as she moved closer, the male made a half-hearted show of studying the whale carcass, then deliberately hovered over it. Drawing it beneath him with several of his tentacles, he enveloped it and began to bite, the black chitin of his four-foot beak making sharp cracking sounds as he crunched down on innutritious ribs and backbones. A few minutes later, and with his mate still looming over him, he discarded the remnants of his distasteful "meal" and slunk towards their lair, squeezing himself inside.

Uncomfortable at being hedged in, the male settled down on the sandy bottom and compacted himself into a writhing pile of tentacles. Annoyance swept over him, and he blended in with the seafloor, adjusting his color and texture until his gleaming orbs were the only parts that gave him away.

The female contemplated her mate through hooded eyes, gauging his submissiveness. Then, with a rush that caused a shower of reddish-brown dust to descend from the orange rusticles remaining around their lair's entrance, she started to move. With all eight of her arms gathered behind her like an oversized Multiple Launch Rocket System, she soared soundlessly up and over a nearby hillock, then headed toward the shallower waters of the Continental shelf.

The male studied her pensively as she shrank in the distance. Despite her bloated body, she was still ravenous. He could tell.

From the safety of their lair, he continued to watch, until the female had moved completely beyond the range of his senses. Once he was sure she was gone, his skin texture and hues changed. He shook himself free from the gritty midden bottom and rose. His eyes, with their horizontal pupils, angled upward, focusing on the long strands of milky-white eggs that adorned the artificial cave's roof. Through each egg's translucent membrane, he could see the eyes of his future progeny, writhing within their tiny wombs. There were tens of thousands of them, a sea of tiny black dots, peering outward into the watery world that awaited them.

Drawing cold seawater into his mantle, the male targeted the eggs with his yard-thick siphon. He directed his stream gently back and forth, like a low-pressure hose, cleansing and oxygenating them. Eventually satisfied that they were free of contaminants, he glanced down, his attention on the annoying black particles that, despite his best efforts, continued to coat the midden floor like free-floating grains of pepper.

There was something about the glittering granules that made the male uneasy. It was more than the bitter taste his tentacles' chemoreceptors detected when he brushed up against them. The tiny dots brought with them a strange, tingling sensation, one his mollusk's mind interpreted as a threat of some kind. He suspected their presence was at least partly responsible for his mate's increasingly erratic behavior of late, but he lacked the ability to fully comprehend or communicate this.

Extending his arms through their lair's entrance, the male octopus gathered enough sand to fill a good-sized garage and dragged it inside. With surprising gentleness, and taking extra care to ensure his movements did not dislodge or damage any of his fragile larvae, he pushed and pulled the sand carefully across the nursery bottom. With deliberate slowness, so as to not cause the particles to swirl up and onto the eggs, he continued until he'd covered them as best he could.

Then, with an almost human shrug, the father octopus left the nest and settled down in a pile directly outside. His parental instincts ensured that he would not abandon his brood, but the longer he remained inside, the stronger the unusual itchiness became. And with it came bizarre feelings of agitation and anxiety – emotions he was ill-equipped to deal with.

Trembling, as his hunger resurfaced in a fiery rush, the male extended one of his arms and began to poke at the gray whale's skeleton. He turned its arc-shaped skull this way and that, exploring its innermost cavities, in the hope his mate had missed something – something sufficient to warrant his excavating it.

She hadn't. As frenzied as her feeding had been, she'd been quite thorough.

Angry and frustrated, the male *Octopus giganteus* began to corkscrew his way into the gritty seafloor, his suckers helping him auger his way deeper and deeper until, three yards down, he came into contact with the hard stone underneath. Shaking his massive body, he caused the surrounding sand to cloud up and over him, covering himself in a fine layer, then adjusted his color and texture to match. Within moments, he was indistinguishable from the surrounding seabed – a low, rough-hewn ridge of some kind, no different than anything else.

His golden eyes glittering slits now, the male watched and waited. Though desperate to feed, he would not leave. Perhaps a shark, a whale, or any large sea creature, for that matter, would happen by.

If one did, it would find an unpleasant surprise waiting for it.

SIX

As a steaming blob of guano struck his temple and began oozing down his cheek, Martin O'Dare had to bite his tongue to keep from cursing. He wiped away the bat or bird shit – he had no idea which – with his sleeve and shook his ginger head in disgust. He was beginning to have some serious doubts about his decision to explore Rock Key's hidden railway tunnel.

Exploring? More like spelunking!

Bypassing the rock-textured drop gate that warded the thirty-foot tunnel had been as simple as punching Sergeant Wurmer's purloined access code into its camouflaged keypad. Walking in and closing the thick steel portal behind him was even easier; the flipping of a bright yellow lever, located immediately inside, and conveniently marked.

Martin's problems had begun when the door slid down, and he found himself in the dark. He had presumed that the overheads he'd seen lighting up the track when they hauled Nero inside would stay on. They hadn't. And, despite a frantic search, he could find no way to turn them back on.

Left with no choice but to rely on his cell phone's woefully inadequate flashlight function, the stocky trucker crept cautiously along, his shiny aluminum attaché case, crammed with cash, gripped possessively under one arm. He sucked in a breath and resumed stepping, wincing at the painfully loud crunching sounds his work boots produced on the slick mounds of gravel that lined the tracks.

Martin's eyes widened in alarm, as his lead foot suddenly slid out from under him. Thankfully, his reflexes kicked in, and he got his free leg up and under him in time to avoid ending up in a heap in the middle of the tracks.

He whistled low and stood there, grinning and shaking his head in a show of forced levity. Imagine if he'd sprained an ankle or, worse, blew out a knee? The guards would've laughed it up big time as they handcuffed him and turned his ass over to local PD.

Martin ground his molars and continued, praying for the booming echoes of his footfalls to fade before someone heard them. As if the threat of getting busted wasn't bad enough, the unpleasant prospect of electrocution via third rail suddenly popped into his head. He stiffened, but then relaxed, rejecting the worrisome notion. The big flatbed they'd loaded Nero's cage onto had been self-propelled; he'd seen it. Shaking off his apprehension, he swung his phone light left and right, surveying the gloomy tunnel ahead.

God, this place is fucking creepy.

And it was. There were strange sounds and rumbles that he couldn't begin to fathom, not to mention a distant thrumming he could feel through the soles of his feet. Some sort of subterranean machinery, he guessed.

An unexpected barrage of high-pitched squeaks from above caused Martin to stop suddenly. He licked his lips and glanced nervously upward. The thirty-foot tube he was traversing was semicircular in cross-section, and appeared to consist entirely of rough-hewn stone – there were no beams or support columns that he could see. High up, beyond the range of his sad little light, were layers of cobwebs, matted down and plastering the ragged stone as it ascended into darkness. And from that darkness, came a cacophony of loud chittering sounds.

A horde of bats, no doubt. Hopefully, the non-vampiric kind . . .

Martin resisted the urge to cross himself, and instead wiped his dripping brow with the back of one hand. The air inside the tunnel was warm. Not sauna temp, like the midday sun baking Rock Key's barren exterior, but definitely not welcoming and cool, as he'd expected. It was tepid and had a clamminess to it that made your skin feel as if it was two sizes too small.

The worst part was the odor. There was a dank mustiness about the place, a smell that went beyond the powder-dry deposits of manure and guano he occasionally dodged, or the rust-colored scrape marks that decorated the rugged stone walls every few feet.

To Martin, the stink was reminiscent of the inside of a crypt.

He paused to check his cell's power reserves, then rechecked that the ringer was muted, before continuing. His whorish ex had unexpectedly called him a few minutes ago, nearly giving him a coronary, and sending echoes of her saucy ring tone bouncing up and down the nearby passageway. He'd hung up on her at once, of course, before she'd got him caught. It was just like Meg to somehow realize he was riding high, and to try and figure out some way to bring him down.

Not this time, bitch.

Leaning against the dampness of a nearby wall, Martin rested his briefcase on the ground and scanned the tunnel ahead. As far as he could figure, it had run straight for a good hundred yards. Now, it was finally beginning to veer. In fact, there was a Y-shaped split up ahead. The left passage was an extension of the one he was currently on, with the rails continuing seamlessly on. The right one, on the other hand, appeared track-free, just ragged stone and barren concrete. A utility tube, most likely, but it was hard to tell from that distance.

Frustrated that he couldn't see further ahead, and worrying more and more about being discovered, Martin considered giving up his quest. His romanticized notions aside, Rock Key was beginning to look more and more like an abandoned subway tunnel – hardly worth the risk of continuing.

When he reached the junction, Martin paused to weigh his options. He still had a full sixty percent charge on his phone, which was good; the last thing he needed to worry about was stumbling around in the dark, screaming for help.

He decided to give his little expedition just five more minutes. If nothing of interest happened by then, it was game over. He'd return to his waiting boat, hop in, and haul ass back to Matilda, loot in hand.

And, speaking of loot . . .

Suddenly, the thought of losing his footing and watching the score of a lifetime tumble down the nearest mineshaft, loomed large in Martin's mind. He disliked the case's shackle – it reminded him too much of his marriage – and had removed it shortly after Wurmer's departure, but right now it made sense. Slipping the steel cuff around his wrist, he tightened it almost to the point of discomfort. That accomplished, he checked his pants pockets to ensure he still had the key, then eyed the twin tunnels.

The rail tunnel proved problematic. Even with his limited light, he could see that, in addition to veering left, it descended at a fairly steep angle. He could also make out a sheen of moisture, coating both the stainless-steel rails and the gravel mounds they rested on. The added sound of dripping water made it a no-brainer. As curious as he was to discover why the base owners would shell out a small fortune for a rogue elephant, he wasn't keen to slip and bust his ass while doing it.

Martin smiled humorlessly as he envisioned where *that* might take him. He'd probably end up strapped to a gurney in the base's medical wing, where a team of doctors would promptly cut his clothes off. Within minutes, every guard in the place would know about his "injury". He could hear their sniggering now.

Fuck that.

Yes. The path to the right definitely looked more promising. Cool, dry, and level too. By comparison, it was downright inviting. And, if his eyes weren't playing tricks on him, there appeared to be doorways dotting the walls.

Looks like it's time to see what's behind door number three!

Martin started eagerly forward. A moment later, his lips parted into a huge grin. His vision had been spot-on. There *were* access doors, spaced roughly fifty feet apart. They were big and constructed from some sort of heavy-gauge metal, like the kind they used to secure utility rooms . . . Or prisons.

Clearing his throat, Martin approached the nearest door. He pressed his ear to it, then gripped its welded handle and gave a powerful tug.

Nothing. As luck would have it, it was secured from the inside. It had to be, because for the life of him, he couldn't find a keyhole.

Shrugging, the tenacious trucker tried the next one, and then the one after that. They were all locked, an endless line of towering, gray-painted dominoes, built to tease and frustrate him, like so many things in his life.

After the tenth attempt, Martin had reached the point of exasperation. He spat irritably at the nearest door, then sighed. A moment later, his jaw dipped, and he wiped a string of spittle from his chin with the back of one hand.

That was it. He'd had enough. It was time to go home.

He was literally turning on his heel, when he spotted a door that wasn't locked. In fact, it was more than that, it was ajar. The invitation couldn't have been more apparent if it was intentional.

Dismissing his innate cautiousness, Martin approached the doorway with a spring in his step. Finally, things were going his way. He reached the partly-open portal in three quicks strides, grabbed it by its reinforced edge, and yanked it the rest of the way open.

Martin shrugged. Like the unlit tunnel it intersected, the room before him was pitch-black, but he didn't care. His phone still had plenty of juice. The spelunking would continue. As he shined his tiny torch into the impenetrable darkness, his lips peeled back into an enormous Cheshire cat smile. At last, he was going to uncover Rock Key's hidden treasures.

When he stepped into the open doorway, and a blast of fetid air hit him square in the face, however, Martin's smile dipped.

There was a foul odor emanating from the chamber beyond, that came and went in waves, like the breath of a living thing. He smelled manure, blood, and some sort of livestock, although what kind he couldn't begin to say. Topping off all of that, was a particularly putrid stench. It was pungent-yet-old, like something had died and its remains left lying there for decades, maybe centuries.

The hairs on the back of Martin's neck pricked up, and he raised one foot to take an involuntary step back.

"Welcome to Tartarus, motherfucker!"

The shove came from out of nowhere, a powerful blow between his shoulder blades that sent him sprawling. He flew forward and landed face-first inside the room, his phone flying from his hand and skittering across the floor until its light flickered and went out.

Martin's eyes widened, more from sheer astonishment than the pain of tearing open his chin on impact. He heard a bellowed guffaw, followed by chuckles, and the loud clang of the door being slammed shut and locked.

"Very funny, jerkoff!" he shouted at his unseen assailant.

Infuriated, he planted his palms on the floor, preparing to rise and unleash hell on the jokester responsible. The air about him shifted suddenly, and he sensed something that caused a cold clump of fear to coalesce inside his bowels.

It wasn't that he was in complete and utter darkness.

It was that there was something in there with him.

He could hear it in the distance, its deep, rhythmic breathing like mournful sighs. Whatever it was, it sounded huge, and he got the distinct impression that, although he couldn't see *it*, it could definitely see *him*.

Martin felt his heart begin to scale his esophagus, and fought to contain his panic. Pulse pounding, he regained his feet so slowly and silently, he would've done a three-toed sloth proud.

A painful tug on his wrist reminded him he was still shackled to his attaché case, and he reached down, carefully gripping its polymer handle. He considered wielding the knurled aluminum case as a bludgeon or shield if he had to – it was certainly weighty enough – but railed at the notion. The thought of it bursting open, and his hard-earned 140K being lost forever, was more than he could bear.

Martin swallowed the growing lump in his throat. He could hear that damn breathing again. What the hell *was* it? It seemed louder now; was it coming closer? He waved his hand in front of his face.

Nothing. He had literally zero visibility. What was he going to do? He chanced a fear-shaken exhalation and tried to think. He had to get out of there, but how? He was completely blind. He--

He needed his phone.

But how could he find it? It could be anywhere, and any sudden noise or movement on his part might cause whatever was out there to come after him.

A twinge of pain from the laceration on his chin brought Martin back to reality and inspired him to man up. He took stock of things. He was hurt, trapped, and locked in a dark, stank-ass room with God-knows-what, presumably by one of those swaggering security guards. He'd heard the laugh clearly. It didn't sound like Wurmer, at least he didn't think so. It didn't matter, charges needed to be filed. But before that could happen, he needed to get the hell out of there.

Gingerly touching his wounded face, Martin realized he had no choice but to try feeling about for his smartphone. If he didn't, for all he knew, he could be trapped there until he died. The wheels in his mind began to rewind, and he focused on rehashing the moment he'd been pushed. As he'd fallen, he remembered seeing the phone go sailing forward, sliding along the floor until its light went out. That was about fifteen feet away. And beyond standing up, he hadn't moved much. Which meant . . . he was still facing in the same general direction; hence, his phone was probably straight ahead, somewhere between his ten and two.

Licking his lips and swallowing, in an attempt to moisten his throat, Martin quietly descended into a crouch, then eased his way into an all-fours position. He paused, listening for the heavy breathing before he started to move. He couldn't tell for sure, but for the moment at least, whatever was out there seemed content to stay in one place.

He drew in a lungful, let it out slow, and then started forward. He crawled a few feet, stopped, then lowered his chest and extended his arms. Each time, he swept his fingertips along the floor in overlapping arcs, like the bands of a rainbow, trying to cover as much ground as possible. It was a laborious process, made more so because the heavy briefcase forced him to rely primarily on his left arm.

The floor was far from bare, Martin soon realized, as he latched onto something stiff and furry. His face contorted in disgust as he realized it was a desiccated rat carcass, and he quickly tossed it aside. Shaking his head, he continued with his pattern - crawling two steps, then bending and sweeping. Crawl, bend and sweep, then repeat.

As his fingers dug into something warm and mushy, Martin's unseeing eyes widened. He brought the unknown mass under his nose and took a whiff. It was a half-gallon-sized hunk of manure. Judging by its temperature and consistency, it was fresh, too.

Gagging, Martin tossed the fly-infested hunk of fecal matter over his shoulder, wiped his hand on his trousers, and continued on. Over the next few yards, he came across more of the same nastiness, squishing like warm clay under his knees and palms. He realized he was crawling through a veritable minefield of feces and stopped. A moment later, his sides began to shake with barely-contained laughter, as he mentally compared his current situation to Bruce Willis's classic air vent scene from the movie "Die Hard".

A lighter to see? Oh, please! You had it easy, brother. Like the man said in Jaws, "Come on down here and chum some of this shit!"

Martin's muted chuckling ceased as he noticed a tiny blue light, like a pinhead-sized sapphire, glowing in the dark. A heartbeat later, his dirty fingers closed on the frame of his trusty smartphone.

As he brushed its screen, the resultant backlight literally blinded him, his pupils were so dilated. It took him a moment, and a barrage of blinking, before he could bear to look at it. He realized the little indicator light was on due to a barrage of profanity-laced texts from his ex-wife.

Bless your black heart, you foul-mouthed gutter snipe.

Overcome with relief that he could finally get his bearings, Martin stood up and carefully brushed himself off. There was no need for the flashlight; with his eyes already so well-adapted to the dark, the screen's illumination alone would let him see enough to navigate. Plus, he didn't want to risk turning on the flashlight app, in case whatever was out there was—

The sounds of heavy footfalls, thudding in his direction, nearly caused Martin to piss himself. He staggered two paces back, half-tripping over a large clump of dung in the process. He could hear the footsteps growing louder, and the deep exhalation that accompanied them.

It was coming.

Like a child denying the existence of a "monster" by throwing the covers up over its head, Martin pressed the phone screen tightly to his chest, praying that the resultant darkness would somehow save him.

The breathing grew louder, and his pulse raced like a rabbit's in a trap. Whatever it was, it was close, *very* close. It was coming . . . coming for him. He could hear it, sense it, *smell* it.

Too terrified to turn the light on, Martin stood there shaking, his eyes scrunched closed, his heart jackhammering in his chest. He started to pray, then heard what sounded like a shuddering sigh. He felt a sudden sense of warmth.

Oh God, it's right next to me, he thought. *I can feel its body heat!*

Something prickly rubbed up against Martin's forearm, and he screamed. Panic took the reins and he backed hurriedly away, only to slam into something hard and unyielding. He thought it was a wall, but then, to his horror, the "wall" began to move. He started to whimper.

It was the monster! It was right beside him and it was *huge*!

Martin's mind teetered on the brink. Unable to handle the fear and uncertainty any longer, he ripped the phone from his chest and aimed it like a gun at his monstrous adversary. Like a searchlight, the cell's dazzling radiance illuminated the nearby chamber, and the thing that towered over him like some drooling colossus.

It was Nero.

———

His brow beetling, Garm Braddock rose from his captain's chair and took up position between *Gryphon's* illuminated sonar and helm stations. As he folded his arms across his barrel-like chest, Ensigns Ramirez and Ho glanced up, gauging their captain's mood. They exchanged looks, before turning back to their respective screens.

Garm peered up at the live-feed of his brother, Dirk, dominating the ORION-class sub's twenty-foot bow viewer, and shook his head. His twin rarely brought him bad news, but when he did, it came by the containerload.

"So, this thing's appearance has basically shot our plan to hell," he said.

"I'm afraid so," Dirk replied.

Garm could see he was seated in the office portion of his private quarters, wearing a white polo shirt, and sipping coffee from his favorite mug. His hair was more disheveled than normal, and he looked worried.

"I ran security checks on everything," Dirk stated, one hand disappearing off screen as he reached up and swept a finger down his own viewer. "Media, social media, even military channels. I found a lot. And none of it good."

"Is it all the same animal?" Garm asked. He hadn't informed the majority of his crew yet as to the identity of their pending target. But on a submarine *Gryphon*'s size, he didn't need to.

"It must be," Dirk replied, his eyes tightening as they scanned an unseen image. "Just last night, there were two vessels lost: the *Ignominious Fate*, a research trawler situated twelve miles offshore, in the Florida Straits, and the *Knot Me*, a mega-yacht anchored near the drop-off, just outside of Alligator Reef."

The young scientist checked another screen before continuing. "Frankly, I don't like the ramifications. Both of those vessels were steel-hulled ships in excess of four hundred tons, a size considered to be more or less immune to pliosaur attacks." He licked his lips. "The trawler got in one distress call before it was pulled under. The yacht, nothing. It was found stripped and picked clean, just like *Pride of Arabia*."

"How many lives were lost?"

"We don't have an exact tally. Several dozen at least. The media's going to go into a feeding frenzy, once word gets out."

Garm ground his teeth. "So, it's hunting territory is in deep water, out toward the Atlantic?"

"Absolutely not. There's more. A lot more."

"Like what?" Garm's keen eyes shot to Ramirez's station, watching as the astute sonar tech focused on, but then dismissed, a distant fathometer reading.

"We've got a deluge of bizarre disappearances, in and around the Keys."

"How close?"

"Too close," Dirk said. "Apparently, our 'Kraken' broke through the pliosaur net twice. The first time it must've gotten entangled; the netting was torn apart. The second, an entire tower was twisted into a pretzel and then uprooted."

"Holy shit! That leaves us wide open."

"And not just from *it*. Until the damage is repaired, anything can get through."

An unpleasant possibility dawned on Garm. "You, um . . . don't think it's using Jörmungandr to sneak in and out, do you?" As he said it, he had a vision of his sub getting caught flatfooted in the narrow tunnel, unable to fight or even turn around, and a chill crept up and down the big submariner's spine.

"It may well be; it's a fast learner. I've got social media reports from yesterday about a group of paddleboarders disappearing off Duck Key, and a news report from early this morning, showing three Jet Ski's being pulled under by a mysterious undertow, off Islamorada."

"Shit, that means--"

"Wait, there's more," Dirk interjected, his eyes grave. "Just an hour ago, *this* happened by Coffin's Patch."

His brother hit a key, remotely causing *Gryphon*'s monitor to split in two. On the second window was a YouTube channel, showcasing a new download titled 'Kraken Attackin?' Garm blinked when he saw the numbers. In forty minutes, the amateur video had already surpassed a half-million views. The footage showed a couple holding a sign that said 'newlyweds' and squealing with delight as they engaged in some early morning parasailing.

He braced himself for what was coming. Lit by the morning sun, the towboat gradually decelerated, the forty-foot, multi-colored canopy that supported the pair flattening as they descended toward the water. Within ten seconds, the tandem passengers' altitude had dropped from one hundred feet to less than ten. They were giddy as could be, kicking their bare feet in anticipation of getting wet.

They got more than they'd paid for.

The cheering suddenly stopped, and you could tell from the angle of their heads that husband and wife had both spotted something below them. Whatever it was, sent them into hysterics. They began waving frantically at whoever was taping them, screaming for the boat to reaccelerate.

Despite the wind, you could hear the captain's voice in the background, his tone one of obvious annoyance as he muttered something colorful. A moment later, a slimy brown tentacle as thick as a couch exploded up and out of the water, curling around the shrieking parasailors and yanking them under with unbelievable force.

The video went off-kilter crazy then, with a lot of banging, crying, and cursing, and the captain bellowing at his shocked crew to retrieve their passengers. The videographer managed to regain his composure at that point and focused his lens on the boat's big hydraulic winch, and the steel cable coming off it.

The cable began to shiver and, despite the smoke coming from it, the winch appeared unable to regain line. Then, to the utter astonishment of all present, the boat started to move. It began to be towed backward, like it was a big-game charter, backing down on a marlin. A few seconds later, the pull inexplicably ceased. The cable went slack, and they were finally able to retrieve it.

What they got back looked like it'd gotten jammed up inside a wood chipper. The harness webbing was ripped and torn, and the sturdy aluminum bars that had connected the couple to one another were twisted and bent. Worst of all, the only thing that remained of the parasail's jubilant passengers was a bloody strip of skin and fat, wedged in the conjoining point of their mangled safety belts.

Dirk froze the video, just as the couples' friends started to wail. He cleared his throat noisily. "Uh, sorry about that. But you see what's going on."

His jaw set, Garm nodded. Out of the corner of his eye, he noticed Ensign Rush at communications, wiping away a tear.

"Dirk, how do I find this thing?"

"Hard to say. It's got a big appetite, and it's getting bolder. Initial attacks, like on the *Rorqual*, were on large, slow-moving or stopped vessels, and in deep water. They were also at night. Now, it seems comfortable hunting in broad daylight, wherever and for whatever it likes."

As his tactician's mind whirred through *Gryphon*'s strengths and weaknesses, Garm threw a glance at Cunningham on fire control, before turning back to his brother. "How shallow can this thing go?"

"Despite its size, very," Dirk said. "Octopuses are like liquid rubber when they want to be. They can flatten themselves like a pancake, and squeeze through any opening their beak can fit through. Remember that video of one springing out of the water to seize a crab?"

Garm nodded, not liking the implications.

"They can even go on land. At least, temporarily."

"Wonderful . . . just don't tell me they can drive stick, okay?"

On the viewer, Dirk's resultant grin faded. He straightened up and took a breath. "I'm sorry, Captain Braddock, but effective immediately, the hunt for *Typhon* is officially aborted. The CDF cannot allow this creature to continue its rampage. It isn't afraid of us, or our machines. And it's going to keep on feeding, until we either declare our coastal waters off limits or it's killed. I choose the latter. And it's up to you to do the job."

"No problem. Any suggestions on how to find it?" Garm gestured toward his 3D sonar screen. "It's a big ocean, and your monster is all over the map. Not to mention, those last attacks happened in water too shallow for *Gryphon* to even *think* of venturing."

"You've been authorized for unlimited global satellite access, including covert-ops, and I've requested a pair of fully-armed Bearcats to assist you," Dirk advised. "Their long-range optronics will be at your beck and call. With their speed and mobility, to help hem it in, not to mention the added firepower, I'm sure it will narrow things down a bit."

"Much appreciated," Garm said. He started gnawing his lower lip. The anticipation of facing a new and dangerous opponent was beginning to build, but he felt a growing sense of apprehension, as well. Which made sense. Except in old sci-fi movies like *"It Came From Beneath the Sea"* and *"War of the Gargantuas"*, he'd never heard of anyone taking on a giant octopus before.

"Hey, Dirk?"

"Yes?"

"Any advice on facing this thing?"

His twin's chest rose and fell in slow motion before he replied. "Be careful. You know how intelligent Einstein is, right?"

"Smarter than me, I've heard," Garm said with a chuckle.

"Picture a much more mature animal – one that thrives in the abyssopelagic zone and stalks the largest odontocetes on the planet. Then, add on that it's got adaptive camouflage like nothing you've ever seen. You're familiar with *Proteus*'s abilities."

"I have some experience, yes."

"For all her gifts, our captive mutant can only alter her pigmentation – hues and patterns. The octopus is the true master of disguise. It can change not only its color, but its shape and texture. It can match anything it chooses – sand, rock, coral . . . it could appear as a giant sea cucumber if it wanted to."

"Lovely."

"The point is, it's Nature's ultimate ambush predator. So, when you go looking for it, be ready. Odds are it'll be waiting for you. And, as fast as they are, you'll probably only get one shot."

"Got it. Thanks."

"Oh, and Garm?"

"Yeah?"

"Whatever you do, don't pull any punches."

Garm smiled mirthlessly. "I never do, Dirk . . . I never do."

SEVEN

Martin's heart had plummeted so far into his colon, it felt like it was going to come out his ass. His neck ached from craning his head back so far, but he was too terrified to even think about moving. All he could do was gaze up in horror at the elephant as it loomed over him; its huge head, covered with concrete-like hide, shone a dull bluish-gray in his cell phone's light.

Martin's entire life – screenshots of humiliation, conniving, and conflict – swirled before his eyes in a fleshy kaleidoscope. And at the end of that sorry montage, he saw himself being torn limb from bloody limb by the very animal he'd sacrificed to line his pockets.

He swallowed hard. This close, there would be no escape. And the ironic thing was, it wasn't the elephant's fault; Nero was what he was because of human beings: the byproduct of a lifetime of unmitigated abuse that had turned the tractor-sized beast into the sadistic mankiller that he was. And, the former circus elephant knew full well that the urine-soaked human standing before him was the wellspring of his recent sufferings.

Martin's fate was sealed. The question running wind sprints through his terror-stricken mind wasn't *whether* Nero would kill him. It was *how* he would go about doing it.

He envisioned a dozen different ways the monstrous pachyderm would end his pathetic existence, with each more agonizing than the last. Crushing him against the nearest wall, goring him with those mammoth tusks, stepping on him like a tube of toothpaste, or just seizing his ankles in that iron-hard trunk and dashing his brains out against the cement floor, were just a few possible scenarios. And in every one of them, the animal trafficker's precious briefcase of cash was thrown clear and sat there, watching him.

Suddenly, Nero uttered a deep-throated rumble and changed position.

This is it, Martin thought. Shaking like that last leaf of autumn that clings to its branch in the face of winter's wind, he closed his eyes and waited for the end.

The end.

Five seconds passed, then ten. Even with his adrenalized hearing, the only sounds he could make out were the deep-drawn whooshes generated by Nero's enormous lungs.

Something was wrong. For some reason, the bull wasn't moving to attack.

At the thirty-second mark, Martin screwed up his courage and cranked open his eyelids enough to peek. The elephant was barely five feet away, staring contemplatively down with those red-rimmed eyes of his, at the pale primate that had kidnapped him.

Still unable to move, Martin remained where he was, staring back up at Nero with a befuddled look on his face. He didn't understand the delay. Was it some kind of sadistic game? Why wasn't he already dead?

Then, as the towering ungulate emitted an out-of-character groan, and a series of shudders began to wrack its massive frame, a bizarre possibility occurred to him. Nero wasn't shaking like that because he was enraged. He was trembling because he was . . . afraid.

He's afraid!

Martin's jaw touched his chest, and he blinked as he tried and failed to wrap his head around what was happening. Finally, he settled for shaking his head in bewilderment. The biggest, strongest, most badass land animal on the planet was standing right next to him, quaking with fear.

But fear of what? Can it be the dart gun? Maybe he's addicted to the Carfentanil and he's dying for a fix?

Martin started to scratch his head, then froze. There was a tremendous thump, like something huge had struck the concrete floor beneath their feet. Nero shifted in response to the impact, moving closer to his former captor.

What is he doing?

As the quivering elephant pressed one columnar forelimb against his hip, Martin couldn't believe it. This creature, this 24,000-pound terror, whose musth-fueled rage made him a threat to every living thing around him, was seeking solace from a defenseless human being, who could have walked beneath his cavernous belly without mussing his hair.

Dazed and disbelieving, Martin did the insane then – he stretched out a trembling hand and touched Nero's rock-like skin, in an effort to ground himself. A moment later, he pulled back in wonderment.

It was true. The bull was acting like his skittish old Labrador retriever used to do during a bad thunderstorm – pressing himself tightly against his master's thigh, looking for comfort and reassurance.

Suddenly, there was another sound – this one a definite banging of some kind – followed by a rumble that felt like an aftershock. A moment later, a blinding layer of light lanced into the room, lighting up Martin's feet and the floor beneath him like a rapidly-expanding plasma torch.

He squinted, gritting his teeth and shielding his face with his briefcase, while his still-dilated pupils struggled to adapt. The rumbling increased, and the chamber's overall illumination with it. Through slitted eyes, he discerned that what he'd assumed to be an oblong-shaped, oversized closet, was actually a steel-walled box, some fifty feet wide and twenty feet high.

Around him, Martin saw stamped-down piles of dung, scattered across the floor like flattened, tan-colored hillocks, and here and there, the dried-out remains of crushed rats. There were plenty of stains marring the concrete as well, including old bloodstains, from the look of it, and some nasty drag marks, too. In a few places, he even spotted rust-colored claw marks gouged into the concrete, like the kind a big bear makes on trees.

As his eyes finally adjusted to the light, the bleary-eyed trucker was able to detect its source. A forty-foot section of the far wall was rumbling noisily upward, like a metal curtain going up for a Broadway show.

Apparently, it was showtime.

Martin continued to shield his eyes with his free hand, to compensate for the ever-increasing brightness. As the wall continued to rise, a sudden breeze kicked up, pushing back his hair and sweeping away the stifling dankness of the room. In its place, he smelled seawater, a sprinkling of fish, and something pungent that he couldn't identify.

Nero apparently could, however, because he went crazy.

Fan ears flapping, and trumpeting so loudly that he ruptured one of Martin's eardrums, the giant pachyderm began stomping noisily back and forth. There was a series of sharp, splintering sounds, like ice makes when you pour tepid water over it.

Nero's immense mass and sudden movements were causing stress cracks to appear in the concrete floor beneath his padded feet.

Paling, Martin stepped hurriedly back. He drew in a breath and raised his hands, trying to figure out something he could shout over the din that might calm the agitated elephant.

Then, a second wall started to move.

This one was at the chamber's opposite end, and stretched its entire width.

Confused, Martin moved toward it and glanced down, only to gape in disbelief at the situation he now found himself in. It was like something out of an "Indiana Jones" movie. Instead of rising, the back wall was grinding noisily forward, its immense weight propped up on two-foot-wide steel grooves, inlaid into the cement floor. Martin's eyes swept across the manure and bloodstained cement as he did some quick calculating. The wall stretched the width of the chamber; there was no getting around it, and only two inches of clearance underneath it . . .

He snapped his fingers. Suddenly, the flattened piles of dung and the claw and drag marks all made sense – even the rats. When activated, the wall pushed everything in its path relentlessly forward, forcing it--

Aaaaarrrrgh!

Martin's scream as Nero stepped squarely on his foot reverberated inside the enclosed space like a frightened schoolgirl's shriek. The huge bull was in full panic mode, emitting deafening bellows and rushing back and forth across the room, desperately looking for a way out.

Martin staggered two steps back, before catching himself on his uninjured side. He drew in a breath, then peered down at the blood-soaked mess that had been his right foot. His exhalation was a pain-filled hiss. The injury was bad. As in, "Sorry, old man, we've got to amputate," bad.

Then, the full agony of his shattered tarsal and metatarsal bones hit him, and he started to sag. Fighting to stay conscious, he moved laterally, limping as fast as he could toward the room's far corner, and away from the moving wall. He needed to buy himself time, but also, he needed to steer clear of Nero.

The great bull was about to go berserk. Lowering his head and shaking his massive tusks from side to side in full-on threat display, he uttered a tremendous bellow. A moment later, he threw himself against the encroaching wall. There was a thunderous boom as irresistible force ran smack into its immovable object – twelve tons of steely-sinew, pitted against a matched volume of concrete and rebar.

His eyes glazed-over from the pain, Martin watched as the wall emitted a low creaking noise and came to a shaky stop. He shook his head in amazement.

Incredibly, Nero had done it.

But only for a moment.

There was another, louder bang, audible even over the enraged bull's bugles and trumpets, and the wall resumed its methodical march. One by one, the elephant's barrel-like feet lost traction and slid slowly backward. Quaking with fear and fury, he dug in again and again, setting and resetting himself, and pushing with all his might.

It was to no avail. The cement and steel barrier continued its inexorable roll.

Nothing could stop it.

Biting his lip to keep from fading out, Martin realized he was literally running out of room. The approaching wall was moving steadily now, with less than twenty feet remaining before it impacted on its opposing side, pushing anything and everything in its way through the forty-foot opening. And turning anything that tried to avoid the portal, by hiding on either side of it, into a pancake.

Having no desire to end up a butterfly, pressed in someone's scrapbook, Martin took one agonizing step after another, heading straight for the brightly-lit opening. The pain from his mashed foot was astounding, but he found if he kept his weight on his largely-intact heel, he could at least hobble. Behind him, Nero stubbornly continued fighting. He had turned his back to the wall and placed his immense hindquarters against it, leaning into it and pushing with all his might, in a frantic attempt to keep it from continuing.

Meanwhile, Martin rested one forearm against the left side of the opening's yard-thick frame and gazed down in abject wonder. There was water barely ten feet below him, a crystal-clear pool of sparkling seawater that, surrounded by an immense cavern, stretched far into the distance. It was as big as a lake but, from what he could see, mad-made. It had a semi-circular shape to it, and measured at least three football fields in length. On one side, its arc-shaped borders were warded by a wall constructed of some sort of clear material, like plexiglass. It was thick, too, a good ten feet, he estimated. Outside the wall, there were immense support columns, riveted steel arms reinforcing it every hundred feet or so – he could see them arcing into the distance, like the raised arms of some immense octopus.

Martin shook his head. Even without Nero's distracting bellows of rage, he would've had a hard time comprehending what he was looking at. The pool – and he assumed that was what it was – was far too big for people to frolic in. Not unless there were thousands of them, that is. It was incredibly deep, and the only discernable diving spot was hundreds of feet away, a tiny concrete dock that extended only part of the way out. Moreover, he saw no paddleboards, kayaks, or skimmers: no watercraft of any kind.

It was definitely designed for human use, however. It was brilliantly lit by powerful overheads, and heated, too, he could tell. There were cameras rigged up above, and a system of huge monitors, not to mention stadium-style seats ringing the center portion of its curved wall.

The seats were empty now, but Martin imagined they drew quite the crowd when whatever competitions they hosted went live. Or, maybe it was some kind of testing pool for technology? Hell, you could move a destroyer around in there, it was so big--

Holy shit!

The moment he saw the wake, and the gigantic shadow accompanying it, Martin knew what he was looking at.

The place wasn't a pool. At least, not for people. It was some sort of hellish aquarium. An aquarium that housed something – something huge and hungry. Hungry for--

The realization that Nero had been purchased as take-out, and he'd inadvertently added himself on as an hors d'oeuvre, struck home. His dignity be damned, Martin began screaming for help. He quickly realized he'd never be heard over the elephant's frightened trumpets, however, so he leaned against the portal's steel frame and extended his left arm, waving it wildly in the hope someone manning the cameras would notice.

It was at that moment that the thing that called the pool home showed itself.

If Martin hadn't pissed his pants earlier, he would've done so now. Spouting forty-foot columns of compressed water vapor, like it was the mother of all whales, the scaly titan gave off a thunderous snort. Water streamed off its broad back like it was a submarine, and it began emitting a series of loud clicking sounds as it floated lazily at the surface. It held position there, a good three hundred feet way, but based on the size and musculature of its four, broad flippers, Martin had a feeling it could close that distance in the blink of an eye.

It was a pliosaur, one of those *Kronosaurus imperators* you saw every other day on the news. He'd seen videos of them on *Pliosaur Wars*, usually after they'd been shot to hell, as jubilant fighter pilots from their respective squadrons took turns posing with the bloody remains of their kill.

Martin nodded through a haze of pain. They'd blown away some real monsters on that show, but they'd never seen anything like this behemoth. Its glittering scales were the color of polished obsidian, and it looked like a battleship at berth. It's crocodile-like jaws bristled with ivory fangs, each as long as his forearm, and its head was as big as Matilda. The most frightening part of it, however, were its oval-shaped eyes. They were a glittering reddish-orange, with sinister black centers that made it look like a demon from the depths of hell.

Actually, for all he knew, maybe it was.

As the monster hissed and submerged, Nero acted like he'd lost what little remained of his mind. Forced to turn sideways, the poor elephant had been pushed to the point that his thick toenails were beginning to extend over the edge. He had only moments, before he dropped in on some very unpleasant company.

Martin wouldn't want to be in his shoes when that happened. On land, the huge bull was a force to be reckoned with. But in the water, against *that* thing . . . he doubted the elephant would stand a chance.

Fighting to focus past the pain radiating from his foot, the traumatized trucker considered his options. He was sure someone was aware of what was going on. Obviously, the people he'd sold Nero and those other animals to spent a boatload of money feeding their monstrous pet. They'd invested heavily in it, which meant someone monitored its meals – probably at that very moment.

Martin figured that, although the asshat who'd pushed him into the "feeding trough" was a real SOB, the odds of him being the one running the place were slim. In fact, whoever he was, he was in for some real trouble, once his superiors found out about his little stunt.

Martin just needed to stay alive long enough for someone to became aware of his predicament. He glanced down, checked his footing, and did some quick calculating. There was just enough space on the spot where he was perched, that, with a little luck, he could hold on after the wall had completed its relentless forward march. A thought came to him and, after a moment's deliberation, he hefted his briefcase in his right hand. Holding it at arm's length, like a flag of truce, he waved it back and forth, in the hope that someone would take the bait.

With his ass on the line, Martin was more than willing to give up his score. It was only money. But, in the back of his mind, he was hoping he wouldn't have to. He figured the potential trouble he could cause the place might let him turn the tables on them, maybe allow him to negotiate an under-the-table settlement with whoever was in charge. Hell, if pressed, they might double his recent payday, just to make him go away.

Oh, yeah. This could actually work.

Martin was in the middle of a pain-reduced grin when Nero struck.

The bush elephant's muscular trunk lashed out like a striking anaconda, encircling his waist so fast, he didn't realize what was happening. He barely managed a "woof!" of surprise as he was yanked off his feet. A split-second later, he heard a loud popping sound, followed by agonizing pressure, as the trunk's iron grip tightened around his midsection.

Martin uttered a guttural shriek of anguish as he felt his rib cage collapse.

A moment later, he was airborne.

Through a cloud of pain, his world spun like an out-of-control amusement park ride. He was face-down when the water rose up to meet him, its surprisingly hard surface slamming the wind from his sails and stifling his gurgled cries. Fear of drowning rose to the pinnacle of his rapidly growing mountain of terror, and a surge of adrenaline coursed through his veins. A moment later, and despite his collective misery, he made it to the surface and started treading water.

Martin tasted two things at once then – a nasty mouthful of brine and the most bitter of ironies. He glanced up at Nero, seventy feet away and teetering on the brink, as the bull tried and failed to grasp the slippery wall with his trunk. The fear-stricken pachyderm seemed so human then and, like many people would have done under those circumstances, had tossed his former captor into the pool, to save himself.

A sudden shift in the water around him drew Martin back from his impromptu moralizing. He licked his lips and looked fearfully about. A powerful displacement wave, like the kind created by a surfacing submarine, was causing him to bob up and down.

The pliosaur was directly beneath him.

Martin's heart started pounding in his ears so loudly, he couldn't hear himself think. He couldn't decide whether to swim for it or remain still, in the hope of avoiding detection.

His breathing became a series of harsh gasps and, as he scanned the water with dread-filled eyes, he noticed a layer of pale green leaves littering the pool's surface for thirty yards in every direction.

He cursed at the realization. Those weren't leaves.

That was money. *His* money.

Denial tried buoying him, but as he raised his right hand up out of the water, a bolt of dismay shot up his herniated spine. He realized Nero's trunk had shattered not only his ribs, but his attaché case as well. All that remained was the stainless-steel shackle, locked around his badly-bruised wrist.

Martin's disgust turned to terror as the colossal predator surfaced in a watery blast. From ten yards away, all he could see was the top of its misshapen head, but that was enough. It was even bigger than he thought and had an indestructible look to it: like some armored sea dragon, its body coated with interlocking scales. He recoiled as it angled its huge head to the side, and one of luminescent eyes broke the surface. Their eyes met, and he felt his heart turn to ice. Like an entomologist examining an insect, it studied him, its wrinkled eyelid compressing inward, its slitted black pupil contracting.

A whimper escaped Martin's bone-dry mouth, and the pain of his injuries was forgotten. Any thoughts of trying to swim for it evaporated, and he started treading water in slow motion. It was more than just the fear of being devoured; he felt mesmerized by the monster's blazing orb, like it was boring into him, feeding on his very soul.

When he caught a glimpse of the behemoth's arsenal of teeth, visible just beneath the surface, Martin realized his soul was the last thing it was after. He couldn't tell it if was deciding whether it was worth snapping him up, or if it was relishing the fear that streamed out of him, along with the contents of his bowels.

He had just started praying when the pliosaur, with what he swore was an amused expression on its crocodile-like face, swam slowly away. The bugled bellow and prodigious splash that followed told him why he'd been spared. Nero had reached the end of the line.

Twisting his head to and fro, in the hopes of spotting some movement from the cameras, high above, Martin felt reality's crushing weight bear down on him. The cavalry wasn't coming. Nobody was. Either they didn't know or didn't care. Either way, he was on his own. His only chance was to swim for it. And maybe, just maybe, the luckless elephant's sacrifice would give him the break he needed.

In the distance, the monster turned lazily into a wide arc. It was definitely closing on Nero, but it was taking its sweet time doing so. Like a saltwater croc approaching a tortoise that has blundered into its domain, it moved with methodic slowness, secure in the knowledge its slow-moving prey could not escape.

Martin saw his chance and struck out, swimming for all he was worth. His crushed foot screamed from the effort, and he could feel his fragmented ribs tearing away at the inside of his chest like a meatgrinder. He coughed, tasted blood, coughed again, and spat out a mouthful of burgundy-colored nastiness. He grimaced, realizing that Nero had definitely punctured one, if not both, of his lungs.

It didn't matter. The cement pier he'd spotted was a full city block away. If he didn't get there fast, drowning in his own blood would be the least of his problems.

Behind him, he heard a titanic splash, followed by a tremendous thump. Nero gave out the most God-awful cry, a bellow of agony that filled the colossal pool chamber and reverberated off its granite walls.

Too terrified to look back, Martin focused on swimming. His breathing became more and more wheezy, and bright red blood began to stream from his ears and nostrils, creating a trail of crimson that spread in bright billows behind him. He must've looked like a stuck pig, oozing its life out. With an effort, he pushed the image from his mind and kept on stroking.

Only seventy-five yards to go. Come on, old man, you can make it!

Based on the unbelievable racket, Martin couldn't believe the struggle Nero was putting up. After hearing a nauseating crunch, that sounded like a redwood being split apart, he'd assumed the stricken bull was done for. Yet his frantic bugling and thrashing continued, interrupted intermittently by thunderous rumblings from his oversized attacker. Despite the sheer mass of the predator that had latched onto him, the elephant was giving a remarkable account of himself.

Either that, or the pliosaur was simply playing with its food. It was a horrifying thought, one that made the wounded trucker shiver as he swam. Maybe it *was* relishing its kill, enjoying its prey's pain and suffering . . .

Jesus, stow that shit and focus, you pussy!

As Martin crossed the fifty-yard mark, Nero's boisterous struggles suddenly ceased. The horrifying sounds of mastication soon followed, repeated gnashing noises that echoed across the surface of the pool's now-pinkish waters.

Unable to resist any longer, Martin glanced back to see what was happening. He immediately wished he hadn't. The *Kronosaurus imperator* was in the process of biting its dying victim into manageable portions.

Martin blanched as its fang-lined mandibles yawned wide and then closed like a colossal pair of shears, severing Nero's head and forelimbs as easily as a cleaver hacks through a block of cheese. From a hundred yards away, he could feel the raw power of the titan's jaws, each bite sending shockwaves through the pool, like ripples on a pond.

Pale as paper, Martin turned back and resumed his desperate flailing. Thirty seconds later, the sounds of feeding began to fade.

He was out of time.

With less than twenty-five yards separating him from the T-shaped dock, the trucker experienced the familiar sensation of water pushing against him. This time, however, it was from behind. Apparently, twelve tons of fresh elephant wasn't sufficient for the giant predator's needs. It had picked up the smell of his blood in the water and was coming for him.

Martin threw a furtive glance back over one shoulder and started to cry. He could see his adversary's wedge-shaped head, cruising effortlessly along just below the surface, as it systematically closed the distance. Like Nero, it knew he didn't have a prayer of escaping.

"We'll see about that!"

With a defiant cry, Martin doubled his efforts, crawl-stroking like an Olympic hopeful. He could feel his foot and ribs throbbing, even the burn of saltwater eating into the cut on his chin, but he separated himself from the pain. His speed started to mysteriously increase, and he realized why; the bow wave generated by the beast's tremendous mass was propelling him along, like dolphins coasting in front of a luxury liner. The stupid thing was inadvertently helping him. His eyes lit up with the realization that he had a chance.

C'mon, Stumpy! Don't give up!

Mouth open wide and sucking wind, Martin swam for his life. He was less than ten yards away from the dock's reinforced edge when something distasteful unexpectedly lodged in his mouth. He spat it out and swore – a waterlogged one-hundred-dollar bill, of all things. Just then, he felt the pressure wave behind him dramatically increase. He looked back.

The sight that greeted Martin made him scream at the top of his lungs. What looked like the opening of a cave – its roof dripping with fat ivory stalactites – surged powerfully toward him.

Then, there was a thunderous rush and he was enveloped.

Martin heard a loud cracking sound that drowned out even his hysterical cries, and he found himself under bizarre, twilight-like conditions. The disgusting stench of rancid meat filled his nasal passages, and he gagged as he gazed, terror-stricken, left and right. He was surrounded by white, rubbery tissue, and row after row of machete-sized fangs.

It was the nightmare of all nightmares.

He was in the monster's mouth.

Yet, for some insane reason, Martin was still alive. Then he realized why. Eager to inhale him before he reached the refuge of the dock, the creature had overshot its mark. In addition to its target, it had clamped down on an eight-foot-wide section of the pier. Five feet of reinforced concrete was preventing it from closing its jaws. He could hear the behemoth's displeasure, deep-throated growls so low and loud that they threatened to sunder his bones. Its displeasure rapidly increased, and it started shifting its scale-covered jaws this way and that, flexing its Mini-Cooper-sized jaw muscles as it tried to bite through the dock's stony lip.

Martin was in marine hell. Surrounded by sharp-ridged teeth, each capable of eviscerating him, he gripped whatever he could, frantically trying to remain in the bowl-shaped center of the pliosaur's cavernous lower jaw. Its thrashing movements became too much, however, and as its raised its head, and the seawater in its mouth drained through its palisade of teeth, he did the only thing he could.

He climbed atop the thing's Corvette-sized tongue. Latching onto it with both hands and feet, he dug in like he was riding one of those towable tubes he'd seen overindulged teens drag behind their parents' pleasure boats.

All of a sudden, the giant reptile ceased its thrashing. The cracking sound its teeth were making as they punched holes in the pier's edge stopped, and he could feel its steely muscles relax.

Martin's heart fell into his colon. It had detected his changed position in its mouth. It was up to something.

He had to make a move. And he had to do it now.

A quick sideways glance revealed a long, triangular-shaped gap between two rows of its oozing fangs. The opening was wide, but narrow – barely a yard-high at its widest point. It was as close to a no-win scenario as you could ask for, but with a desperate dive, coupled with a shitload of praying, Martin figured he could thread that needle. He might get ripped up in the process, but if he pulled it off, he had a chance. The dock had enormous pilings, supporting and surrounding it – cement and steel cores too tough for even the giant marine reptile to penetrate. If he could get to them he—

Oh, shit.

A sudden contraction from the titan's pulsating throat muscles was the only warning Martin had. He felt himself begin to rise, and a split second later, the monster's surprisingly warm tongue hoisted him up and back. He had time for just one blood-curdling scream, before it tossed him head over heels down its gullet.

As the burning blackness caved in on him, three fast-fading thoughts swept through Martin O'Dare's traumatized mind. He realized that he'd been reunited with poor Nero, he worried about what would become of Matilda, and he remembered removing Meg from his life insurance policy.

Despite all the pain, that last one made him smile.

———

Seventy feet above the still-frothy surface of the amphitheater pool, and shielded by ten-foot-thick walls of ultra-reinforced concrete that would've done a WWII pillbox proud, acting Security Chief Oleg Smirnov struggled to put a damper on his temper. He settled for snorting in disgust, then turned and threw a baleful gaze at Sergeant Bryan Wurmer, who stood in an at-ease pose beside the auxiliary dispensary control desk. The post was currently manned by one of the new recruits – an O'Neil something-or-other. At least, according to his nametag.

He resumed doing the caged lion thing, pacing irritably back and forth, while pondering his next course of action. To say he was pissed would have been an understatement; his expression was reminiscent of storm clouds on the horizon. Yet, for all his pent-up fury, the ex-pugilist's size-fourteen combat boots made almost no sound, as he spun and stalked up to Wurmer, getting right in his face.

"You were responsible for thees, da?" he said, an accusatory finger pointing at the foot-thick, clear-titanium window that overlooked both the thousand-foot pool and *Tiamat*'s adjacent paddock.

Directly below them, the bloodstained waters of the amphitheater were still sprinkled with cash, the scattered bills like pale-green jimmies, topping the world's largest cherry smoothie. And in the middle of that lethal beverage, the pliosaur queen's 400+ tons submerged with deathly silence.

"Yes, sir," Wurmer said. He tensed as he suppressed a headshake.

Despite the concealment provided by the sergeant's thick salt-and-pepper mustache, Smirnov could tell from the set of his lantern jaw that he was furious at having been discovered.

"You know thees ees ground for expulsion, da?"

"He was snooping around the facility, sir," Wurmer replied. "He would've--"

Smirnov held up a meaty index finger. "Stop. How do you say, 'spare me your bullsheet?'"

Wurmer started to open his mouth, but then closed it.

"I watched closed-circuit cameras," Smirnov advised. "I saw you make eet easy for heem to get your access code, *and* I saw you lift hees keys from pocket."

"W-what?"

Smirnov glanced down at cadet O'Neil, suddenly enthralled by the texture of the water on his monitors, before moving closer to Wurmer. At six-foot-four, he was three inches taller than the cruel-faced sergeant, but he knew better than to let his guard down. Wurmer might've been a disgraced ex-marine, but he was still an ex-marine – a threat not to be taken lightly.

"You heard me," Smirnov said, pegging him with a hard stare. "You are not exactly hugger, now are you?"

Wurmer's thin lips compressed inward, a sure tell of his mounting fury. "No, I am not."

"Good." He extended a meaty paw, palm up. "Now, give me keys for dead man's expensive truck."

Wurmer sighed resignedly, then reached into his pocket before depositing the tractor's keys in his superior's hand. As Smirnov's fingers closed on them, their eyes met.

"You know, 'acting chief', you're *really* not one of us."

"Oh?" Smirnov said, amused. "And how is that?"

"I mean, sure, you've killed a few *women*, but that's as far as it goes. Hell, you're not even on the *shit*. If Dwyer were here--"

"I am not on 'the sheet' because, unlike *you*, I am already 240 pounds of man," he indicated, tapping his broad chest. "I don't need."

"Yeah, sure. I bet that's why your late wife turned lap-licker," Wurmer retorted. His bloodshot eyes became suddenly feral. "Tell me, where was your '240 pounds' when Garm Braddock was giving our boss a beat-down? I heard you high-tailed it outta there."

At the mention of his dead wife, Smirnov felt a murderous rage begin to well up within him. He clamped down hard, channeling it where it might do some good.

"You know," he began with a dismissive scoff, "I don't fight Captain Garm Braddock because many reasons. One, I theenk two against one is already unfair fight. Two, I respect heem – he is great boxer and good man. And three, and ees most important, I have no desire to go back to gen pop, just because of Angus Dwyer's obsession weeth other Braddock brother. You understand thees, da?"

"Tell that to Dwyer when he gets back."

"Oh, *if* he gets back, I promise I weel."

"Yeah, right."

Smirnov wore a predatory expression as he contemplated the ongoing insubordination. "You know, I theenk maybe you want to do something here, da?"

Wurmer's expression, as his head swiveled toward his boss, was evocative of an angry lizard. Unfortunately for him, he'd made the mistake of remaining in an at-ease pose the entire time – a difficult position from which to make a move.

"C'mon, *worm*," Smirnov taunted from less than a foot away. He made a show of resting his hand atop his holstered side-arm. "You have gun, I have gun. You wish to make move? Go ahead . . . *try*. But, I promise you, before you clear holster, I heat you so hard, I make your jaw look like 'Daffy Duck's'."

Wurmer's eyes blazed with fury, but he hesitated, realizing his miscalculation. A moment later, he turned face forward with his head up, swallowing his pride and anger.

"Nyet?" Smirnov inquired from under raised eyebrows. Still seated at his nearby desk, O'Neil looked like he was searching for a hole to crawl into. "Good, then we make equitable solution to problem."

"What does that mean?"

"Way I see it, we have two choices. Option one, I tell Dr. Grayson what you deed, and let cheeps fall where they may. Of course, you know what weel happen, and unlike me, you don't have option to go back to beeg house . . ."

". . . and option two?"

Smirnov may have appeared unemotional, but inwardly he chuckled at the rangy sergeant's tenseness. Every one of Grayson's 'last chancers' knew full well that the old man was not to be trifled with. "Some friends of mine have market for used vehicles. I geev them keys, they make truck go away, we share cash."

"Share how?" Wurmer asked. His eyes were still intense, but he was noticeably calmer.

"You and I each get forty percent. O'Neil gets twenty."

Eyes peeled wide, the black-haired cadet twisted around in his chair. "Me? B-but I'm not a part of this. I didn't do anything."

Smirnov gave him a friendly smile, before resting a callused hand on the newbie's shoulder. "Dees ees true, ex-corrections officer. But you weel have, once you've edited out certain . . . unnecessary portions of feeding video, da?"

O'Neil swallowed nervously. "Uh, just how much is this twenty percent you're talking about?"

"Hmm. Let me theenk. Classic vehicle like that, excellent condition and upkeep . . . I theenk you get, maybe, fifteen thousand?"

"Dollars?"

"Da."

O'Neil hadn't even finished his whistled exhale before his hands became a blur on the keyboard. "Oh, comrade, I am *so* your guy."

Amused, Smirnov pretended to watch him work.

As he did, Wurmer took a step toward the nearby window and gestured at the water, far below. "What about the cash?"

"What about eet?" Smirnov remarked. He indicated *Tiamat*'s vast shadow cruising past, just below the surface. "You want, go get."

"But, we can wait until she's back in her pad--"

"Only Doctor Braddock or Doctor Grayson can use helmet to control queen," he reminded. "Either one would see money floating on surface, da?"

Wurmer flushed, realizing how royally he could've fucked up.

With a dismissive headshake, Smirnov peered over O'Neil's shoulder. "Turn paddock filters to maximum, to clean out blood and tissue fragments and . . . eencriminating paper." He eyed Wurmer contemplatively, then the nearby door. Straightening up, he gestured for the sergeant to join him. Once they were out of earshot, he checked to make sure they had privacy, then leaned in close.

"You know, Wurmer, eet is true; we are bad people here, you and I. We say bad theengs, we *do* bad theengs . . . eet is likely we deserve our lot in life," he said, as the two shared a nod. "I theenk we understand one another. I have no desire to rock boat, or to lose my freedom again. And, I am sure you feel the same, da?"

"Okay . . ."

"Good," he said. Then he fixed the smaller man with a look so cold, it could've come from one of Tartarus's captive saurians. "But I warn you now, eef you ever make comment about my Tatiana again, the next person to do swan dive into queen's paddock weel be you," he advised. "And, believe me . . . I weel keep copy of video."

EIGHT

"Helm, depth and distance to target," Garm Braddock ordered. He leaned back in his oversized captain's chair, his alert eyes alternating between keeping tabs on *Gryphon*'s hard-working bridge crew and scanning the relentless barrage of nutrient-rich seawater, swirling around the sub's transparent bow.

"We're fourteen miles out, sir," Ho replied from her lit-up station. "Holding steady at three hundred feet, speed thirty knots."

"Maintain both. Sonar, readings?"

Ramirez discontinued tweaking his Don Juan mustache and gave his instruments a quick recheck. "A large billfish just cut across our baffles and, five minutes before that, we had a good-size school of bigeye tuna running parallel to our portside at 500 yards. They got spooked by a pack of *Xiphactinus* and got out of Dodge quick."

"Nothing sizable?"

"So far, I'm picking up only one notable biologic," the sonar tech replied, his shoulder blades contracting inward as he turned a dial and increased his screen's sensitivity. "Designate is a . . . pliosaur. Looks like a good-sized male, estimated size . . . just under sixty feet." He spun in his seat. "It could be one on our hit list, sir."

Garm frowned. "Position?"

"He's a thousand yards out and veering away at high speed. Bearing is two-two-zero. He's . . . heading out to sea, sir."

163

Ramirez's goatee-framed lips dipped into a frown as he watched the bearing recede. "He must've detected us."

"At the velocity we're traveling, I'm not surprised," Garm remarked. He made a dismissive gesture. "Ignore the lizard." Eager to accelerate the hunt, he stood up and moved a step closer to the bow, his brow furrowing as he strove to peer further into oncoming seas than human vision allowed.

After wasting an hour, scouring the undersea canyons surrounding the wreck of *Pride of Arabia*, *Gryphon* had been hauling ass for the past forty minutes. They'd hurtled through the waters of the Continental shelf like a 435-ton torpedo, terrorizing any marine life that got in their way. On the sub's portside lay the fertile waters of the Florida Keys National Marine Sanctuary, to starboard, the foreboding depths of the Straits of Florida. Her target was the schooner *Rorqual*'s last reported position off Marathon, a location Garm figured was as good as any to begin his Kraken quest.

"Fire control, status?" Garm asked over his shoulder.

"LADON is locked and loaded, sir," Cunningham called back, "I've got all tubes flooded, with NAEGLINGs primed. Targeting options?"

"For now, infrared/ultraviolet homing seekers only," Garm replied. "Safeties will be addressed once target has been acquired."

"Aye, aye, captain," the CSO affirmed, his long fingers doing a jig across his control panel, as he made the requisite changes.

Garm grinned. He could tell from Kyle's jauntiness that his old friend was in good spirits. In fact, the whole bridge crew was. He didn't know if it was because of the unexpected mission change, that they had a once-in-a-lifetime opportunity to take on a mythical marine monster, or the fact that, after having seen some of the blood it had spilled, they were eager to return the favor.

Probably a combination of all three. But it didn't matter. Ho and the rest of his primaries were the pick of the litter, and the finest in the fleet. If they couldn't do the job, nobody could.

"Helm, increase speed to thirty-five knots and make your depth two hundred feet," Garm ordered. "When we're a mile out, reduce to ten and notify me."

"Yes, captain," Ho replied. The corners of her mouth pricked up as she pushed forward on the yoke. With a barely noticeable hum, the sub's eight, 1,500 horsepower Mako M69 MHD pump jet propulsors increased their output, propelling the streamlined anti-biologic sub even faster through the water.

Garm shut his eyes, reveling in the faint vibration that shimmied through his iron mistress's armored skin, as he put her through her paces.

"Communications," he said, eyes still closed. "Any action from our satellites?"

Ensign Heather Rush removed one half of her headset, pushing a lock of strawberry-blonde hair away from her eyes with it before replying. "I'm on it, but no confirmed sightings yet, sir. I did, however, just get an update on the Bearcats."

"And?"

"They deployed from MacDill Air Force Base ten minutes ago. ETA our current position, ninety minutes – give or take."

"Excellent." Garm nodded approvingly. "Tell them to split up and commence spiral-pattern overflights, focusing on where the three most recent incidents took place: Duck Key, Islamorada, and Coffin's Patch."

"Yes, sir."

"Also, inform them that I want all potential sightings streamed straight to the main for confirmation," he added. "And if target *is* confirmed, they're to clear with me before engaging."

"Yes, captain," Rush said. She glanced sideways at Cunningham, before speaking into her chin mike.

Impatient and eager, Garm took to cracking his knuckles to let off steam. He'd been trying to figure out a way to expedite the confrontation his instincts told him was coming, but he kept drawing a blank. He wasn't worried about the Air Force pilots stealing his thunder – annihilating the overgrown pile of sushi that liked treating people like potato chips was the most important thing. He just figured the Bearcats' chances of success were slim. If the beast they sought was as resourceful and cunning as Dirk made it out to be, it would hear the noisy aircraft from five miles out, and either blend in with the bottom or go deep.

Still, if a little rotor noise or a few well-placed warning shots help herd the damn thing, the choppers might prove useful.

Garm nodded to himself, then headed for the prow. Squeezing past sonar, he reached *Gryphon*'s curved observation window in three brisk steps, then turned his back on the sapphire seas beyond. "Okay, people," he spoke up. "You all know what we're hunting: an octopus big enough to feed on a *Kronosaurus imperator* cow. It's big, it's nasty, and it's crafty. And we're going to blow it to bits and dip what's left in soy sauce. The only question is, how the *hell* do we find it. Any ideas?"

He studied each of their faces in turn.

Nothing. He needed a volunteer.

"Ensign Ho, how about you. Suggestions?"

The petite helmswoman's bow-shaped lips contracted inward. "We could just lie in wait for it, by that destroyed tower. It'll probably use the same route to bypass the pliosaur nets over and over."

Garm nodded. "Excellent tactic, but too time consuming. We'll save that as a fallback position. Anyone else?"

Ramirez hesitated, then raised his hand. "We could map all the reported incidents and see if there's a pattern, a central hub, so to speak. Octopuses usually have a nest where they take their food, right? A . . . mitten?"

"Midden," Rush corrected, averting her eyes as everyone turned to her.

"I like it," Garm said, encouraged. "Get started on that immediately. We don't have enough info to hit the ten-ring, but that could eliminate a lot of wasted water."

"We'd still be scanning a good ten to fifteen square miles," Cunningham pointed out. "For a moving target that looks like any other coral reef."

"Humph. Well, then, how about you, Lieutenant Killjoy?" Garm pressed. "As I recall, you used to be quite the cryptozoology nut, back in the day. What's your take?"

Cunningham's lips betrayed the faintest hint of a grin. "Actually, I have an idea, but . . ."

"But what?"

"You're not gonna like it."

"We'll see. Spit it out."

"Normally, this thing eats whales, right?" Cunningham ventured.

"Reputedly."

"So, we bait it. We kill a big, fat humpback, and let it bleed out in whatever area we've cordoned off as this thing's backyard. It'll smell dinner and come running. Then, I'll do what I do best."

"Tell mother-in-law jokes?" Ho quipped.

"Exactly."

Garm drew a breath. "That's an amazing idea, but also an idiotic one. Grayson would fire every one of us, and we'd get six months in the brig to boot, for killing an endangered species."

"Well, what if the whale was already--"

"Captain?" Ho said, twisting in her seat.

"Yes, ensign?"

"We've reached the one-mile mark. Shall I adjust course as ordered?"

"Affirmative."

"Uh, captain?" Ensign Rush asked from her station.

"Yes?"

"I have Sam Mot on intercom. He's asking to speak to you."

Garm braced himself. "Fine, patch him through."

"You're on, sir."

"Sam, this is your captain speaking, how's it going down there?"

"Gee, boss man, let me think. Besides me going stir crazy, it's going great!"

Garm felt his jaw begin to drop. *Is he drunk? And why the hell do I keep putting him on speaker?* "Very funny. So, I take it a change of scenery is in order?"

"Scenery? You mean, as opposed to the superfluous vista of Yeoman Perkins' pimply plumber's crack that I'm currently being treated to, every time he takes something out of the oven? Oh, don't spoil me, now!"

Momentarily speechless, Garm weathered the bridge crew's combined guffaws and, in the background, what sounded like Sam apologizing to Perkins for demeaning his rear end so harshly.

He literally groaned into his facepalm.

Thank <u>God</u> Commander Morgan isn't here.

"I tell you what, Sam," he offered, trying to restore order. "I'm taking suggestions right now on how to pinpoint our Kraken. You read the report on the *Pride of Arabia* attack. If you can come up with something of merit, I'll have you brought up to the bridge, and you can man the jump seat until you're needed elsewhere."

"Seriously?"

"Absolutely."

"Actually, I may have the solution to your problem."

"Do tell," Garm grinned, wondering where this was going. "Go on . . ."

"Well, you see, I poked my head into your quarters a little while ago," Sam said. "You know, to get an idea of how the other half lives."

"I hope you knocked first."

"Of course. And while I was in there, I couldn't help noticing that big piece of metal you've got propped up; you know, the one with that thing's fingerprints all over it?"

Garm sighed, hoping that was *all* he'd done in there. "Get to the point, Sam."

"Well, when I saw it, I worried about you. I mean, the report you gave me said that party yacht that got attacked was radioactive, right?"

"Yes," Garm replied. "But our exposure was brief. And, that section of aluminum – which was from a freezer – was hosed down to remove contaminants."

"Oh, good. So, I don't have to worry about your ovaries falling out," Sam said with an audible chuckle. "That's a relief."

"Is that *it*?"

"No. You see, I was sitting here wondering, where did all that radiation come from?" he continued. "I mean, it was all over the ship, right?"

"Right . . ."

"So, how did it get there?" Sam asked. "See, a man in my position tends to watch a lot of television. Old movies. Old *sci-fi* movies. You know, like the ones where the monster is spawned by--"

"Radiation," Garm breathed. "Holy shit! Sam, you're a goddamn genius."

"Obviously. So, you think that--"

"Hang on," he said, trying to contain his excitement as he signaled Rush to put him on hold. "Communications, key in the nearest military satellite, and get me scan results from that other yacht that was attacked. The, um . . ."

"The *Knot Me*?" she offered, her fingers already moving at sub-light.

"Yes," Garm nodded. He could feel his adrenaline kicking in. "Check for radiation readings. If there are any, is the signature a match for--"

"Bingo!" Rush spouted. She pinked from the combination of excitement, and the realization she'd interrupted her captain. "Geez, I'm so sorry, sir."

"No worries, ensign. What've you got?"

"Both yachts were peppered with radioactive particles," she announced. "Granules of Uranium-235 ore with traces of Uranium-238." She paused on her board, then hit one more key. "And . . . isotopic analysis indicates a match."

We've got the bastard.

Garm's narrowed eyes gleamed as he exhaled hard through his teeth. "Put that crazy son of a bitch back on."

"You're connected, sir."

"Sam, you still there?"

"Hey, good timing; Yeoman Perkins and I were about to start doing the Limbo," Sam snorted. "Of *course*, I'm still here. I'm a *prisoner* in this place!"

"Not anymore; you've just been paroled," Garm said with a huge smile.

"Seriously?"

"Absolutely. You just scored one for the team."

"Well, it's about time someone started appreciating my greatness," Sam touted. "Now, besides bringing me *carefully* up to the helm, how about arranging for some real food, a beer, and maybe an intro to some of the ladies on this heap?"

Garm sighed. "I'll send someone down for you shortly. Braddock out." He signaled for Rush to kill the conversation, then turned to fire control, "Lieutenant, have you got a location on Lieutenant Blair?"

"Uh, he said he had abdominal cramps and was heading for his bunk, sir," Cunningham offered. "Apparently, the breakfast burritos disagreed with him." As he spoke, the CSO's eyes drifted down to his seat cushion and his nose crinkled up.

"Perfect," Garm said, trying and failing to stop a chuckle. "Rush, please send Blair to the galley, and tell him to 'carefully' pick up Sam Mot and carry him to the bridge."

"Uh, yes, sir," Rush said, her blue eyes wide with merriment.

"Next, I want satellite scans of the surrounding seas, out to a radius of thirty miles," Garm ordered. "Key in on the radiation readings present on both *Pride of Arabia* and *Knot Me*.

Input all findings into navigation, and then send them to sonar, directly."

"I'm on it, captain."

"Ramirez," Garm continued. "I'm assuming you've got your chart underway – the one plotting all reported sightings?"

"Already completed," Ramirez said. "It was pretty simple stuff."

"Well, things are about to become more interesting. Once Rush sends you the U-235 trace trails, I want you to drop those radioactive breadcrumbs into your chart. Map everything, and compare notes with Ensign Ho."

"We're all over it, sir," Ramirez said, exchanging a nod of familiarity with the stern-faced helmswoman.

"We're looking for that 'central hub', as you put it," Garm stated. "Unless I've missed my guess, our shy and reserved TALOS jockey just gave us the means to go knocking on our Kraken's door."

"You mean, bust it down, don't you, sir?" Ho asked, twisting in her seat.

"Oh, we're going to do more than *that*," Garm said, squeezing between her station and communications, before he settled down into his own chair. He glanced up at *Gryphon*'s clear prow, and the frightened school of baitfish, fleeing before her. "We're going to tear its house down around it, and then blow it to pieces as it tries to flee."

It was midday, with the Caribbean sun burning bright overhead, and a brisk breeze adding a sprinkling of chop to otherwise flat seas, as Captain Dennis "Salty" Morton laid in a course for home. He and the crew of *Tons of Fun* had been at sea for three days straight, and with the sixty-six-foot trawler's freezer holds packed almost to capacity with stacks of fresh fish, everyone was looking forward to a nice, fat payday, and a few days off in which to spend it.

Sitting back in his worn captain's chair, in the center of the vessel's recently-upgraded pilothouse, Salty rested his prescription sunglasses atop his head like a tiara, before giving the boat's steering wheel an affectionate squeeze. At sixty-six years of age, the vintage Nordhavn fishing yacht was as old as he was. Of course, as he was fond of pointing out, usually while tapping his recently-replaced knees, a little loving maintenance, and periodic upgrades, kept both of them seaworthy.

Salty checked their location on the GPS, then swung his grizzled head from port to starboard, double-checking their position by line of sight. Normally, he'd have preferred to navigate Nicholas Channel on their journey home, but that would've brought them closer to Cuba. Nowadays, with armed conflict tearing up what was left of the already war-torn island nation, the farther from her shores they were, the safer he felt.

They were currently hugging the northern edge of Santaren Channel, just off the Grand Bahama Banks, and about seventy-five miles from Andros Island. Whereas the banks, themselves, were relatively shallow – eighty feet at most – the channel plummeted down to well over three thousand. Right now, they were running in three hundred feet of plankton-rich water, which suited Salty just fine.

"Pardon me, Captain Morton, but are you sure you still want to bother with the trawl?" Carl asked, wiping the sweat from his brow with a lean forearm, as he purloined a bottle of water from the bridge's cooler. "I mean, we're pretty much stoked to the gills, down below. Shouldn't we just make for home?"

"You really miss those Miami clubs, don't you, kiddo?" Salty said, giving the curly-haired teen a smile. "Don't worry, the chicas will still be there when you get back. Our course is already set, but I'm still seeing a lot of activity on the fish finder. If we can manage one more netful en route, what's the harm?"

"You're the boss", Carl nodded, chugging half the bottle in one long swig. "So, how much do those fangers go for, nowadays?"

Fangers . . . Salty smiled. The nickname was apropos. Although one of the smaller and less dramatic of Diablo Caldera's escapees, it was estimated that the hordes of five-foot *Enchodus petrosus* that swarmed many of the world's oceans had done as much ecological damage as the monstrous *Kronosaurus imperators* had – maybe more. With the exception of speed demons like wahoo, tuna, and most species of billfish, whose numbers had actually rebounded, native fish species like herring, mackerel, and menhaden couldn't keep up with the ravenous invaders. Many staple stocks had crashed hard into the seabed, and most had yet to recover.

On the bright side, as opposed to the overgrown and deadly X-fish, whose meat was not only tough and stringy, but bland, Sabretooth salmon were delicious, not to mention rich in fatty acids. And, unlike many trawler captains, he knew where and how to catch them.

"We're looking at a good ten bucks a pound, my intrepid first mate."

"And how--"

"We're toting at least twelve tons," Salty said, grinning as he saw the youngster's face scrunch up, trying to do the math. "That's almost a quarter million – minus fuel, docking fees, 'political contributions', taxes, and assorted other expenses, of course."

"Wow, that's amazing," Carl said, wide-eyed.

"And, just think, if we bring in a few more, en route, the crews' bonus keeps on growing."

"And, on that note, we're all over it!" the fresh-faced teen declared, finishing his water, and tossing the empty into a nearby recycling bag. With a smart salute, he headed out, closing the door carefully behind him.

Salty grinned at the anticipated enthusiasm. Unlike most captains, who paid their crews set wages, and paltry ones at that, he preferred to give a share of the profits, like the old-time whalers had. He paid each of his regular crew one percent of the gross take, and his second-in-command twice that. In this case, it meant paying them around three grand a head – in Carl's case, six – for just three days work. But, what the hell; it kept them motivated, and they damn sure deserved it.

Not because the job was particularly grueling. Because it was dangerous.

Very.

Trawling waters inhabited by hungry sea dragons bigger than your boat meant taking your life, and the lives of your crew, in your hands.

And then juggling them.

Salty peered back, through the wheelhouse's salt-stained windows, and glanced left and right, giving their gear a quick perusal.

Unlike now-outlawed benthic trawlers, which, for over a century, had dragged their nets along the bottom, ripping up the seafloor and inflicting irreparable damage on marine eco-systems worldwide, *Tons of Fun* was a pelagic huntress. She stalked the midwater, towing the gaping mouths of her cone-shaped nets high above any vulnerable – not to mention ensnar-ing – coral reefs. With her advanced electronics, including the best in-hull cameras money could buy, she captured fish by the thousands – all ensnared within the diamond-mesh of her fun-neling nets.

Although Salty had complete confidence in his crew, not to mention sensors that measured everything from rate of catch, to net geometry, to the precise tension of their trawl lines, the old captain left nothing to chance. He preferred to personally check the readings on the paired Gilson winches that drew in his nets, as well as the angle of the thick towing warps that ran off them like tightropes – just to make sure. Some things, no machine could tell you.

Satisfied with the current track and the gape of their trawl, Salty focused on the fish finder, hoping for one final school to envelop. Like any other otter trawler, his boat used a pair of trawl doors, more popularly known as otter boards, made of sturdy timber and steel, to keep the net's sprawling mouth spread horizontally while it was being towed. The vertical spread was accomplished with floats, attached to the trawl's topline, and a series of weighted bobbins that drew down its foot rope. Hydrostatic pressure, generated by the boat's pull, did the rest. Like wings spreading out, the faster they went, the further apart the doors spread, and the wider the trap's mouth opened.

After that, it was a "simple" matter of finding the fish, and surrounding and keeping pace with them until, exhausted, they were drawn back into the trawl and trapped. Finally, when the tapered end was filled, the engorged net was cranked up over the stern for unloading.

Like the ladies say, 'nothing beats a big cod end', Salty thought, his grin widening as he turned back to the bow and reached for his coffee. Yes, it was a good time to be out on the water, enjoying the sun and sea, and to be the boss of his own business.

Of course, there were downsides to the whole thing. Especially nowadays.

Most people thought he was insane, traversing known pliosaur hunting grounds in an aluminum-hulled boat, with a gross displacement of less than 190,000 pounds.

And maybe he was, he thought. But, then, he had something they didn't know about. Or rather, someone.

Salty nodded as he clocked Nash Hunterdon standing by the portside bow railing, the wind converting an escaped lock of his tied-back hair into a blonde-colored whiplash. Nash had his booted feet spread for balance, his hazel eyes concealed behind a pair of metallic-blue polarized sunglasses. With his lean face and frame, he reminded Salty of one of those cyborgs from the old "Terminator" movies, his head sweeping mechanically back and forth, as he scanned the area for potential threats.

Nash was his captain's life insurance policy, and an expensive one, at that. At three percent of the gross, with the exception of Salty's take, the kid was the highest paid member of *Tons of Fun*'s crew. And he was well worth it.

Thrown out of the military after basic, because they'd deemed him "mentally unfit for service", the twenty-two-year-old orphan was a handful, and then some. Taciturn and withdrawn by nature, when provoked he had a vicious temper, and a violent streak to match. Salty discovered that the moment he and his crew found him hiding out on the boat, following a Miami barroom brawl. Rather than turn him in, however, the old man had given him a stern talking to, followed by a job.

It worked out nicely. Because, for all his flaws, Nash was the greatest marksman the aging trawler captain had ever seen. A trained sharpshooter, he was cool under pressure – something he'd demonstrated more than once. To date, he'd gunned down at least twenty net-invading *Xiphactinus* and six marauding pliosaurs, five of the latter with single shots from the semi-automatic rifle he kept slung over one shoulder. It was a beast of a gun – a custom-made AR-15 clone with a reinforced shock-stock, and loaded with 400 grain, .50 caliber Beowulf rounds that could shatter an engine block.

Or a hungry marine reptile's skull.

Thankfully, the *Kronosaurus imperators* typically attracted to the fish they trawled weren't the largest of the species; but even an Orca-sized one was a threat not to be ignored. The last one they'd encountered was the biggest to date, a forty-foot monster that had gotten entangled in *Tons of Fun*'s nets. Flailing around at the surface, it nearly capsized the boat before Nash put it down with five shots to its exposed chest, followed by two more to its wedge-shaped head.

Two things changed after that. Carl, Jack, and the rest of the crew stopped complaining about Nash's cut. And Salty installed remote-controlled detonators on his towing warp connectors. Better to blow the lines and lose a few thousand dollars of mesh, then to end up in the drink with a pissed-off sea monster and anything accompanying it.

Salty scrutinized his net sounder screen, and then frowned. He'd hoped the initial concentration of fish he'd seen at the mouth of the trawl was an indicator of more to come, but now the waters ahead were practically barren. He shook his head and headed for the pilothouse door.

Ah, well. I better go check on John Dillinger, see if he's thirsty, and make sure he doesn't hurt anybody . . .

Salty chuckled to himself at the thought. Actually, since coming aboard, and after he'd had the chance to kill something, Nash had been fairly calm. He'd had words only once or twice with the other members of the crew, and had calmed down as soon as his captain got involved. Hell, he'd even apologized.

Salty didn't know if it was the military in him, or if he just needed a father figure in his life. He'd gotten his hands on the kid's psych report, and it listed him as a sociopath.

Whatever that means.

It didn't matter. Nash needed a job, and they needed him. As long as he didn't hurt anyone, prevented the boat from being sunk, and kept everyone on it from getting eaten, the old man didn't give a rat's ass what the army's excuse-for-shrinks called him. Half of those guys were nuts, anyway.

"Hey, kiddo, how's it going?" Salty opened up. He held out the sweating bottle of spring water he'd brought along.

"Thank you, Captain Morton; it's been quiet," Nash said, accepting it and cracking the nozzle. He took a swig, then set it down and resumed his scanning.

"A good haul, today," Salty opined, eyeing a few gulls circling high above them. As all captains knew, seabirds were a useful marker when it came to locating feeding fish. But they could be a royal pain in the ass, too. Once they'd learned to associate the trawler with free scraps and bycatch, they followed it day and night, squawking, squabbling, even defecating on the crew at times.

At least there are only a few of the little shitburgers, right now.

"I saw," Nash replied. "I, uh, feel bad. Like, I'm the only one onboard who's not doing any work."

"But you *are* working, son," Salty said, resting a hand on his shoulder. "Right at this moment."

Nash's gaze shifted momentarily from the waves, down to the painted floorboards. "Yeah, I suppose."

"By the way, before we set sail, I spoke to the families of those three guys that jumped you in that bar."

"What for?"

"Well, considering all you did was bloody a few noses, over a girl, and in a fracas that *they* actually started, I figured there was more than meets the eye to their desire to 'see justice served.'"

Nash's brow tightened. "I, uh . . . don't understand, captain."

Salty looked him in the eye. "It means, they were hoping for money in a civil case. And, once they realized they had no case, they decided to press charges, in the hopes you'd give them cash."

"I . . . don't, really. So, what did they say to you?"

"It was more like, what I said to *them*."

Nash scratched his head, obviously not getting it. "And, what was that?"

Salty shrugged. "I offered them each five-grand cash to drop the charges. As expected, they took it."

"W-what?"

"You heard me," the old man said, grinning. "All charges have been dropped. Now, you can stop hiding out, and sleeping on *Tons of Fun* every night."

"Th-thank you, captain," Nash managed, still perplexed, and now embarrassed, too. Suddenly, he turned pale. "Wait, you gave them *fifteen thousand dollars?*"

"Yep."

"But I, uh . . . I don't have that kind of money. I mean, I-I'll pay you back, of course," he said, "You can dock my pay if you want, or take all of it until--"

"Relax, kid," Salty said, clapping him amiably on the shoulder. "It's on me. Last trip, you saved all our lives. Besides, I'm writing it off as an . . . insurance expense."

"Really? B-but--"

"Case closed," Salty said, then lowered his voice. "Just be more careful in the future. We need you and--" he paused in mid-sentence, his attention drawn to the graffiti scrawled on the pilothouse's nearest bulkhead. Drawn in permanent marker was a score of large "X's", each with a red universal "no" symbol encircling it. Above them, were six upward-pointing, crocodile-like mouths, similarly prohibited.

"I see you've been keeping score," Salty indicated.

"Yeah, uh, Carl said it would be okay," Nash said in a rush. "If it's a problem, I can clean it off as soon as we're docked."

The old man thought it over, then smirked. "No, I actually like it. Gives the boat more personality, like we're one of those WWII bombers that kept track of all the enemy fighters they'd shot down."

"Wow, you know, that's exactly what I was thinking," Nash exclaimed.

"Well, then, I guess that makes you our ace. I think--"

Salty's smile evaporated as a shrill alarm went off. Tightlipped, he rushed back into the wheelhouse.

"What is it?" Nash asked, following him, but remaining in the doorway.

"Proximity alarm," Carl answered over his shoulder.

Salty leaned forward, his eyes locked onto their long-range sonar screen.

"We've got a contact coming up behind us," he said, indicating an amorphous reading at the bottom of the scope. "A damn big one."

He saw Nash's eyes widen, then narrow, as he took in the sonar image.

"I'm on it," the kid said, unshouldering his rifle and pulling its charger handle back.

"Easy," Salty said, inspecting the readout. He did a doubletake. *What the hell?* Whatever it was, it was coming up beneath them at a leisurely pace of ten, no, twelve knots. But the *size* . . . "That's impossible!"

Carl squeezed past Nash and stood beside him. "What is it?"

Salty took two steps back from his screens, as if a little distance might alter things. It didn't.

"Get everybody up on deck," he ordered, "And have them put on life preservers." Before asked, he tagged on, "According to the readout, we've got a bio-mass angling up under us. And if the readings are correct, it's in excess of two hundred tons."

"W-wait, what?" Carl and Nash said in unison.

"How can that be?" the first mate asked. "It must be a blue whale, right?"

Salty shook his head. "It's too broad, and too big to be a pliosaur. Whatever it is, it's the biggest thing I've ever seen."

Nash's eyes were iron rifle sights. "What should we do, captain?" He cradled his heavy weapon. "Run or fight?"

Salty considered his towing warp detonator switch, then checked his other screens. "No good; it's too close to make a break for it."

"Should we kill the engines?" Carl asked, halfway out the door, and signaling the rest of the crew.

The old man shook his head. "No. A sudden change in noise or vibration might be an attractant, or be interpreted as vulnerability." He inhaled deeply, trying to pull warm air into his suddenly cold lungs. "It's nearly two hundred feet down – a hundred feet beneath our trawl and rising slowly. Let's go out and meet it."

"Now, you're talking," Nash announced, his jaw set.

Salty caught him by the arm, before he could rush off. "Easy, there, Doc Holliday. We never fire a shot in anger; you get me?"

"Yes, captain."

With Nash at his side, and Carl, Jack, and the rest of the crew busy donning life-jackets and securing anything that wasn't already tied down, Salty threw his sonar screens one final look, then hightailed it to the nearest gunnels.

Suddenly, the water all around them swirled, and *Tons of Fun* started wobbling from side to side. The old man shook his head in incredulity, watching as his ninety-ton vessel bobbed up and down like an apple in a hot tub.

Whatever was beneath them had to be *enormous* to produce such a displacement wave. He glanced back at the bridge, wishing he'd brought the detonator with him. If the intruder got tangled in their nets, it would go berserk. The old trawler would get flipped over like it was a bath toy, and there was nothing they could do about it.

Even Nash's big gun was useless against a creature that size.

I wonder, could it be a Lusca? Salty considered the legendary sea monsters that were said to lurk in Caribbean waters, especially the Bahamas' infamous Blue Holes. Supposedly, it was some sort of giant octopus.

"I see it!" Carl cried from the stern. As he pointed down into the depths, he was so excited, his feet seemed to have sprouted springs. Above them, scores of seabirds appeared, hovering a hundred feet up, as they eagerly eyed the whitecapped waves below.

They see it too.

"I've got eyes on it," Nash announced, shouldering his heavy rifle and training it on the water.

Salty leaned over the side, and for the second time in the past three months, his heart leapt into his throat. He could just barely make it out – a vast, grayish form, cruising effortlessly along. It was barely a hundred feet below their keel, but in the murky water, still too far down to identify.

"Should I take a shot?" Nash asked, his weapon trained on the menacing shadow.

"Absolutely not," the captain said, his pulse tapdancing in his ears. He indicated his security officer's rifle. "Even *those* rounds lose effectiveness at the ten-foot mark. Best you'll do is let it know we're here. Worst, you'll piss it off."

Nash didn't seem to hear him as he checked his target. His eyes were like a hunting jaguar's, poised to strike.

Oh, God. He's going to do it.

Salty reached over and rested a staying hand on the kid's shoulder. Below them, the monstrous form leveled off, its speed steady as it overtook them and began to pull ahead.

"Don't do it, son," he whispered. "It's moving off. If you anger it, it could kill us all."

Nash gnawed his lip, his need to lash out waging a tug-o-war against common sense and his captain's orders. Suddenly, his narrowed hazel eyes peeled wide and he pulled back.

"Look!" he exclaimed, pointing down. "It's not an animal!"

Salty followed his gaze. "What do you . . . son of a *bitch*!"

The old man exhaled so hard to expel all the stress he had pent-up, he felt light-headed. The kid was right. Far below, a bright red beacon glimmered in the darkness. It was like a ruby-colored strobe, there for a split-second, then gone, only to re-appear fifty feet away. Within minutes, the light vanished from sight, and the mysterious intruder with it.

As *Tons of Fun*'s swaying slowly subsided, Carl walked over, obviously shaken. "What the hell *was* that?"

Salty wore a nonplussed look. "Beats me, kid. Some sort of military weapon – a submarine, most likely."

Nash nodded. "That'd be my guess, but whose?"

The old man put on his sunglasses and peered toward the horizon. "Based on its current path, it looks like it's headed toward Cay Sal Bank. And after that, maybe the Keys."

"So, it's American?"

"Could be," Salty said. "But, given our proximity to Havana, and everything going on there, I don't plan on waiting around to find out," He turned to his crew, hands on his hips. "Okay, I think that's enough excitement for one lifetime. You fellas ready for our return cruise?"

The murmured cheers coming from ten haunted faces spoke tomes.

"Okay, then," Salty said. "Carl, get all your scallywags in line and moving. Bring the trawl in and secure it, then batten down the hatches. I want us rigged for full-speed running. We're going home, boys!"

As his first mate moved off, directing the now-whooping members of the crew to their appointed tasks, Salty gestured for Nash.

"C'mon, kid. You're coming with me."

Nash's brow lifted. "But, captain, shouldn't I stand guard, just in case?"

Salty's years suddenly weighed in on him, and he gave a vigorous headshake. "Take a break, son. And speaking of cases, I've got a case of apple brandy stashed in the wheelhouse, that's just begging to be opened."

"But, uh, I don't drink, captain."

"That figures," the old man said, laughing uproariously. "But, right now, I don't need a drinking buddy. I need a *bartender*. And, Nash, my man, *you* are pouring!"

As they headed into the pilothouse, Salty couldn't believe his eyes.

For the first time since they'd met, Nash Hunterdon was smiling.

NINE

Like a leviathan on the hunt, the anti-biologic submarine *Gryphon* arced up and over a towering undersea rise. Despite tipping the scales at over 435 tons of submerged displacement, the sleek, 132-foot pliosaur killer moved with an uncanny silence. Her active sonar emitters were dormant, and the acoustic cladding that coated her shock-absorbing ceramic-steel outer hull reduced even the loudest of engine sounds to a whisper.

To the region's resident marine life, viewing the dark-hued colossus through the gloom, with rays of sunlight dancing along her nearly-indestructible hull, *Gryphon* was a shimmering shadow – a ghost, creeping forward with questionable intent.

"Helm, confirm distance to target," Garm Braddock said from his chair. Eyes narrowed and hands gripping his armrests, he leaned attentively forward.

Time was literally of the essence. Once they'd pinpointed the location of the *Octopus giganteus*' lair, reality's fangs sank in. The brazen beast had set up shop not far from where it first encountered the *Rorqual* – barely twelve miles from Marathon's shores – and had effectively laid claim to the entire Florida Keys National Marine Sanctuary.

It had to be stopped. And quickly.

Garm had barely given his crew time to plot a course, before he ordered *Gryphon* ahead at flank. Jaws set, they'd hurtled through the Straits of Florida like a runaway ICBM, covering twenty-three miles in less than thirty minutes. It was one of the few times in the ORION-class sub's illustrious history that she'd had the opportunity to exploit her maximum speed – a teeth-rattling forty-one knots – and the crew was exhilarated by the experience.

Her stressed-out Reactor Control Officer, not so much.

"Less than two miles, captain. Reducing speed to four knots, as ordered," helmswoman Connie Ho replied. Her almond-shaped eyes were intense as she gripped the yoke and pulled back slow. Without turning her head, she asked, "Positive shield, sir?"

"Why not?" Garm replied. A moment later, the curved, foot-thick laminate barrier that reinforced *Gryphon*'s clear-titanium prow rumbled slowly down and locked into place.

As much as the former pugilist preferred to see the whites of his enemies' eyes, the creature they hunted was an unknown commodity. They had no idea what it was capable of, and it made sense to take precautions.

The same applied to the sub's assorted sonar systems. Based on what Dirk had told them about an octopus's concealment ca-pabilities, Garm figured stealth was the name of the game. As a result, from this point forward, they'd rely almost entirely on their passive sonar processing system – at least until they were in the strike zone.

"Communications, transfer forward view to the main, 2X zoom," Garm ordered.

"Yes, sir," Rush replied, hitting a key and watching as the bow window turned black and crackled with static. A moment later, its opaqueness was replaced by an enlarged HD view of the seas, directly ahead.

Strangely, there were no discernable fish. Just the craggy cliff's edge, a hundred yards to starboard, and the blue-to-in-digo water of the drop-off, extending as far as the eye could see.

"Sir, I'm noting a surprising absence of marine life," Ensign Ramirez commented from sonar. He twisted around to meet his captain's gaze. "We must be close."

"Agreed," Garm replied, exhaling some of the anticipatory stress he was feeling. "Transfer chart overlay to the main, upper left corner. Rush, any update on those Bearcats?"

"Yes, sir. They've finished refueling and are forty-five minutes out."

"Good. Keep me posted."

Garm focused on Ramirez's topographical map – a satellite view of the region's seafloor, and assorted landmasses. On it, each of the cephalopod's known attacks and sightings, as well as a dozen probables, were marked in bright reds and yellows.

"Sonar, overlay radiation trails."

Ramirez flipped a switch and, like a nest of wintering garter snakes, a convoluted series of twisting and turning trails pretzeled their way across the map. There were literally scores of them, and each one glowed a brilliant blue from the radiation it emitted. Garm smiled, pleased with how useful the top-secret military satellites were proving to be. The readings were like sapphire breadcrumbs, ready to guide them home.

"Well, Sam, what do you think?" he asked, spinning in his chair to face the bridge's normally empty jump seat. "You've been surprisingly quiet since you got here." He studied his long-time friend, wondering if they might need him, and worried that he was hung-over.

Dressed in a pinned-back jumpsuit, Sam Mot twisted his limbless torso against the X-shaped safety harness that held him in place, until he was comfortable. "Sorry, it took me a while to recover from 'Pepé Le Pew' bringing me here," he remarked, fake-smiling as he threw a glance at the illuminated chart. "And, I didn't want to interfere with your operation."

"Thank you," Garm said, cocking his head to one side as he continued to gauge his friend's functionality. "We're glad you're here."

"Not as glad as I am. The galley sucks!"

"Wait until you try the food," Ensign Ho remarked from her station.

"Why, Connie; is that a dinner invitation?"

Garm almost groaned. From his vantage point, Sam didn't catch Ho's annoyed eye roll, but he did. "Let's keep it professional," he said. "So, what do you think?"

"Of the twinkling thingamajigs on your board?" Sam made a face and shrugged. "It's very pretty. But where, in that big, beautiful Christmas tree, is this thing we're supposed to be hunting?"

"Ramirez, bring our AWES operator up to speed, please," Garm said.

"Yes, captain," the sonar tech replied, rising stiffly to his feet.

Humph. Adolfo looks annoyed, Garm thought. *Must not like someone hitting on his woman. Not that Connie can't take care of herself . . .*

Ramirez cleared his throat and indicated the assorted sections of the map. "As you can see, the radiation trails coincide perfectly with each attack we know of. However, our boy's been busy. There are many more tracks than attacks."

"So, it's hunting, and not always successfully," Sam offered.

"Could be. Or, it's establishing its territory. Or, many of its attacks haven't been reported. No witnesses, so to speak. And there's also the possibility that most of its victims have been local marine life – whales, sea lions, maybe even pliosaurs."

Sam nodded. "Why do many of the trails sort of 'fade out' at the ends?" he asked, using his nose to indicate the glittering blue lines.

Ramirez stroked his goatee contemplatively, then turned to communications. "Uh, Rush, could you zoom in, please?"

Garm watched with interest, as a section of the map tripled in size.

"Thank you," the sonar tech said. He cleared his throat and turned back to Sam. "We've concluded that the radioactive material is dust. It's being continuously shed by our octopus as it moves. At a certain point or distance, it just runs out of it."

Garm shifted position. "Thank you, ensign." He inclined his head toward Cunningham. "You're up, CSO. This next part was your discovery."

"Uh, thanks, captain," Cunningham said, happy to be mentioned. He remained seated and, with the touch of a screen, transmitted a red targeting scope to the main, directing it from his station like a cursor. "You may have also noticed that the radiation readings all originate from a central location, which is right about . . . *here*."

"So, that's where the thing hangs out," Sam said.

"We're betting that's its larder, yes," Cunningham concurred, glancing down at his instruments. "Also, if you look closely, you'll see that the radiation readings are at their brightest and most concentrated when it first leaves home." He used his red bullseye to circle an area at the center of the map.

"Which means that--"

"The source of the radiation is its lair," Cunningham finished.

Garm cut in. "Which *means*, that this thing may be sitting on a mountain of Uranium-235."

"Is that a problem?" Sam asked.

"Not for us," Garm said. "But there may be some serious cleanup, once it's dead. Which means the EPA will most likely get involved, which could get ugly. Grayson absolutely *loves* those guys."

"Yeah, I heard," Sam shrugged. "So, what's the plan? And, while we're at it, why are we going so slow?"

"The element of surprise, my young Padawan," Garm said, grinning. "Helm, distance to target?"

"Just hitting the one-mile mark, sir," Ho replied.

"Excellent. Ramirez, initiate iridophores."

"Yes, sir."

Sam's lips parted. "Wait, I forgot . . . this sub has a cloaking device, right?"

"She does indeed, my boy," Garm said, clicking his tongue. "She does indeed."

Ramirez turned sideways in his seat. "Iridophores are at 100%, captain. System recommendations are: floating mass of kelp, school of--"

"Make us a blue whale, ensign."

"A . . . but, sir, doesn't this thing *eat* whales?"

"Exactly," Garm said, smirking. "I want it drawn to us, like our new AWES operator is to a stripper in a Catholic schoolgirl outfit."

"Now, *that* was a cheap shot," Sam commented, amidst all the snickers.

"Payback, old friend. Payback."

Garm watched with amusement as the steadily-increasing hum of the ship's cloak engaging caused Sam's eyes to widen with undisguised nervousness. *They* always *do that the first time. What do they think is going to happen, something out of "The Philadelphia Experiment"?*

Outside, *Gryphon*'s slate-gray hull shimmered and then vanished. In its place appeared the largest *Balaenoptera musculus* the world had ever seen – a sulfur-bottomed giant almost a half-football field in length.

"Fire control, weapon's status?" Garm asked. He chuckled as he saw Sam finally release the breath he'd been holding.

Just wait until we bring the REAPER online.

"Same as earlier, captain," Cunningham said. "LADON gun system is primed and active, fish are ready, and all tubes are flooded. Shall I set safeties?"

"For fifty yards, and flood outer doors."

"Aye, sir."

Sam angled his dirty-blonde tresses toward the captain's chair. "Hey, Garm-- I mean, *captain*, what kind of torpedoes does this boat carry?"

Garm signaled to Cunningham, who sat up proudly as he replied.

"We're equipped with America-made NAEGLING M9 ADCAP rocket-propelled torpedoes, with acoustic tracking and infrared/ultraviolet homing seekers. They're supercavitating, with a top speed of almost 350 miles per hour."

"Holy shit!"

"Yeah, that's probably the last thing that goes through a pliosaur's mind, as it sees a pair of them coming at it."

Garm rested a heavy forearm on one of his armrests. "But not *Typhon*," he reminded.

"No, sir," Cunningham said quietly.

Not satisfied with their preparations, Garm contemplated *Gryphon*'s sonar station. He hated having to rely solely on the less-combat-oriented fathometer. Given that no octopus he'd ever heard of possessed, or could detect, active sonar, he decided to gamble.

"Ramirez, activate OMNI ADCAP sonar, including active search and attack, but keep it low. I don't want this thing to know we're here until it lays eyes on us."

"Aye, sir. Should I bring ANCILE online, too?"

Garm ruminated. As much as he wanted their obstacle avoidance system, complete with acoustic intercept, up and running, he'd risk their enemy being alerted by the tracking pings emanating from its active sonar projector, once it went live.

"Not yet. Helm, make your depth 100 feet and hold position."

"Yes, sir," Ho replied, making quick course adjustments.

His lips pursing, Garm noted the topographical chart, still on the main.

"Sonar, lose the trail map. Transfer all details to POSEIDON, and give me a 3D view of the target, on the main. Let's see what how big of a ring we're dealing with."

"Aye, sir," Ramirez said, hitting a few keys on his touchscreen. "Water depth precludes any detailed satellite imagery, so, topography-wise, we're relying entirely on POSEIDON's passive sonar readings. Ready . . . now."

The sonar tech flipped a switch, and the glittering, black and gold 3D fathometer screen that hung suspended between his station and navigation morphed rapidly in response, reforming as a huge swathe of the targeted seafloor. An instant later, a far larger duplicate of it dominated their darkened bow viewer.

Garm rose from his chair and took a step forward, his pale eyes tight. One eyebrow arched as he observed the bright white blip that pulsed directly atop an undersea ridge – a lonely ghost, suspended in the dark.

"Sonar, are we able to get more detailing on the region adjacent to the bullseye?" he asked.

"Negative, sir," Ramirez replied, trying and failing to increase gain. "Marine snow is limiting effectivity of the fathometer trace, and the increased radiation is impeding our sensors. Barring OMNI ADCAP going fully active--"

"No, this will do."

Garm contemplated the readings for a few more seconds, before returning to his chair. "Okay, team. As its lair, our quarry has apparently chosen an uncharted shipwreck," he announced, indicating the ghostly beacon. "Whatever type of vessel it is, it's draped across the edge of an undersea ridge, in approximately 450 feet of water."

He nodded as Ho's chair swiveled in his direction and she raised her hand.

"How deep is the drop-off?" the petite helmswoman asked, gesturing at the foreboding region beyond their target.

"Another thousand feet or so," Garm replied, scrutinizing the readouts further, "before it slopes down and dumps into the Straits of Florida. We're in luck. The shoreward region around the target is barren for a radius of several hundred yards – some low-lying coral reefs, but no significant structure. That gives us plenty of maneuvering room, and no place for it to hide."

Cunningham cleared his throat. "Unless it's disguised as part of the seabed," he reminded.

"Good point," Garm concurred, nodding.

Sam spoke up, his green eyes focused on the seafloor image, as it did a slow rotation. "What's that area that looks like a bunch of broken railroad spikes, about a thousand yards to the right?"

"That's the Tombs, and it's a place we'd do well to avoid."

The AWES' operator's eyes went wide. "Yeah, good idea."

There was a moment of silence as the bridge crew eyed the spot Sam mentioned. The "Tombs" were an infamous series of seamounts; an extinct volcanic ridge that stretched nearly fifteen miles along the edge of the Continental Shelf. The pushed-up mountains formed a natural barrier, beyond which water depths plummeted from a few hundred feet, to the Florida Strait's reputed maximum of over six thousand.

Individually, the headstone-shaped hills and knolls were small as seamounts went – most between a thousand and fifteen hundred feet. But, together, they were an imposing sight. To Garm, the arc-shaped forest of shattered peaks had an almost smile-like look to it, like the curved mandible of some colossal crocodile: a tooth-filled opening, eager to destroy and devour any vessel and crew foolish enough to enter their domain.

And devour they had.

With its powerful cross currents, and the fast-narrowing spaces between many of its rocky "teeth", the Tombs had claimed nearly a dozen submarines in the last century.

Garm shook his head vehemently.

He had no intention of being swallowed up by that blackened maw.

"Sonar, is there any indication our quarry utilizes the Tombs?"

"I'm showing just two trails," Ramirez replied, indicating a pair of glittering blue paths leading from the monster's lair, into the abyssal caverns. "In fact, there are very few readings descending into the deepwater, period. Most of the evidence suggests foraging in the shallows."

"That makes sense. The Tombs aren't known to be the home of any large life forms," Garm observed. "Not since our resident sperm whales abandoned it in favor of safer hunting grounds. Same holds true for the abyss."

Sam shifted in his seat. "So, what's the plan?"

"Helm, confirm position," Garm said.

"Still holding, sir," Ho replied. "Distance to target, fifteen hundred yards. Depth, one hundred feet."

"Sonar, how's our cloak holding up?"

"Iridophores are at one hundred percent and stable, sir."

"Good. It's time for this big 'ol blue whale to make a krill," Garm said, giving Sam a wink. "Helm, down five and ease us forward at six knots. Make your depth three hundred, and set course two-one-zero, right standard rudder."

"Aye, sir."

"Once we're two hundred yards out, change course to bearing one-three-one and hold position."

"Yes, sir," Ho confirmed, her dark eyes unblinking as she worked her touchscreen with one hand, and the yoke with the other.

"We're coming in from seaward?" Cunningham interjected.

"That's correct," Garm replied.

"But, if we miss with the NAEGLINGS . . ."

"I thought you 'never' miss," Ho remarked over her shoulder.

"I--"

Sam's expression became alarmed, as he clocked the look of chagrin on Cunningham's face. He cleared his throat hastily. "Wait, if you use those high-speed torpedoes you were talking about and they miss the target, they could go all the way up the beach, couldn't they?"

"All NAEGLING M9 ADCAP's have a built-in auto-destruct," Garm stated. He regarded first Sam, then Kyle. "I prefer to have plenty of maneuvering room, and a safety margin of water under my keel. Again, we don't know what this thing is capable of," he reminded. "I'd prefer not to learn through trial and error."

"Yes, sir," Cunningham said. Head down, he tapped a few keys.

Rush spun in her seat. "Captain, I have an update from the Bearcats."

"Let's hear it."

"They're fifteen miles out. ETA our location, six minutes."

Garm pondered his options. "Transmit our target's coordinates to them, and tell them to hold position at the five-mile mark and await further instructions."

"Five miles away, sir?"

"Bearcats were originally designed for anti-materiel use, ensign," Garm advised. "They're far from stealthy, and I don't want them alerting the target. Send the command."

"Yes, sir."

Ensign Ho's head spun in her captain's direction. "Sir, we're two hundred yards from target. Altering course to one-three-one and holding position."

"Excellent," Garm said, feeling *Gryphon* move smoothly beneath him. He leaned forward in his chair, focusing on the main's 3D fathomer image of what awaited them. "Sonar, give me infrared overlay on the main."

"Aye, sir."

Garm nodded as the bow image shimmered, its detailing increasing. Six hundred feet away, and angling away from their position, the seaweed-littered precipice where their foe slept jutted up from the deep like the towering crest of some stone tsunami, frozen in time.

He could just make out the outline of the wreck, a large, tubular structure that appeared in shades of teal, whereas the seafloor it lay across was highlighted in darker greens and blues. Around the wreck, and running down the cliff's face, was a veritable starfield of tiny gold flecks – sea anemones and other innocuous life forms, wriggling in the dark.

"Communications, take over; give me full forward on the main, high-def and no zoom," he said.

"Yes, sir."

Garm watched as *Gryphon*'s twenty-foot bow window image dissolved, then rematerialized as a real-time view of the sea outside. He half-smiled. No matter how many times he saw it, he couldn't get over how incredible the iridophore-generated monitor images were – comparable to the real thing. Technically, it *was* the real thing, he reminded himself, just reimaged. Still, he preferred the shield up, and being able to stare directly through their transparent titanium bow, at whatever was on the other side.

Soon . . .

"Helm, maintain depth. Let's start our run," he said. "Ahead, four knots."

"Yes, sir," Ho nodded.

"Stand ready, people," Garm said, swiveling in his seat, and eyeing Cunningham in particular. "We're entering the lion's den."

Seen from outside, the illusory blue whale that was the *Gryphon* moved ponderously forward. Its barnacle-edged flippers shifted as it swam, and, although their range of motion was limited, its huge flukes moved slowly up and down.

Ahead, the ridge hove into view. And with it, some otherworldly monster.

"What the hell *is* that?" Garm asked no one in particular, eyeing the wreck's visible hump. "Weapons ready." They got closer and closer, but nothing sprang out at them. Impatient, he turned to Ramirez. "Anything?"

"Strong radiation readings, sir," the sonar tech replied. "Definitely coming from the shipwreck."

"Biologics?"

"Nothing big. There's something inside the wreck," Ramirez continued, wiping the moisture from his mustache with an index finger, while eyeing his screens. "A good-sized bio-mass, but it's . . . not a single animal."

"Details?"

The sonar tech shook his head. "I don't know. The radiation's making it hard to tell. It's a bunch of small life forms, sir," he said, rechecking his screens and hitting keys. "Could be a school of fish or shrimp – definitely not our Kraken."

Garm could feel his chest muscles beginning to tense from all the epinephrine his adrenal glands were producing. "Okay, maybe it's out grocery shopping," he commented. "Let's get a closer look at its living quarters, see if we can get confirmation. Helm, maintain depth and circle the wreck from 100 yards out, maneuvering thrusters only."

"Yes, captain," Ho said, tabbing a few keys.

There was a slight shimmy as *Gryphon*'s powerful hull thrusters, drawing power directly from her primary magneto-hydrodynamic propulsors, kicked in. Stern out and bow forward, she began to swing sideways, running in a tight arc. With her sensors straining, and her torpedo tubes barely three boat lengths from her target, the sleek pliosaur killer swung soundlessly around.

"Fire control, stand ready on LADON," Garm ordered. He licked his lips in anticipation. Sonar might've said the monster's midden was uninhabited, but with all the interference the structure was putting out, he was far from convinced.

"Just say the word," Cunningham replied, his targeting systems online, and the joystick for the big Gatling cannon gripped firmly in one hand.

On their viewer, directly ahead, the aged shipwreck finally came clear of the surrounding coral reefs.

"What the--" Garm gripped his armrests. "Is that a *sub* of some kind?"

"Madre de Dios," Ramirez muttered.

Draped along the edge of the drop-off, like some fallen monolith, was the biggest diesel-powered submarine Garm had ever seen. She was a full football field in length and incredibly massive. In the scant places where a crust of barnacles and seaweed had failed to take hold, her hull appeared a dull-gray color. Her bow was badly crumpled and all but buried in silt and sand, the result of impacting on the bottom, no doubt. Her tail section was also twisted and bent, like a roll of aluminum foil someone grabbed too tightly. She had no props, at least none that he could make out, and her back was broken. The most impressive damage, however, started at the base of her antiquated conning tower – an enormous rent that split her side from sail to keel. At least, he figured as much, as the gaping forty-foot opening terminated at the seafloor, with the vessel's belly embedded in the sand.

Although, from a moral perspective, the big submariner understood that he was staring at a mass grave, in his warrior's mind, it was like finding the remains of some long-dead Titan, slain on the summit of Mount Olympus, and left to rot.

Sam shook his head in wonder. "Wow. Now *that* alone was worth the trip." He turned to his captain. "Kinda looks like a giant version of one of those little dioramas you put in fish tanks, doesn't it?"

Garm fought the obligatory eyeroll. *"The sea, once it casts its spell, holds one in its net of wonder forever."* He gave Sam an inscrutable look, then turned back toward the bow. "Jacques Cousteau."

"Shall I continue orbiting the wreck, sir?" Ensign Ho asked.

"No. Full stop and hold position," Garm replied, rising from his chair. As he took in the sub's tremendous mass, something started to click. A moment later, a ping of excitement shot up his spine. He did a double-take, to make sure he wasn't imagining things, and then grinned. His hobby of studying all things military had finally paid off.

"Communications," he said, not taking his eyes off the viewer. "Run a scan of the wreck and find me an ID." He pursed his lips, then added, "And, send a secure transmission to Dr. Braddock, back at Tartarus."

"Message, sir?" Rush asked, already tapping keys.

"Tell him we found a missing U-boat."

"What?" five mouths echoed simultaneously.

Sam sputtered. "W-wait, are you saying that's some sort of Nazi sub? Like, from World War Two?"

With a chuckle, Garm pointed at the viewer image. "What, you think some drunken teens, maybe as a college fraternity prank, swam to the bottom of the sea a hundred years ago, using air hoses, and, with some sort of water-repelling semi-gloss, painted that aged shield emblem, complete with lightning bolts, sword, and swastika, on the front of her bridge?"

Sam's jaw dropped as he laid eyes on the faded crest, barely visible on the front of the sub's dilapidated conning tower. He sank back in his seat, his webbed restraining belts keeping his limbless torso in place. For the first time since he'd come aboard, the former LifeGiver was speechless.

"Captain, Dr. Braddock requests more information," Rush said.

"Send him everything," Garm stated. "Coordinates, photos, fathometer scan, the whole kit-and-caboodle." He thought for a moment, then added, "Also, tell him is appears the U-boat is our Kraken's lair, and the source of the radiation signature we've been tracking."

"Yes, sir."

Garm stepped between sonar and navigation, his torso momentarily disrupting their shared 3D screen. "Ramirez, still no life signs from inside the hull?"

"Negative, sir. Just that school of fish we picked up before."

"Right. Maintain cloak until I tell you otherwise. Fire control, stay sharp. I want LADON doing intermittent sweeps, but primarily trained on our six. Don't want that thing blindsiding us."

"Affirmative, sir," Cunningham concurred, his eyes alert and glued to his myriad targeting screens.

"Helm, maintain position, maneuvering thrusters only," Garm said. He nodded to himself. Their current location was an ideal spot from which to survey the wreckage, and without stirring up the seabed.

Rush turned in her seat, one hand cupping her headset. "Sir, no records exist for this particular submarine," she said. "I ran the conning tower numbers four-two-zero and got a hit. But the records indicate U-420 was a lot smaller, and was reported lost in the North Atlantic, in October of 1943."

Garm scanned his internal memory banks. "Let's see. The U-420 was a Type VIIC. That means she measured, what . . . two hundred feet in overall length?"

"220 feet and two inches," Rush replied, obviously impressed. "And 871 tons submerged displacement."

"And this beast?"

"Running computer scan now," A moment later, the comms tech recoiled in her seat. "Wow."

"Ensign?"

"Sorry, sir," she apologized. "*This* U-420 measures approximately 332 feet in length and 46 feet in height – that's an estimate, with possible inaccuracies from keel distortion and compression. Total mass is around . . . 2,763 short tons."

"Wow, indeed."

Rush continued. "According to records, that makes it the--"

"The largest U-boat the Third Reich ever built," Garm finished. "Bigger even than their Type-X versions, which were mine layers."

Ramirez cleared his throat before speaking. "Uh, captain, this thing has eight tubes in the bow alone. I . . . don't think she was laying eggs all day."

Garm focused on the visible torpedo tubes, many of them ruptured from the boat's initial collision with the seabed.

Impressive. I bet you were a badass bitch, back in your day.

"Captain?"

"Yes, Ensign Ho?"

"Why would they assign two submarines the same designation?" she asked. "Isn't that unusual?"

Garm pondered the question. Then it hit him like a stiff jab to the nose. "Because April 20th was Adolf Hitler's birthday," he realized, pointing at the conning tower numerals. "With the other one lost, I'd bet good money that had something to do with it."

"You know a lot about World War Two," Sam observed.

"I know a lot about *every* war," Garm said. "Combat strategy is my area of expertise, and I've studied every aspect of it."

"Boning up on the bad guys, eh?"

"It is good to know one's enemy. It is better to know one's self."

Sam looked up, contemplatively. "Who said that, Sun Tzu?"

"No, Jake Braddock," Garm replied, grinning.

"Captain," Rush spoke up. "Doctor Braddock states there is no known record of this particular U-boat, or even its hull design. He suspects it may be the prototype for their . . . Type-Z?"

Garm's whistle sounded like a bomb falling. A few years prior, and with Eric Grayson's backing, he'd gotten permission to peruse a stack of high-level Nazi communiques, several of which mentioned just such a submarine. The records had been heavily redacted, however, and he'd eventually assumed the whole thing was a smokescreen, or, like America's 72,000-ton *Montana*-class super-battleships – which never made it past the planning stage – just a paper concept.

What he was looking at now, however, was decidedly *not* paper.

"Captain," Rush continued. "Dr. Braddock asks if we've done a scan of the vessel's interior."

"Send: 'Have done fathometer scan of exterior, but interior radiation levels prevent detailed readings. Am hesitant to use OMNI ADCAP, due to possibility of alerting target to our presence. Please advise.'"

"Sending, sir."

Garm turned toward sonar, his moist lips compressing in anticipation of what was coming. "Ramirez, prepare to--"

"Captain . . ." Rush began.

And, here it comes.

"Dr. Braddock requests active sonar scan of the hull, including confirmation of presence of radioactive materials."

Garm turned, giving Cunningham a "make sure you're ready" look, before he gave the order. "You heard the man, Ramirez; bring active sonar online, and give me a complete broadband scan of the wreck." He leaned forward and rested a hand on the primary's shoulder. "And, uh, do it *quietly*."

Ramirez swallowed. "Um, yes, sir."

As the wiry sonar tech worked his magic, Garm signaled Ho. "Keep a sharp watch on POSEIDON," he said, indicated the 3D screen. "Especially, the seabed. If you see anything that looks like a section of seafloor changing shape or slithering in our direction, sing out."

"Yes, sir." Ho replied.

"I have scan results," Ramirez announced. "We've got large quantities of concentrated Uranium-235 ore present inside the wreck and scattered outside. Unable to provide an exact volume, however, due to much of it being buried."

"Very well," Garm said, signaling to Rush.

"I've also managed to ID the life forms congregated inside," the sonar tech added. He slid a finger down one of his screens, shaking his head in bemusement.

"Squid, snappers?"

"No, sir. They're eggs!"

Garm's big head swiveled in his direction. "What kind of eggs?"

"Designate: cephalopod eggs, sir. They're . . . octopus eggs. The biggest I've ever seen."

Garm turned back to the main, trying in vain to peer inside the lightless crack that split U-420's corroded flank like a giant's axe stroke. "How many of them are there?"

Ramirez blinked, checking his scanner. "Thousands . . . tens of . . . no, wait, hundreds of thousands!"

"Are you serious?"

"Captain, there are over 200,000 eggs in there, and they're ready to hatch!"

Garm felt a headache coming on. On one hand, this unexpected development was a plus. The fact that their Kraken was an expectant mama, with a clutch to take care of, meant she'd definitely be back.

But, it also meant that, within a few years, they could be inundated with an army of the whale-sized beasts, tearing up not only the Gulf, but the entire Eastern seaboard. They could be looking at a worse plague than the one they were already facing.

"Communications, tell Dr. Braddock I recommend destroying the wreck at once, and waiting for the female octopus to return. When she does, we'll be--"

Rush held up a hesitant finger.

"Yes, ensign?"

"Dr. Braddock said that, due to the historical significance of the wreck, as well as its potential scientific importance, it is not to be destroyed or damaged."

Garm heard the rest of the bridge crew suck in a collective breath, and held up his hands for calm.

"Your orders are to utilize the TALOS Mark VII AWES to neutralize the nest. If possible, please retain several of the unhatched eggs, to be kept in stasis until your return."

"Okay . . ."

Eyes pensive, Rush drew in a lungful, then said on her exhale. "Once the larvae are eradicated, you are to camouflage your vessel and lie in wait for the mother octopus. And kill her."

"Will do," Garm said. "Okay--"

"I'm sorry, sir," Rush cut in.

"Go on."

"Lastly, Dr. Braddock said to remind you of U-234. Once you have confirmation the parent octopus has been terminated, you're to send your AWES pilot back into the wreck and use the Mark VII to explore the interior, documenting all finds."

Well, looks like Typhon gets a pass this time. "Anything else, ensign?"

She shook her head.

"Orders received and preparing to implement. *Gryphon* out."

Suddenly tired, Garm strode the two steps back to his captain's chair and plopped down into it. His inability to speak directly to his brother was annoying, but formalities or no, Dirk was right. He'd been so focused on making his kill, he hadn't considered the possibility of there being anything valuable – or dangerous – inside U-420's aged hull.

He should have. The U-234 incident was legendary. If memory served, when her crew surrendered to the U.S. Navy in 1945, she'd been en route to Japan and carrying over a thousand pounds of uranium oxide, two Messerschmitt jet fighters, and a slew of jet engines.

Garm's eyes swung back up to the fallen warship. *Lord only knows what secrets she has inside of her. And what the* hell *was she doing off the coast of Florida? Were they bound for South America, or were they planning something nasty, here? Maybe they were hoping to surrender the boat to the authorities, defecting, with a gift of technology? And who or what sank her?*

Garm snorted irritably and filed all his pressing questions in his *"I'll deal with you later"* bin. They had a job to do, and it was time to do it. He turned to the left, finding and catching his oldest friend's gaze.

"Looks like you're up, "Samwise". You finally get to earn your keep."

TEN

The Devil's banquet awaited, and *Antrodemus* was eager to partake of it.

With her vessel having covered nearly three hundred nautical miles in the last ten hours, Captain Natalya Dragunova was both tired and irritable. After veering off from their sister ship, *Gryphon*, they'd cruised at near flank speed through the night, running on the surface whenever possible, and making stops as needed. The surface stops had been solely to enable her crew to effect repairs to the crimson-hulled sub's battle-damaged photonics assembly.

"Helm, deestance to Diablo Caldera," Natalya said, turning away from the helm's clear bow window, and reclining back in her shock-absorbing captain's chair like some six-foot-two tigress. She shifted to relieve an ache in her back, then let her head tilt to one side, her tawny blonde tresses cascading down like an amber-colored waterfall.

Normally, Natalya kept her hair up in a tight military bun, per protocol. But after having spent the night alternating between staring at fish and pacing the bridge, she needed to let her hair down – literally and figuratively.

Too bad Wolfie isn't stashed in my cabin, she pined.

We're fifteen miles out, ma'am," Ensign Jackson said, checking her screens. "We're maintaining thirty-five knots. At our current speed, ETA at our targeted coordinates . . . ten minutes."

"And depth?"

Jackson's eyes shone against her milk chocolate colored skin, and her lips compressed. "Sorry, ma'am. We're at 500 feet, with 6,000 more below the keel and shallowing."

"Maintain course and speed." Natalya inhaled deeply, wincing a bit as she felt her breasts complain from the pressure of her sports bra. She realized she was still sore from her recent lovemaking with Garm, and allowed herself the briefest of smiles.

Then she focused her attention back on her crew. The fact that fatigue might affect their alertness and efficiency was a growing concern. They were in dangerous waters – even more so than a pliosaur killer like *Antrodemus* would normally traverse. Now was not the time for carelessness.

Ensign Laverne Jackson was good at her job, and had been with her for a year now. At age thirty-five, she was Natalya's primary helmswoman, and a talented one at that. A former NYC taxi driver, of all things, she was a self-proclaimed survivor from Bedford Stuyvesant who, after being held up one time too many, gave up her cab. She packed up her kids and her mother, and drove all the way to Florida, enlisting in the CDC the following day. As it turned out, five years of navigating Manhattan rush hour traffic in a speeding taxi loaned itself remarkably well toward learning how to drive an anti-biologic submarine.

Of course, it also helped that single moms were notoriously tough bitches.

"Sonar," Natalya said. "Any transients?"

"We left the last US naval ships behind an hour ago, captain," Ensign Suzanne Meyers responded, her blue-gray eyes widening as she watched multiple screens simultaneously. "OMNI ADCAP shows the usual schools of fish and squid. No biologics of any consequence." She cocked her lean head to one side. "I'm picking up a lot of surface activity around the Sabana-Camagüey Archipelago, however."

"What kind?"

"Warships, ma'am. From both sides." She licked her lips. "I'm detecting multiple shockwaves – designate, military ordnance, surface batteries firing."

Natalya's gray eyes intensified. The ongoing and bloody power struggle between Cuba's divided military forces was of no consequence to her, as long as it didn't interfere with their mission.

"How close to the caldera?"

"About thirty miles. So far, the rebels appear to be holding the line."

"Khorosho," Natalya nodded. "Let's hope eet stays good."

"Don't worry, captain. I'll keep them monitored."

She gave Meyers a nod of approval. Suzanne "Susie" Meyers was a recent add-on to her crew. A bouncy little thing with a willowy-but-chiseled frame, she'd been recommended a month prior, by both Garm and Derek Braddock, after *Antrodemus*'s previous sonar tech left on maternity leave and never came back.

Coincidentally, Meyers was also the daughter of a close Braddock family friend: the soon-to-be-retired mayor of Paradise Cove. She was a likable sort, a vegan and into Yoga, but her true passion was surfing – sadly, an almost extinct sport, nowadays.

Natalya hit her chair's intercom tab, to order coffee for her bridge crew. She already knew how Jackson liked hers. "Ensign Meyers, how do you take eet?" she asked.

"Cream and sugar, ma'am."

"How about you, Bender?" she asked, bracing herself.

Ensign Bartholomew "Bart" Bender turned in his chair, one of his trademark smirks already in place. *Antrodemus*'s primary communications officer, the freckle-faced Irish-American was, by far, the most loquacious member of her crew. To call him gabby would've been an understatement. Far worse than his incessant, know-it-all need to provide everyone with useless bits of marine trivia, however, was his shameless obsession with his captain.

Horny men finding ways to appease themselves on a submarine was nothing new – anyone in the service could tell horror stories of discovering "deposits" on shower walls that would turn one's stomach. But, in the CDF, where regulations were not as strict, and with men and women working together, side by side, things could get ... distracting.

Bender was obviously finding it difficult to stay focused.

Natalya had spoken to him about his behavior privately; even reprimanded him publicly, thinking it would solve the problem. It hadn't. He simply had no respect for the chain of command. All balls and no brains, as they said. More than once, she'd considered disciplinary action against him, or, alternately, catching him alone in Tartarus and beating the snot out of him. But, either way, she knew there would be repercussions. The worst of which would be having to explain her actions, not to mention the details of his piggish persistence, to that arrogant mudak, Eric Grayson.

It wasn't that Bender was unattractive. Facially, he wasn't bad, he had a so-so physique, and Natalya definitely wasn't married. If she and Garm discontinued their "theeng", she could and would do as she pleased. But she liked her men fierce, brave, and most of all, tall. The ginger was painfully short, to the point that, when he tried stepping up, she felt like a Leprechaun was hitting on her. It was all she could do to keep from giggling.

The biggest turnoff, however, was the hair.

Like his face, Bender's body was covered with freckles. There were literally thousands of them. And the only thing he had in greater abundance was body hair: thick, sweaty layers of it.

Natalya shuddered at the thought. Bestiality and her were *so* not a fit.

"I'll take it light and sweet," Bender snickered. "Like my women."

"Or your *men*," she countered, with a slight grin and a not-so-slight headshake. "And you, Guerrero?" she asked, spinning her chair a quarter-turn so she could face her CSO.

"Black, like my hair. Or soul," she replied with a shrug, her deadpan expression hinting at some inner merriment as she adjusted her tied-back locks.

Natalya smiled as she finished placing the galley order. Lieutenant Amanda Guerrero, her veteran Combat Systems Officer, had been with her since the beginning. She was her favorite crewmember, and as close as she'd come to having a friend aboard.

The two had a lot in common. At five-foot-eleven, the square-jawed Guerrero was almost as tall, and equally athletic. As a teen, growing up in Spain, she'd won an amateur kickboxing championship and numerous archery titles. She was intelligent, had a collegiate background in botany, and was a talented gymnast who, twice, came close to making her country's Olympic team.

All that changed four years prior, when her beachcombing parents fell prey to a prowling pliosaur. It was a gamechanger for the girl, one Natalya could very much relate to. Guerrero did more than change after that, however. She rose like a Phoenix from its ashes. Flushing her chance at Olympic stardom, like Garm's father had done, decades earlier, she emigrated to the US. Her goal was to extract revenge, pure and simple – something she planned to accomplish by offering her services to the CDF. She applied for a gunner's position and, as it turned out, was terrific at it. Her simulator scores and, later, real-life kills, rivaled or exceeded even Kyle Cunningham's, aboard *Gryphon*.

The only problems Natalya faced with Guerrero came from their military superiors. According to her initial performance reviews, they felt the twenty-five-year-old orphan with the scarred chin enjoyed her work a bit too much. She liked to kill, they said. In fact, she reveled in it. There were concerns. Especially, when they saw a pattern of sadistic behavior emerging from someone who had the ability to launch nuclear torpedoes.

A psych eval was ordered. The next thing you knew, the word *psychopath* was being passed around.

Natalya didn't buy it. She felt there was a huge difference between being damaged and being broken. She'd lived on that difference.

She went to bat for her then-fledgling CSO, as did Garm, and even that scaredy-cat Derek. In the end, they'd won. Guerrero was hers, with the caveat that, as her captain, she, and she alone, was responsible for her behavior.

She'd kept her close ever since.

"Helm, geev me ten up to periscope depth," Natalya said. "Maintain current heading, but reduce speed to twenty knots."

"Yes, captain," Jackson replied. "Reducing speed and shallowing."

"Communications, prepare to extend photonics mast."

"Yes, ma'am," Bender replied, donning his headset and tracking their rise. "Are we sending?"

"No, and no active transmeetting. I want only satellite over-view of our position." Natalya swiveled in her seat. "Sonar, once we're at periscope depth, transfer overview to the main." She rolled out tense shoulders. "Let's get a good look at what we're up against."

Jackson's head popped up. "Depth is sixty . . . forty . . . we are at periscope depth, ma'am."

Natalya signaled to Bender, who flipped the switch. There was a barely perceptible vibration, that signaled *Antrodemus*'s optronics mast was extending to the surface. Once it did, they'd be able to access full-color, high-def images of anywhere on the planet, as well as low-light and thermographic cameras.

Natalya felt a sudden change in cabin pressure, as the bridge's armored exit door whooshed outward on heavy hydraulic hinges. She glanced back, expecting to see Yeoman Percy, their culinary specialist. To her surprise, her second-in-command, Javier Gonzalez, was standing there, balancing a cardboard tray of coffees and bagels on one vascular forearm.

The dark-skinned Cuban flashed her an, "I'll be your waiter tonight, ma'am," smile, then turned his rawboned frame sideways, to ease his passage through the bridge's narrow doorway.

"I was in the galley when Patsy got the call," he said. "Figured I'd give her a break, and myself a chance to get an update."

"Good, I would have needed you, regardless," Natalya said, smiling as he handed her a steaming mug. "Spasiba."

Gonzalez nodded and went about the bridge, handing out food and flagons of much-needed caffeine. Bender was the last.

"Much obliged, commander," the communications officer said, taking a careful sip and eyeing his bagel, while simultaneously touch-typing with his free hand. "By the way, did you know," he mentioned, "that only one percent of the water on this planet is drinkable?"

"Are you insulting my coffee?" Gonzalez asked, feigning offense. "Because I brewed this batch myself, and it's the good stuff, my chatty friend."

"No, I'm serious," Bender persevered. "Ninety-seven percent of Earth's aqua is saltwater, and of the remaining three, two-thirds of it is locked up in glaciers. That means we drink, shower, wash our cars, fill our swimming pools, and flush our toilets, with the one percent that's left."

"Well, I don't know about you," Jackson chimed in, chewing contentedly, and cradling a mug of Kona like it was a newborn, "but I'm loving my share of that one percent, right now!"

"Bender, that ees truly fascinating," Natalya commented, gesturing for Gonzalez to sit beside her in the vacant jump seat. "Now, tell me how thees topic relates to my last command."

"Already done, captain," he said, grinning and indicating the glittering image that had replaced the screen-saver seas, dominating their bow window for the last few hours. "And, waiting on Meyers, too."

"Very good," Natalya commended, giving him a cool look in response to his smugness. Bender could be a little shit at times, but he *was* good at what he did.

She took a quick sip and set her mug in its armrest holder, then, in one fluid motion, rose and moved toward the bow, stopping between Meyers' and Jackson's stations.

She looked up, giving the main a quick once-over, then turned back toward Bender. "Zoom een. Geev me ten-mile view from our position forward."

A second later, the amount of visible sea increased dramatically. Far to port, a small cluster of ships hove into view, and an equal distance to starboard, a separate, and significantly larger, force. Center screen, and far in the distance, a vast and ominous outline began to shape. Although shrouded by mist and clouds, there was no mistaking Diablo Caldera's plateau-like slopes.

"Helm, what ees maximum depth?" Natalya asked.

"Still shallowing, ma'am," Jackson replied. "We're at twenty-seven hundred feet and dropping."

Natalya nodded. "As you can see," she said, placing her hands on her hips and speaking loud enough that the entire bridge could hear, "We are *there*." She indicated the pulsing red icon that represented *Antrodemus*. "About feefty miles from Andros Island, heading straight toward the caldera." She gestured at the distant volcano. "Eet ees isolated, and approximately fourteen miles from the closest islets of the Archipelago de Camagüey."

She pointed at the two groups of naval ships. "The place has always had a bad reputation, and even weeth the accepted theories that the pliosaurs that stalk our oceans most likely came from there, the Cuban government remains een no hurry to explore the place."

"Chickens," Bender muttered.

She shot him a reproving look. "Or, they weesh to avoid confirmation of thees, and prefer to maintain a . . . specter of doubt."

Gonzalez stood up. "Although I was born in the USA, a year after the Paradise Cove incident, in fact, my roots are Cuban." He indicated Diablo's fast-approaching outline. "The island has always been regarded with superstition by my people, and with good reason. For as long as anyone can remember, fishermen that braved its reefs have never come back. Knowing that, and political posturing be as it may, I think it's a safe assumption that, wherever we find in there, it's not going to be a walk in the park – Jurassic or otherwise."

"Agreed," Natalya said. She indicated the ships on the viewer. "See? The naval forces from both sides geev the place a wide berth. Thees ees to our advantage. At the three-mile mark, the waters around the island are less than one thousand feet deep, and een some places, as little as one hundred."

She acknowledged Meyers' raised hand.

"Yeah, we definitely don't want any problems in water that shallow," the sonar tech stated. "We'd be like fish in a barrel, or maybe bathtub."

Suddenly, Bender's spine straightened, and he gripped his headset with both hands. "What the . . .?"

"What ees it?" Natalya prodded.

He turned to face her, uncharacteristically tense. "Captain, I'm getting a message from our base, on a secure channel. Should I--"

"Do nothing," she commanded, holding up a warning finger. "Who ees message from, and what does eet say?"

"There's no name attached. The message reads, '*Attention, Antrodemus. Please confirm your current location and heading.*' It's signed only, '*Tartarus*'."

Natalya and Gonzalez exchanged glances, then she turned back to Bender. "Do not answer. Ignore message."

"Ignore it, ma'am?"

"That ees right. Eet was never received."

"But how are--"

"Our photonics mast ees not yet repaired. Correct, Commander?"

Gonzalez gave her a conspiratorial look and nodded. "That's correct, captain. I'll make sure the log is updated personally, so that we have a record of precisely when repairs *have* been completed."

"Good," Natalya said, then glanced back down at communications. "Retract photonics mast and forget any more messages. Understand?"

Bender swallowed nervously, but nodded. "Understood, ma'am."

"Good. Helm, geev me current max depth, and deestance to target."

"Seafloor is now at eleven hundred feet, ma'am," Jackson replied. "We're two-point-seven miles out, and most of that is, like you said, between nine hundred and a thousand feet. Until we hit the slopes, that is. Then it goes up fast."

"Captain, we've got a change in surface activity," Meyers advised.

"How so?"

The sonar tech indicated her POSEIDON 3D screen, and the flotillas of ships they planned to bypass.

"This larger group," she said, "Are apparently the rebels. They're the ones--"

"That gave us permission to explore the island," Natalya finished.

"Right. They've got the superior numbers: four turn-of-the-century destroyers, a slightly more modern guided missile cruiser, and a dozen smaller ships. They seem content to hold position, after having inflicted serious damage on the government forces."

"Da, and?"

"Well, the government ships – three destroyers in all – have disengaged and are no longer firing at the rebels."

Natalya shook her head. "They are surrendering, da?"

"No, they're spreading out and scanning the surrounding water with active sonar, and at the widest possible patterns. Which makes no sense, because according to our records, neither side has any active-duty submarines."

A chilling thought crept into Natalya's head. *Could they be tracking Typhon?*

Bender cut in. "Something's up. I've breached their secure channels, and am monitoring their ship-to-ship communications; the rebel commander thinks it's a trick of some kind."

Natalya moved to Meyers' side, scrutinizing the destroyers' movements. Her sonar specialist was correct. For ships that had just engaged in mortal combat with a superior force – a force that was still within range of their cruise missiles, and vice versa – the government fleet was acting very strangely.

Meyers cleared her throat. "I'm picking up a lot of rotor noise. They just launched a trio of helicopters. Very noisy. Checking machine profiles . . ." She hesitated, rechecking her screens and pressing a finger to her earpiece. "Designate, Kamov Ka-27's . . . the old Helix models. They're dropping active pinger sonar buoys, ma'am. A lot of them."

"They're looking for someone," Natalya said, her gaze finding Gonzales's.

"Three guesses who that is," he commented.

Bender shifted in his seat. "Wait, they're after *us*?" His voice had that same whiny tone he'd used the last time she'd shot him down. "I thought this mission was top-secret and had government approval?"

"Eet *does*. But we're dealing weeth two governments."

Gonzalez stood beside his captain. "Looks like one of the rebels flipped on us. Should we bag it?"

"Nyet." Natalya practically spat the word. "They weel never find my boat."

Guerrero spoke up for the first time. "If it's a fight they want, why not give it to them? No one can prove we were here. I say we show those losers, with their hand-me-down ships, what *Antrodemus* is capable of." Her shocking blue eyes were even more intense than normal as she leaned casually back in her chair, the fingers of one hand tap-dancing across her weapons console. "How about it, captain; shall we strike a blow for freedom?"

Natalya did an involuntary facepalm. *Maybe the CDF doctors were onto something, after all . . .*

"Maybe next time, lieutenant," she said, giving her a reproachful look. She stepped to her chair and flipped the ship-wide intercom switch. "Thees ees the captain: battle stations. I repeat, battle stations. Thees is not a drill."

The bridge's lighting automatically dimmed, and the shrill cry of a warning claxon could be heard in the hallway outside. Natalya signaled Gonzalez to secure the bridge door, then addressed navigation. "Helm, down fifteen and reduce speed to five knots; take us to the bottom."

"Aye, captain," Jackson said, hitting keys left and right and working the yoke. Natalya grinned as she heard the former Brooklynite mutter, *"Oh, no you don't. You crazy Cubanos ain't getting this mama bear . . . no way, no how."*

"Sonar, geev me all-around coverage on OMNI ADCAP with active search and attack, and increase POSEIDON to maximum gain," Natalya commanded. "Once we've leveled out, breeng SVALINN online. Suppress all active sonar pings targeting us weeth out-of-phase emissions."

She signaled Jackson. "Remember, to be eenvisible to their sonar, we must be near full stop. Eef Meyers tells you to, you stop fast and use maneuvering thrusters to hold. Once sonar pings pass by, you resume course, da?"

"Got it, captain," Jackson said, her jaw set as she exchanged nods with a noticeably tense Meyers. "Don't worry, girlfriend. We got this."

"And ensign, once max-depth reaches three hundred feet, you come to full stop and hold position. Understand?"

"Yes, captain."

Natalya nodded, then turned to Gonzalez. "What do you theenk?"

The broad-chested Cuban shrugged. "Grayson always sells foreign powers outdated crap. I'm familiar with their sonar and, compared to ours, it's junk." He reached up and grabbed an overhead handhold as *Antrodemus*'s nose angled steeply downward. "Between our acoustic cladding and SVALINN arrays, unless we host a rock concert or make sudden, erratic moves, their active pinging should be useless. We're a needle in a haystack, as far as they're concerned."

"A needle, da?" she replied, envying his confidence, as she watched the sunlight outside their bow fade, and the infrareds take over. "Good. Let's just hope we're not the ones that get pricked."

———

Seated at the helm of his private quarters' work station, Dirk Braddock stared in frustration, up at the mammoth monitor before him. His lips did the motorboat thing as he blew out his breath, and he shook his head in disgust.

This totally sucks. There's all this action and discovery going on, and here I am, sitting at my desk like some oversexed nerd, stuck watching internet porn, with nothing but my fossil collection for company.

Dirk turned momentarily contemplative, then grinned and corrected himself. A nerd he might be, but with Stacy's overzealous assistance, his sex life had certainly improved, lately. He *was*, however, definitely frustrated that he was left sitting in his office, "calling the shots", while the more physically gifted and courageous got to enjoy the wonder and adrenaline rush that came with being in the thick of things.

He grabbed his self-heating mug, considered a refill, then checked the time and decided no, placing it back on its polished petrified wood coaster. He'd been downing way too much caffeine of late, and it was almost lunchtime.

Lunchtime already?

There were barely twelve hours to go on the agreement he'd brokered – make that *bought* – from the Cuban resistance. Based on the position of the two transponder symbols he'd been tracking for the last twelve hours, things were about to get interesting.

Glancing up, Dirk rechecked on *Gryphon* and *Antrodemus*'s locations. Dragunova was steaming toward Diablo Caldera and, if all went well, would soon commence her expedition to uncover its secrets. Meanwhile, his brother was holding position near Marathon, and preparing to deal with a very large and hungry cephalopod.

Very large.

Now, *there* was an understatement. Dirk made a Jedi-like hand gesture at his fancy new monitor, opening a file folder marked *Octopus giganteus*. In it, were all the images and data Garm had sent him. The sucker imprints, pictures of the damage to that ruined yacht . . . if his calculations were correct, the sheer size of the female octopus was mind blowing, like something from an old Ray Harryhausen movie.

It was a shame she had to be destroyed. Besides being an incredible scientific oddity, there was so much they could learn from such a creature. He stroked his chin, wondering if there were any other titans of the deep that the pliosaurs' impact on the world's oceans might force to the surface.

Of course, the octopus's death wouldn't be a complete loss. If Garm's AWES operator did his job, they'd bring back several hatchlings for him to raise and study. Dirk's thoughts drifted to Einstein, sitting in his fish tank in Grayson's museum of an office, stuck doing tricks for crabs.

For a mollusk, the yard-long *Octopus vulgaris* was certainly a mental marvel. What would it be like, he wondered, interacting with a pair of them over thirty times the length, and tens of thousands of times the mass? What would they eat, and could they be trained?

Grayson will certainly be tickled pink with the discovery.

Dirk smiled. His mentor would be beside himself with excitement when he found out about the hatchlings. Any concerns the aged CEO might have had about them sending his submarines off on different missions, instead of a combined effort to capture *Typhon*, would be dismissed out of hand. And, there certainly wasn't any need to mention that they still planned to kill the rogue bull, as soon as an opportunity presented itself.

And speaking of pliosaurs . . .

Dirk glanced up just in time to see *Typhon*'s would-be mate swim past his bedroom wall. *Tiamat*. She looked like an obsidian-colored Russian Topol-M ICBM, only double the length, and eight times the mass.

And almost as deadly.

Dirk waited until the last of the queen's 400+ tons finished cruising by, then pulled his shoulders back and refocused on his research. He was proud of himself, sitting there, with the thick aluminum slab that served as a privacy guard raised. Normally, just the thought of laying eyes on the demon that murdered his mother would send his blood pressure into the red, let alone the effect her "accidentally" nudging the PBU barrier had.

But, now, he seemed to be getting used to her. And she knew it.

It was the strangest thing, but Dirk felt like he was coming into his own, of late. He was braver, more brazen. Or was it just stupidity? He hadn't sensed the actual change when it happened, but it was definitely there. He didn't know if it was the result of him finally working up the nerve to enter his deceased mother's quarters or, perhaps, him using the new control helmet to wrangle *Tiamat* during that big presentation for Admiral Callahan.

Now, *that* had been a "moving" experience. Like the part where he'd stepped into the scaly titan's mouth to rescue Stacy? His *bowels* had tried to move, that was for sure.

Talk about entering the lion's den.

Dirk shook his head, bemused. Yeah, he was definitely not himself of late. The way he'd circumvented Grayson's orders, altering the mission parameters? That was something he wouldn't have done a month ago. And that incident where he stood up to that thug Dwyer in the gym? He had no idea what had come over him, but once the goon tried denigrating Natalya Dragunova, he suddenly wanted to jump the guy.

His face reddened, as he recalled the incident in its entirety. Actually, he'd been damn lucky his brother showed up. Otherwise, he'd have ended up in the infirmary. No doubt about it.

Yeah, don't know what *I was thinking there!*

As Dirk chuckled to himself, something dawned on him; maybe his sudden change was because of Dragunova? Could it be one of those "little head overpowering the big head" kind of things? He'd finally come to terms with his obsession over her, chalking it up as an unrequited love interest, but could she have such a profound effect on him that he'd risk ending up in a body cast?

Maybe she could; she is amazing. It's probably some sort of caveman thing, like imprinting on a potential mate. He'd read up on it recently. People did crazy things when it came to procreation.

All of a sudden, Stacy Daniels popped into Dirk's mind, and a rogue wave of guilt accompanied her. He tapped his fingers on his desk, ruminating on their "friendship's" recent upgrade. He didn't buy the whole, "I'm just using you for sex" routine she'd been feeding him lately – along with mouthfuls of her voluminous breasts – but then again, he wasn't an idiot. He wasn't about to say no.

Seriously, what man in his right mind would? Or woman, for that matter?

Last night *had* been amazing, Dirk thought, grinning like a teenager who'd just gotten to second base for the first time. He reached over to the wooden desk rack that housed his collection of prehistoric predator teeth and absentmindedly touched the pointy tip of his seventeen-inch *Kronosaurus imperator* fang with a nervous finger.

God, the way she'd ridden his—

Dirk blinked and shrugged off the normally-welcome image. He felt a sudden chill pierce him to the core and got the distinct impression he was being observed.

He was.

Hovering directly outside his window, the width of her wedge-shaped head and massive neck practically filling its fifteen-foot frame, was *Tiamat*. Like Death does all of us, she'd been watching him.

With her twenty-five-foot pectoral fins slowly undulating to keep her in place, and her battle-scarred lips peeled back just enough to reveal a battery of flesh-rending fangs, she zeroed him with those baleful orange eyes of hers.

"Fuck you, bitch. I'm not afraid of you."

Dirk glanced up at the prototype cybernetic helmet, sitting on a shelf above his desk, and considered using it to make her bash her head against her paddock's far wall a few times. Just to teach her a lesson.

He shook his head. Lord knew how many times he'd wished that he, or anyone that could've used it, had had that helmet on and been there, the night his mother had been taken. What a difference it would've made.

Dirk stood up and locked eyes with the pliosaur queen. He wasn't going to abuse Grayson's prize pet; but on the other hand, and despite his newfound gumption, there was no way he would get any work done with her sizing him up as a midday snack.

He walked toward her, trying to portray confidence, but feeling the tenseness build. He reminded himself that her implant protocols prevented her from coming closer than fifteen feet to the PBU barrier. He wondered, given free rein and the room to build up enough speed, could she shatter it?

Stop thinking like that. You're just playing into her game.

Dirk stopped a yard back from the Celazole wall, his arms folded defiantly across his chest, and his dark eyes trying their best to bore their way into her fiery orbs. He felt like an ant trying to intimidate an elephant, but he wasn't about to back down. Not this time, and not anymore.

"Shield," he commanded, a minute later.

As the foot-thick aluminum barrier descended between them, he did something he never would have thought himself capable of. He smiled at the world's deadliest predator. And then he blew her a kiss.

Knowing she could still see his feet, he remained where he was until the shield had completely lowered. Then he turned on his heel and headed back to his station. A moment later, the watery whoosh behind him showed she'd grown tired of the game and moved off.

For now.

Dirk glanced back up at the prototype cybernetic helmet. Hopefully, after this latest incident, the mutant *Kronosaurus imperator* cow knew better than to continue harassing him. If she didn't, he'd have no choice but to punish her again, either by reducing her virtual paddock size or worse.

Out of the corner of his eye, Dirk spotted the two-foot window he'd opened in the upper-right corner of his monitor. On it, was what he subconsciously referred to as his mother's death video – the black and white security footage documenting her cataclysmic drop into Tartarus's amphitheater pool, followed by *Tiamat*'s subsequent entry and the nightmare that ensued.

At this point, he'd seen the clip so many times that he knew it by heart. He was still convinced that the circumstances surrounding Amara Braddock's death overwhelmingly suggested it was no accident, despite what Dr. Grayson believed. Still, he had to concede, however grudgingly, that any evidence he had was based on coincidence, and was entirely circumstantial.

Dirk sighed as he mentally flipflopped once more. Maybe his mentor was right. Maybe he was just seeing ghosts, or worse, in his grief, trying to invent some malevolent entity, someone or some*thing* to blame.

Out of habit, he gestured for the security video to initiate. Lately, he'd been focused on – make that *obsessing* over – its final ten seconds.

It was the view from the auxiliary camera as it swept slowly back and forth, swiveling away from the spot where his mom was killed, and ending on the damp concrete lip of the amphitheater pool's maintenance ledge. In the background, the lower portion of a locked security door was visible, and, at the very bottom of the screen, you could see the rushing water created by the current generators. According to the official report, the generators' unscheduled activation had been an accident – a side effect of one of the rolling blackouts that plagued Tartarus back then.

Dirk's frown deepened. It was yet another disturbing, albeit confirmed, coincidence. At least he knew that Stacy hadn't been involved.

He sighed, his gaze finally falling away. As always, nothing was amiss. Everything on the recording was the same as it had been every other time.

His fingers tap-danced on an invisible keypad, as he reduced the window size to fifty percent and allowed the footage to run. He'd set the final segment to a play/rewind loop that rewound and repeated. At some point, he'd figured watching it backwards might make a difference. It hadn't.

Turning back to his research, Dirk focused on the collection of computer-generated U-boats that now dominated his monitor. He had them stacked in size order and, as he started at the bottom and worked his way up, he whistled softly. From Germany's smaller coastal and long-range attack boats, to the huge XB-class, originally designed as minelayers, and then relegated to transports, the U-420 his brother had found topped them all.

If she was, indeed, a prototype of the never completed Z-class, she was an incredible find.

Dirk stroked his chin as he reviewed assorted blueprints and schematics, trying to unravel the mystery of the mammoth submarine. What was she designed for? At well over 300 feet in length, and with a hefty beam to boot, she would've been capable of transporting an entire company of heavily-armed commandos. Heck, they could have thrown in a few armored half-tracks, to boot.

But her battery of bow-mounted torpedo tubes indicated a vessel meant for more than just troop transport. With the ability to launch eight of the *Kriegsmarine*'s most devastating "fish" at the same time, U-420 would've been a formidable adversary. Hell, she could've been a battleship killer. Or, more likely, designed to target America's irreplaceable aircraft carriers – the key to bringing the war in the Pacific to Imperial Japan's doorstep.

But what the hell was she doing in the Keys? And who sunk her?

Dirk had a momentary image of the monstrous U-boat creeping toward Jacksonville's Naval Station Mayport, under cover of darkness, and unleashing her lethal arsenal on a slew of slumbering warships. For a mentally unbalanced and battle-weary Adolf Hitler, it would've been the Third Reich's version of the Japanese attack on Pearl Harbor: quite the coup.

He shook his head. No, that wasn't it. If that had been their goal, why the Uranium-235? And what else was stored in her holds?

Dirk scanned his records. As he'd intimated to Garm, the U-234, a Type-X sub, almost as big as U-420, had surrendered in 1945, while en route to Japan. In her holds, besides an assortment of advanced weaponry, she carried 560 kg. of yellowcake – uranium oxide concentrate powder, ready for enrichment.

With the war all but lost, the Nazis had apparently planned on turning over their greatest secrets to their Nipponese allies. Given time, it could've changed the course of the war. Thankfully, fate dictated otherwise. Could the captain and crew of U-420 have also been planning to turn their vessel over to the United States in exchange for asylum – sort of a WWII real-life version of the Tom Clancy classic *"The Hunt for Red October"*?

Dirk's imagination got the better of him, and he imagined a German version of Sean Connery at the helm of the big submarine, his vessel crammed with what was then state-of-the-art weapons technology, sitting less than twenty miles from the coastline.

Whoever her captain was, he must've had contacts here. Some sort of cloak-and-dagger types, no doubt, waiting in the shadows—

The . . . shadows?

Dirk's head snapped up toward the window replaying the security footage. His eyes went wide, then narrowed. He could've *sworn* he'd seen something with his peripherals that stood out, something different from one moment to the next. But what was it? And where?

He ran through that last ten seconds, watching the back and forth sweep of the camera as it played, rewound, then played again. He saw nothing. Frustrated, he tried focusing his gaze straight ahead, relying once more on his side-vision. Back and forth, rewind. Back and forth . . .

Then he saw it.

He was right. There *was* something different. Some sort of discrepancy between the first and second sweeps of the camera. It was hardly noticeable; a shadowy haze, barely visible, on the far-right side of the screen, near eye level.

Dirk stared at it, blinked to clear his vision, and then stared again. Whatever it was had to have been close to the camera, so close that it was blurred. But it was there. An out-of-focus edge of something; it was there one moment and gone the next. But what the hell *was* it?

A sudden adrenaline rush caused the young scientist to start panting, and he reached for his virtual keyboard. He was onto something; he was positive. With fumbling hands, he enlarged the video to half-screen, then froze it and isolated the two best possible frames, outlining the portions in question.

As he put the two frames side-by-side, enlarging them and maximizing their resolution, he realized his hands were trembling.

"Computer, activate voice command prompts," he said.

"Voice command online. What is your command?" the mechanized feminine voice asked.

"Analyze images A and B."

"Images analyzed."

Dirk licked his lips. "Comparative analysis. Is there a difference between the two images?"

"Image A was taken from a lens angle with a variance of approximate point-six degrees--"

"Cancel. Comparative analysis of encircled portions of two images. Analyze the blurred portion on image A versus its absence in image B. Does blurred portion of A represent the presence of a physical object not found in B?"

The system hesitated for a moment. "Confirmed."

I knew it! I knew there was something!

Dirk glanced at his empty mug, then swallowed to moisten his throat. "Computer, analysis of object. What is it?"

"Insufficient data."

"Fuck!"

"Unable to comply. System--"

"I'm, uh . . . system pause," Dirk said. He shook his head, realizing he'd almost apologized to his PC. He thought for a moment.

"Computer, calculate distance of object from lens."

"Unable to calculate specific distance, due to focal length limitations."

"Okay, approximate distance."

"Object is at or near ground level, approximately three to six inches from lens."

Now we're getting somewhere.

Dirk took a few quick breaths. "Computer, attempt recreation of object."

"Insufficient data. Identity of object would be required to proceed."

Damn it!

"Computer, calculate approximate *size* of object."

"Size estimate: object possesses an estimated vertical height ranging from two to six inches. Horizontal or overall mass estimates impossible due to insufficient data."

"Computer, best guess as to identity of object."

"Insufficient data."

"Is object living matter?"

"Insufficient data."

"Is object inanimate matter?"

"Insufficient data."

Dirk's hands balled into fists, and he dug his bottom incisors into his upper lip to keep from screaming. He drew in a breath and held it until it hurt, then leaned forward and keyed the final portion of the video into the system for analysis.

"Computer, analyze footage frame by frame; reanalyze frames in question, and calculate camera positioning." He hesitated, fearful of the answer he might get. "Based on field of view and framing, does camera positioning in frame A, versus frame B, preclude the possibility of a simple variance in camera arc?"

The system hesitated once more. "Camera model in question has no propensity for deviation. Background image comparison confirms presence of object in frame A, and absence of object in frame B."

"So, there *is* something in A, and in B it's gone."

"Confirmed."

"But you cannot tell me what it is?"

"Insufficient data."

"And you can't provide any possibilities as to *what* it might be?"

"Insufficient data."

Exasperated, Dirk threw his forearms onto the desk before him. A moment later, his aching head cascaded down to meet them. "Computer?" he groaned.

"Yes?"

"I need a drink."

"Insuffi--"

"Oh, shut the hell up."

ELEVEN

"**L**ooks like it's time to separate the men from the boys," Sam Mot said from the open cockpit of his TALOS Mark VII Armored Weaponized Exoskeleton System. "You know how they do that in Greece, right?" he remarked, smirking in Garm and Jayla Morgan's direction. "With a crowbar!"

Garm shook his head and grinned. Jayla just groaned.

The three of them were standing in the heart of *Gryphon*'s underwater airlock – a cramped, twelve-by-sixteen-foot chamber, located forty feet back from the sub's armored prow, and situated directly behind its currently retracted labium's housing.

Garm made a face as he looked around. He hated being inside the floodable airlock, and not just because he knew that the yard-thick pressure door to his left was the only thing holding back the entire ocean. Granted, the thought of drowning or being crushed to death wasn't appealing, but it was the eerie lighting, the eternal wetness, and the pungent odor of rusting metal and sea salt that really got to him. Reinforced girders that made it stronger than a bunker or no, as an athlete who loved the outdoors and regularly did ten miles of roadwork a day, the place was anathema to him.

Of course, there was also the REAPER. Garm glanced pensively upward. The encapsulated barrel of their monstrous rail gun ran right over the airlock's ceiling. Literally.

600 megajoules of energy blasting by, right over your head? Yeah, fuck that. You can keep your "blast shielding". Short of staring down the barrel, the airlock was the last place he wanted to be when the rail-energized, armor-piercing, electromagnetic repulsion gun fired.

"Okay, Sam, you about ready?" Garm asked, moving close and standing on tiptoe, so he could see inside the eight-foot TALOS's illuminated cockpit. His limbless friend appeared well-situated; he was wearing a skin-tight, protective bodysuit, with a padded restraining harness holding him in place, and had the weaponized exoskeleton's sleek cybernetic control helmet strapped on tight.

"I'm good, oh, pal-o-mine," Sam said, smiling. "It even has air conditioning." He made a show of glancing down inside the suit's lit-up interior and whistled. "Boy, look at the size of those . . . *shock absorbers.*" He glanced over at Jayla and winked. "Hey, Morgan, thanks again for helping ol' Garm here get me into this thing." He gave her an appraising look. "Dang, nice muscles, girl. Did I tell you, I'm attracted to women with strong backs?"

"Oh, Lord," she mumbled, her cheeks reddening.

"Seriously," Sam persisted. "You're not seeing anybody . . . am I right?"

Jayla hesitated, obviously caught off guard.

"That's what I thought," Sam continued. "Not a bad thing, having high standards and all that. But, it does make you tense after a while."

"W-what?"

"Don't sweat it, pretty lady. When we get back, if you're game, it'd be my privilege to take you out for a night on the town."

Garm cleared his throat. "Uh, in the . . . AWES, Sam?"

The former LifeGiver turned momentarily contemplative. "Yeah, you're right. No problem. We'll eat in, before we eat out."

"Okay, enough small talk," Garm said, stepping forward and closing the armored suit's rugged titanium-steel hatch with a loud thump. He heard a low hiss, as the interior sealed and pressurized itself, and stepped back to give Sam room to maneuver.

"Watch your head," he advised, indicating the exterior pressure door.

"So, let's review this one more time," Sam said, his face hidden behind a mirrored, oval-shaped panel, his amplified voice emanating from TALOS's external speakers. "I go out and pluck a couple of octopus eggs from the bunch, and store them in *this*," he said. In the menacing steel talons of his suit's right hand, he cradled what looked like a foot-thick, yard-long test tube with heavy silver endcaps.

"*Carefully*," Garm reminded.

"Right. Then, I activate the suit's primary weapon," he continued, holding up its cannon-like left arm, "And use it to torch the remainder of the eggs."

The AWES's massive upper body leaned back at the waist as he peered upward. "Isn't that going to be a stretch? I saw the video, and the inside of that opening must go a good thirty feet."

Morgan interjected, her South African accent more pronounced than normal. "It should be relatively simple. The actual plasma blade you'll be wielding has an effective range of ten feet, but it emits so much heat that anything within five feet of it will be instantly parboiled. You should be able to make short work of the nest."

"Just keep in mind," Garm reminded, "The U-420 has been officially labeled an historical site. "Your weapon radiates a temperature of ten thousand degrees Kelvin. That's double the surface temperature of the sun, so try not to do any damage."

The hulking suit's nod was reminiscent of a robotic Sasquatch. "Got it; fry the eggs, don't burn down the kitchen."

"Exactly," Garm said, grinning. As Sam took a preparatory step, he added, "One more thing."

"Yes?"

"An old Japanese proverb my mom told me: 'A father's goodness is higher than the mountain, a mother's goodness deeper than the sea'."

When Sam stared at him quizzically, he explained. "Moms don't like people messing with their kids. So, get in, do your job, and get your ass back aboard *Gryphon* like the Devil itself was after you. Because she well may be."

"Gotcha."

There was a sudden wheeze of depressurizing air, as TALOS's three-inch-thick titanium face plate unexpectedly opened. He could see Sam's lit-up face. He was wearing a peculiar look.

"I, um . . ."

Garm's head cocked to one side. For the first time he could remember, the ever-jocular former LifeGiver seemed both serious and at a loss for words.

"I've never told you this," Sam struggled. "But, just in case things go bad out there, I want to clear the air."

"Okay . . ."

"Although it may've cost me an arm and a leg – or *two*," he said, doing an exaggerated eye roll, "I want you to know, I've never regretted saving your life." He met and held his best friend's gaze. "And, I also want you to know, if I had to do it again, I would. Although, next time, I'd definitely prefer to be shit-faced!"

Garm's jaw muscles tensed as he grappled with unfamiliar emotions. "Thank you, Sam," he said. "I'm touched. But, if this is your way of trying to get me to kiss you, forget it!"

"Damnit, he's on to me!" Sam chuckled, exhaling to ease the tension. He glanced at Morgan and winked. "How about you, girlfriend? A kiss for luck?"

The dusky-hued South African sputtered, and then, to her captain's complete surprise, gave the AWES operator a tentative smile. "Maybe when you get back."

"Hell, yeah," Sam exclaimed, willing his faceplate closed, then turning and clomping toward the nearby pressure door.

"And, FYI, you two. I worked out a deal with Grayson. You're gonna have a new Sam Mot on your hands, come this time next year. So, look out!"

"Okay, you Hellraiser," Garm said, chuckling. He gestured to Jayla, who joined him in splashing through ankle-high brownish water, as they retreated back outside the underwater airlock's interior pressure door.

"Good luck!" Garm shouted, then turned and closed the foot-thick barrier. He swung the sealing lever down hard, checked to make sure all the backup seals were in place, armed the system, and then gave a quick look through the tiny window, to make absolutely sure Sam was prepared.

Then he hit the switch.

There was a shuddering metallic rumble, as the eight-foot external airlock door's seals parted, and it began to lower outward like a drawbridge on giant hydraulic pistons. Pressurized seawater blasted in, nearly toppling Sam despite TALOS's six tons, and filled the compartment to the ceiling.

Unable to see through the murk, Garm and Jayla abandoned the window and took to watching the airlock's internal camera monitor. Inside, Sam took his first tentative steps, the AWES's huge booted feet keeping him surprisingly stable as he moved toward the ramp-like edge of the armored outer door.

A moment later, he stepped off the door's edge and into the infinite blue beyond, like it was a diving board. At the same time, he willed the suit's Mako M65 Pump Jet Propulsors to life. With the soles of his feet blazing a bright electric blue, he rose effortlessly up and held position, a gray-colored colossus, suspended in the current.

He's got the stabilizer thrusters completely under control, Garm noted, watching the monitor intently as Sam maneuvered around. *Glad to see he took the training simulations seriously.*

As the mechanized marvel veered off and accelerated toward the nearby wreck, Garm tapped Jayla on the shoulder and grinned. "C'mon, 'girlfriend'. Let's get back up front and watch your man work."

"Oh, blerrie hell," she muttered. "I know I'm never living this down."

A thousand feet below, in the chilled blackness of the abyss, the male *Octopus giganteus* lay in wait.

After a seeming eternity, he'd come to the conclusion that his mate had either been killed or had abandoned their clutch. His century-old mollusk's mind very much doubted the former, but with her unstable behavior of late, the other possibility loomed large.

Under normal circumstances, it would've been unlike the female to leave the nest for any extended period. In fact, throughout their long history together, she almost always relied on him to forage for prey, while she stood guard. But her recent habit of prowling on her own, combined with her increasingly vicious temperament, was disturbing.

The male hunkered down atop the submarine ridge he had chosen, the papillae coating his gnarled skin altering in color and texture. Even in sunlight, it would've been difficult to distinguish his gray, green, and brown body from the surrounding rock. But here, in the darkness of the deep, it was all but impossible.

His decision to leave the nursery, however briefly, weighed heavily on the protective father. But, with his mate failing to reappear, and his own strength beginning to fade, he realized he had no choice. For his clutch to live, *he* must live.

That meant he had to eat.

His worries about leaving to forage were mitigated, at least in part, by the fact that the usual egg thieves – the reef's resident fish – completely avoided the ancient iron construct the two octopi had chosen for a lair. At a subconscious level, the male believed the unpalatable black granules littering their midden were, at least partially, to blame. If they were, however, and if their presence granted him the respite he needed to feed himself, their presence was tolerable.

Opening his gleaming golden eyes, the male surveyed the trap he'd set. The bait was the gnawed-on remnants of the gray whale he'd given his mate the previous evening: at this point, little more than the skull, rib cage, and backbone. Although bereft of any real substance, the decaying gristle and tiny scraps of flesh that still clung to the carcass exuded a strong scent.

It was a dinner bell few scavengers could resist.

He had chosen his ambush spot well, a low-lying ridge overlooking an open stretch of stone and sand, and adjacent to a nearby canyon. With his superior multilayered vision, it gave him the ability to spot potential prey from far off. Best of all, a cold current moved briskly through the region, and would carry the smell of the cetacean's remains far and wide. Soon, he would--

The male's eyes narrowed. His first guest was already approaching.

Consciously calming his burning stomach, the colossal cephalopod studied the approaching prey item. It was a shark, and a large one at that. Known to the tiny warm-bloods above as *Carcharodon megalodon*, the ghostlike hunter swimming stealthily closer was actually the smaller of the ancient fish's two surviving sub-species. A true testimony to the power of evolution, and despite a laundry list of environmental changes that had, over millions of years, all but annihilated their kind, the Megalodons had soldiered on.

With his rapacious appetite temporarily quelled, the male octopus remained as rigid as the stone he imitated. He could tell, even from this distance, that the shark was an ideal meal. At fifty feet in length, it was not as large as some of the pelagic versions he'd encountered in the past, but still tipped the scales at over forty tons. Its pale, mottled hide had lost much of its ancestors' slate-gray coloration – one of its many adaptions to a deepwater existence. Its dorsal and pectoral fins were also shorter, its caudal fin longer, and its eyes substantially larger – a necessary adaptation to a life lived near the bottom, and in perpetual darkness.

Of course, one thing about the great fish that had *not* changed, were its six-inch teeth. Primarily a scavenger, the deepwater Megalodon's jaws were like a seven-foot mouthful of serrated chisels. They were designed for one thing: to crush the rib cages of sunken whale carcasses and shear what organs remained into mincemeat.

They could do the same thing to an octopus.

Like an otherworldly apparition, the pale-hued shark drew steadily closer. Its huge nostrils, and the magnetically sensitive pores on its blunt snout, were infallible range finders, allowing it to scent its way along the bottom like some gigantic six-gill.

With its prey only fifty yards from the carrion that had drawn it, the male octopus saw the Megalodon's mood begin to change. Its broad pectoral fins extended out from its flanks like circular sawblades, and its back began to hump. The fish's innate wariness had begun to ebb, and a powerful feeding response was beginning to build.

Suddenly, with a flick of its mighty tail, the shark accelerated and slammed into the chewed-up rib cage of the skeletonized gray whale. It began to bite, all the while powering itself against its target with repeated sweeps of its scythe-like tail. Its thick enameled teeth, their tapered points designed to fit between cetacean ribs, to make splitting them apart easier, began to dig in, and a loud cracking sound resonated through the water – like a dead tree, felled by a lumberjack's axe.

Seconds later, the huge shark's tail stopped its frantic thrusting and its withdrawn snout wrinkled up in frustration. It realized no meaty prize remained inside the dead whale's rib cage.

At that moment, the male octopus struck.

As he jetted forward like a 134-ton torpedo, his eighty-foot tentacles flared out in every direction at once. Parachuting down, he landed square on the giant fish's broad back and enveloped it.

The Megalodon, its oil-colored eyes widening as it realized its mistake, went berserk. It flailed and snapped wildly, heaving its mammoth body to and fro, its scarred snout slashing desperately at anything that came within range, as it tried to bring its mighty jaws to bear.

It was useless. Too wily and experienced to make mistakes, the male octopus had sprung his trap perfectly. He had wrapped the shark's rough-skinned body from gills to caudal fin in a deadly cocoon of clinging tentacles.

The battle was already decided.

Not waiting for his venom to finish off the rival predator, the ravenous cephalopod began eating it alive. His four-foot raptor's beak yawned wide and he bit down, tearing mouthful after mouthful of still-twitching flesh from his hysterical victim. Soon, the male's hunger was all he knew, and he began to lose himself. He spun the hapless shark belly-up to induce a state of torpor and pinned it to the bottom. A moment later, he began to eviscerate it, his insatiable maw gulping down its oozing intestines as its dying eyes watched.

Long minutes passed, until, finally, the male's feeding frenzy began to fade. Seated in a cloud of blood and scraps of skin and flesh, he could feel his strength returning. And with it, a cool calmness swept over him. He shifted position, his mantle bulging to the limit as he drew in thousands of gallons of seawater. He expelled it from his siphon in a rush – the octopus equivalent of a sigh of contentment.

As he flirted with his own lethargy, the male pondered the half-eaten Megalodon. Caution dictated he bring it with him. Should the female return, it would make a good gift to appease her. Especially, if her own hunting had proven fruitless. And, if she did not come back, he could consume the remains himself.

All of a sudden, a sensation akin to alarm resonated through the octopus. He felt a familiar tingle ripple across his bark-like skin, and began to cast about. Evolution's perfect sperm whale slayers, one of the many gifts his species had evolved was the ability to detect the long-range sonar emissions of their prey. It was a useful tool, both for the adults of their kind, when it came to hunting, and the young, when the tables were turned. At smaller sizes, even an *Octopus giganteus* could fall prey to their narrow-jawed adversaries.

The male was detecting whale sonar now. Lots of it. But there was something unusual about the sound waves. They were less focused, louder, and more regimented. They were also distant and emanating from higher up. They were coming from--

The octopus's glittering gaze swept up and up, eventually focusing on the pinnacle of a nearby cliff. His eyes flew open wide and his thick skin paled as he realized where the sonar pulses were coming from. Accompanying them, was some sort of bioluminescence. He could see it, even from a thousand feet down.

A sudden rush of rage filled the male and his mighty tentacles contracted like a colossal fist. A second later, he exploded violently upward in a swirl of suckers. Stealth and subterfuge were abandoned and, as he accelerated to full speed, a powerful pressure wave proceeded him. Far below, and shrinking rapidly, lay the abandoned remains of the Megalodon, a swarm of hungry hagfish already gathering.

Food mattered not now. Some creature had dared to invade the nest.

And it was going to pay.

With its flesh.

Still smarting from his failed attempt to decipher the mysterious "shadow" in Amara Braddock's death footage, Dirk Braddock sat back in his ergonomic office chair and resumed slow-sipping his drink.

He hadn't been kidding, earlier, when he told his PC he needed one. And the 50-year-old Glenmorangie Scotch Single Malt 1995 he'd opened had definitely done the trick. Hefting the weighty bottle in his free hand, Dirk studied its accompanying ingredients card and whistled, before setting it carefully back down on his desk.

An extravagant birthday gift from Eric Grayson, the whisky cost ten thousand dollars; an outrageous sum for even the eccentric billionaire to spend, in his humble opinion. His eyes wide, he rotated the bottom-heavy glass in his palm, watching the ice cubes swirl and crackle, as the amber-hued single-blend they battled diluted.

Dirk grinned at the thought of "neat" drinker Grayson catching him enjoying his precious, cask-matured scotch chilled. Boy, would he hear it. He shook his head and chuckled aloud.

Fine, so I'm a heathen. Whatever.

Still grinning, he turned back to the welcome distraction of his U-boat research. Anything to take his mind off that damned video. He glanced at the wall clock, his lips pursing contemplatively. Garm's friend Sam – the unfortunate quadruple amputee – should be finished clearing out the *Octopus giganteus* nest soon. Once that was done, and the parent dealt with, *Gryphon* could head back to base with the remaining hatchlings. Something new and exciting to address.

Enlarging one of the stills of U-420 on his screen, Dirk focused on the enormous gash in her steel flank, followed by her caved-in bow section and collapsed stern. Deciphering the mystery of the mammoth submarine intrigued him, and his scientific mind was obsessed with solving it.

The gash was definitely secondary damage, caused as U-420 dropped onto the stony ridge, adjacent to the drop-off. Dirk's eyes swept across the sub's considerable length, scrutinizing every part of it. He held up his hands, trying to imitate what he believed had occurred. The boat had come down at speed, probably at a steep angle, and hit nose first. Her vulnerable prow had crumpled like an accordion, simultaneously burying itself in the seabed. Then, the rest of her had followed.

Her rigid keel, unable to conform to the curvature of the drop-off, promptly shattered, and her spine along with it. The stern was the last to strike the bottom, slapping down hard and casting up silt and sediment for a hundred yards in every direction. But how did she sink?

That was the mystery.

All the damage that Dirk could see matched known impact parameters. Which meant that, whatever fatal wounds the submarine sustained were either on her starboard side or belly, and concealed beneath ten feet of sand.

Then again, it could've been sabotage, or leaked toxins, or even something as inane as someone inadvertently leaving a hatch open.

Dirk shook his head and smiled grimly. No. He couldn't picture experienced sailors of the *Kriegsmarine* being that careless.

A brutal vision of U-420's envisioned demise began to creep into the young scientist's head, and he shivered at the thought. Modern subs like the ORION-class, although smaller, used advanced materials and technology to maximize space, reduce crew complement, and even provide some much-needed, albeit minor, creature comforts. But a hundred-year-old dreadnought like the Z-class sub – constantly on the run and targeted by bombs and depth charges – was a cramped and crowded tomb, a mobile mausoleum, just waiting for its permanent residents.

Dirk pictured the huge U-boat's final moments; her terrified sailors, clinging to whatever handholds they could find, screaming as she did a high-speed death roll, straight to the bottom. There would've been that terrible, deafening impact, followed by a tsunami of pressurized seawater, blasting into her fractured hull and drowning everyone in its path.

The lights might have stayed on briefly, the emergency ones, but then, darkness and death. Any crewmen in the bow section got off easy. Their ends came quickly. But anyone still "safe", huddled behind whatever watertight hatches they'd managed to close in time, suffered a slow and horrible death, immersed to their necks in icy seawater, with nothing but a flashlight to illuminate the utter hopelessness of their situation. One by one, they succumbed to hypothermia, drowned, or suffocated as their air supply ran out.

Their pleas and prayers went unanswered. No one would come. No one would have even known. And even if they had, no one could have possibly saved them. A horrifying way to go.

"Poor bastards," Dirk said aloud.

He shook it off with a shudder, and for the umpteenth time, wondered how his brother Garm did it. He sure as hell wouldn't want to be down in a submarine – not under combat conditions. Not even in the newest models, with their high-tech pressure hulls and automated escape pods. No way, no how.

And how the old-timers did it, back during the first and second world wars, was beyond him. They must've been made of sterner stuff. He remembered watching that old Wolfgang Petersen film, *Das Boot*, recently, and cringing at not only the inhuman conditions the men endured, but the mental tortures they suffered during combat. The stress, the fear, the never knowing when the end would come.

Das Boot . . . Dirk shook his head.

Suddenly, something sparked.

Das . . . *Boot*.

Boot?

Dirk's head whipped to the right so hard he nearly herniated a disc, and he clicked on the link to the amphitheater security footage. His lips were dry, and he swallowed his remaining scotch in one huge mouthful. When he tried to speak, his voice came out as a frog-like croak.

"Computer . . ." he began, then paused and swallowed. "Activate voice command prompts."

"Voice command online. What is your command?" the emotionless female voice asked. Dirk made a mental note to change "her" speech pattern to something more pleasant. Maybe a nice Russian accent?

"Revisit analysis of most recent images A and B."

On the screen, the two frames from the security footage reappeared, complete with the portions he'd boxed for investigation.

"Images analyzed."

"Computer, attempt recreation of unknown object."

"Insufficient data. Identity of object required to proceed."

Dirk drew in a breath and held it. "Computer, calculate object as being someone's footwear."

There was a momentary delay. "Specify type of footwear."

"A boot."

"Specify type of boot and gender of wearer."

"A . . . military-style boot, adult male."

"Scanning."

Dirk watched the system initiate a high-speed scan of the blurred object's visible edge, followed by a blinding-fast series of bright-red, blue-print-style outlines as it attempted multiple reconstructions. A moment later, it paused.

"Analysis complete."

"Results?"

A series of dark pixels materialized on the screen and swirled around the shadowy image Dirk had isolated, hovering over it, and then compressing inward. They began to coalesce. A moment later, they solidified, and the completed image shrank to fit and crept sideways across the screen, hovering beside the footage frame.

He was right. What he'd seen next to the camera was the outer edge of someone's boot – the heel, to be exact – so close that it had been blurred beyond recognition.

"Object confirmed as the left side of a Mark-V combat boot, standard military issue. Left foot. Gender: male. Size estimate: eleven to thirteen. Color: black. Manufacturer: Grayson Defense Technologies."

Dirk sagged back in his chair, the wind practically knocked out of him. He couldn't believe it. He'd been right all along. Someone *had* been there the night his mother was killed. Right there, in the shallows, watching her as she swam for her life.

Watching her die.

In fact, he reconsidered, that same person might well have been the reason why Amara Braddock aborted her initial attempt at the maintenance ledge. He remembered her expression as she'd hesitated, already halfway there, only to turn inexplicably away.

She'd seen something. Something that scared her, scared her enough to make her abandon the ledge and try for the far more distant amphitheater dock instead.

No, not something. *Someone.*

The realization hit Dirk like an uppercut to the stomach. Borderline nauseous, he hunched forward, his hands on his knees as he sucked in slow, soothing breaths. He looked up, determination on his face as he considered the situation. And his options.

Finally.

Dr. Grayson would finally see proof that his mother's death was not as cut and dried as the old man believed. But who was responsible? How was he to narrow the field? There were literally *hundreds* of those boots stomping around Tartarus. The technicians wore them, the submarine crews, the captains . . . even the guards.

The guards.

"Computer," Dirk rasped, clearing his throat. "Scan list of Tartarus security personnel."

"List scanned."

"How many male guards wear Mark-V combat boots, between sizes eleven and thirteen."

"Sixteen active officers, three active sergeants, and acting Security Chief Oleg Smirnov."

Smirnov? Okay, looks like I'm going to him with this. Dirk frowned at the notion of being alone with a convicted killer. *Well, at least he's better than Dwyer. Assuming, of course, that he's not the one I'm looking for . . .*

He sat back, arms folded, as the gears in his head turned.

One of his eyebrows suddenly rose. "Computer, is there anything out of the ordinary about the boot in question? Any, I don't know, unusual wear pattern on the sole or heel?"

"Confirmed."

He waited impatiently. "Can you . . . *tell* me?"

"Affirmative. Mark-V boot recreation possesses an augmented heel. Heel height has been increased by thirty-seven millimeters versus standard issue."

"Conclusion?"

"Medical customization to compensate for leg-length discrepancy."

Bingo.

All of a sudden, Dirk found it hard to breathe. He was *so* close; he could feel it. He gripped his chair's padded armrests and leaned forward. "Computer, scan medical records of active Tartarus personnel."

"Scan complete."

"How many personnel exhibit congenital leg-length discrepancies in the ranges suggested by the Mark-V recreation?"

"Six personnel. Candice Jameson, electrician. Age twenty-six--"

Dirk wrung his hands in exasperation. "Computer, modify query. How many *male* personnel, wearing Mark-V combat boots, in size range eleven to thirteen, exhibit leg-length discrepancy in the suggested range, on the *left* side?"

There was a long pause, almost as if the system was hesitating.

"One individual."

Finally . . . "And, *who* is this person?"

"Unable to comply."

"What? What do you mean unable to comply?"

"Individual listed is a member of Tartarus's security staff. Medical records for security officers are classified."

"Come again?" Dirk's face contorted angrily. "Override security classification, voice command authorization: Braddock, Doctor Derek J."

"Request denied."

What the-- Dirk felt like the system was screwing with him. He was an officer of the company, currently in command of all Tartarus, and he couldn't access the medical records of his own personnel?

"Computer, on whose authority are security staff member records sealed?"

"Grayson, Doctor Eric M., Chief Executive Officer."

Dirk sank back into his chair, a 'wow' expression on his face. Apparently, Grayson's overprotectiveness when it came to his "last chancers" knew no bounds.

He thought for a moment, then his brown eyes twinkled with ill-contained mirth. There was more than one way to skin a cat. Or a rat.

"Computer, scan commissary purchase orders for all Mark-V combat boots in the last twelve months."

"Completed."

"List recipients of any special request, custom-order boots – security and combat personnel *only.*"

"Two recipients: March 15th, 2045. Captain Natalya Dragunova, commanding officer, *USS Antrodemus.* Request for Mark-V boots, heelless women's model . . ."

Dirk smirked as the system droned on. Yeah, Dragunova *was* quite tall.

"Continue."

"June 10th, 2045. Security Officer Jonah McHale. Request for Mark-V boots, modified heel."

Dirk sprang out of his chair so fast it looked like he'd sat on a thumbtack. *McHale?* Wait, that was the guard who'd gone rogue, the one Grayson told him about. They'd found him in the basement, after he went AWOL. The SOB had chewed out his locator!

"I've got you now, *asshole*," he snarled. Grabbing his radio off its cradle, he paused for a moment to compose himself, then held it to his lips.

"Attention, security: this is Dr. Derek Braddock. Acting Security Chief Smirnov, please respond. Over."

Dirk leaned forward at the waist and rested his palm heels on the edge of his desk. His impatience was rewarded.

"Doctor Braddock," Smirnov radioed quickly back. "Thees is Acting Chief Smirnov. Over."

"I need to speak with you," Dirk said as calmly as he could. "Please come to my office and . . . actually, better yet, contact me via private video conference."

"Very good. Geev me a few meenutes to get to private location. Smirnov out."

Dirk placed the radio back in its charging cradle and straightened up. His lips pursed to one side as he surveyed his desk. Then, he reached for the discus-shaped bottle of scotch, making sure its lid was sealed tight, and stashed it away.

It wouldn't do for the chief of security to see he'd been drinking. The guy might think he was intoxicated and imagining wild and horrible things.

Nix that. They weren't wild at all. Just horrible.

While he waited for the call, Dirk stepped into his bathroom. He checked his appearance, made sure his nametag was in place, and then headed back to his desk. He had just started drumming his fingers on its hard surface, when the incoming video call announced itself with a loud ping.

"Good morning, Acting Chief," he opened, starting the call with a wave of his hand.

"Good morning, Dr. Braddock," Smirnov replied. "What can I do for you thees fine day?"

Dirk studied the ex-heavyweight's face. His big, squarish head looked even larger on the five-foot monitor, and he was surprised he'd never noticed the guard's cauliflower ear, twice-broken nose, or the trio of scars decorating his heavy brow ridge. Obviously, he'd fought a few wars in the ring. Or outside of it.

"I'm transferring a security personnel file to you," he said, tapping a key.

Smirnov glanced down. "Officer McHale, da? Thees ees guard who go bad."

"I know. I want him taken into custody."

"I . . . am sorry, but I cannot do thees, Dr. Braddock."

Dirk felt his temper rise, but checked himself. "Explain."

"McHale ees no longer here, on base."

"Where is he?"

The big Ukrainian shrugged. "I honestly don't know. Dwyer had heem sheeped out after what happened een basement. You know about thees, da?"

Dirk exhaled irritably and nodded. "Shipped out where?"

"I am not sure, probably back eenside."

"Inside? Inside where?"

"You know, the . . . beeg house? He ees probably back on dead row."

Dirk formed a steeple with his fingers and rested his lips momentarily against it. If he recalled correctly, Jonah McHale was the former bouncer who'd stomped a drunken girl to death outside a Chicago club. Another winner; death row was too good for him. "Acting chief, are you telling me you don't even know *which* prison one of your people was sent to?"

Smirnov appeared genuinely flustered. "I am sorry, Dr. Braddock. I am new to thees position. And they have not yet geev me access to Dwyer's files." He glanced back over his shoulder, then moved closer to the camera. "Can I ask, what thees ees about?"

Dirk hesitated, not sure how much he should say. He did a mental rewind of Smirnov's behavior from the other day, however, back when Garm confronted Dwyer and White. He wasn't certain, but his overall impression was the former pugilist could be trusted.

"You're familiar with my mother's death, yes?"

Smirnov's face turned solemn and he nodded. "Da, I saw footage. Eet was terrible loss. Please accept my overdue condolences."

Dirk sighed. "Thank you. But new evidence has come to light that suggests McHale was *in* the amphitheater when she was killed."

"*Bozhe moi*, are you sure?"

"Pretty sure."

Smirnov shook his grizzled head from side to side. "Thees ees bad. You must speak to Dr. Grayson at once. He can help."

"I'm going to. But I was hoping to have McHale in custody, and have the chance to debrief him, before I made that call."

"I understand. Ees beeg problem."

"It is indeed," Dirk said. "Thank you for the information. I assume, *Chief* Smirnov, that I can count on you to keep this information confidential, until such time as it may become public knowledge."

"Da, of course, Dr. Braddock. I am at your service."

"Braddock out," Dirk said, killing the call.

He glanced at his waiting cellphone, then decided to stall by heading for the kitchen, snatching up his self-heating coffee cup on the way. He programmed his usual insta-mug's worth – high-end Columbian this time – and yanked open the fridge as it brewed. He was too worked up to make a sandwich, so he settled for a yogurt, scarfing it down like he had a tapeworm, while his caffeine finished trickling down.

Depositing the empty yogurt tub in his recycling bin, he grabbed his mug, tossed in his usual splash of half-and-half and a dollop of pure cane sugar, and was back at his desk and ready for action. When he sat down, his phone was still sitting there, glaring at him.

Dirk slowly sipped his coffee and glared back at it. His own hesitation began mocking him, and he put the mug back on its coaster, before reaching for the phone. He stared at it, contemplating his reflection in its glossy black surface. Finally, his lips formed a tight "O" as he sucked in a slow breath.

He let it out in a rush. *Okay, let's get this over with.*

He hit Grayson's auto-dial and waited. He was away on business and, not surprisingly, it went straight to voice mail.

"Hello. You've reached the voicemail of GDT founder, Dr. Eric Grayson. My regular business hours are ten-to-four, Monday to Friday, Eastern time. If you're an authorized party, kindly leave a message."

Dirk cleared his throat. "Hi, Dr. Grayson, it's Derek. It may come as a surprise, but I've . . . stumbled upon evidence that appears to implicate Officer Jonah McHale in my mother's death. At a minimum, he was there, watching, as she was taken. Acting Chief Oleg Smirnov has informed me that McHale's already been shipped out. I need your assistance in finding him, and in arranging for him to be questioned. Thank you."

As he hung up the phone, Dirk suddenly realized how drained he felt. He didn't know where things might end up after this, but he did know that the stress of bearing the weight of it, day to day, was literally sucking the life out of him. He needed resolution, so he could move on. There was no way around it.

Dirk almost jumped as his phone vibrated from an incoming text message.

"Derek, I am both astonished and outraged by this news. Please rest assured that you and I will, together, investigate this immediately upon my return. I promise you will have GDT's full legal resources at your disposal. One way or another, we will get to the bottom of things."

Dirk's lips formed a seamless line as he nodded and set the phone back down. He reached for his coffee, relished a long draught, then nodded in satisfaction. He'd always known in his heart that he could count on the old man's backing, once he'd found the proof he needed. And he had.

Everything was going to be okay. Or, at least, as well as it could be.

A second text came through, drawing him back from his musings.

"I forgot to ask. How's the hunt for future groom Typhon going?"

Dirk interlocked his fingers, rapping them gently against his chin as he weighed his response. Because of their little octopus "problem", their clandestine plans for *Typhon* had, obviously, been put on hold. And, he was hardly in a position to let the Diablo thing out of the bag.

At least, not yet. A little bit of misdirection was in order.

But not too much. His aged mentor was incredibly astute.

"No progress yet, sir. However, we have something coming in, a new biologic, that could have a substantial impact on things."

Grayson's reply came through surprisingly fast.

"Fantastic. By all means, keep me posted. I know I can always count on you."

TWELVE

Eyes locked onto *Gryphon*'s high-definition bow images, Captain Garm Braddock, his first mate, Jayla Morgan, and the ORION-class sub's entire primary bridge crew – except for Ensign Adolfo Ramirez – watched with bated breath, as AWES operator Sam Mot manipulated the TALOS Mark VII underwater combat chassis toward the U-420 wreck.

With little more disturbance than a puff of sand, Sam touched down on the seabed, fifty feet from the WW2 sub's shattered flank. A moment later, the AWES's powerful leg pistons began to pump, and he started clomping methodically toward the giant octopus's front door.

Garm's opalescent eyes barely blinked as he observed the pending drama, and he found himself wishing he had Ensign Ho's "lazy eye problem", so he could watch two screens simultaneously. To avoid missing anything of import, he'd had Rush split the main, dividing the twenty-foot titanium bow window that formed the upper portion of their vessel's prow into two separate screens. On the left, was a zoomed in view of U-420's exterior, as seen from *Gryphon*'s powerful front and sail-based optronics. On the right, the real-time footage from TALOS's integrated high-speed cameras.

As a precaution, and to make sure they had room to fight, Garm had ordered *Gryphon* suspended in the current, a hundred yards from the wreck. With her powerful floodlights illuminating a five-hundred-foot swathe of seafloor, the entire

WW2 submarine, and a good portion of its surrounding stone and coral crypt, stood out in stark relief.

It was a desolate graveyard, to be sure. Not even a fish.

"Sonar," he said quietly, his gaze never leaving the monitors. "How are we looking?"

"So far, so good," Ramirez said, stroking his goatee with his thumb and forefinger. He was hunched forward in his seat, his eyes preternaturally wide as he scanned both his active and passive sonar systems. "Cloak is holding at one hundred percent. Nothing of significance on either OMNI ADCAP or POSEIDON."

"Good," Garm nodded. "Remember, the mother octopus could be disguised as almost anything – a mound of sand, coral – even that big boulder over there. Without us going full-active search-and-attack, a reading from her might look like little more than a sudden change in topography. So, stay frosty."

"Don't worry, sir. She's not sneaking up on me."

Garm nodded, then swiveled his seat as quietly as possible and turned to Cunningham. "We good?"

The CSO nodded, his blue eyes intense. He was obviously anticipating a fight. "Just say the word, and I'll light up what-ever comes our way like it's Independence Day."

"Captain?" Ensign Rush whispered from communications.

"Yes?"

"I've read that mother octopuses typically die after their eggs hatch," the willowy blonde said softly. "So, if we destroy all the eggs, why do we have to bother killing her?"

"Because we don't know if that holds true for this species," Garm said. "And, if it does, we don't know how long it will take her to expire, or how many people she might kill before that happens. And, lastly, because we have orders."

"Yes, sir."

Standing in an at-ease pose beside her captain, Jayla Morgan started to speak, but he signaled for silence. "He's reached the entrance," Garm advised.

On the left-side monitor, the powerhouse AWES had stopped walking, its infrared and thermal systems exploring the enormous rent in the Z-class boat's hull. The sound of Sam's respiration inside the robotic suit was negligible – a few bubbles at best – and his voice came in clear through the microphones.

"Position, approximately twenty feet from the entrance to the lair," he said. His POV shifted from side to side as he continued scanning the opening. "Doesn't seem to be anyone home," he noted, then cleared his throat. "Thank God."

Garm's mandible muscles jutted out as he saw TALOS take a step and stagger suddenly to one side. A cloud of dust and rust flew up, as the mechanized suit righted itself.

"Sorry, a little slippery, there," Sam radioed. "A lot of Uranium-235 ore outside the wreck . . . radiation readings are high, but only minimal interference with non-essential systems." His cameras dipped downward as he studied the debris-strewn seabed, directly outside the midden opening.

"Noting a large number of broken-off rusticles, some up to three feet in diameter, scattered around the entrance." He took a step, the booster-rocket-shaped foot of the AWES coming slowly down atop one. It crumbled beneath the suit's six-ton weight, spreading additional rust particles into the surrounding water.

Sam's breathing became more labored as he moved forward. "Also, a lot of whale bone outside: ribs, vertebrae . . . looks like fragments from a large baleen whale." His cameras panned left to right, zooming in on the ivory-colored bone pile. "Remains are heavily gnawed on, some snapped in two and – holy crap, is that a killer whale's skull?"

In his captain's chair, Garm's eyes narrowed as Sam enlarged the image of what had to be a four-foot *Orcinus orca* skull, sans mandible.

"Stay focused, Sam," he radioed.

"Roger that."

Moving carefully inside the ragged outer edge of the U-boat's failed pressure hull, Sam leaned back, striving to fully take in the cavernous interior. With his suit's high-intensity searchlights illuminating everything, his lens array swept smoothly back and forth, documenting everything at 200,000 fps. Inside the forty-by-sixty-foot space – barren except for a handful of rusted girders and some bunches of aged wiring – countless strands of foot-long ovoid structures draped down on glistening gelatinous strands. It was a veritable jungle of white vines, overladen with an assembly line of milk-colored grapes.

But they weren't grapes. They were eggs.

More eggs than one could count.

"Holy fucking shit," Sam muttered. "Th-this is like a maternity ward from hell. *Gryphon*, are you seeing this?"

"That's a copy," Garm replied.

Sam extended his cannon-like left arm and gave the nearest strand of eggs an exploratory prod. The disturbed baby octopi recoiled, their tiny tentacles swirling and black beaks snapping inside their tiny wombs.

"Hey, uh, captain . . . these things look like they're ready to pop!"

"I'd say our timing was fortuitous, then." Garm glanced at Ramirez and got a reassuring thumbs-up. "Okay, Sam. Collect the samples, as requested, and let's finish up."

"You got it, boss."

As the bridge crew watched, enthralled, the TALOS suit drew closer to the strand of *Octopus giganteus* eggs. Shifting his capture tube into the crook of his left arm, Sam used his right hand to carefully unscrew the nearest silver endcap, enabling the device to flood with seawater. He then reached up and, one by one, plucked three eggs from their stalks and eased them carefully inside.

A moment later, he screwed the endcap back in place and touched its tiny keypad with the tip of one armor-piercing talon. A matched series of LEDS on both ends lit up in response, and the contents began to cloud over and congeal. The stasis refrigerants were kicking in.

"Samples secured," Sam radioed.

"Good job," Garm said into his intercom mike. "Commence phase two."

"Roger that. I'm going to stash the sample tube a safe distance from the nursery," Sam said. "It's gonna get pretty hot in here, and I don't want to hear your brother complaining that I brought him three pieces of poached calamari."

Garm grinned, watching on *Gryphon*'s monitor, now, as the hulking TALOS suit stomped slowly back out of the nest, its "bundle of joys" gripped in a hand that, with its actuators online, could twist the barrel of a Sherman tank into a pretzel.

"Man, it feels good moving around in this thing," Sam commented, his breath a bit labored as he trudged and kicked his way through the boneyard once more. "The visuals, smells, doing the underwater 'Superman' thing . . . and the *strength*. Boy, you wouldn't want to compete for babes with me wearing *this*, old pal!"

"Whatever," Garm sniggered.

"Hey, remember that contest we had during basic training, you and I?"

Oh, God. He's not going to go there, is he?

"You know what I mean," Sam said. "Did you tell your crew who the crowned 'king of conquest' really is?"

Garm flushed, torn between avoiding a U-boatload of embarrassment, and allowing Sam the leeway to continue letting off steam, while he finished what was, essentially, the most dangerous job on the planet.

Then, as he saw every pair of eyes on the bridge turn in his direction, he knew there was no escaping it.

"Go ahead," he drawled, shaking his head. "Tell them who it is . . ."

"I *will*," the now-sweating AWES operator said, approaching a tiny alcove, about sixty feet from U-420's hull, and inserting the capture tube carefully inside. "You see, bridge crew, in our younger days, your illustrious captain and I were best buds.

We were also what you'd call 'babe hounds'. We loved women – worshipped them, in fact – and the more hotties we hooked up with, the happier we were."

Garm started to speak, but then sank back in his seat. This had to be payback for sending a protein-packed Brody Blair, AKA the 'father of flatulence', to Sam's aid before. *So be it.*

"Now, some of you will look at your captain and think, 'Who could compete with him?' I mean, he's big, built, and *vaguely* attractive, and he's got those icy blue eyes that he hypnotizes poor, innocent waifs with . . ."

"Hey, we all have our crosses to bear," Garm remarked from the shelter of his facepalm.

On the screen, Sam began the trudge back toward the mother Kraken's nursery, his mechanical stride eating up the yards. "Mind you, before I lost my limbs, I was nothing to sneeze at. Kind of a green-eyed 'Baywatch' beefcake, if you will."

The TALOS Mark VII stopped, ten feet from the opening, its armored torso swiveling slowly as it scanned the surrounding area for threats.

"But, it was my superior intellect that allowed me to take the title, and prove once and for all who the ultimate stud was," Sam resumed, chuckling over the radio. "Ain't that right, captain, oh-my-captain?"

Garm sighed. "I think what you meant to say was, you cheated."

"Cheated? No, I *innovated.*"

To her captain's surprise, Ensign Ho unexpectedly twisted in her seat, her hands still grasping *Gryphon*'s yoke. Her eyes shone with need-to-know, and she flashed him a rare smile. "Can you give us the details, sir. Please?"

As Garm cleared his throat, he realized things would be infinitely calmer on his boat, once Sam Mot's "tour" was completed.

"It's simple. Our illustrious AWES operator broke the rules of dating."

Sam shot back, "I did not. The contest was who could 'hook up' with the most girls in a month. *You* made the mistake of wining and dining them, whereas *I* just got down to business. Hence, I kicked your overgrown butt."

Garm rubbed his temples with one big hand, then leaned forward in his chair. "Okay, so here's what happened . . . Ten miles from the base, there's a local town where, during weekends or furloughs, guys and girls go to party and hang out. The contest – which *Sam* suggested – required us to 'hookup with' girls from that town. So, what he did was, every chance he got, he went there, either at lunchtime or right after work, and stood on the busiest street corner he could find."

Ramirez angled his head quizzically. "And did what, rap to girls?"

"Oh, he did more than that," Garm said. "He took the direct approach."

"Ah, I remember *this*," Cunningham interjected.

"Yep," Garm continued. "He'd walk right up to a cute girl – *any* cute girl – and tell her she was the most beautiful woman he'd ever seen, and that she'd make his life complete, if she'd only sleep with him."

Morgan started. "Wait, what? And that worked?"

Sam's chuckling came through loud and clear. "It sure did. Every day!"

Garm's brows hiked toward his hairline as he nodded. "Yes, it worked. Oh, he got slapped, punched, kicked, screamed at, and even spat on a few times, but sooner or later, one of them would think he was cute, and find his line of BS flattering, and she'd take him back to her place."

"Wow, he saved all that bread?" Ramirez said. "Why didn't *I* think of that?"

Garm had to bite his tongue as he caught the venomous, "Oh, you are *so* not getting any later," look Ho shot her partner-in-crime.

"It was a . . . unique approach, I admit," he said. "So, Sam, are you through humiliating a superior officer and ready to get down to business?"

"Does *this* not look ready to you?" Sam's amplified voice replied over the loudspeaker. On the viewer, he could be seen standing in the center of the crack in U-420's side, his back to the darkness within, and his activated plasma torch blazing like a purple and white broadsword blade.

"Man, look at this thing!" Sam said. He muttered something about being glad for his viewing port's auto-dimming feature and started swinging the ten-foot blade in huge arcs, relishing the superheated swaths it cut in the seawater all around him.

He glanced down, spotted a twisted iron beam protruding from the wreckage, and took a swipe at it. The plasma weapon severed it almost immediately, like an electric knife carving a pot roast.

"Man, this is some real 'Jedi' shit," Sam said, shaking his head as he watched the glowing red edges of the two hunks of girder cool and fade.

Garm chuckled. "Yeah, you're a regular 'Darth' Mot."

Sam twisted at the waist, making a show of patting TALOS's considerable titanium-steel buttocks with the suit's huge right hand, and quipped, "Hey, I got your 'dark side' right here, pal!"

"Just get to work . . ."

After swinging his blade for what felt like the thousandth time, Sam Mot decided it was time to take a break. He held the ten-foot jet of seawater-stabilized plasma away from himself, mentally reducing its length, then extinguished it altogether. He paused, contemplating the weapon's housing, as its super-hot nozzle faded from white to red to gray. Sensing the sudden reduction in illumination, the TALOS system's exterior floodlights flipped back on, lighting up the surrounding seabed.

Sam whistled, then willed the AWES's internal temperature down a few degrees, before taking a sip of water from one of its internal drinking tubes. He'd been working at burning away the contents of the *Octopus giganteus* nest for a good ten minutes now. That, and torturing *Gryphon*'s bridge crew with his adulterated version of the Beatles' song *Yellow Submarine*. He smiled. That girl Jayla, the diesel one with the Aussie-style accent and the booty that wouldn't quit, might've been uptight, but she was into it – and him; he could tell.

Yeah, for a limbless man, life was good.

Sam paused, gazing up at the last strands of foot-long cephalopod eggs, suspended high above, inside the hollowed-out heart of the U-420 wreck. Out of curiosity, he zoomed in on the three hundred remaining ovules, using a combination of night, infrared, and magnetic resonance imagery. As he watched, the tiny soon-to-be man-eaters, sensing the heated water all around them, squirmed and snapped inside their melon-like wombs.

Nasty little buggers. Can't afford to let one *of them get away.*

Suddenly, a thick piece of bone snapped under one of the AWES's titanium-steel feet, causing Sam to look down. As he caught himself amid a cloud of uranium dust, he had a momentary vision of the hatchling's monstrous mother. He could picture her, a vast pile of putrescent protoplasm, munching away atop an ever-growing mountain of human skeletons, her ravenous offspring looking on.

Sam shuddered. "Man, this is definitely one nightmarish nursery."

"Progress report, Dr. Mot?" Garm's voice suddenly said.

Sam chuckled, realizing he'd gotten so distracted, he'd forgotten they were still connected. "Almost there, boss man," he said, reigniting his plasma blade and swinging it high overhead. "Just a few ... more ... strokes."

"Don't do it."

"Do what? Say, 'that's what she said'?" Sam snickered. "Come on, now. What do you think I am, some kind of pervert?"

Relishing his old friend's sigh, the former LifeGiver continued moving around U-420's insides, prepping his final sweeps.
At first, given the near forty-foot-high, multi-decked space the
octopi had chosen as a nest, he thought he'd be forced to use the
Mark VII's propulsors, in order to reach the ceiling portions.
But the cute redhead back at Tartarus had been right. His hy-
brid plasma weapon generated so much heat, that any organic
matter within ten feet of it was instantly broiled. And, within
five, the temps showing up on the inside of his mirrored faceplate were off the charts.

Yeah, heat did rise. So much so that, with his combat suit's
twelve-foot reach, combined with the plasma torch's ten, annihilating the uppermost regions of the next was as simple as
extending his arm. The laws of thermal radiation did the rest.

Sam's head angled upward, his mind momentarily on the
poor bastards who'd gone down with U-420, a hundred years
earlier. He shook it off, then stepped slowly around the near-
empty lair, watching impassively as the last of the octopus eggs
literally burst from the heat he directed at them. In grotesque
waves, their gelatinous exteriors popped like goo-filled bal-
loons, the writhing larva within shriveling up into nothingness,
a split-second later.

It was as easy as taking a blow torch to cobwebs. In minutes,
it was over.

Sam stepped back, waiting for the organic "dust" he'd created to clear, and surveyed his handiwork. Satisfied, he headed
back out the rust-rimmed crack in the ancient U-boat's hull.

*Man, momma octopus is gonna be in for an unpleasant sur-
prise when she gets home. Besides the armor-piercing one Garm
has waiting for her, that is.*

Outside, Sam stopped in the center of the boneyard and
looked around. Protected from the sea's deadly effects, and em-
powered by his strength-amplified exoskeleton, to boot, he felt
like Poseidon, overlooking his watery domain. A hundred yards
away, he could see *Gryphon*, suspended in the current, and for

the first time took note of the ORION-class sub's iridophore-based camouflage.

"AWES to *Gryphon*," he radioed.

"Go ahead," Garm replied.

"Mission complete, nest eradicated."

"Good job. You have the samples?"

"I'm about to retrieve them. By the way," Sam commented, zooming in on the anti-biologic submarine. "You guys really *do* look like some sort of gigantic whale, hovering out there. It's *very* convincing. Of course," he reached up, tapping the side of TALOS's robotic head with one talon tip, "You wouldn't fool *me*."

"That's a relief," Garm said. "How did the Mark VII perform?"

"Aces," Sam replied, holding up his cannon-like left arm and reigniting its blazing purple blade. A flashing warning notice popped up on the inside of his visor. "Humph. It says plasma reserves are down to just four percent. Definitely due for a reload, but beyond that, I've got no complaints."

"Holy shit!"

Sam started. The shocked voice he'd just heard wasn't Garm's. It sounded like that sonar guy . . . Ramirez? He heard multiple individuals fast-talking in the background, but with the combined chatter, couldn't make out what was said.

"Uh, captain, what was that about?"

There was a moment's pause, then Garm came back on the multiband. "Sam, get back to *Gryphon*, ASAP!"

"No problem. What's going on?" he asked, starting forward.

"No discussion, just move your ass. I mean it!"

Shaken by the uncharacteristic franticness in his friend's voice, Sam decided to forego walking and willed his boot propulsors to life. Around him, clouds of sand and detritus swirled as he lifted up off the boneyard bed like a Cape Canaveral rocket. "I'm up and away. What the hell is happening?"

"Sam, listen – there's something coming up the wall!"

The ... wall?

Already twenty feet off the bottom, Sam twisted around, his maneuvering thrusters letting him hold and hover as he gazed back at the seaweed-tufted cliff U-420 rested upon. Beyond it there was nothing.

Just endless ocean and a thousand-foot freefall into darkness.

Suddenly, from out of that darkness, an immense tentacle arced up and over the cliff's edge, slapping down and latching onto the surrounding coral reef with suckers the size of SUV tires. Sam's eyes went wide with astonishment. The tendril was as thick as a suspension bridge cable, its writhing surface twisted and knotted and coated with some sort of gelatinous slime.

A moment later, a second tentacle followed it, and then a third. Soon, it was like a writhing nest of colossal sea serpents had fastened their boneless grip onto the ridge.

A dark, dome-like shape the size of a cottage followed, and in the center of that domicile, a pair of monstrous yellow eyes glared down at him with murderous intent. As the realization he was caught between *Gryphon* and the intruder hit home, Sam felt the blood drain from his face. A moment later, his fear was upgraded to pure terror, as he realized he'd lost the ability to move.

A voice began bellowing from his internal speakers, but the AWES operator failed to respond. Unable to comprehend the speaker's increasingly frantic commands, he was aware of one thing and one thing only.

The parent *Octopus giganteus* had come home.

Spinning his wheels had never been Dirk Braddock's strong suit, and, as he did the caged lion thing, pausing only to flip *Tiamat* the bird as the mutant pliosaur swam enigmatically past, he concluded he absolutely sucked at it. The notion that he'd found, at a minimum, an eye witness to his mother's death, and at maximum, an actual contributor, occupied his every thought. Running Tartarus from his office had run a distant second.

Not that, as the facility's Acting Director, there hadn't been a laundry list of problems to deal with. He'd already resolved issues involving the pliosaur queen's filtration system (clogged again), and the inventory for all pliosaur food items on site (X-fish stocks were dwindling, and a new order was placed with the supplier). Most importantly, he'd taken care of Rear Admiral Ward Callahan and his 500-million-dollar purchase, the freshly-implanted, 136-ton *Kronosaurus imperator* cow, *Goliath*.

When asked about his latest acquisition, the admiral had been beyond ecstatic. Moreover, the 80-foot pliosaur, herself, seemed in good health and spirits. Especially, when the emergency valve to her holding tank was opened, allowing her to "escape" out through its corresponding tunnel, and into the nearby sea.

Of course, there was no actual escape. The dark-hued cow was corralled by Callahan, himself, the moment she left Tartarus. Standing feet apart, with his pricy cybernetic control helmet in place, it was obvious the brash and outspoken navy man was relishing the degree of control GDT's new technology gave him over history's deadliest predator. In fact, while boarding a runabout, scheduled to deliver him to his flagship, the carrier *Independence*, he'd announced that, rather than assigning one of his minions to run herd over the huge female, en route, he planned on doing it himself.

Between Callahan's obnoxious alpha male assertiveness, body odor, and non-stop attempts at reliving his brother Garm's assorted boxing matches, Dirk was far from sorry to see him go. He just hoped the admiral didn't get too exuberant and decide to test *Goliath* out on one of the local fishing boats.

Extracting his cell phone from his lab coat pocket, Dirk ran a quick scan on his to-do list, and then frowned. That was odd. His mother's friend, Dr. Kimberly Bane, was still MIA. She'd missed their meeting the evening before, bless her cougar heart, and hadn't responded to emails or voice messages since then. And now, it seemed no one could find hide nor hair of her.

Hide nor hair.

A worrisome thought came to Dirk, and he started wondering if Bane might have somehow ended up in one of the pliosaur paddocks. No, that was impossible. They were too elevated. Except for *Gretchen*'s or . . .

Dirk reached for his radio, then pursed his lips tight. He disliked using public relay systems, with the exception of the most mundane of communications. Better to use the phone instead.

It was picked up on the first ring.

"Hello, Dr. Braddock, thees ees Acting Chief Smirnov," the big Ukrainian said. The man seemed to worry a lot. He looked tense, even on the cell's tiny video screen.

"Hi, AC Smirnov. Thanks again for your help, earlier," Dirk said.

"Just doing my job. I double-checked any records I could find, but there ees no eenformation available. I am sorry."

"No worries. Along those lines, I'd like you to start a missing persons investigation for me, please."

Smirnov nodded. "Da, but we know McHale was sent back."

"Not him," Dirk said, cricking his neck to one side. "Our new epidemiologist, Dr. Kimberly Bane, appears to have gone missing. She was absent from a meeting we had scheduled yesterday, and it's been a good twenty-four hours since anyone's seen her."

"Does she have--"

"No," Dirk anticipated. "Her locator has not been implanted yet, so we're talking search party."

"Okay, boss. I weel assign two reliable men, and lead investigation, personally."

"Thanks, AC. I have every faith in you."

As he cut the video call, Dirk shook his head and grinned, realizing he was starting to sound more and more like his mentor. He stepped back behind his desk and plopped down hard into his beckoning chair. Restlessness won out, and he sat up straight and started drumming his fingers on his thighs as he pondered the situation.

Kimberly, you naughty girl; you better be passed out in some guard's bed, after a night of drinking and depravity. Because, if I have to tell Grayson he's lost another *epidemiologist, he's going to have a stroke.*

Dirk's eyebrows scaled his forehead. All jokes aside, the old man just might. Especially with the breakthroughs on Cretaceous Cancer Dr. Bane had already come up with. The woman was brilliant. A horny pain-in-the-butt, but brilliant, nonetheless.

He waved a dismissive hand and scoffed. He was sure she was fine. After the experiences she had during her first day on the docks, there was no way she'd have gone wandering down there. Not alone, at least. And, it's not like she could get into any trouble in her lab or private quarters . . .

Now, how am I going to get my hands on this McHale character? I have a long list of questions he needs to answer. And I'm sure Garm will want to "speak" with him, too.

Dirk heaved himself back, feeling the ergonomic chair's shock absorbers take the hit, and uttered a growl of frustration. He'd been tempted to reach out to GDT's contacts at the Department of Corrections, but he didn't want to step on Eric Grayson's toes. The old man had already pledged his full support, and the last thing he needed right now was to rock the boat.

It's bad enough I already hatched a plot to kill the bull pliosaur he's counting on for his breeding program, sent one of his submarines to explore Diablo, without his knowledge, and ordered the other one to seek and destroy the proverbial Kraken. I think we'll hold off on making any more off-the-wall moves for now.

All of that would be fine, Dirk thought, filing away his concerns. The octopus obviously had to be dealt with, and he'd tried bringing up the caldera opportunity during their meeting.

Sure, he anticipated a stern lecture from the CEO regarding the power of communication, but once the old man found out about the potential treasure trove Diablo held, not to mention the trio of giant octopus larvae his protégé had en route, he was sure all would be forgiven.

McHale . . .

Cursing to himself, Dirk stood up and reached for his cell. He dialed Stacy Daniels' quarters, figuring he'd invite himself over. If he couldn't do anything right now about the suspected ex-con, he could at least vent to his best friend about it. After all, he had to talk to *someone* with a sympathetic ear. If he didn't, he'd go nuts.

My best friend?

Dirk pondered the thought as the phone rang and rang. Truth be told, he realized that was how he felt about Stacy. Oh, the attraction was certainly there, but he didn't consider her a "fuck buddy", as she'd put it. He had more respect for her than that. He just didn't love her the way she obviously loved him.

Yeah, best friend with benefits would have to do.

It was funny. He'd never had a BFWB before. It wasn't such a bad thing.

On the seventh ring, Dirk gave up on Stacy's quarters and dialed her cell. He frowned as it went straight to voicemail.

Great, don't tell me she's gone missing, too! he joked.

Real concern overshadowed him, and he turned to his computer screen. His fingers a blur, he started pounding his virtual keyboard, pulling up Tartarus's private personnel directory. He ran down the list, found Stacy's name, and touched the locator tab. Thankfully, unlike Bane, she'd had one of the itchy things implanted in her forearm, six months earlier.

A moment later, Dirk nodded. His BFWB was on dock level, moving around *Gretchen*'s paddock. As usual. He reddened with embarrassment, remembering how he'd sneaked down there the other day, thinking Stacy was somehow involved in Amara Braddock's death. He'd expected to catch her in a seditious act. What an idiot he'd been.

She'd been mad as hell, of course. But, with them eventually ending up in the shed together, it hadn't been a total loss.

Dirk sighed. It turned out, the only infraction Willie Daniels' daughter was guilty of was keeping secrets about her fifty-ton pet pliosaur. He chuckled. If he didn't know better, he'd have sworn she loved Gretchen more than she did him.

Actually, she undoubtedly __does__ love her more than you, you idiot.

He made a face, then licked his lips and closed the personnel program. He reached down and started slipping into his loafers. His plan was simple: he'd go down to the paddocks, find Stacy, offer her a late lunch at his place, and then make her sit and listen to his tale of conspiracy and woe.

As he closed and sealed his quarters' door, he fought down a smirk. With *Gretchen* as competition, he'd probably have to promise to put out, too, but what the heck. Sacrifices must be made.

Whistling to himself, Dirk moved jauntily toward the nearest lift.

A few minutes later, his forgotten cell phone started vibrating atop the smooth surface of his desk, its illuminated screen a dancing nightlight in the darkened room. On it, an icon indicated an incoming text message from Dr. Eric Grayson.

It was marked urgent.

———

Their enemy had found them.

A hundred yards from *Gryphon*'s bow, the colossal octopus loomed over the rust-tinged wreck of U-420 like some impossibly large tarantula, its eight legs straddling its prey. The skin covering its pulsating body was the color and texture of a black oak tree, and its golden eyes shone like torches in the near-darkness.

Garm exhaled through bowed lips, then leaned forward in his captain's chair as he sized up his adversary. The octopus was larger than he'd expected, its mantle alone the size a two-car garage, and each of its sprawling tentacles stretched at least twenty-five yards in length.

For some reason, the huge predator hadn't rushed in to attack them yet – probably because it hadn't caught them in the act. That, or it was trying to figure out why the biggest blue whale it had ever seen was staying so close to its nest, instead of running for its life.

"Captain, shall I drop our cloak?" Ramirez asked. The bridge was a beehive bustle, as everyone readied themselves for the inevitable. A warning claxon sounded, followed by flashing overheads and a harp-like series of loud pings, as both OMNI ADCAP and ANCILE went live. The anti-biologic sub's bow sphere and external arrays were blanketing their target with a barrage of active search-and-attack and obstacle avoidance sonar pings.

"Not yet," Garm said, still eyeing what he realized would be his deadliest adversary to date. He figured they had about twenty seconds before the damn thing realized its offspring were gone, and the gates of hell got knocked clean off their hinges.

"She's not sure what to make of us yet," he remarked, then turned to Ensign Rush, "Communications, I need intel. Get me everything you can on normal-sized versions of this thing: strengths, weaknesses. Find me its vulnerable spots."

"On it, sir."

"Sonar, what do your readings say?"

Ramirez's eyes dropped from the live feed on *Gryphon*'s bow window, back down to his station. "Bio mass is . . . *mierda*! 130-plus tons, sir. She's as heavy as a big Gen-1 cow, and considerably longer."

Finally, a worthy adversary; something worth killing.

"Rush, put me on shipwide."

"Done, sir."

"Attention, crew," Garm announced. "This is the captain. Battle stations, repeat, *full-secure* for battle stations. *This is not a drill.*"

He signaled for her to cut the feed, then licked his lips as he and the rest of the bridge crew clicked into their crisscrossed padded restraining harnesses. Unlike most naval vessels, on *Gryphon*, the term "full-secure for battle stations" had a special meaning. The ORION-class subs had beefier hulls, and were faster and far more maneuverable than standard military boats.

They had to be – they hunted surprisingly agile sea dragons for a living.

As a result, during combat, there were often sudden and unexpected directional shifts and drops that could slam an unprepared crewmember against a steel bulkhead, or launch them straight up, to smash into lethal protrusions from the ceiling above. Secured battle stations meant not only reporting to one's station, but also strapping in, in anticipation of risky maneuvers to come.

Cunningham swiveled in his seat. "Captain, I have sonar lock. Permission to engage?"

"Negative," Garm said, indicating the tiny form standing before them on the seabed, in a direct line between them and the lurking octopus. "Our AWES operator is in our field of fire."

Cunningham snorted irritably and turned away, muttering something about Sam Mot still owing him fifty dollars from years ago.

Garm hit a tab on his armrest. "Sam, how you doing out there?"

"Um, besides hoping this suit's waste disposal system is fully operational, how do you *think* I'm doing?"

"Just hold position," Garm said, grinning. "No sudden moves. I don't think it's figured out that its nest has been destroyed. Not yet. We may still be able to get you back aboard."

"Roger that."

As if reading the captain's mind, the octopus suddenly changed position. Shifting its body up and forward, it plopped down directly atop U-420's barnacle-coated conning tower. There was an otherworldly metallic moan, audible even through

Gryphon's state-of-the-art acoustic cladding, and a moment later, the conn collapsed under its weight.

Well, so much for Dirk's desire to keep the wreck intact.

The moment it had settled into place, two of the giant mollusk's lead tentacles slithered down like a pair of primeval pythons, worming their way inside the rent in the U-boat's hull. They began to stretch and extend, feeling their way further and further inside the darkened opening.

"Captain," Rush said, her blue eyes wide with fright as she glanced up at the viewer. "It says that they can *taste* with their suckers?"

Suddenly, the octopus's body stiffened and its tendrils retreated from the now-empty nursery. Its eyes widened, and the tips of its arms began exploring the nearby seafloor, searching, touching, smelling . . .

Soon, they were pointing directly at Sam.

Uh oh.

"It's *on*, people!" Garm shouted, his own eyes tightening as the cephalopod's orbs narrowed into yellowed slits. A split-second later, its enormous body swelled with rage and it lifted off U-420 like some deranged dirigible. Dropping down, it landed on the nearby sand with a frightful thump, displacing thousands of cubic yards of seawater as it started moving forward at high speed.

Its target was obvious.

"Sam, she's coming for you!" Garm bellowed.

"Shit!"

THIRTEEN

His opaline eyes intense, Garm spun toward Ensign Ho. There were mere seconds to act, to prevent Sam Mot from being torn to pieces before their eyes. And there was no way in hell he was going through *that* a second time.

"Helm, searchlights, now!" he yelled. "Sonar, deactivate iridophores! Make her focus on us!"

On the viewer, the eight-foot TALOS Mark VII looked like a Lego action figure, its tiny legs pumping as Sam desperately dove for cover. The mother Kraken was closing on him fast. Its huge body swept forward, gliding fluidly over the seabed, its deadly tentacles reaching.

Sam's panicky voice suddenly emanated from the bridge speakers. "Uh, a little help?"

Fifty feet over his head, *Gryphon*'s powerful searchlights flipped on and lanced through the murk. Like pure white tractor beams, they struck the mollusk's exposed head region, momentarily blinding it.

Garm bellowed, "Sam, hit the deck!" then barked at Ho. "Helm, break hard to port, maneuvering thrusters at *full* power. Keep her in our sights. Fire Control, prepare to engage!"

"NAEGLINGs, sir?" Cunningham asked.

"Negative, the blast wave would envelope Sam – LADON only!"

"Ready, sir!"

Garm gripped his armrests tight, as *Gryphon* powered left at high speed. He could feel her 435 tons groan as she was pushed through a wide arc, her bow still pointed at the enraged octopus. From her station, Connie Ho was the epitome of concentration. Her angular jaw set, she worked the yoke like the pro she was.

On the viewer, the Kraken's enormous body rippled like jelly and it began to creep sideways, its eyes partly closed and its body low to the ground. It seemed to have forgotten about the tiny figure before it, its attention focused instead on the gleaming submarine that had replaced its anticipated meal.

Its enormous body suddenly changed shape, and its mantle rose up like a hot air balloon on rubbery stilts. Garm got the distinct impression it was standing on tiptoe, striving for a better look. Its skin started to become rougher and more bark-like, and its glittering eyes widened. A heartbeat later, their horizontal pupils zeroed *Gryphon*. There was an impossibly low-frequency rumbling sound, like an underwater landslide, that vibrated through the submarine's reinforced hull.

Then, with a watery whoosh, the octopus's colossal body flew straight at them, its tentacles coiling and uncoiling in anticipation as it hurled itself forward. The distance between them began to shrink, and the bridge crew grabbed hold of anything they could, bracing for impact. Soon, all Garm could see on the bow viewer was a wall of sucker-lined tentacles, eager to envelope them all.

"Fire control, light her up!" he commanded.

"Engaging!" Cunningham shouted.

BRRRRRRRRRRRRRRRT!

The bridge vibrated with the high-speed thrumming of the LADON Gatling cannon's full-auto bursts. On the viewer, bright red tracer rounds marked the gun's lethal stream of 30 mm cannon shells like a laser beam, slamming into a spiraling section of the octopus's exposed underside.

"Direct hit!" Ramirez cried out. "Target veering!"

Garm's jaw muscles bulged as the octopus paused in mid-charge, then pulled back. It seemed surprised, but then shrugged off the impacts of the depleted uranium rounds as if they were snowflakes. Its wrath returned even greater than before, and it snapped its black beak like a pair of giant shears as it gathered itself. A second later, it charged again.

What the hell?

"Engaging!" Cunningham yelled from his station.

BRRRRRRRRRRRRRRRRRRRRRT!

This time, Garm watched the entire salvo of supercavitating rounds as they hit home, their blunt tips tearing into the uppermost portions of several of the giant cephalopod's tentacles, right where they connected to its body. Bits of tissue burst outward with each strike, along with spurts of bluish blood, but the explosive, tissue-devastating effect he was used to seeing when LADON tore into a *Kronosaurus imperator* didn't happen.

The octopus veered away again, this time in the opposite direction. There was the familiar hum of LADON's actuators, as Cunningham swept the big Gatling cannon's barrel back toward it and then fired again.

BRRRRRRRRRRRRT!

"Holy shit, d-did you see that?" the CSO sputtered.

Garm's eyes narrowed. The octopus had changed direction again, but this time the instant *before* LADON fired. Its hose-like siphon had acted like a jet, launching it backwards with incredible speed.

It was 150 yards away now, and doing a fast-zigzag pattern as it moved laterally to *Gryphon*'s position.

"Fast learner," Garm muttered. "Communications, why aren't our shells having any effect?"

Rush shook her head as she eyed the data she'd compiled. "I-I'm not sure, captain. They don't have any bones, for starters. We use penetrator rounds and, apparently, they aren't striking anything solid enough to cause expansion. It's like shooting into foam rubber; the animal's body is being punctured, but the shells aren't able to fragment."

BRRRRRRRRRRRRT!

"Oh, you think you're slick, eh?" Cunningham snarled, his hand gripping his joystick. On the screen, the octopus shot up and down, like a horse on a giant merry-go-round. It was circling them now. "Try *this* on for size . . ."

BRRRRRT! BRRRRRRRRRRRRRRRRRRRT!

"Gotcha!" the CSO exulted, as his fake to one side allowed him to catch the wily cephalopod right in his crosshairs. "Shit! I hit her dead center, captain. Why isn't she dead?"

Garm looked at Rush, his left eyebrow doing the inquisitive "Spock" thing.

"I, um, I honestly don't know," she admitted. "The anatomy is very bizarre. They've got three hearts, and most of their brain tissue is in the tentacles."

Ho's voice rang out. "Captain, it's circling us, trying for an opening." Her shoulders tensed but her eyes remained locked on their viewer. "I think it's trying to get under us!"

"What's our depth?" Garm asked.

"A hundred feet under the keel – water depth is four-fifty, max."

"Down fifteen on the bow. Drop our nose to fifty and pop our ass up," Garm said. A hundred yards away, the infuriated octopus continued its stalking: feinting, then jetting one way or the other, the moment it was targeted. Each move brought it another ten yards closer.

Ho was right. It knew LADON could cause it pain, if not kill it outright. It was attacking like a wolf, trying to get at its prey's vulnerable underside.

"Keep our bow angled down so fire control has a clear field of fire," Garm continued, unbuckling his harness and rising to his feet. "Do *not* let her under us!"

He moved between sonar and the helm, feet spread and braced, big hands resting on the backs of their chairs, as *Gryphon*'s rubberized floor angled sharply downward. As Ho twisted the yoke hard, the sub shifted violently to port, forcing him to grip the chair backs tightly to avoid being thrown to the deck.

"Sorry, captain."

"Fuck this shit!" Garm shouted, watching as the octopus zipped left, then right. "We're done playing her game. Fire control, get back on the offensive – short bursts, anytime you can get close. Just enough to keep her off of us."

"Engaging," Cunningham said.

BRRRRT!

"Helm," Garm said, feeling the reassuring vibration of LADON's high-speed bursts. "We're changing tactics."

"Talk to me."

BRRRRT!

On the screen, the octopus began to fall back. A moment later, it was on the run, with Cunningham doggedly pursuing it. Burst after burst of high-density rounds streamed after it, tearing up the seabed all around them, and occasionally ripping into its tough tissues.

"We need to do more damage than we've been able to do," Garm said. "But we need to clear U-420 and Sam in order to do it."

"I'm with you, sir."

BRRRRT! BRRRRT!

"When I give the word, you're to level off and then back full," he began. "Maintain depth, but keep us away from the wreck, and either parallel to the drop-off or pointed out to sea."

"Yes, sir," she said, one hand making quick adjustments.

"CSO, safeties are still set for fifty yards, correct?"

"Yes, captain!" Cunningham's brow was furrowed and beaded with sweat as he continued his bizarre duel.

"Good," Garm said, moving back to his seat and strapping himself in. "The moment we start to fall back, you're to cease fire and prep NAEGLINGs. This thing knows about LADON; it doesn't know our M9's."

"Yes, sir!"

"Infrared/ultraviolet homing seekers *only*," Garm ordered. "Remember, it's got no sonar. And, helm?"

"Yes, captain?" Ho replied.

"Back *full*. I want distance; make her think we're making a run for it."

"Yes, sir."

Garm waited for Cunningham's next full burst, then snapped his fingers. "Helm, *now!*" He felt the pressure in his groin build as *Gryphon* exploded backward at a full 25 knots, her bow angling back up at the same time.

The moment the discomfort eased, he swiveled to the right, watching out of the corner of one eye as Cunningham made minute adjustments on their torpedoes. On the bow viewer, the *Octopus giganteus* seemed confused. Its bulbous head was cocked to one side, like a dog listening to a whistle. A moment later, it rose up off the seabed and jetted toward them at breakneck speed.

It's taken the bait.

Garm hit a tab on his armrest. "Sam, you read me?"

"Loud and clear! Jesus, that thing won't die!" his friend radioed back.

"Just keep your head down," Garm advised. "Things are about to get hard around here."

"Sounds hot."

"Target approaching at substantial velocity," Ramirez announced. "I'm clocking fifty-two knots . . . impact in twelve seconds."

"Mister Cunningham," Garm said, watching as their adversary's mantle expanded across their viewer. "You may fire when ready."

"Roger that," the CSO replied. His finger jabbed a bright red button. "Tubes one and four . . . firing!"

There was the familiar, high-pitched whoosh as the NAEGLING M9 ADCAP torpedoes burst from their tubes, followed by a low rumble as their powerful boosters kicked in.

"Distance to target, four hundred yards," Ramirez said.

"Helm, full stop," Garm ordered. On the main, he could see the white bubble trails created by their supercavitating, rocket-propelled torpedoes as they raced toward their target at a blinding 350 mph. The octopus, spotting their approach, ceased its pursuit, its tentacles spreading out like an immense umbrella.

"Two hundred yards," Ramirez said. "Impact in five, four, three--"

At the last possible moment, the giant predator's tentacles dropped hard and it jetted upward like the space shuttle, the two torpedoes zipping between the tips of its elongated arms. A split-second later, the NAEGLINGs smashed into the stony rim of the drop-off, eighty yards away, and detonated like miniature suns.

"You missed again, Cunningham," Ho remarked over her shoulder.

Garm shielded his eyes with one palm, as the combined fire-ball lit up their viewer. A moment later, a low rumble rocked *Gryphon* as the explosion's shockwave rolled over them. He glanced at Cunningham, throwing him a 'what happened?' look.

"It's apparently smart and . . . very fast," the CSO said, his exasperation obvious. "It's throwing off our homing seekers. Infrared can't get a lock because its body temperature is the same as the surrounding seawater, and ultra-violet's having a tough time because its body keeps changing shape. Octopi aren't listed among our anti-biologic profiles."

Garm exhaled through clenched teeth. "Can you reprogram the UV seekers to target just a part of it? Like, maybe its head, which doesn't alter in shape as much?"

"Sure, if I have time," Cunningham said. "It'll take hours!"

"Captain, look!" Rush shouted.

On the viewer, 150 yards away, the octopus had stopped swimming. It was sitting on the seabed, its tentacles curling and uncurling all around it. Its color had changed too, from a char-coal gray to a far lighter hue.

"What's it doing?" Ramirez asked.

"It's stunned," Garm realized, perking up. He knew a hurt opponent when he saw one. "The shockwave must've thrown it for a loop. Helm, ahead full, intercept course. Fire control, you may fire when--"

"Captain, it's moving!" Ho yelled, pointing at the bow viewer.

Garm cursed. The damn thing was already back on its "feet" and making a break for it. He could see its mantle expand and contract as it jetted seawater, its speed increasing steadily. It was moving parallel to the deepwater, with Sam and U-420 a hundred yards to its right.

"Helm, intercept course," he ordered. "Fire control, we're too close to the wreck to fire fish. Target her ass with LADON and indulge yourself."

"With pleasure, captain," Cunningham replied, grabbing the Gatling cannon's joystick and bringing its targeting system back online.

"Captain, it's accelerating," Ramirez said. "Speed is thirty knots and increasing."

"Helm, ahead flank, run her down," Garm commanded.

"Ahead flank, sir."

BRRRRRRRRT! BRRRRRRT! BRRRRRRRRRT!

The bridge began to hum as the LADON gun system opened up on the fleeing Kraken. In his mind's eye, Garm had a momentary image of them as a supersized Spitfire, spitting lead at a wounded Messerschmitt Me 262.

It wasn't an altogether inappropriate comparison. Similar in overall length, *Gryphon* was barely ninety yards behind their adversary and peppering it. Soon, it was trailing bluish blood, and he could see chunks of rubbery tissue, small pieces of tendril, and even a few suckers flying off its enormous arms as their repeated bursts took effect.

BRRRRRT!

"Ha, take that!" Cunningham exclaimed gleefully. He turned wide-eyed to his captain, then indicated their opponent. On the viewer, an amputated ten-foot section of one of the mollusk's arms writhed wormlike in the current. The beast continued along, leaving it behind.

A minor wound, but I'll take it, Garm acknowledged.

Suddenly, the octopus changed direction and began picking up speed.

"She's heading for the Tombs!" Ho warned, her angular jaw set. "Distance 800 yards and closing!"

"Cut her off!" Garm demanded.

"Impossible, sir," she replied. "I've got the pedal down and the damn thing's still pulling away from us."

BRRRRRRRRT!

Garm's face darkened. Despite being loopy from the explosion, the octopus's top speed still exceeded theirs.

"Cease fire."

"Sir?" Cunningham asked, confusedly.

"She's outside LADON's effective range. You're just wasting brass. How many shells left?"

Cunningham checked his screen. "2,467, sir."

Garm exhaled through his nostrils, his pale eyes still targeting their fast-shrinking enemy. A lot of ammunition expended, and very little to show for it. Ahead, the seemingly endless volcanic ridge known as the Tombs drew progressively closer – a series of ragged, headstone-shaped seamounts that, with an average height of over a thousand feet, looked like an oceanic kaiju cemetery.

He had no intention of going in there. With the powerful rip-currents racing through the narrow gorges that separated the jagged black peaks, the fifteen-mile-long stone forest was one of the most dangerous places on earth. And that was without the addition of a vengeful, bullet-resistant sea monster that could appear as anything it desired, waiting to spring out and destroy them.

"Fire control," Garm said. "Fire tubes two and three, then reload all tubes."

"Tubes two and three . . . firing!"

Gryphon's captain watched intently as the pair of NAEGLING M9s screamed toward their target: a 130-ton horror, its billowing, brown and tan tentacles backed by a field of ever-darkening azure. As it had before, the giant cephalopod waited with impressive calmness until the approaching torpedoes were within fifty yards; then it jetted upward at an odd angle, causing them to zip harmlessly past.

Garm's look of disgust tagged on a squint as the M9s' twin warheads smashed into the nearest peak, a second later. As their combined fireballs flared and faded, they left a hole in its stony flank nearly a hundred feet across. Black volcanic rock crumbled noisily downward, spewing from the jagged wound, and forming a slow-moving avalanche.

"Missed again, sir," Cunningham lamented. "Sorry, it's just impossible to lock onto it."

"Helm, distance to target, and its distance to the Tombs," Garm requested.

"We're four hundred yards back," Ho said, eyeing her gauges. "The octopus is just under three hundred yards from the nearest ravine." She turned toward him, wearing a *'Please don't make me go in there'* look. "Once she gets inside, we'll lose her for sure."

"Well, then, I guess we'll just have to "encourage" her not to."

"Sir?"

Garm twisted toward Cunningham. "Set your next four fish with safeties off, and target Madame Kraken's starboard side," he instructed. "I want you to come as close as you can, without scoring a direct hit."

Cunningham blinked. "You want me to miss . . . on *purpose*?"

"Finger on the self-destruct, commander," Garm instructed. "Empty one tube at a time, and detonate each one as close as you can to the target."

The CSO's eyes went wide as realization hit him like a kick to the kiwis. "You're looking to--"

"Lay down some flack," his captain finished.

"Aye, sir. Making adjustments!"

An evil grin crawled across Garm's countenance. Each NAEGLING's warhead packed 50 kg of high-density GDT-C7

– enough to shatter a Coast Guard cutter's keel, if detonated underneath. He was betting, even with a near-miss, the concussive force would wreak havoc with the giant mollusk's central nervous system – possibly stun or even kill it.

And, besides, it wasn't like he had a lot of options.

"Captain, 'Madame Kraken's' distance to the Tombs is now only 150 yards," Ho advised.

"Ready to fire, sir," Cunningham announced.

"Fire one," Garm said.

Fwoosh . . . BOOM!

As the M9 ADCAP exploded, the bow viewer flared white. As the blast faded, Garm watched grimly as his opponent turned sharply to starboard. It jetted one hundred yards ahead, then turned and started back toward the shelter of the Tombs.

It's working. She just needs a little more encouragement.

"Hit her again," he commanded, feeling his boat shiver as they rode out their own weapon's shockwave.

Fwoosh . . . BOOM!

As the second NAEGLING exploded less than thirty yards from the octopus's flank, it changed course again. This time, however, it angled away from the Tombs, heading out to sea.

"Keep on her, Mister Cunningham," Garm ordered. "Fire three!"

Fwoosh . . . BOOM!"

"It's working just like you said!" Cunningham exclaimed over the bridge's rattling. "Uh oh, looks like she's going deep!"

Garm's eyes hardened. On the viewer, the giant octopus was shooting away from them, moving at a steep downward angle.

It was seeking the refuge of the lightless abyssal zone.

"Tell her she's going the wrong way," he said, his index finger wagging. "Put this one *under* her. Fire four!"

"Number four, firing!"

Fwoosh . . . . . . BOOM!

"Bingo!" Cunningham exulted. "Initiating reload procedures for all tubes."

"Sir," Ramirez said, clearing his throat. "Target is holding position. I'm not sure if it's stunned or disoriented. Distance is now 250 yards and . . ."

"And?" Garm asked.

"Shit!" the sonar tech spouted. "She just flipped a bitch! Sorry, I meant target is on an intercept course, bearing zero-two-zero. She's attacking us, sir!"

"Helm, back full!" Garm bellowed. "Fire control, where are we with those M9's?"

"Sixty seconds to full reload," Cunningham said, programming the ORION-class sub's torpedo auto-loader as fast as his fingers could type.

"Helm, distance to target?" Garm asked. On the viewer, the octopus's mantle resembled a rough-skinned hot air balloon, coming at them. It had dipped down, and was now curving back up in a steep arc, instead of a straight-line rush.

"She's at two hundred yards and rising fast," Ho growled. Her dark eyes looked like an angry Peregrine falcon's as she pulled back hard on the yoke. "She's trying to get under us. Unless you come up with something, estimated impact in twenty seconds!"

Garm ground his molars. He could feel everything on the bridge rattle as *Gryphon* raced backwards, but it was no good. The octopus was faster. "CSO, forget the fish. Ready LADON!"

"On it, sir!"

"Communications, give me shipwide."

"Shipwide, sir," Rush said, her glistening eyes betraying her fright.

"This is the captain," Garm announced. "Brace for collision. I repeat, brace for collision."

Ignoring the collective breath his bridge crew drew, he turned back to Ho.

"Helm, continue back full; on my command, you're to roll hard to starboard and execute a complete inversion. Understood?"

Ensign Ho's jaw dropped, then reformed as a huge grin as she flipped a pair of switches. "Understood, captain! Ready when you are!"

Garm watched the viewer, gauging his enemy's velocity and angle of attack as it closed on them. Yes, Madame Kraken was slick all right. She was already familiar with LADON, and she knew they shot torpedoes, too. She was planning on striking their vulnerable underbelly, where the big Gatling cannon couldn't reach her, and their ADCAP torpedoes were useless.

Four seconds to impact . . . three . . .

"Full inversion, NOW!" Garm bellowed, grabbing his armrests. "CSO, fire at will!"

There was a tremendous roar as *Gryphon's* eight MAKO M69 pump jet propulsors exerted their combined 12,000 horsepower, followed by a metallic groan so loud it loosened the fillings in one's teeth. Then, like a spiraling 435-ton leviathan, the backpedaling submarine rolled completely upside down, going belly-up and turret-down, at the precise moment the infuriated octopus's tentacles were reaching hungrily for it.

BRRRRRRRRRRRT! BRRRRRRRRRRRRRT!

Garm's hands dug into his armrests like meat hooks, and his insides felt like he was on some hellish amusement park ride. His tactician's mind absorbed a dozen things at the same time: the sound of LADON's supercavitating rounds firing, the vibrations of the bridge, the creaks and pops of their inner and outer hulls flexing, the yells and cries of alarm coming from the bridge crew, the sound of his coffee mug flying from his chair and shattering, and loose items tumbling and flying left and right.

Most importantly, his brain registered the thudding impacts of their 30 mm depleted uranium shells striking at point-blank range. The pummeling they dished out sounded like devastating body blows. A muffled, bloop-like roar accompanied them. Then there was a loud whooshing sound and *Gryphon's* hull shook violently.

"We did it, sir!" a red-faced Cunningham yelled. He was holding the bottom of his seat with one hand, his other still gripping LADON's joystick, and his auburn hair hanging down. "Scored two center mass hits and she's breaking off!"

"Helm, right us," Garm said, feeling the blood beginning to rush to his brain.

"Yes, sir," Ho said, upside down and smiling.

There was another bone-aching metallic moan as the submarine righted itself, backed by expletives and the sounds of loose objects once again rolling and crashing all over the bridge.

"Sonar," Garm said, no longer able to see their adversary on the main. "Locate target. Has it been neutralized?"

"Negative," Ramirez replied, his sweaty hands clutching his station tightly as everything jostled right-side up. "Target is angling away from the Tombs, sir. Current trajectory suggests it's returning to U-420."

"Very well. Helm--"

"Captain!" Ramirez interrupted. "Look, sir. I-I think it's hurt!"

Eyes intense, Garm leaned hard against his restraining harness. *Gryphon's* sonar tech was correct. Although its thrusting movements still gave it a velocity approaching sixty miles an hour, one of the octopus's huge tentacles had suffered a gaping wound at the point where it joined its body. It was shot to hell – literally hanging by a thread.

Time to finish this.

"Intercept course," he commanded. "Ahead flank!"

Garm sat back, considered releasing his harness, but then thought better of it.

"Communications, send a message ahead to Sam," he said. "Tell him to keep his head down. He's got company due any minute."

"Aye, sir," Rush said, cupping half her headset with one hand, and talking in quick, low tones into her chin mike.

"Maintain battle stations. And give me a damage report," Garm continued. "I want crew status; find out who's hurt and how badly."

"Yes, sir," Rush replied, eyeing her screens and working her keyboard. "Reactor is at 96% capacity. We lost a few iridophores during that last maneuver, and I've got readings indicating a level one leak in pressure hull number four, sir . . . it's the sail."

"Looks like we won't be cloaking any time soon," he acknowledged, then mentally dismissed the problem. The leak was also minor; with the pumps running at even half capacity, it could easily wait until they made port. "Injuries?"

Rush cupped her padded earphones with both hands now, listening. "Ensign Akio and Commander Morgan both suffered minor slip-and-fall injuries during our inversion. They weren't fully strapped in. Also, Yeoman Perkins reports a wrenched shoulder, a harness-related injury."

"Note to log," Garm said. "Helm, time to intercept."

"Fifteen seconds," Ho replied. She glanced at the fathometer screen to her left. "Target appears to be stationary, and . . . what the hell? Sir, I'm no longer seeing it on my screens."

"Sonar?"

"I . . . I'm not sure what happened, sir," Ramirez admitted. "I lost it the moment it passed the wreck. In fact, that entire section of the drop-off just blacked out on me."

"Continue on intercept course," Garm ordered. "Reduce speed to twenty knots. Fire control, are we ready on all four tubes?"

"Yes, captain," Cunningham said, his eyes fierce as he eyed his targeting systems. "We've got sixteen NAEGLINGs remaining."

"Plenty to do the job," Garm said, contemplating the looming underwater ridge where U-420 rested. He leaned forward in his seat, mouthing a curse as the padded restraining belt once again restricted his movements. Suddenly, his eyes widened. "What in the . . . ? Helm, full stop!"

"Full stop, sir."

Garm felt the sudden change in inertia compress his lower abdomen as *Gryphon*'s combined maneuvering thrusters fired in reverse, to offset their forward momentum. "Communications, zoom in on the region directly behind the U-boat. 3X magnification."

Rush touched her screen, and the view of what lay beyond U-420 tripled in size. Starting two hundred yards back from the ancient submarine, and covering an area equally as wide, stood a towering wall of absolute blackness. It ran from the surface to the seafloor and hovered there like a black hole; a lightless window into the void.

Garm cocked an eyebrow. "Is that . . . ink?"

"Yes, sir," Ramirez replied, his back as straight as a board. "Origin is confirmed biologic. It must've excreted it as a means of hiding," He threw his captain a quick glance. "I think it's sensitive to our sonar, sir."

"Can you scan inside the cloud?"

"Negative. It's too dense and obscuring for POSEIDON to penetrate, and active sonar is reading it as one huge mass."

"Is it in there?"

"Impossible to say, sir. But my guess would be, yes."

Garm frowned, then unclicked his harness and stood up. He walked over and laid a hand on his sonar tech's shoulder. "Keep an eye on the cloud, but give me active scans of the surrounding area, too, in case it's hiding nearby."

"Yes, sir."

"Helm, hold position. Maneuvering thrusters only."

"Yes, sir."

"Communications," Garm said. "Prep a pair of LOKI's for launch."

"On it, sir," Rush said, suddenly lively. "Settings and program?"

He considered for a moment. "Set acoustic signatures to match those given off by our AWES," he replied, an impish grin tugging at the corners of his mouth. "She didn't seem very fond of Sam and TALOS. Maybe we can entice her into doing something rash."

Garm nodded approvingly as Rush threw herself into her work. If nothing else, the LOKIs would stir things up, running around inside the giant cephalopod's lightless hideout with their sonar emitters and strobe lights banging away. From the annoyance factor alone, she'd probably lash out at them, and in doing so, give them the opportunity to zero her.

It'll be worth losing a LOKI to kill the damn thing.

"Captain," Ramirez advised. "Tide is receding. Although the octopus ink has a higher specific gravity than the surrounding water, it *is* beginning to dissipate. In a few minutes, we should have a confirmed visual, even without sonar."

"Good. Stay on it. Fire control," Garm turned, looking over his shoulder at his CSO. "I want one eye on the cloud and the other on LADON's crosshairs. Sweep the entire area, just in case."

"Aye, sir," Cunningham nodded. "I'm not Ensign Ho, but I'll do my best."

Garm gave him a look, then turned back, just in time to see Connie Ho's upper back grow noticeably rigid. It was a surprisingly cheap shot from Kyle – picking on the diminutive helmswoman's lazy eye condition – but then again, she'd been riding him hard for the last month.

Riding him hard . . .

The possibility there'd been a one-night-stand between his CSO and Ho, presumably before she started dating Ramirez, made its way into Garm's mind. He dismissed the thought. Kyle had an attractive wife and was happily married. Still, there had to be something behind the ongoing hostility. Ah, well. It was an issue he'd consider prying into at a later date.

"Captain!" Ho shouted, her head inclining toward their bow viewer. "Look!"

As he stared, Garm felt excitement shoot up his spine like an express elevator, headed non-stop for the penthouse. Protruding from the very bottom of the gradually-dispersing ink cloud was the terminus of one of the giant octopus's eighty-foot tentacles.

He could make out a good twenty feet of it, slowly curling and uncurling as the behemoth remained hunkered down in its hiding spot.

Checkmate.

"Fire control," Garm asked. "Distance to target?"

"150 yards, sir."

"Charge REAPER and prepare to fire."

"Seriously?"

Garm targeted him with a look he usually reserved for stare-downs in the ring. "To quote Rocky Marciano, 'Why waltz with a guy for ten rounds if you can knock him out in one?'" He touched the bruise still adorning his temple, then shook his big head. "I'm through pussyfooting around with this thing. We're going for the knockout."

Cunningham nodded as he tapped a few keys. "A 2,000-pound tungsten projectile moving at 5,000 miles an hour ought to do it, sir." He paused, licking his lips thoughtfully. "Are you concerned about what might happen if I . . . *we* miss?"

"Not at all; the continental shelf's incline will disperse any kinetic energy not absorbed by the target. Relax, Kyle. It's not a nuke."

"Yes, sir," Cunningham replied. On the main viewer, the REAPER's glowing crosshairs materialized as an overlay, and a second later, the familiar rhythmic vibrations it generated could be felt building beneath the bridge's thick rubberized flooring. The acrid smell of ionized air began to fill the room, and Garm got that godawful metallic taste once again in the back of his throat.

His wolfish eyes gradually narrowed, and he relished the feeling of immense power as the sixty-foot rail gun's energy levels began to build. When he gave the order, *Gryphon* would spew an annihilating 600 megajoules of kinetic energy, directly at their oversized adversary. It would be a ten-foot wide, three-hundred-foot-long superheated blast of destruction, that would literally turn the surrounding stone to magma.

When the dust settled, they'd be lucky if there was enough of Madame Kraken left to dip in soy sauce and wasabi at the victory party he planned on throwing.

"Status?" Garm asked.

"REAPER at 78% and building, sir."

"Target the cloud, twenty feet directly above that tendril's thickest part," Garm instructed. "Maximum penetration."

He watched, as the illuminated crosshairs shifted and refocused. Based on the giant octopus's body design, he calculated their aim was spot-on. But even if it wasn't, with a shotgun blast that big and bad, even a near miss would be fatal.

Ramirez cleared his throat. "Ink cloud continuing to dissipate, sir. Dimensions are now eighty yards in diameter and decreasing steadily."

Garm nodded. With the tide's inevitable pull, the mollusk's viscous blind was beginning to break up and disperse into the surrounding seawater. Much of the upper region had already cleared, but the heavier portions at the bottom still maintained much of their density. He could make out a good thirty feet of at least one of the creature's squirming tentacles now.

"REAPER at 89%, captain," Cunningham advised.

"Stay on her," Garm said, his anticipation building every bit as much as the energy stored in their weapon's pulsed power system.

Just stay right *there, you murderous bitch. Stay* <u>right</u> *there . . .*

Suddenly, Ramirez's head started doing the pendulum thing, whipping from sonar screen to sonar screen, before ping-ponging back up to the main.

"Uh, captain . . ."

"REAPER at 97%, sir!" Cunningham yelled. "We won't be able to hold her much longer!"

Ramirez's head whipped toward his captain's, his eyes as big as teacups. "Captain, look!" he yelled, pointing at the very bottom of the ink cloud.

"Captain, REAPER at 100%!" Cunningham cried out. His finger was suspended over the trigger and, all around them, the bridge began to shake.

As Garm's eyes found the spot Ramirez was indicating, the noises around him suddenly ceased. His sonar tech's yelling, Kyle's bellowing – even the vibrations that shook the bridge to the point anyone not belted in would be shaken from their seat – all of them were muted. The only sound he could hear was the bass beating of his heart.

Boom-boom. Boom-boom. Boom-boom.

On the bow viewer, the shrinking ink cloud had risen sufficiently that the octopus's entire tentacle was now visible.

And it was *just* a tentacle.

Twisting and writhing on the seabed, the severed arm moved with a mind of its own. As he noted the pale suckers lining its near 80-foot length, Garm was reminded of one of those lizard's tails that popped off in a predator's mouth, allowing it to escape. His rib cage felt like it had transformed into constricting bands of ice as the realization hit home.

They'd been suckered.

"Captain, incoming!"

KABOOM!

The impact against *Gryphon*'s armored hull was so devastating, if Garm hadn't managed to lunge for one arm of his wildly swiveling chair, he'd have crashed into Ensign Heather Rush's station hard enough to kill her. As it was, the burning spasm of pain that paralyzed his right shoulder like a hit from a Taser told him he'd torn his rotator cuff.

"We're hit!" Ensign Ho cried out, as the big submarine lurched sideways. "Target was lying in wait off the portside. She's on us, sir!"

Garm made a frantic leap, miraculously landing in his command chair, and managed to fasten his harness, despite the pain. "CSO, can you fire LADON?"

"LADON?" Cunningham sputtered. "May I remind you, REAPER is ready to explode!"

Garm experienced a moment of disorientation as *Gryphon* rolled wildly to starboard, then heaved back. Kyle was right. Their thermal management systems could only handle the rail gun's full charge for a few more seconds. They had to fire it or shut it down.

Meanwhile, on the bow viewer, the only thing he could see besides water was a section of clinging tentacle, as thick as his king-sized mattress. Plastered across the screen, its huge white suckers expanded and contracted like gaping mouths, each one eager to take a bite.

"Then fire!"

"What?"

"You heard me!" Gritting his teeth, Garm clamped down on his pain as they began to be wrenched back and forth. "She's at least partly by the bow! Fire, goddamnit!"

Cunningham closed his eyes, mouthed a prayer. Then he pushed the button.

Instantly, the main's external view was replaced by a pitch-black, vision-saving tint: the equivalent of welder's glass. Accompanying it was a tremendous sucking sound which, to the uninitiated, made it seem as if all the air in the bridge had been drawn out, leaving an airless vacuum behind. The bridge floor vibrated so hard, it felt like the decking beneath everyone's feet was being hit with triphammers.

Then the REAPER projectile rocketed down its titanium-steel barrel.

Like a volcano erupting, a searing stream of power exploded from *Gryphon*'s prow. Even with the main's protective shielding, the blast was impossible to stare at, a pure white energy pulse that annihilated everything in its path: flesh, bone, stone . . . even the water all around it.

Garm blinked to clear the colored motes dancing before his eyes, then felt a spike of panic skyrocket. He'd forgotten about Sam! He'd been so disoriented, he had no idea what direction their bow had been pointing when he gave the order.

What if the blast was directed at Sam? Had he just killed his best friend?

There was a tremendous rocking and *Gryphon* torqued hard on her axis. The safety tint vanished from the main and, along with a violently churning sea, Garm spotted a fifteen-foot free-floating section of tentacle. It drifted past the bow, along with dozens of scorched, fleshy fragments.

"Fire control!" Garm called out. "Did we get her?"

His answer was a staggering hit that turned the ORION-class submarine almost completely on her side. The sounds of straining steel and titanium were deafening, and the 435-ton ship began to move laterally.

"Just winged her, captain!" Cunningham yelled back, both hands on his station, and relying on his safety harness to hold him in place. "I-I think she's pissed!"

With her hull still twisted at a ninety-degree angle, *Gryphon* continued to be pulled sideways. Suddenly, she slowed, then began to shake and shimmy. Garm could tell his vessel was being manhandled, and shook his head in disgust.

"Helm, full power to maneuvering thrusters! Right us!"

"I'm . . . trying, sir!" Ho replied, her teeth clenched as she wrestled with the yoke. "It's got us keeled over and I-I think it's using the seabed as an anchor!"

"Get us free! Pull as much power from the engines as you can!"

"I am, sir!"

Garm's shoulder was killing him from gripping his armrests, but he ignored it. Being sidewise was definitely better than being upside down.

"Communications!" he yelled. "Get me Sam on the horn!"

Too terrified to reply, Rush hit a few switches and gave him a thumbs-up.

"Jesus, Garm, are you guys alright?" Sam's voice blurted from the bridge's speakers. "You wounded it with that big gun, but not enough! It's got a couple of tentacles wrapped around the reef, and the rest around you good and tight!" The panting AWES operator hesitated for a moment, then added, "I think it's trying to figure out what you guys *are*! It's feeling its way around the hull, like it's exploring! Should I take a slice at it with my plasma torch?"

"You will do no such thing!" Garm thundered, sweat running down his face. The bridge lights were set on full combat mode, and both ANCILE and OMNI ADCAP were pinging away nonstop. "I'm just glad you're alive, old buddy. I was worried we might have had you in our sights when we fired the REAPER."

"W-wait, what? You mean, you didn't even know if I was downrange when you pulled the trigger? Why, you son of a--"

Sam's curse was cut short by a metallic creak as *Gryphon* fought to right herself. She succeeded, but only for a moment, before being yanked violently back down, this time nose first. There was a thunderous crash, and Garm saw sand, seaweed, and another monstrous tentacle snake its way across the sub's bow.

"It just slammed us prow-first into the seabed!" Ho yelled out. She twisted the yoke left and right, causing the submarine to sway sickeningly from side to side as she continued to fight. "I can't break free! Not with it holding onto the bottom!"

Garm mouthed a curse. "Sonar, show me our position on POSEIDON!"

"Full overview, sir!" Ramirez shouted.

The image on the 3D fathometer screen was exactly as Sam and Ho had described. They were midpoint between the nearly-dissipated ink cloud and U-420, their nose partially embedded in the bottom, and their stern sticking up at a forty-five-degree angle. They'd been lucky. Between their advanced hull design and superior construction materials, the armored ORION-class subs were five times stronger than any comparably-sized boat on the planet. If they weren't, Garm and his crew would've been dead already.

As he watched the fathometer version of the octopus poring over *Gryphon*'s exterior, searching for weak spots, it occurred to him their demise might not be far off, regardless. They had to break free – bring weapons to bear.

"Fire control!" he bellowed, his eyes on the main. "Get on LADON and--"

Garm's command was cut short as the sub was abruptly yanked up off the bottom amid a shower of sand. A moment later, she tilted 45 degrees to starboard and then began to track sideways at high speed. Loose items crashed to the floor, and the several members of the bridge crew uttered cries of alarm.

Suddenly, a computerized voice began to speak.

"Danger: collision imminent. Danger: collision imminent."

Garm cocked his head to one side. "Helm?"

"She's . . . dragging us toward the . . . drop-off!" Ho replied, her brow damp with sweat as she hauled back on the controls, pulling for all she was worth. "I . . . can't stop her! We're . . . heading right for the . . . damn U-boat!"

Garm gripped his armrests tightly. Through the bow window, all he could see was churning sea and the seafloor zipping by. He glanced at POSEIDON instead, and what he saw chilled his blood.

The beast had latched onto their hull with several of its arms and was jetting backwards, hauling *Gryphon* behind it like some jumbo suitcase up a flight of stairs. He could tell from the thing's trajectory that it would clear U-420's mashed conning tower.

But they wouldn't.

"Everyone, brace for collision!" Garm shouted. He hit the emergency button on his armrest, activating shipwide warning lights and a claxon that resounded throughout the sub.

"Brace!"

A second later, *Gryphon*'s entire portside plowed into the rusted remains of the 330-foot U-boat. The explosive impact drowned out the frightened cries of the bridge crew and shook the sleek pliosaur killer to her core. It was followed by an impossibly loud wrenching noise, and a rumbling reminiscent of an earthquake.

As his world shuddered and spun all around him, Garm gaped in disbelief.

The force of the collision had caved in a hundred-foot section of the far larger U-420's aged hull and dislodged her from her sandy grave. Pushed to the precipice, there was an ear-splitting reverberation as she teetered back and forth. A moment later, gravity demanded its due, and the century-old warship tumbled over the edge.

With a debris trail churning in her wake, she descended like some murdered monolith, twisting and turning as she plummeted toward the beckoning darkness of the deep. After a hundred years of waiting, the pride of the *Kriegsmarine* was headed for her final resting place.

And *Gryphon* was going with her.

FOURTEEN

As he exited the lift and hit the docks of Tartarus, the first thing Dirk Braddock saw made him chortle. It was a first for him, laughing aloud as he eyed the enormous pliosaur tanks, each one "home" to one of the deadliest predators on the planet. Around him, the place was remarkably subdued – at least in terms of the human element. That was probably due to the final cords of *"Danger Zone"*, by Kenny Loggins, blasting out of the facility's ceiling-based speakers. Tartarus's resident saurians had just completed their latest exercise interval.

It wasn't Stacy's often unpredictable song choices that made Dirk crack up. Nor was it that her preprogrammed workout music was so loud it sent every technician, janitor, and security staff member within earshot into hiding. He was laughing because of the visitor he had deposited in *Charybdis*'s sand-strewn tank the night before.

Or rather, the Gen-2 cow's reaction to it.

Dirk stopped fifty feet from the dockside wall of the pliosaur's aquarium and stared up at the new addition. Sharing the ten-story-high tank with the 70-foot *Kronosaurus imperator* was the biggest *Mola mola* he could get his hands on.

Known as an Ocean sunfish, the eleven-foot, 5,000-pound Mola was, with the possible exception of their genetically enhanced bluefin tunas, the heaviest bony fish on the planet. It was also one of the ugliest. With its caudal fin replaced by a rather butt-like clavus, and its elongated dorsal and anal fins stretching some fourteen feet from tip to tip, to Dirk it looked like an enormous, disembodied head, swimming along with its mouth open, wondering where its body was.

What was amusing, even puzzling, was the fact that, despite the Mola having a swimming speed of only two mph, and no defensive capabilities whatsoever, it somehow remained un-touched. In fact, as a species, the pelagic fish's numbers had been unaffected by pliosaurs reclaiming their role as apex pred-ators throughout the world's oceans. True, packs of *Xiphactinus* preyed on the smaller sunfish at times, but the 2,000+ lb. adults were generally ignored. And the saurians weren't eating them, either, and Dirk wanted to know why.

Slow-swimming, innocuous sea creatures like manta rays, manatees, and basking sharks had been virtually annihilated by the rapacious reptiles. Even that notorious man-eater, the great white shark, was either extinct or hanging by a fin. But not the *Mola mola*; they remained unmolested. Just last week, Dirk had seen drone footage of a bull pliosaur swimming right past one, without giving it a second glance.

And, despite remaining unfed, *Charybdis* was exhibiting similar tendencies.

Squinting, Dirk could just make out the gray-hued behe-moth, lurking near the bottom of her paddock, as she was wont to do. It was obvious that she was staying as far as possible from the googly-eyed sunfish. In fact, she was avoiding it like the plague, to the point that, if it swam sluggishly in her direction, she gave ground.

Dirk shook his head, then smacked his palm heel against the eight-foot-thick clear polybenzimidazole wall of the pliosaur's enclosure, as if to knock some sense into her. It was unbeliev-able. Her territory was being flagrantly violated, yet the mighty *Charybdis* would do nothing.

The young scientist was fascinated. Maybe the Mola smelled and tasted repulsive to pliosaurs – like a person consuming their own feces? Or, perhaps, its freakish appearance somehow unnerved them? More likely the former than the latter, he mused. He began to wonder if solving the mystery of the sunfish might offer up some practical applications, maybe lead to a chemical deterrent that could keep the huge marine reptiles away from beaches and boats – the Thalassophonean version of shark repellent. If so, it would be a tremendous boon to GDT's burgeoning consumer division.

Dirk studied *Charybdis*, rising for a breath and giving her unwelcome roommate the *Kronosaurus* version of a side-eye, and sniggered. He'd have the big sunfish dumped in *Tiamat*'s enclosure, later that evening. If it survived the night with *her*, they were looking at a potential goldmine.

Striding past the empty submarine slips and turntable, Dirk headed toward the fenced-in portion of the complex that included the *Xiphactinus* tank, the surgical center and its healing pool, the *Colossus* lift system, and, of course, *Gretchen*'s enclosure. As it loomed in the distance, he eyed the foreboding black curtain that cordoned off a 300-foot section of the dock. Behind its warning signs lay Tartarus's colossal amphitheater, and the pliosaur queen's connected paddock.

Memories of his mother, and thoughts of her killer, began to joust in Dirk's mind, and his grin drooped. Grayson would never allow anything to happen to his prize pet, so direct revenge was impossible. But he'd be damned if he didn't do his best to uncover exactly what happened that night and bring anyone even remotely responsible to justice.

As for *Tiamat*, well, he could always slip a Mola or two in her tank whenever Grayson wasn't looking.

With the current generators switching to maintenance mode, and the music dying down, Dirk could hear the *slip-slap* of his tennis shoes as they impacted on the moist concrete of the dock. High overhead, a hoist zipped by, slowing and changing direction as it navigated the complex latticework of well-oiled girders that spread, web-like, fifteen stories above his head. The smell of filtered seawater grew stronger as he drew nearer to the chain-link fence surrounding *Gretchen*'s dimly-lit pool.

There was a sudden crackling sound, and Dirk paused, still fifty feet away. Behind him, static hissed and cleared on the trio of enormous monitors that hung suspended from the center of the complex's roof and, with Stacy still not present, he paused to watch.

The monitors were programmed to auto-activate when GDT's media surveillance systems intercepted newsworthy, pliosaur-relevant events – a common occurrence, even with the huge reptiles' numbers reduced by CDF "intervention".

The initial piece was interesting. It had been filmed the previous day, on a small marina in the San Francisco Bay Area. A charter boat had been preparing to load clients and tackle, only to discover a juvenile *Kronosaurus imperator* squabbling over dock rights with the area's resident pinnipeds. The marine reptile was small, only seven feet or so, but with its fanged jaws and foul disposition, it was holding its own against a pair of far bulkier Steller's sea lion bulls.

That was, until the charter boat captain stormed to the transom of his boat and fired over its head with a pump-action shotgun.

Dirk shook his head as he turned and made his way to *Gretchen*'s gate. You knew things were bad when smallish pliosaurs were bold enough to climb out of the water and start sunning themselves, right next to a retiree's houseboat.

Lips pursed, he pressed his thumb to the Bioscan padlock that warded the steel-framed gate, then paused and took stock. He could see *Gretchen* lounging at the opposite end of her pool, her wedge-shaped head and muscular neck protruding just above the surface, as she took slow, relaxing breaths.

Stacy was nowhere in sight, but the oversized wheelbarrow parked five feet from the pool's nearest corner, and the trail of fish slime and blood leading from it to the water, proved she'd been there mere moments ago. Not one to leave a mess behind, she'd undoubtedly return. In fact, he surmised with a twinkle in his eye, she was probably in the tiny shed by the pool's opposite end at that very moment.

Probably changing out of her wetsuit.

Mentally revisiting their impromptu tryst from a few days prior, Dirk grinned and reached for a nearby controller. With any luck, he might catch her naked.

Setting the unit to maximum, he clipped it on his belt and eased the chain-link gate open, taking care not to bang anything. *Gretchen* had obviously just fed, and would undoubtedly be lethargic. If he moved slowly, with the controller masking his presence, odds were she wouldn't even notice him.

If she did, or if things took a turn, there was always the reserve button. A development he and Stacy had engineered, back when GDT's neural-interface helmet was still in its infancy, the newer controllers had a built-in failsafe. In an emergency – meaning one of their resident sea monsters had you cornered and was about to devour your sorry ass – it was the Tartarus equivalent of a dead man's switch.

Literally.

Once held and released, the controller emitted a powerful pulse that caused the brain of any cybernetically implanted pliosaur within fifty yards to flood with gamma-aminobutyric acid and glycine, the neurotransmitters that cause sleep paralysis.

The affected animal immediately experienced the same type of immobility a human being does during REM. The consciously controlled/voluntary muscles of the body, in this case the flippers and jaws, were temporarily paralyzed.

The battery-draining discharge would only work once, and the effects lasted a mere thirty seconds, but if a 100-ton sea monster was about to sink its teeth into you, it could literally mean the difference between watching television later that evening and being buried in a shoebox.

Momentarily resting his palm on his controller for reassurance, Dirk stepped cautiously into *Gretchen*'s domain. To his right, stood the fortified underwater gates that separated the pliosaur's 200-foot pool from the tunnel that transported clean water into her enclosure. Like a subway entering a station, it flowed in one end and continued out the other. During the saurian's daily exercise intervals, the current tearing through the pool was strong enough to topple a tractor trailer. Right now, it was quiet.

Dirk's burgeoning lust grappled with the notion of calling out to Stacy. He realized it was a very bad idea and started tiptoeing his way along instead. Although he was confident that the controller would keep him safe, he was ever mindful of the colossal carnivore reposing at the opposite end, and kept a respectful distance from the water's edge.

Six paces later, Dirk stopped in mid-step.

A new image had appeared on the ceiling monitors and, as he read the closed-captioning, he hesitated. This report carried far more weight than the previous one.

In fact, it was downright disturbing.

Stopping with his back six feet from the pool's edge, he stared up at the distant screen and scratched his head. The news report was from one of the Great Lakes: Lake Erie, to be exact. It featured footage from someone's cell phone, a family outing at a local beach. There was a barbecue, some picnic tables, and some kids shore fishing and playing; a nice scene.

Suddenly, a sub-adult *Kronosaurus imperator*, maybe twenty feet long by Dirk's estimate, exploded up out of the shallows like an ambushing Nile crocodile and seized a young boy in its four-foot jaws. At this point, the footage had been stabilized, but it was still jumpy. There was a lot of screaming and running and, despite what must have been the child's father, beating on the three-ton predator with a beach umbrella, it choked the kid down in seconds.

Obviously still hungry, the emboldened saurian proceeded to waddle up and out of the water like a scaly elephant seal, using its four flippers to propel itself. Scattering terrified civilians like a bowling ball does ten-pins, it seized a hapless woman – the dead child's mother – by the legs and started dragging her back towards the lake.

Someone showed up with a revolver at this point, possibly an off-duty police officer, Dirk surmised, and emptied his weapon into the thick skin of the pliosaur's flanks.

It was useless. Even after absorbing six rounds at point-blank range, and despite the heroic efforts of several other chair-wielding adults, the marine reptile hauled its hysterically struggling victim back into the water and vanished in a tremendous splash. The woman's screaming face as she was drawn under was the last thing anyone would see; the footage ended at that point, the final frame showing nothing but crimson water.

Dirk's jaw hung down, and his mind spun as he absorbed the enormity of what had happened. Besides the fact every media outlet was already going apeshit over it, the odds against such an attack taking place were mind boggling.

In fact, it was all but impossible.

How the _hell_ did a pliosaur get into Lake Erie?

He stood there, gesticulating at an invisible audience. Granted, the Niagara river connected Lake Erie to Lake Ontario, and the Saint Lawrence river linked Lake Ontario to the sea, but there was a plethora of barriers in the way, including a series of man-made ones, specifically designed to ensure such a thing never happened. There were canal lochs, dams, electrical barriers, nets . . . Hell, just to get into Ontario undetected was incredible, especially for an animal the size of a cow Orca.

And even if it *had* found its way into the lake, how the *hell* could it make it into Erie with Niagara Falls in the way? Did it levitate? Did it sprout wings and fly?

Dirk mouthed a curse, as the awful possibility that someone had *deliberately* put the creature in there dawned on him.

Dumping one or more *Kronosaurus imperator* hatchlings into the Great Lakes? Now, *that* would be one of the sickest pranks imaginable. The kind that would garner the comedian responsible a hefty prison term.

Dirk's eyes bugged out as the broadcast continued, with some talking head introducing an additional video clip. This one had been taken head-on, right as the hungry pliosaur charged its second victim. The footage was better – high-def and surprisingly stable – and as the fanged jaws flew right at the screen, practically enveloping the lens, he sprang back reflexively.

A look of surprise came over Dirk, as he felt his back foot slip out from under him, and he stepped hurriedly back to catch himself. He glanced down and grimaced. He was standing in a big patch of bloody fish slime, a leftover from *Gretchen's* recent feeding.

He started to step, only to have his look of disgust convert to astonishment, as both of his feet flew out from under him. He toppled backwards and, for a moment, had a spectacular view of the underside of the old Gen-1 skeleton, suspended directly overhead. Then, he felt a hard slap to his occipital and everything turned gray and gurgled. He uttered a muffled cry of panic as he realized he couldn't breathe.

Spouting saltwater and gasping for air, Dirk surfaced. His fingertips shook as he used them to clear his vision, and he glanced around.

A moment later, his heartrate spiked. He'd managed to cushion his landing by falling headfirst into the pool.

Gretchen's pool.

An instant and impressive shift in the surrounding seawater told the frightened scientist something he would rather not have known. The saurian had sensed the splash caused by something invading her domain, and was turning to investigate.

Dirk's eyes were the size of saucers as the humpback-sized predator swiveled in his direction, propelled by a casual flick from one of her ten-foot pectoral fins. She was a hundred feet away and facing him head-on, her fang-filled cranium like a giant spearhead, aimed at his heart.

He froze, confident that the combination of his immobility and the white controller clipped to his belt would disguise him from the inquisitive carnivore.

It didn't. With her football-shaped eyes breaking the surface like those of some monstrous crocodile, the pubescent *Kronosaurus imperator* began to move in his direction. She came on unhurriedly, draped with an air of casualness with which he was all too familiar. It was a look he'd seen countless times during Tartarus's scheduled feedings; the superlative confidence of a predator that knows its prey cannot escape.

The mottle-hued goliath was now fifty feet away and closing.

Dirk's panic upgraded to primal fear as he was confronted with the possibility every creature dreads – being devoured. He reached underwater with trembling hands and unclipped his controller, checking its settings and power levels to make sure it hadn't gotten waterlogged. It seemed fine.

It occurred to him he could be panicking for no reason. *Gretchen* might have felt the splash and, not detecting anything, was simply curious. Maybe she couldn't even see him.

As he turned to gauge the distance to the pool's edge, however, that notion evaporated like a drop of water landing in a hot skillet. The moment his head moved, the pliosaur's blood-red eyes contracted, her slitted pupils meeting his as she focused on her target.

Shit, she can *see me. Worse, she looks interested . . .*

Dirk's next exhalation was a shudder, and he kicked hard with his feet as he readied the failsafe on his controller. As much as he hated scrambling one of their resident *Thalassophoneans'* brains, he had no choice. He hit the switch and braced himself as the device's LEDs flared like miniature stars.

Nothing happened. *Gretchen* kept on coming.

In fact, if anything, she seemed even more attracted.

Dirk's heart started banging so hard, it felt like it was trying to claw its way past his ribcage. He gazed frantically around. There was nobody. No one to help or even report what was happening. He was about to die, and no one would even know. That is, not until they ran a scan on his locator, and discovered his mangled remains nestled inside the fifty-foot marine reptile's stomach.

Suddenly, the young scientist's lips curled defiantly back.

It's not going to be as easy as your aunt had it with my mom, you bitch!

Teeth clenched, he began taking deep breaths, readying himself. He had a plan; he was going to dive for it.

It was nuts, Dirk knew. He'd always been a champion swimmer, and could hold his breath longer than anyone, even Garm. But none of that made a difference. He had no illusions about outdistancing or hiding from his pursuer. The water might be murky, a few feet of visibility at most, but he knew that wouldn't matter. Even sans sonar, he would stand out to *Gretchen*'s superb underwater vision like a chartreuse fishing lure does to a Northern pike in a clear mountain lake.

His only chance was that the behemoth might be so well-fed already, she might be too lazy to submerge for another tidbit. He hoped so. Because he planned on swimming right under her.

As if recognizing his intent, *Gretchen* drew closer. Her eyes never leaving his, she lowered her monstrous jaws until her submerged muzzle was angled steeply downward, with only the immense mandibular muscles bulging from the rear of her skull still visible.

He realized then that the bitch was playing with him. She was waiting for him to dive, and would strike the moment he did.

With his plan thwarted, Dirk felt desperation take over. There was only twenty feet still separating them, and he was out of time. He could feel sheer animal stubbornness still trying to inspire him to look for an alternative means of escape, but in his heart of hearts, he knew he'd never find one.

Then he saw something. Something that sickened him.

Floating three feet away was a pale-gray patch of dead pliosaur skin. No surprise there; *Gretchen* shed constantly.

This piece was larger than the norm, however, about a yard across and, judging by the big, interlocking scales, had come from the crown of the creature's head. In fact, it was the exact region where the Y-shaped scar was – the result of the laser-made cranial incision, done during her implant surgery.

Despite the fear the saurian instilled as it floated barely fifteen feet away, Dirk's adrenalized mind sensed there was something strange about the scar, and he found himself reaching for the waterlogged piece of epidermis. Hoisting it clear of the water, he held it at arm's length and turned it to the light. As he did, *Gretchen* remained motionless, watching him intently with her jaws slightly agape.

Suddenly, Dirk's heart leapt into his throat and, as his eyes flitted to the pristine new scales atop the *Kronosaurus*'s head, he could swear she was smiling.

The "scar" was fake.

It had been painted on, using some sort of whitish adhesive. Probably silicone. Which meant that—

As *Gretchen* emitted a deep-throated rumble that shook his intestines and nearly caused him to defecate, Dirk realized the true depth of his predicament. The controller wasn't activating *Gretchen*'s implant because she didn't have one.

He was in the water with an unrestrained pliosaur.

Cold fear, accompanied by an unfettered sense of betrayal, took over, and Dirk's limbs lost the ability to move. He couldn't speak or swim, could barely kick to keep from sinking. A bizarre sense of calm came over him then, and he waited for the inevitable strike.

"Dirk? What the hell are--"

As he imagined hearing Stacy calling out to him, Dirk shook his head. Along with his life, he was losing his mind.

"*Gretchen,* <u>no</u>!"

There was a big splash and Dirk closed his eyes, waiting for the pliosaur's razor-sharp six-inch crowns to sink deeply into his body. With her jaw power, she would instantly sever his flesh and bones into bloody fragments. At least it would be quick.

Ah, there it was . . . He felt a sudden warmth around him, encircling his neck, his shoulders. Probably his blood, he reasoned. Curiously, there was no pain.

At least, not yet.

"Stay, *Gretchen*! I said STAY!"

His eyes twitched like he was experiencing REM sleep. He heard a voice.

"Dirk, open your eyes! Dirk!"

He cranked open his lids and stared dazedly at Stacy's face. She was in the water with him, one arm cradling his neck and keeping him afloat.

"What the hell are you doing?" she demanded. "What happened?"

He felt bewildered, unsure where he was. Was he dreaming? Were they in his quarters? Spotting *Gretchen* looming over Stacy's shoulder snapped him back.

"J-Jesus!" he sputtered. "Th-that <u>thing</u>! She--"

"Shh!" Stacy hushed. "Don't move. Do you hear me? Don't move an inch!"

Treading water, she turned back to the lurking *Kronosaurus* with a stern look on her face. "Bad girl, *Gretchen*! Bad!"

She waved one hand back and forth at the water's surface, as if slapping and then backhanding it. "No!" She turned back toward Dirk, one arm curled possessively around his neck, then glanced back at her monstrous ward. "Mine!" she yelled, then kissed Dirk on the temple. "Mine!"

As Dirk gaped in disbelief, *Gretchen* blinked, then uttered a snorty sigh of acquiescence and turned away, paddling resignedly toward the other end of the pool. Her back was turned, almost as if to give them privacy, and she remained there.

"Come on," Stacy said, half pushing and half shoving him toward the pool's reinforced lip. "It's time to go."

He went along in a daze, partly hoisting himself, and partly being hoisted, up out of the water, and onto the wet concrete. Soaked to the bone and in shock, he collapsed onto his back and lay there, staring wide-eyed up at the web-like network of lift girders.

Stacy propped herself up, her amber eyes overflowing with concern. "Are you okay?" she asked, inspecting him for possible injuries. "Did she bite you? I was changing and--"

Dirk sat up as if he'd been lying on a bed of nails. "What th-the fuck?" he stammered, then sprang unsteadily to his feet. His face contorted with fury and, trailing seawater, he staggered back, all the way to the chain-link fence. When he felt it strike his back, he wheeled on her.

"Are you *insane*?" he yelled. "That-that *thing*, she's not even implanted!"

"Keep your voice down," Stacy said disapprovingly, looking around to see if anyone was nearby.

"Keep my . . . is *this* what you've been doing all this time?" Dirk demanded, indicating the pool. "Y-you *never* performed her procedure, a-and you've been covering it up all this time?"

"Stacy stared at the floor. "I didn't want her to be affected. She's--"

"My God! You've been swimming with a wild pliosaur!" he exclaimed, his headshake so spasmodic it was painful. "You've been *playing* with it, *scratching* it like it was one of Grayson's dogs . . ." He paused to facepalm himself. "Jesus fucking Christ, you lay in its *mouth* with a raw *tuna*!"

Her jaw set, Stacy met his gaze. "Yes. And now you know they *can* be tamed. There *is* more to them than just mindless eating machines."

Dirk's hands reached up, clawing frenziedly at the air. He had an urge to grab her by the shoulder and shake some sense into her, but he knew better. "Stace, you mean the world to me, but you're out of your mind. You've been at this for *years*. She could've killed you a *hundred* times over. A _thousand_ times over!"

"But she *didn't*."

Dirk stopped talking and started taking slow, steadying breaths, trying to rein in his racing heart. Then he realized that, despite the danger she'd been in, Stacy was right. She'd had Gretchen all this time and had never had a problem with her. In fact, the two were practically inseparable. She could do virtually anything with her outsized pet – ride it like a horse, swim with it – hell, she'd just taken an easy meal away from the damn thing, and it had submitted to her and left, after being scolded like a child!

A child.

"That's right, Derek Braddock," Stacy said knowingly. Her beauteous face wore a haunted look as she faced him, hands on her hips. "She *is* a child. *My* child. Probably the only one I'll ever have."

"Now, what's *that* supposed to mean?"

"Never mind. What are you doing down here, anyway?"

"I . . . I was looking for you."

She gave him an inscrutable look. "Well, ya found me. What's up?"

Dirk wiped away some of the seawater from his face and ran his hands back through his hair. There was too much happening; he felt dizzy and lightheaded and had one hell of a headache coming on.

"I found a witness who saw my mother die."

Stacy's lips parted and her bronzed face flushed. "What? Who?"

It was his turn to ask her to lower her voice. "McHale, one of the guards. He was there watching from ground level. He saw the whole thing."

"Wait, he saw and did . . . *nothing*?"

"No," Dirk said bitterly. "In fact, I think he might've been responsible. Or at least involved."

Stacy drew in a breath, her jaw muscles knotting up as her familiar temper began to build. "Okay, where is that fucking cunt cake?"

"Gone. He went AWOL a few days ago, and as soon as they caught up with him they shipped him out."

"Where to?"

"We don't know."

Stacy looked at him like he was an idiot. "What do you mean, 'we don't know.' *Someone* has to know. This is a military-based corporation that does heavy R&D. There are *records*."

Dirk nodded. "Dr. Grayson will, undoubtedly. I told him, and he's pledged his help."

"Good."

"But I can't wait that long," he said. "I-I feel like I'm going to burst."

"But, he's back in a few days, right?"

"Too long for my tastes. I'm going to do a little investigating on my own."

Stacy arced an eyebrow. "Investigate how?"

"First, I'm going to my quarters to shower and change," Dirk said, half-grinning as he indicated his drenched outfit. "I stink like pliosaur piss. And maybe my own."

"Agreed. And then?"

"Then, I'm going back to my mother's private office." He glanced around and lowered his voice. "I found one mystery file stashed on her computer already. I have a feeling there may be more."

"Do you want me to go with you?"

Dirk thought it over, then shook his head. "No, it's better if you stay here." He indicated the nearby marine reptile. "I suspect you need to reapply *Gretchen*'s 'makeup.'"

Stacy smiled. "As a matter of fact, I do." Her eyes shone as she studied him. "Thank you," she said, leaning in and giving him a quick peck.

Dirk flushed, then indicated the fish scales, blood, and slime that coated a good ten-foot section of nearby concrete. "And clean up this mess, will you? Someone could fall and get hurt!"

Stacy's amber eyes danced with merriment. "You're the boss."

Dirk turned to leave, then looked back at her. "Am I?"

"As long as *Gretchen*'s not around," she said, winking.

Smirking, Dirk headed back toward the nearby lift, the sounds of Stacy wrestling with the overturned wheelbarrow fading behind him.

After a few steps, he realized he felt discombobulated, like his legs were trying to remember how to walk again. It wasn't surprising, considering how close he'd come to dying. It also wasn't funny; what would Garm say when he heard? He paused for a moment, hands on his hips, and took a breath, letting it out slowly before he started up again.

A minute later, Dirk shook his head and chuckled. Shit, working where he did, it was no wonder he hadn't feared Dwyer the other day. He faced horror every day. Actually, every *hour*. Hell, after what he'd just been through, he doubted he'd ever be scared of anything ever again.

Suddenly, a cool breeze wafted down from one of the overhead fans, boring into him, and he shivered. It would feel good to get out of his soaked clothes and rinse off. The ammonia in pliosaur urine was particularly pungent, and he definitely smelled.

Sniff, sniff. No, change that. He reeked, big time.

Dirk snickered. At least he'd been lucky and hadn't soiled himself.

An alarmed thought came to him, and he reached back and cupped the soggy seat of his trousers.

He hadn't, right?

━━━◆━━━

Dirk's "quick rinse" ended up being the Tartarus equivalent of a thirty-minute spa treatment. Staring death in the face had had a profound effect on the young scientist, and he'd spent the first ten minutes in the shower just standing there, allowing the massaging hot water jets to beat down upon his tension-filled frame.

After his muscles finally relaxed, came the scrubbing of a lifetime. Being immersed in seawater that, despite the filtration system, was laden with pliosaur dermal tissue, feces, saliva, and worse, required one hell of a cleanup. Dirk spent so much time working the loofah, his skin felt like he'd taken coarse-grit sandpaper to it. Eventually, after he'd gotten down to his "base layer", a final soaping, shampoo, and rinse, topped off with a comforting shave from his always-reliable thermal razor, enabled him to feel human again.

By the time he finally stepped out of the shower, pausing, per force, to admire his Bruce Lee-esque physique in the vanity mirror, he was close to his old self. He whistled merrily as he slipped into a luxurious bathrobe, then finished up what amounted to his regular morning routine by dabbing on some of the pricey cologne Stacy had given him for his-and-Garm's birthday. After that, it was clean slacks, a new pair of tennis shoes, and his favorite polo shirt; he felt like a new man.

Smiling now, Dirk pranced into the kitchen, snagged an ice-cold bottle of his favorite electrolyte-enhanced water from the fridge, and headed into his office with a well-oiled spring in his step.

He was halfway there when he stopped suddenly, drew in a breath, and took a moment to assess himself.

He needed to let it sink in that he was alive, that he'd survived a face-to-face encounter with history's deadliest predator, and with no technology to save him. He knew now that he could conquer anything. That included his pending trip to his mother's quarters, where he would soon find out if there was any other information that might point him in the direction of their missing security guard, or maybe a reason that McHale – or *anyone*, for that matter – would want to see Amara Braddock dead.

Cracking open his water, Dirk guzzled a third of it, then walked into his office to do a quick log-on. He figured an update on both *Gryphon* and *Antrodemus* was appropriate, before he headed to his mom's.

A quick palm-wave in front of the new monitor's sensor, coupled with his spoken password, and he was online. Still standing, his eyes fell on the wooden shelf that displayed his collection of giant predator teeth, and he hesitated. He reached out, an index finger running along the ridged edge of the seventeen-inch *Kronosaurus imperator* tooth his twin had brought him, a few months back. He stopped when he got to the huge fang's bone-shattering tip and pulled away, afraid of puncturing his skin.

An image of *Gretchen*'s still-formidable twelve-inch teeth, backed by thirty tons of pressure and ready to pierce him like alabaster Bowie knives, played in his mind, and he shuddered. There was no denying it; Stacy Daniels had literally saved his life. And it wasn't like what he'd done for her with *Tiamat*, back when they'd put on their show for the military.

His paramour's arrival had been unplanned. And if she *hadn't* been there . . .

Shaking it off, Dirk scanned his assorted screens for a general update. Per media broadcasts, the bloody fighting in Cuba continued, with no sign of abating. Tanks, planes, Humvees . . . there were even signs of offshore activity: a naval battle of some kind.

Disturbingly, some of the warships weren't far from Diablo Caldera.

Dirk stroked his chin as he pondered this unexpected development. His rebel contacts had assured him that his people would have uninterrupted access to the volcanic island for a full twenty-four hours. That was the deal. He imagined the rebel fleet taking up position nearby – ostensibly, to protect the visiting survey team – must have attracted the attention of the current regime. It made sense. Regardless, the fighting would continue until one side annihilated the other.

Such was the way of the world; humanity's never-ending willingness to trade innocent lives for money and power could always be counted on.

As far as *Antrodemus* was concerned, it appeared Dragunova's vessel was already in position. Regardless of their intent, the Cuban surface fleet posed no threat to the towering Russian and her crew. With the ORION-class submarine's advanced sonar-absorption capabilities and cloaking system, she could be right under their noses and they wouldn't know it. They had no means of locating her.

Dirk was about to check on *Gryphon*, when he noticed his cell phone resting beside his virtual keyboard. He realized that in his haste to find Stacy earlier, he'd forgotten it. He clocked the flashing blue light that indicated missed messages and scooped it up, slapping his thumbprint on it to open the device, and taking another draught of water at the same time.

He had messages, all right. They were from Dr. Grayson and marked urgent. When he keyed the missed messages, Dirk's heart sank into his stomach.

'*Derek, I just received word that* Antrodemus *is off-mission. In fact, her present location indicates she is at the caldera. Diablo Caldera. What in the world is going on? What have you done?*'

There was a second message, some fifty minutes after the first.

'*You're ignoring me? Derek, I cannot believe that you would go ahead and do something like this. You have no idea of the position you've put me in, or the problems you've caused. I am shocked and* very *disappointed in you.*'

His face a mask of confusion, Dirk tried typing a reply, but his fingers shook too much. He tried calling, but it went straight to voicemail.

He tried again. Same thing.

He shook his head, picturing his aged mentor, busy facing a hostile DOC oversight committee, and receiving this kind of news. The old man must've been stunned. Especially, if *Antrodemus's* location had somehow gone public.

Lord, he must be furious.

Dirk knew there was no point in repeatedly calling. The CEO's phone was obviously turned off, and he was leery of leaving a voicemail. He switched to voice texting instead.

"Doctor Grayson, I'm sorry I just got your messages, and for any miscommunication. We had a sudden and unexpected opportunity to send a survey team to investigate Diablo Caldera. I found out about it after you left, and automatically assumed that you would approve, as exploring the island has been one of our oft-stated long-term goals."

He clicked send and sat there fretting. A few minutes later, with no response, he continued.

"I did try to mention at our last meeting that there was the possibility of such an opportunity, but you seemed disinclined to discuss. And, I thought it would make a great surprise for you upon your return. Besides confirming that the caldera was the source point for our assorted new oceanic denizens, there may be any number of opportunities to be gained from its exploration, including our struggling pharma division."

He clicked send again and stood there pacing. After five more minutes and still no reply, he sat down at his desk, his fingers playing piano on its polished surface.

Something was wrong. If he was able to, Grayson always responded. This was out of character. He must be genuinely upset. Worse, he was hurt and disappointed.

Dirk exhaled heavily, as a wall of guilt began to build, right before his mind's eye. Brick by brick it grew, until it towered over him. He realized then that he'd gone too far. He'd adopted his brother's cavalier attitude when it came to procedures and authority, and overstepped himself in the process. Worse, he'd let down the person who, since Jake Braddock's death, had been like a father to him. The person who'd been there for him when his dad lay dying, and after.

Grayson had also been there when his mother was taken from him. He'd been a veritable rock for the young scientist, one that he could and would cling to, and had been his staunchest supporter in everything he'd done since.

Not only hadn't Dirk appreciated all of that, from a company perspective, he'd used up valuable resources, and, technically, without approval. God, for all he knew, he'd caused an international incident with Cuba, and the media just hadn't found out about it yet! He shook his head ruefully. God, the old man was right. He really *was* a disappointment.

Smarting from his perceived betrayal, Dirk licked his surprisingly crusty lips, then took a sip of water and sent a final text by hand, apologizing if he'd acted inappropriately. He hit send, finished his water, and tossed the bottle in a nearby wastebasket. Then he stood up, straightened his shirt, and grabbed his radio, phone, and ID badge.

It was time to investigate his mother's computer. He still had a few days before Grayson's scheduled return to Tartarus. Maybe he was overthinking things. Maybe it was all nothing and would blow over.

Maybe.

But, in the unlikely event that his actions did end up costing him his position, before that happened, and while he still had unlimited access, he planned on finding and saving any and all evidence even remotely related to his mother's death – everything he could get his hands on.

Checking his phone one last time, Dirk pursed his lips before shoving it in his pants pocket and rushing out the door. In the dark, on the big monitor behind him, *Gryphon*'s red transponder signal began to flash.

FIFTEEN

"There it is, waiting for us, captain," Commander Javier Gonzalez announced. He gestured at *Antrodemus*'s main viewer, his dour expression making his mahogany-colored face appear even darker. "La Boca del Infierno--"

"The Mouth of Hell," Natalya finished, rising lithely from her captain's chair.

Her gray eyes widened as she took in the sight. Surrounded by an outward-pointing field of razor-tipped obsidian spires, some big enough to puncture her submarine's hull, the eighty-foot lava tube opening that was the only navigable access into Diablo Caldera looked far from welcoming.

Far more worrisome than the black volcanic glass shards that hung from its roof, like the pharyngeal teeth in a leather-back's mouth, was the seawater directly outside the lightless opening. It violently swirled and bubbled, like a beaker of boiling acid.

"LOKI number one is fifty yards out, captain, and already reporting temperatures in excess of 260 degrees Fahrenheit," Ensign Meyers reported from her station. She touched a few keys and her eyes popped. "Wow. Uh, it appears the seawater inside the tube is not only superheated, it's pressurized. Initial scans indicate internal temperatures of over 600 degrees. That's near critical."

"Six hundred . . . shit, we're not going in *there*, are we?" Ensign Jackson muttered from the helm. "Cause if we are, I feel a sick day coming on!"

Natalya nodded at Meyers, then said aloud, "I weel determine who ees to be een landing party."

To her surprise, Jackson swiveled in her direction. "Captain, with all due respect, everyone knows how these things go down. You know I ain't no coward, and this ain't a black thing."

Natalya shot her a perplexed look.

Jackson took a breath. "Come on, you've seen how those TV shows work. People always die in these situations, *especially* when there's dinosaurs involved. I got kids. So, if you need a couple of red shirts, I'd just as soon pass."

Natalya glanced down to hide her grin. "Feedback noted, ensign." She turned to her first mate. "Commander Gonzalez, you're most familiar with the LOKI M22 stats. Can our decoys survive a test run eenside the tube?"

Gonzalez answered without hesitation. "Negative, captain. Temperatures exceeding four hundred degrees will disrupt most of the M22's systems. At six hundred we'll lose every seal, and the unit to boot."

Natalya sighed. Half the reason she'd stopped, a thousand yards from the caldera, was to send two of her DSROV's in for a peek. She'd hoped to at least partially explore the three-mile-long lava tube with a disposable decoy, before committing a landing party, aboard the *Remora*.

"Sonar, initiate active sonar interface on both M22's," she ordered, stepping forward and standing beside her second-in-command. "Tight beams and set acoustic projectors for maximum. Give me a detailed map of the tunnel, all the way een, and scan for possible geothermal activity, along weeth any loss of structural integrity."

"Yes, ma'am," Meyers replied, pushing a loose lock of dirty-blonde hair back behind one ear as she worked.

Gonzalez leaned in close to his captain and whispered. "You know, LOKI sonar is not ADCAP. If they're listening hard enough, those surface ships may just pick it up."

Natalya shook her head. "Nyet, emitters are too small. The noise generated by turbulence from the mouth weel disguise." She winked at him. "I checked."

Gonzalez gave her an admiring nod.

"Helm," Natalya said. "Status report."

"Yes, ma'am." Jackson sat posture perfect. "We're fifty feet from the bottom, suspended in just under four hundred feet of water."

"And the surface vessels?"

"The government ships are still keeping a respectable distance from the rebel fleet," she replied, checking her screens. "There's a good ten miles between the two groups. Those sonar buoys they dropped, however, have gone live and are making a helluva racket, and their Helix choppers are still circling the area. They're definitely hunting for something." She licked her lips and added. "I assume it's us . . ."

"Like Benny Hill said, don't assume any theeng," Natalya said wryly. "And eef they are, too bad. Sonar, how ees scan coming?"

"Just finished, ma'am," Meyers said, her incisors digging into her upper lip. "On the main?"

"Da. Communications, geev me split-screen."

From his station, Bart Bender touched a key and the main viewer divided in two. On the left, the lava tube's ominous opening continued to do the witch's cauldron thing. On the right, a convoluted network of glittering gold tunnels appeared. Sitting on a black background, they meshed like an oft-patched fishing net.

"Humph, well *that's* nice and confusing," Bender commented.

"Show best route," Natalya said, ignoring him.

A moment later, a red line overlaid the tunnel map, starting at the opening and extending inward. The selected route had a few twists and turns, but seemed fairly straightforward. As long as it was mapped, that is. Without it, the surrounding lava tubes could easily become a broiling maze of death.

Natalya turned to Gonzalez. "Well, what do you theenk?"

The big Cuban's lips compressed as he digested the tube's topography. "The *Remora* was designed to study black smokers, 10,000 feet down, where temps hit 750 degrees. She's up to the task, as long as you don't spend the night there." He stepped closer to the viewer, his dark eyes pinpointing key features. "Tunnel diameter and clearance look sufficient, and I don't see any regions that show signs of pending collapse."

He turned to her and shrugged. "As long as you don't go too fast and start careening off the walls, I'd say we're a go."

"Excellent." Natalya turned to Bender. "Communications, kindly tell Petty Officer Sato that he ees to prep *Remora* for a landing team."

"On it, captain," the red-haired Irishman said, reaching for his headset. "Standard gear and equipment?"

"Da. Plus, specimen stasis units in assorted sizes, bodycams, emergency rations, and full medical keet weeth surgical supplies."

Bender nodded, preparing to speak into his chin mike. He hesitated. "Arms and ammunition?"

Natalya's mind raced, as she imagined the fauna they might encounter in the forested portion of Diablo Caldera. If the *water* held marine reptiles, giant proto squid, and man-eating fish, what terrestrial horrors might they encounter?

"There ees arsenal in arms locker of *Remora*," she replied. "Issue full body armor to all landing party members, including ADCAP goggles, helmets, and sidearm of choice."

Gonzalez cleared his throat. "Who will the landing party consist of?"

Natalya considered her first officer's unspoken request. His eagerness was palpable, but it was impossible. She needed him there. "I weel lead the team," she announced. "PO Sato will accompany us. I don't want to have any mechanical problems and not have my electronics tech present."

Her lips compressed as she considered her remaining options. Crew-wise, she had limited resources, and she had to weigh the landing party's needs, versus the needs of her boat while she was away.

"Also, Lieutenant Archer," she said, pleased with her choice. Aboard an ORION-class submarine, an Independent Duty Corpsman was equivalent to a doctor. If a member of the landing team was injured, help might not be forthcoming. "He ees good weeth a gun, and has extensive knowledge of zoology."

Lieutenant Guerrero spoke up from Fire Control. "With your permission, I'd like to go too, ma'am. I minored in botany in college, and--"

"Nyet," Natalya said, "We are steel under battle stations. I need you and Gonzalez here, onboard *Antrodemus*, een case something goes wrong."

"Oh. Uh, yes, ma'am."

"You still need one more," Gonzalez advised. He was undoubtedly disappointed, but too disciplined and professional to show it.

Hmm . . ."

Natalya sauntered around the bridge, eyeing her remaining primaries. She was surprised. She had expected them to be climbing over one another for the chance to visit a real-life "*Jurassic World*". They hadn't. Instead, she felt like a high school calculus teacher, posing a murderous equation to a fear-filled classroom, and deciding which "volunteer" she would choose.

They were smarter than she thought.

Natalya's eyes twinkled with amusement, as Ensign Meyers managed to avoid her gaze by faking a sneeze. Jackson was a bit subtler, immersing herself in calculations for the power consumption coils of their maneuvering thrusters.

Only Ensign Bender could look her in the eye. Or would have, if he hadn't been ogling her breasts.

"Okay, Bender . . ." she drawled, "You're weeth me."

"Yes! I knew that--" The communications officer's excitement vanished as one hand leapt to his earpiece.

"Something wrong, ensign?"

"Yes, captain. We're getting a text message on the secure digital acoustic link. It's from Tartarus."

"What ees it?"

"Our mandate has been temporarily suspended, and any previous orders countermanded, effective immediate. We are ordered to abandon our mission and return to base, ASAP."

"Who ees order from?"

"Eric Grayson, CEO."

Natalya's eyes hardened as her primaries uttered a collective gasp.

Bender swallowed nervously. "Shall I acknowledge?"

"Nyet." Natalya wore a deadpan expression as she cricked her neck to one side. "Photonics assembly repairs are not yet complete. We weel complete our meeshun before acknowledging orders."

To his credit, Bender simply nodded. "Yes, captain."

She surveyed the remainder of her bridge crew, gauging their reactions to this development. She wondered if it would be wise to give them a quick pep talk before--

"Captain, I'm getting major chatter from the rebel fleet!" Bender cut in. His eyes were bugged out as he listened. "Good thing Spanish is one of the six languages I speak!"

"And . . ."

"They've got incoming!"

Natalya's body tensed as she spun towards sonar. "Ensign?"

"I've got multiple bogeys, inbound at high speed," Meyers advised, her headset donned and hazel eyes locked onto her screens. "The rebel destroyers and their missile frigate are taking evasive action . . . their anti-missile systems are arming!"

"Helm, emergency rise, bring us to periscope depth!" Natalya barked.

Taking a step sideways, she peered over the back of Jackson's chair, watching the depth gauge as the former Brooklynite worked the yoke. With surprising silence, *Antrodemus*'s 440 tons rose smoothly upward, her shark-like sail slicing through the 200+ feet of seawater that stood between her and a detailed view of the surface.

"Six seconds to periscope depth, captain," Jackson advised.

"Communications, prepare to extend photonics mast," Natalya instructed. She felt the pressure in her lower abdomen build, then lessen, as they hurtled upward and then slowed.

"Prepped and ready, captain."

"Extend photonics mast; show me the rebel fleet."

"Yes, ma'am." Bender's freckled fingers danced across his keypad. There was that familiar hum, as the photonics array extended, coupled with a slight shiver as *Antrodemus* came to a full stop, hovering thirty feet below the surface.

"On the main, captain," Bender said.

The submarine's clear titanium bow, darkened with their ceramic-composite shield lowered, shimmered as images coalesced across its sleek surface. In an instant, they could see clear blue skies and glittering ocean. The view was spectacular and extended all the way to the horizon. But there were no ships.

Natalya exhaled irritably. "Geev me satellite overview of the battlefield, quickly!"

"You got it," Bender said, pressing a few keys. "Linking . . . uh . . ."

"Uh?"

The comms tech looked bewildered. "Th-there's something wrong, captain," he said. He tapped a key, then tapped it several more times, harder. His freckly face scrunched up. "I can't get satellite linkup."

"Why not?"

"I don't know; it's like we've been shut out!" He jabbed the key in an adversarial manner, then turned to her. "Could someone at Tartarus have done this? I mean, the message did say our mandate was suspended . . ."

Natalya uttered a growl of irritation. "Stupid mudak! Ees he trying to blind us?" She waved a dismissive hand. "Use optical zoom. Get me as close to action as possible."

"Complying."

At the turn of a dial, their view rose and flew forward at a ridiculously high speed. The rapidly-enlarging images made it seem as if they were riding a cruise missile into battle. In the distance, they could just make out what was, presumably, the rebel fleet: a small group of destroyers, a large guided missile frigate, and numerous support ships. The fleet had broken formation and was scattering at flank speed.

"Can you get closer?" Natalya asked.

"Sorry, captain. We're at max zoom."

Meyers stiffened. "I'm detecting a lot of military ordnance, ma'am. The ships' Phalanx systems and anti-missile batteries are all firing!"

Natalya sprang out of her seat and, with Gonzalez following, made her way past the helm, moving closer to the main. She spotted a series of bright flashes coming from the rebel ships – children's sparklers, at this distance – as their defensive weapons went live.

Suddenly, two of the destroyers shuddered, nearly keeling over as their sturdy frames were rocked by powerful explosions. On *Antrodemus*'s bridge, the sounds registered as dull thumps. Thrown high by the shockwaves, huge fireballs, combined with ship and body parts, plumed into the air.

A split-second later, the choking smokescreen that formed was parted by two jet fighters, zipping overhead at incredible speed. In their wake, the third destroyer literally blew apart, shattered amidships by a single detonation that cut the streamlined warship in two, and left its flaming halves wallowing in the whitecaps. The bow and stern portions bobbed on the surface, the surviving seamen that still clung to them leaping frantically into the sea, as the fires that all but covered their dying vessel's decks raged out of control.

"What the hell were *those*?" Natalya pointed at the blurred images on their viewer. "Those are *not* Cuban fighters!"

"Not traveling at Mach 5 they weren't, ma'am," Meyers replied. "Designate: F-60's. They're . . . American?"

Mere specks in the distance now, the twin jets spiraled lazily in the sun, before pinwheeling back. They leveled off as they prepared for another attack run.

Natalya wheeled on her. "Are you saying those are American planes?"

"I-I don't know," Meyers admitted, the incredulity on her face giving way to confusion. "They're not wearing any insignia, and I'm not getting a call sign or transponder code from either!"

Bender cleared his throat. "Should I make contact?" he asked, his hand cupping his earpiece.

"Nyet!"

Natalya's steely eyes narrowed as the guided missile frigate *Hemingway*, her name now visible as she chugged toward them, weapons blazing, was bludgeoned by rapid-sequence missile fire. One, two, three . . . at least four advanced cruise missiles slammed into her armored superstructure like high-speed dominoes, each explosion gaining power from its predecessor. The combined flash on *Antrodemus*'s viewer was blinding, the destruction all-encompassing. In an instant, the aged 440-foot frigate – in her day, a state-of-the-art warship – was annihilated.

Her ruined hull a series of fifty-foot, blackened craters, from which smoke and flames spewed, and seawater rushed in unchecked, the flagship of the rebel fleet flopped over onto her side and sank in seconds. To Natalya's astonishment, as she studied the burning debris field surrounding *Hemingway*'s final resting place, she saw no life rafts; there were no arms waving, no brightly-colored lifejackets bobbing up and down.

The frigate had gone down with all hands.

Her mind raced. Had the world gone *bezumnyy*? Could Grayson have done this: clandestinely send American planes to attack the Cuban fleet? He, or someone, had obviously found out where GDT's missing submarine was; their transponder alone made it easy to ascertain their location, but it still made no sense.

Grayson was arrogant, but he was a cautious, calculating man, and the potential risk involved was too great. Plus, why decimate the rebels, who were actually helping them? Had the fighters targeted the wrong ships, or was this someone new altogether? Could the Cuban government have brokered a deal to acquire some of the best warplanes in the world?

That was a distinct possibility. If it *was* a recent purchase, that would at least explain the lack of markings.

Ensign Jackson spoke up. "Captain, I'm getting increased activity from the government destroyers and choppers. They're continuing to steer clear of the battle and increasing their sonar sweeps. If they continue on their anticipated course, they will be over our current position in approximately twenty minutes."

"And the fighters?"

Meyers said, "It, uh, looks like they've settled into a holding pattern, fifteen miles out."

Natalya inhaled through her teeth. The Cubans might have fancy planes, but they'd never hunted an ORION-class anti-biologic submarine before. They were in for a surprise.

"Communications, retract photonics mast. Helm, take us to the bottom and prepare to initiate cloak."

His brow beetling, Gonzalez's head swiveled from the main toward his captain. "Are we proceeding with the mission?"

"As you like to say, you bet your sweet ass we are," Natalya said, her angry eyes miniature storm clouds. "There ees nothing een thees universe that weel stop me from getting eenside that fucking island now." She threw him a grin and added. "Please excuse my language."

Gonzalez's amused chuckle was waylaid by Bender's alarmed cry.

"Captain, I'm getting an SOS from another CDF vessel!"

"What vessel, ensign?"

"It's the *Gryphon*, ma'am."

Wolfie? Natalya straightened. "What ees message?"

Bender shook his head. "There's no message. It's an auto-mated distress call . . . a beacon."

"Send hail to them on secure acoustic link," she replied, reaching her captain's chair in three quick strides and situating herself. "Find out situation."

This is odd, she thought. Could their sister ship have found *Typhon* so quickly? She doubted it. And even if they had, Garm was a superb tactician; she refused to believe he'd gotten him-self into a situation. Then again, the big galoot was not only as strong as a yak, he was as headstrong and stubborn as one.

Bender's head pulled back on his shoulders and he blinked. "I don't believe this. I-I can't get through."

"Why not?"

"I don't know. It's like the link is being blocked, somehow."

Although, outwardly, she forced herself to appear calm, Natalya's fists were balled so tightly her nails were embedded in her palms. Her gut told her something was seriously amiss. Pieces on her chessboard were making dramatic moves – pieces she wasn't even aware of. And she had no idea who her oppo-nent was.

Someone was looking to isolate her and her crew. To cut off their communication lines and resources. Why, she didn't know. But she did know things that most people didn't.

"Communications, send to *Gryphon* typed acoustic link com-mand I-C-U-W-U-L-F-Y, authorization: Dragunova, Natalya," she said, licking her lips.

Bender looked at her as if she had two heads. "What is that?"

"Just do eet."

Her befuddled communications officer tapped in the coded message, then gave an expectant shrug when nothing happened. A moment later, however, his jaw dropped.

"Holy shit!" he exclaimed. "That just got us remote access to the security camera inside their bridge, and the external one, atop the sail. How the hell did you do or even *know* that?"

Natalya grinned hugely. "Ees what happens when engineer who designed submarine tries to eempress woman by opening beeg mouth," she replied. Then she turned to Lieutenant Guerrero, winked and whispered, "Man's mouth ees better for *other* theengs."

Her good mood disintegrated, as a view of *Gryphon*'s bridge suddenly filled their main. The camera was situated directly above and behind Garm Braddock's captain's chair, and she could see his head and shoulders as the image shifted.

Then the sound kicked in. And chaos with it.

The submarine was in trouble. A collision claxon was blasting, and their combat lights were on. Everyone on the bridge was clinging to their stations, as they fought to do their jobs, and, from the seesawing motion of the bow, the boat appeared to be wobbling from port to starboard, and then back again.

No. Not wobbling. It was being pulled, or rather, *heaved*.

Slapped across their bow viewer lay a gigantic tentacle. It was blackish-brown in color and huge, at least five feet in diameter, and lined with suction cups the size of car tires. Natalya gasped despite herself, watching in disbelief as the arm slimed its way offscreen, only to be replaced by another, that slid into its place like some Brobdingnagian sea snake.

It was unbelievable. *Gryphon* was under attack by some kind of immense squid or octopus; the biggest there ever was, from the look of things. The sub was prow-down and, judging by the ever-increasing darkness that hurtled past their viewer, being dragged bow-first into the abyss.

If she couldn't break free she was doomed.

And there was nothing *Antrodemus* could do to help.

———

"Communications, damage report!" Garm bellowed. Strapped into his chair like the rest of the bridge crew was, it was all he could do to hold on, as *Gryphon* alternated being shaken and rolled from side to side.

On the main viewer was a whitish wall of tentacles that moved and swirled like a den of angry serpents. Garm's teeth ached from clenching so hard. Despite the direness of their situation, he had to give the mother octopus a grudging nod of admiration. She had pulled off a cunning sleight of hand on her human adversaries, severing her damaged tentacle like she had, and leaving it protruding from a cloud of ink, to distract them.

It was a masterful ambush. And now that she had the upper hand, she was dragging them on a nightmarish Nantucket sleigh ride into the forever blackness of the deep, stopping every so often to take out her frustrations on her hard-shelled opponent.

"Ensign . . ."

"Working on it, captain!" Ensign Heather Rush yelled.

Shielding his eyes against the bridge's glaring combat lights, Garm's gaze flitted to a nearby wall claxon. It had been shrieking a collision alarm ever since their impact with the wreck of U-420. Combined with the incessant pinging from *Gryphon's* sonar systems, every one of which had gone haywire, the piercing noise added to the non-stop barrage of stimuli he was dealing with.

His face contorted angrily. "Silence that racket!" he yelled.

Whump! His teeth gritted as *Gryphon* was dealt another vicious blow. This one came from starboard.

"Jesus, she's all over us!" Ramirez cried out.

"Stay frosty," Garm ordered. "This boat's got twelve inches of ceramic-steel laminate in her outer hull, backed by another foot of the finest titanium-steel on the inner; we'll be fine."

He turned back toward Rush, hoping he sounded more confident than he felt. "Communications, where's my report?"

"Got it, sir!" she said, obviously frazzled, but doing her best to remain calm. "The impact on the U-boat did serious damage, sir. Our starboard-side outer hull has been compromised over an area nearly sixty feet across, including the starboard torpedo bay," she paused, double-checking her readings. "Pressure hull number two has failed and that area is flooding rapidly. So far, we've lost ballast tanks two and six, and torpedo tube number four is non-operational. The loss of ballast is also throwing off our trim, and we've lost 23% reserve buoyancy."

Garm's face darkened. At least they hadn't hit head-on. Is they had, they'd have lost their bow-mounted OMNI ADCAP sonar dome, the REAPER . . . maybe even flooded the bridge. "Helm, adjust buoyancy to compensate; what's our status?"

"She's got us by the nose and is . . . ugh, dragging us down at a steep angle!" Ho said, grappling with the controls. "I am . . . unable to give precise calculations. I'm trying to compensate for the downward pull, but each time I bring the nose up, she . . . spins us and starts taking us down again!"

His tenacious helmswoman was right about that. Another corkscrew like the last one, and Garm was worried his lunch would come back up.

"What's our depth?"

"Fourteen-hundred feet and dropping!" Ho replied. She grimaced as *Gryphon* torqued to port and twisted the wheel hard in the opposite direction, then hit a pair of keys to fire their portside thrusters. Her face was damp with sweat. "We've entered the Straits of Florida; max depth is over 6,000 feet!"

Garm's brow tightened. Ho knew as well as he did that six thousand feet was also their crush depth, although, with the damage they'd already sustained, he was betting they wouldn't survive two-thirds that. Their side and rear viewers were useless – obscured by tentacles – and he was forced to rely on POSEIDON's fathometer 3D hologram to see what was going on, namely gauging his enemy's position on their hull. Its spike-covered, sack-shaped head was underneath them now, and it appeared to be gnawing on *Gryphon*'s armored belly, probing for a weak spot.

Garm remembered watching a video of an octopus opening a water-filled mason jar to get at a tasty crab inside. Now he knew how the crab felt.

"Helm, on my command, fifteen up bubble and ahead flank," he ordered. "Fire control, LADON's status?"

"We've got 1,246 shells remaining, sir," Cunningham replied eagerly.

"Then make 'em count. Stand ready." He eyed the fathometer and felt *Gryphon* shudder as the giant cephalopod slithered up along their portside. It was creeping up . . . up . . . "Fire control, go live! Helm, up now!"

BRRRRRRRRRRRRT! BRRRRRRRRRRRRT!

There was the usual thrum of LADON's eight-barreled Gatling cannon unleashing hell on their adversary, coupled with the sudden increase in inertia as the submarine's engines kicked in hard. He could feel all eight of *Gryphon*'s Mako M69 propulsors fighting to propel them toward the surface. The bridge began to vibrate as they were buffeted by far more than the usual water resistance.

"Scored two partial hits, captain!" Cunningham yelled. His face was flushed with a combination of excitement and fear, and he gripped his joystick so tightly his knuckles were white.

"We're . . . pulling up, sir!" Ho announced, her teeth bared as she hauled back on the yoke so hard, it seemed like she might tear it from its foundation.

Garm could feel *Gryphon* leveling off, the floor under his feet straightening and then angling upward. He eyed the fathometer, watching as the infuriated octopus, its tentacular spread wider than the ORION-class sub was long, hid underneath them, away from LADON's withering field of fire.

Suddenly, the beast sprang upward, latching onto their portside torpedo nacelle with all of its tentacles. He had a bad feeling about what came next.

He was right.

An instant later, the cephalopod executed a mighty yank, its steely sinews backed by a powerful jet of water from its siphon. Garm didn't have to watch the image to know what was happening. He could feel it through the soles of his feet.

There was a painfully loud groan, and *Gryphon* began to swivel sideways. His primaries cried out in alarm, and loose items rolled and slid along the bridge's rubberized deck.

Garm checked his vessel's status and uttered a vile curse. Their upward angle had not only been countered, they were now pointed almost straight down, with only their harnesses keeping them in their seats. Worse, their increased momentum had them hurtling toward the bottom at a good thirty knots.

"Helm, back full!"

He heard a sudden clanging, and on POSEIDON saw the octopus oozing up their portside flank. It was headed for the sail.

Now was their chance.

"Kyle, blow that bitch away!" he roared. "Helm, level us off!"

BRRRRRRRRRRRT!

Cunningham didn't hesitate. He opened up on the encroaching mollusk with everything he had.

BRRRRR—

Then, LADON's lethal stream of 30mm shells inexplicably stopped.

Still suspended, with his harness digging into his chest, Garm turned his head until his neck hurt, in an effort to see whether they'd run out of ammo. His words were drowned out by a series of painfully loud rending sounds, penetrating even *Gryphon*'s soundproof acoustic cladding, and the entire submarine rotated on its axis.

A moment later, the racket stopped.

Cunningham's eyes were the size of ostrich eggs, and his jaw hung so far down, he could've swallowed one. "Jesus fucking Christ!"

"What is it?" Garm demanded. Around them, *Gryphon* leveled out a bit, but she was still going down fast.

"We-we've lost LADON, sir!" Cunningham announced, his leaden tone a byproduct of his disbelief. "It's been ripped right off the sail! It's . . . gone!"

Rush cleared her throat. "Confirmed, sir. Photonics assembly has also been destroyed, and we've suffered critical damage to the sail. Major flooding in--"

"Seal off the affected area," Garm said, the combination of stress and shock weighing on him.

He glanced at the fathometer image and shook his head. They were right. The armored turret had been savaged, then twisted off like a bottle cap. The whole sail was flooded and lost, along with its pressure hull and accompanying ballast tank.

They were in deep shit. With their enemy literally on top of them, LADON had been their best – their *only* – offensive weaponry. They couldn't use torpedoes (that would be suicide), and, for all its power, the REAPER had proven only marginally effective. It couldn't target something behind them, and the octopus, after taking a glancing hit that had disintegrated one of its arms, seemed disinclined to approach the bow again.

"Captain!" Ensign Ho cried out. "I'm getting indicator lights showing outer hull breaches! They're . . . all over the place!"

"How?"

"The, uh, Kraken seems to have something in its suckers, some sort of corrosive agent, like a molecular acid . . ." Her dark eyes widened as she checked her readings. "It's dissolved most of our iridophores and now it's eating through the outer hull!"

Great . . . what else can go wrong?

"Helm, what's our current depth?"

"Passing 3,000 feet, sir!"

"How much time do we have?" Garm pressed. "And don't sugarcoat it."

Ho ran slim fingers over a touchpad, crunching numbers, then bit down on her lower lip. "Assuming it doesn't compromise the inner hull, crush depth is now estimated at just under 4,200 feet, sir."

That's it. Enough of this shit!

Garm gripped his armrests so tightly, his forearm muscles flexed like steel cables. "Emergency blow, ensign!" he shouted.

"Use all air flask reserves and fill all ballast tanks, including trim and auxiliary!"

"Auxiliary, sir?"

"You heard me, do it now!"

As Ho made the necessary preparations, Garm prepared for the worst. At this point, an emergency rise was their only option. By pumping every bit of air on the submarine under high pressure into their surviving ballast tanks, they *might* have enough buoyant force to offset the power of the octopus's organic version of jet propulsion.

The downside was, that much ballast would require even the air they breathed. If the risky maneuver failed, and if they were unable to regain the surface, they'd be left with only whatever ambient oxygen remained. Their O2 generator had been located within the sail and was lost with LADON.

Garm shrugged. It didn't matter. At their current rate of descent, if they didn't break free, they'd all be dead long before they began to suffocate.

"Initiating emergency rise, captain!" Ho shouted. She threw the switch.

"Show me some sky, ensign."

There was a tremendous gurgling noise as *Gryphon* shed her ballast. A second later, the 435-ton warship's reinforced frame emitted an eerie moan, as Ho adjusted their trim and aimed for the stars.

"Full power to the propulsors!" Garm yelled. He could feel a tug-of-war begin as the octopus, suddenly finding itself grappling with a significantly more buoyant opponent, pitted its tremendous strength against the ORION-class's combined horsepower.

"We've leveled off!" Ho shouted, pulling down on the yoke. "Transferring power to ventral thrusters in the bow to increase lift!"

The submarine, not intended to act like a giant tugboat, began to shake, the vibration traveling back and forth along its length. Still in his chair, Garm had to clamp his jaw shut to keep his teeth from chattering.

He glanced forward and saw the blackness outside changing to a field of azure. "You're doing it!" he exclaimed. "What's our depth?"

"2,100 feet!" Despite the sweat dripping down her chin, Ho smiled. "I think we--"

Waaa-crunnnnchhh!

"Son of a bitch!" Garm bellowed. Incredibly, their gargantuan opponent – refusing to allow the creature that murdered its brood to escape – had thrown caution to the wind and pounced on *Gryphon*'s bow. He could see the underside of its enormous body; the central hub where the giant tentacles merged in a deadly pinwheel of acid-oozing suckers.

In the center of those amorphous spokes lay a huge, black beak, big enough to cut a horse in two, that snapped and gnawed at their composite shield. An ear-splitting grating noise assailed everyone's ears, followed by a series of thrashing and crashing sounds as the maddened beast mauled their prow.

"She's tearing up the nose, disabling our bow thrusters!" Ho shrieked. "She must've felt where the push was coming from!"

"Screw that, she's right where we need her," Garm spat. "CSO, charge REAPER!"

"Yes, sir!"

There was another, otherworldly groan, and the bow began to dip again.

Her toned arms shaking from the effort, Ho hissed in exasperation. "Captain, she's pulling us down again! I . . . I can't hold her!"

Cunningham called out. "REAPER at 46%, sir. Estimate--"

Bwaah! Bwaah! Bwaah!

Garm cocked his head to the side, trying to ID the unfamiliar alarm. "Communications, what is that?"

Rush checked her screens, then covered her mouth with her hand. "Oh, God . . ."

"Rush, what is it?"

"Y-you have to shut it down!" she said, indicating a flashing warning sign on one of her monitors. "The barrel's been warped by its attack. If you fire we'll--"

What the hell?

"Kyle, shut it down!" Garm roared, unable to believe their misfortune.

"Yes, sir. Initiating thermal dampeners," Cunningham complied. He looked pale and haggard, and started licking his lips the way he did when he was extremely nervous.

With the deck only slightly inclined, Garm took a chance and unclipped his cross-harness. He leaned forward in his seat, his mind reeling. For the first time in his life, he couldn't figure out how to fight back. LADON was gone, the REAPER disabled, and they were unable to break free from their cold-blooded adversary's deadly embrace.

For the life of him, he didn't know what to do. And the lives of everyone on *Gryphon* hung in the balance.

A sudden, staticky sound drew Garm's eye, and he watched as POSEIDON's 3D hologram started to break down, like virtual building blocks crumbling. Soon, whole sections were missing, like lost pieces of a jigsaw puzzle, and he knew it was just a matter of time before the entire thing went dead.

"Captain," Rush hesitated. "The creature has disabled almost half of our wide-aperture sonar arrays. Also, pressure hull number three is compromised and we've got flooding in ballast tanks four and seven. Reserve buoyancy is now down to 47%."

As if the monster had heard her, *Gryphon*'s down-angle suddenly increased, and she began to descend again. A loud metallic rumble rippled through the bulkheads on either side and Garm's heart sank. He knew a death knell when he heard it.

"I-I'm sorry, captain," Ho said, her heart-shaped face pale and drawn. "We've lost too much buoyancy and can't generate enough thrust. Unless we can break free I . . . I can't bring us back up."

"All back full," Garm said, then added on a heavy exhale. "Buy us as much time as you can."

"Yes, sir."

He heard a deep, burbling sound outside – a grunt of annoyance, from the sound of it – as the frustrated octopus realized its battered opponent was still putting up a fight. He looked around the bridge, studying the fearful faces of his tough-as-nails primaries; men and women who looked up to him and depended on him. And now . . . He leaned forward, eyes narrowed and lips pressed against his interlocked hands as reality sank in. He knew his boat's buoyancy numbers like he knew his own social, knew what they meant.

His iron mistress was doomed.

Sixteen

Gryphon was finished.

There was no escaping it. And it was all his fault.

Garm shook his head in disbelief and dismay. A master tactician and a former heavyweight contender, and he'd been outsmarted by a mollusk, of all things! Worse, his poor crew was going to pay the ultimate price for his cock of the walk demeanor.

Of course, the complete and utter irony was impossible to ignore. He'd always planned on going out with his boots on – slugging it out with a worthy opponent – he just never figured it would be the Kraken of myth and legend.

The Kraken . . .

As his vessel shook from yet another brutal savaging, Garm's mind wandered to the framed antique parchment inking of *The Kraken*, by Lord Alfred Tennyson, that he had hanging in his quarters. Maybe Dirk would want it . . .

His head popped up, and he saw Rush and Ramirez looking over at him with scared-yet-hopeful eyes. He had to do something, perform some rabbit-out-of-a-hat miracle or . . . he shook his head, then swallowed hard and sat upright, bracing his booted feet against the sloped deck.

"Communications, get me Tartarus on a secure line."

"Yes, captain," Rush said, her pale hands trembling as she made the connection. Her shoulders tightened a moment later. "I can't, sir."

"The acoustic link's disabled?"

"No, sir. I'm not getting anything from Tartarus. It's like they've gone dark."

Garm's eyebrows rose. "Are you certain?"

The willowy blonde nodded. "Positive, sir. I don't understand it, it's like they're not transmitting."

"Fine. Patch me through to *Antrodemus*."

Ensign Ho sang out, "Captain, depth is 2,900 feet. I'm slowing us as best I can. She's damaged both bow planes, so steering is compromised, but I'm switching up the propulsors every chance I get, working the angles to offset the pull and push us toward the surface."

"Is it working?" Garm asked.

"Not really, but it's pissing her off," she said, grinning.

He felt the deck move and made a quick lunge for his armrests, just before the sub torqued savagely to port. He grinned back at her. "I think you're right."

"Captain," Rush turned to him with downcast eyes. "I'm sorry; I can't get through to *Antrodemus*."

"Is it their photonics mast?"

"I don't think so, sir. It's like our transmission is being . . . blocked?"

"Mother--" Garm reined in his temper. *What the hell?* It was like the whole world was against him, instead of just a giant octopus. He chuckled maniacally as he once again tried and failed to come up with a solution.

Killed by a Kraken. Tennyson would be impressed. Tennyson . . .

Garm's embattled mind started running through the Poet Laureate's timeless classic. He'd read it so many times while lying in bed, he knew it by heart. The last few lines swam through his head.

There hath he lain for ages, and will lie,
Battening upon huge sea worms in his sleep,
Until the latter fire shall heat the deep;
Then once by man and angels to be seen,
In roaring he shall rise and on the surface die.

Suddenly, it hit him like an uppercut to the chin, and his big head lurched back atop his shoulders. He knew what he had to do.

"Okay, you punk-ass bitch, you wanna dance?" he sneered. "Let's dance."

Ramirez regarded him with nervous eyes. "Captain?"

"Relax, I'm fine," Garm said, stepping forward onto the sloped deck. "Helm, what's our depth?"

"3,300 feet, sir." Ho replied. She gave him a curious look. "You look like you're up to something."

"I am," Garm affirmed. "Is our labium still functioning?"

"Our . . ." Ho shot Ramirez a side-smirk as she swept her finger down one screen, checking her readings. "Yes, sir. She, I mean *it* appears to be."

"Transfer power to it, and program settings for emergency defensive."

The petite helmswoman threw him a briefly bemused look, but then her expression changed and he saw the cage fighter in her regain her feet. "Yes, sir. I like the way you think."

"Tell me when you're ready."

Cunningham spoke up, "Captain, maybe if we--"

"Forget it, Kyle. You've done all you could. It's time to go."

The CSO wore a flabbergasted look. "Go? I don't--"

He stopped talking as Garm moved back to his chair and hit the emergency shipwide. "This is the captain. *Gryphon* is finished; we're in a dive we're not coming out of. It's been an honor being your captain. Please make your way to the nearest escape pod and abandon ship. I repeat, abandon ship."

Garm released the button, envisioning the absolute panic he'd just caused. Not that the remainder of his crew weren't already terror-stricken from being belted in all this time, while their vessel was being systematically dismantled all around them.

He looked around and saw Ramirez, Rush, and Cunningham all staring at him, slack-jawed. He could tell from the dread in their eyes that every one of them wanted to rush out the bridge's armored door, but their fierce loyalty to him kept them in their seats.

Only Ho appeared calm and collected and ready to fight.

"Captain," Rush said quietly. "The board is, uh, indicating several of the escape pods suffered mechanical errors. It's possible, with all the damage we've sustained, that many of them are nonfunctional."

Garm nodded, then turned toward an expectant Ensign Ho.

"Labium is ready to deploy, sir." she said with a grim smirk.

He looked at what remained of their 3D fathometer screen, then chuckled. Screw sonar; one glance at what clung to their bow was all he needed. But just to make sure . . .

"Negative shield, ensign."

Ho did the Vulcan eyebrow thing. "Are you sure, sir?"

"Oh, I'm sure . . . I want to look this fucker in the eye."

She nodded knowingly. "Yes, sir. Raising shield."

The deep hum of their foot-thick ceramic shield was accompanied by a series of startled inhalations from the remainder of his primaries. Foot by foot, the nearly indestructible barrier rumbled upward, like a knight's visor raising, leaving only their twenty-foot bow window between them and the unforgiving sea.

And a far-less-forgiving sea monster.

Drawn to the shield's movement as it arced up over the prow, the behemoth spotted the light emanating from the bridge and moved to investigate.

Rush's whimpered, "Oh, God!" as she spotted the octopus barely registered. Garm had already laid eyes on his cold-blooded adversary. And what eyes they were – swirling yellow firebrands that gleamed with undisguised hatred.

From less than ten feet away, the *Octopus giganteus* loomed over what must have appeared as a group of defenseless bipeds, ripe for the picking. Its gnarled body trembled with rage and it swelled like a water balloon. A moment later, it threw itself at *Gryphon*'s crew, its four-foot beak impacted like a pile driver on the clear titanium barrier, snapping and slashing along its smooth surface.

"It's going to get in!" Rush cried out.

Garm calmed her with a staying hand, then stepped forward, grasping the backs of Ramirez and Ho's chairs for support.

"Madam Kraken, at last," he said, his voice so menacing it sent chills down everyone's spines. The colossal cephalopod, realizing its razor-edged mouthparts could not reach its soon-to-be-victims, and unable to gain any purchase on the slick metal, ceased its assault. It crept closer, one of its window-sized eyes zeroing Garm's face, and it studied the focal point of its enmity.

He smiled up at it, then muttered to Ho through his teeth. "Ready, ensign?"

"Yes, captain."

"Full speed, maximum power and penetration," he said, grinning and nodding at the maddened beast, as if it were an old acquaintance he'd just run into on the street. "We've got one shot; make sure you're going center mass."

"Just say the word, sir."

He pointed his hand at the octopus like it was an imaginary pistol, and clicked his tongue as he pretended to pull the trigger. "Now."

Boom.

As *Gryphon*'s labium fired, what felt like an explosion under everyone's feet made the deck jump. Designed for manipulating captured 100+ ton pliosaurs, the forty-foot mechanical arm, terminating in powerful pincers, and backed by the strongest actuators on the planet, had the power to pull a bank vault door off its hinges.

In emergencies, it could also be used defensively.

Garm was pretty confident this qualified.

Lashing up and out like an inverted scorpion's tail, the robotic claw slammed into the giant cephalopod's exposed underside with the speed and power of a runaway freight train and dug in.

"Direct hit!" Ho exulted. "Pincers embedded!"

The octopus, sensing the twenty-foot metal talons that had buried themselves in its flesh, went mad. With its body flailing and twisting like some titanic cat-o-nine-tails, its tentacles slammed over and over again against the bow and forward nacelles, creating a sound like thunder.

"We've got her, captain!" Ho shouted over the din. She gripped the labium's joystick with both hands and pulled back.

"Maximum power to the manipulator!" Garm yelled, holding the two chair backs tightly as the bridge was buffeted. "Draw it back as far as possible and lock it down!"

"Trying . . . it's working, sir! The actuators are nearly in the red, but they're holding! I don't know how long it'll last, but I've got her pinned!"

I have you now, Garm thought. He gave Ho a heartfelt nod of respect. "Good work, ensign. But, now that we've got her cornered, this is *my* fight."

"Sir?"

"Hey, you know I've always been good in the clinches," he said, winking.

Cunningham swiveled in his seat. "Wait, what are you going to do?"

Garm smiled. "It's time to 'heat the deep', Kyle."

The CSO looked around and shook his head. "I don't get it."

"You know, *'In roaring he shall rise, and on the surface die'* . . ."

"What?"

Garm turned his back on the raging Kraken. "Come on, this is your chance to do what you've always wanted. Load the HARPE MARK 66's into two of our remaining torpedo tubes."

Cunningham sagged in his seat. "You're . . . you're going nuclear?"

He nodded.

"B-but, we need base approval for that. Grayson or--"

"Tartarus has gone dark, my friend," he admonished. "The decision is mine, and mine alone."

346

Cunningham gestured at the monstrous octopus which, unable to free itself, had started gnawing on *Gryphon*'s reinforced prow. As it did, one of its deadly tentacles slimed its way across the bow's titanium portal, leaving chemical burn marks in the clear metal.

"But, it's right *there*!" he sputtered. "We'll all die!"

"No, lieutenant," Garm said. "Flood both tubes, remove all safeties, and keep the outer doors closed. I'll take care of the rest."

"You? Wait, and we're--"

"You and the rest of the bridge crew are leaving. That's an order."

Aghast, Ho spun in her seat. "Captain, no! We stay together! I want to--"

"I already told you, 'short stack'," he said, his amused eyes flitting to Ramirez, "This is *my* fight. Connie, you're the best pilot I've ever seen, and it's been an honor to be your captain, but it's time for you to leave."

Ramirez hesitated, his mouth open.

"Save it, Adolfo," Garm advised. "I'm giving you your last two orders. Number one: get your dice-loving ass off my bridge. Number two: go make an honest woman out of this little wildcat."

Ramirez paled, then glanced toward Ho, as the two of them exchanged looks of uncertainty. "I, uh . . . I will if she will."

"Oh, she will; you *both* will." Garm announced, grabbing their chair tops and spinning them around like they were kids, until they faced the bridge's exit. "Now, go find an escape pod that still works, quit pissing away your money, and go raise a couple of half-Chinese, half-Latino rugrats. You can name one after me."

Ho's eyes shone as she studied her captain's face. After a moment's deliberation, she nodded, unclicked her harness, and got up. "Thank you, sir. For taking a chance on me."

"Are you kidding? Surest bet I ever made," he said. "Now haul ass, before that thing breaks loose!"

As the couple made their way to the exit hatch, Garm started toward Cunningham, but then hesitated. The walls began to quiver, and a low creaking sound filled the bridge, like a towering castle door trying to open on rusty hinges.

His wolf's eyes slitted. The octopus had wrapped its remaining tentacles around the prow like a giant anaconda and was squeezing with all its strength. It was trying to cave in their nose or pop out the viewer plate. "CSO, are my fish ready to swim?"

"Primed and ready, captain," came Cunningham's brooding reply. "I just . . . I can't believe you're *doing* this. Why don't you just leave, too?"

"First off, half the escape pods are down," Garm replied, glancing over Rush's shoulder at her board. "Ramirez and Ho can fit in one together, so that gives you a chance. But, if I take one . . ."

"Fuck that, we're pals! We--"

"And we always *will* be. But I need you to man up now, and help Rush out of here, before you run out of time." He checked their depth gauge. "You've got less than nine hundred feet to go, old friend."

Cunningham rose from his seat, then stepped up and grabbed the larger man in a big bearhug. Then, as Kyle disengaged and extended his hand to Heather Rush, Garm's jaw dropped.

"Come on, hon," Cunningham said, his eyes watering.

Obviously scared out of her wits, Rush flushed, but then undid her harness and took his hand. Her eyes peeled wide as the deck beneath their feet shivered once again, and she threw herself against him.

"What the fuck?" Garm sputtered at the unexpected revelation. "*You* two?"

"What, you thought it was *you* she was following from ship to ship?" Cunningham smirked. "Always the big ego . . ."

Garm facepalmed himself. "But-but what about your wife? And the--"

"Hey, I keep my private life private," Cunningham said. "I love my kids to death; they're my life. But, my marriage? Let's just say that many a healthy union has been destroyed by allowing a disruptive mother-in-law to move in."

Garm pursed his lips. "Good luck to you both." He checked the status of *Gryphon's* labium. "Now, *hurry*. That thing's acid is starting to erode the manipulator at its base. I don't know how much longer it'll last, and I have to finish this."

Rush stepped shyly forward and leaned up to give him a peck on the cheek. "Thank you for everything."

He smiled down at her. "Take care of my pain-in-the-ass friend, will you?"

"I will."

Suddenly, a terrifying wrenching sound reverberated through the bridge, as the octopus intensified its assault. The overheads flickered and went out, and sparks sputtered and sprayed from both sonar and fire control.

"Move it!" he shouted, the alarm in his voice lending impetus to the two. They ran for it, shutting the heavy hatch behind them with an exceptionally loud thump, and leaving him sealed in and alone in the dark.

The emergency lights kicked on almost immediately, bathing the helm in shades of ruby-red, and Garm moved to Kyle's station, checking the status of the two HARPE torpedoes. He grinned. Named after the sword that *Perseus* used to slay *Medusa*, but also coded UPURS – meaning literally, "up yours" – each of the nuclear-tipped torpedoes packed a two-kiloton wallop – the equivalent of two thousand tons of TNT. Just one was enough to reduce an aircraft carrier to a heap of molten slag. Two combined were, well, suffice it to say, if it remained in the blast radius, the octopus didn't have a prayer.

Both weapons were running hot and ready to go at the press of a button. The moment he hit the switch, they would rocket forward, slam into the outer doors, and detonate. The rest would be one big fireball of history.

And his epitaph.

Garm's mind wandered to Kyle and Rush ending up to-gether, and he chuckled. And to think, all this time he really *had* thought she'd been carrying some sappy torch for him. Ah, well, it was just as well. Nat would've killed her if she'd ever thought . . .

Nat!

Garm's eyes tightened, and he rushed to communications, trying to get the acoustic link online. According to the readings, it was functioning fine, but it was like Rush said; they couldn't get through. He thought it over, then decided to gamble. He prepped an emergency MIB for release – literally, a digital mes-sage in a waterproof "bottle", that would float to the surface, emitting a satellite beacon any GDT ship could lock onto – and then grabbed the mike.

"This is Captain Garm Braddock, Commander, USS *Gryphon*, to Captain Natalya Dragunova, Commander, USS *Antrodemus*. Coded transmission to read: Hey, Nat, it's Wolfie," he knew the camera over his chair would be recording and made sure to stay in frame. Behind him, a scalding ten-foot jet of steam exploded from a ruptured overhead pipe and began hosing down the deck. "As you can see, things have gone pretty far south." He indicated the raging monster, peering in the window behind him. "My crew is attempting to abandon ship, but I have to end this. I can't allow this thing to murder anyone else. I want you to know, you're the most amazing woman I've ever known, and I've always regretted not being the settling down type."

He looked down, the bridge's red lighting giving his face a brooding, almost devilish look. He licked his lips, then looked back up. "Do me a favor, if you can; look after Dirk. You know he worships you, and I won't be around to watch his back anymore. If you could do that for me, I'd be eternally grateful."

Garm walked back to communications, set and hit the re-lease, not knowing enough about the system to tell if the hissing sound he heard meant the MIB had launched, or that the system was compromised. He turned back to the bow viewer, stepping close to it as the octopus glared malevolently down at him.

A warning chime began to ring out and he sprang to Ho's station. *Damn it.* The labium's anchorage point was approaching critical; a few more seconds and they'd lose it. And the Kraken, too.

He had to do what the octopus had done, a little sleight of hand, or tentacle. Something to keep her focused away from what mattered, and on something that didn't.

Time for a little rope-a-dope.

"Come on, you fucking twat-waffle!" he yelled, approaching the main in the near-dark. With it being an abyssal hunter, and from the way the thing's nearest eye appeared to glower, he was confident it saw him. He seized his uniform shirt at the collar and ripped it off in two huge pieces, exposing his powerful physique, then held his arms out to the sides in a mocking challenge.

"You want me, *here I am!*" he bellowed, stepping right up to the transparent barrier. He banged on it with a rock-hard hammer fist, surprised at how cold it was. *"I'm* the one who killed your disgusting larvae! I, Garm "the Gate" Braddock, one of the greatest and most feared heavyweights who ever lived. *Now, come and get me!"*

The Kraken accepted his invitation.

In an instant, its colors shifted to a dark crimson with angry black bands, and jagged, horn-like protrusions erupted like spikes, all over its cottage-sized head. A moment later, it uttered a tuba-like rumble and hurled itself once more at the titanium barrier, its monstrous maw gnashing.

Garm staggered sideways as *Gryphon's* already battered prow absorbed the initial impact. The damp floor beneath his feet dipped and shifted so often, it was like trying to stand in a soaked bouncy house. He cursed as he lost his footing and went down. Then, before he could regain his feet, a curved, ten-foot section of steel I-beam came crashing through the ceiling overhead, nearly cutting him in two.

When the dust settled Garm realized he'd been lucky; Ramirez's station had taken the bulk of the hit. Its reinforced structure had crumpled, leaving him pinned, but with a Herculean effort, he was able to hoist one end of the girder and squirm free. Half-stunned and panting, he lay on his side, trying to see through an impenetrable wall of pain. He tried to get up, then uttered an involuntary hiss and clutched his right side.

Garm had seen and inflicted enough broken ribs on other fighters to know when his own were busted. He ran nervous fingers down the bare skin of his flank, then winced. Half his side felt like bubble wrap and he tasted blood.

He was wrong. His ribs weren't broken. They were fragmented. And he had horrific – potentially life threatening – internal injuries as well. Standing was next-to-impossible, and he had to resort to crawling on all fours toward Kyle's chair, in the hope of using it as a crutch.

Around him, the bridge shook repeatedly, as the frenzied octopus renewed its attack. Obsessed with the idea of tearing Garm limb from limb, it resorted to alternately staring inside to pinpoint his location, then hauling back and launching itself at that spot with everything it had. Its tenacity came at a price; its maw bled blue and its black beak was worn and split on the edges; yet still, it refused to stop.

He also noted, with a growing sense of alarm, that its tentacles' repeated strikes had begun to weaken *Gryphon*'s bow window. The metal had softened, and its bites were leaving visible dents in the foot-thick barrier.

Given enough time, it would get through.

Judging by the high-pitched chime that began to sound – a dire indication that the ORION-class submarine's hull integrity was fast approaching the point of no return – it made no difference.

All of them: *Gryphon*, himself, and the Kraken, were out of time.

One of them just didn't know it yet.

Dragging himself through a haze of hurt, Garm managed to make it to fire control and reached up. With his jaw clamped to keep from crying out, he gripped the upper edge of Cunningham's station with one hand, and the CSO's armrest with the other. He drew a quick breath and then, with a pain-filled hiss, hauled himself to his feet.

The octopus, spotting him through the partially-obscured bow window, attacked instantly. It sensed the submarine's hard shell was nearing the point of collapse and threw itself against the main like some blue whale-sized demon.

The impact was reminiscent of a jumbo jet slamming into the side of a mountain, and Garm went flying. For the first time since the *Xiphactinus* attack, his ability to master pain was overcome, and he screamed as his already battered body bounced off a nearby bulkhead, ending up in a heap atop Rush's abandoned station.

The giant cephalopod was far from finished, however, and began a repeated barrage of rushes, smashing itself beak-first against the invisible wall that somehow still managed to resist it. The partially-compromised bow began to push inward from its frenzied blows, and Garm could do nothing but cover up as he was flung like a child's action figure, from station to bulkhead and then back again, until he finally ricocheted off the ceiling.

He came down with devastating force, only to end up prostrate, draped like a discarded rag doll across the top of his own captain's chair.

Smoke and steam filled the bridge and Garm lay there, face-down and barely breathing. Blood streamed from his broken nose and mouth, and his insides felt like someone had shoved a rusty chain saw through his side and left it there, still running.

He sucked in a breath through torn lips. He smelled blood and something burning. He tried to move, only to cry out. It was no good; each impact against *Gryphon*'s unbosoming steel walls and deck had been like falling out of a two-story building and hitting concrete. His athlete's body was broken, finished.

I guess someone else better hit that switch . . .

Garm mind felt like it had been through a blender, yet even so, he managed to raise his aching head and glance toward fire control. Where the *hell* was that slacker, Cunningham? His vision was impaired, and he realized one of his eyes was swollen shut. Afraid of what he might find, he reached up and touched it.

He uttered a sigh of relief. The eyeball was still intact. *Thank God*.

For as long as he could remember, his eyes had been what girls liked most about him. Or, at least, what they noticed first. He always told them they'd been a gift from his mother.

His mother? Where *was* she?

The room shuddered again and again, and as the intracranial pressure in his head increased, Garm became more and more confused. For some reason, his mother wasn't coming to put a Band-Aid on his cuts like she always did.

She wasn't there. Why wasn't she there? Was it because she was . . . dead?

Orange flames began to creep up from Ramirez's abandoned sonar station, and the sight and smell of the fire and smoke gradually brought the mortally wounded ex-pugilist back to his senses. His bloodied countenance turned even grimmer as he took stock of his situation. He was sprawled, face down, over the back of his chair. The shock had caused his already-shattered ribs to explode like shrapnel inside his abdominal cavity, but he'd been lucky.

If he'd landed face-up, his back would've snapped. Like a dry twig.

Ignoring the unbearable jolts of agony that shot through him, Garm grabbed his chair top with one hand and an armrest with the other and started sliding to the left. The slippery blood helped; he wanted to avoid aggravating his crushed right side as much as possible, for fear of passing out.

Stifling the scream of anguish that slipped past his torn lips, Garm finally got his feet back under him. The deck continued to heave and dip, and he staggered like a drunkard toward fire control. His legs were wooden, his kneecaps either dislocated or broken from one of the blows he'd received, and he walked stiff-legged, to avoid collapsing.

Step by step, he worked his way along. What was six feet seemed like six thousand, and he had to pause to breathe. Each inhalation was a throttled wheeze, and the blood that dripped from his nostrils formed gooey crimson bubbles that popped and dripped down his chin on every exhale.

He licked his lips and discovered that several of his teeth were gone, too.

It doesn't matter, you overgrown, egomaniacal ape. You're not posing for prom pictures here!

Garm finally made it to fire control. He wanted to collapse onto it, or at least sink down into its inviting chair, but he was afraid to. He knew if he tried his legs would give out, and, if he missed, he doubted he would have the strength to stand up again.

A standing eight count would have to do.

With his bloodied palms resting on Cunningham's weapons console, Garm used his good eye to scan its surface. Amazingly, all systems were still functional.

Drip . . . drip . . .

Realizing the stream of blood that began to obscure the release switches and levers was coming from his face, he pulled his head up and back and turned toward the bow. The resultant compression his mangled organs suffered made him shriek, but he couldn't hear himself think, let alone speak. The cacophony of dying *Gryphon*'s warning claxons, fire alarms, and surviving sonar systems – still targeting the Kraken with active pings – was an insurmountable barrage. Topping it all were the deafening blows the beast continued to rain down on his doomed vessel.

Boom . . . boom . . . boom . . .

Garm gripped the edges of fire control's main console with surprising strength and watched, with a bizarre sort of detachment, as the obsessed beast continued to hammer away. His body flooded with adrenaline, and everything about him began to be viewed in a dreamlike state.

Boom . . . boom . . . boom . . .

Through an agony-induced fog, Garm regarded his nemesis. It was leaning in close, its glimmering eye fixed on him. It stayed there, and he wondered if it knew how badly hurt he was, or if it was simply relishing its pending victory.

Suddenly, his pain-muddled brain took note of the titanium portal that was the only thing keeping the octopus at bay. Normally clear as glass, its smooth surface was dulled from all the scoring and slashing it had sustained, and there was an enormous dent in it that extended inward nearly three feet.

Despite the insurmountable pain, the big submariner forced himself erect. His pale blue eye met and held the Kraken's monstrous gaze, and he remembered all the brutal battles he'd fought; the punishment he'd endured, both in and out of the ring, and the endless parade of opponents who had tried and failed to put him down.

He had never lost a fight, and he wasn't about to start now.

Like himself, *Gryphon* had also taken one hell of a beating, he realized, as he studied what remained of the conn. The damage was impressive. Yet, despite the titanic cephalopod's vast array of weapons: its corrosive suckers, monstrous strength, and lethal beak, it had failed to finish the job.

It had taken its best shot and *Gryphon*'s defenses had held. But how?

Suddenly, it hit him like a rabbit punch.

It's tired!

A sneer crossed his battered face and Garm stood straight and proud. He spat a nasty combination of blood and spittle in the octopus's direction. Then, with his one good eye latched onto its, he shook his head and smiled.

"My turn."

Then he jabbed the launch button.

There was the familiar whooshing sound and rumble, as the Mark 66's launched, and then a very unfamiliar banging noise. He caught a fleeting glimpse of what looked like fear in the Kraken's glittering eyes.

As he watched, its golden orbs turned jaundiced and started to stretch, becoming impossibly large and diluted, until they finally dissolved into nothingness. At the same time, he felt the floor rise up under him and a sensation of extreme warmth, like he was laying on hot sand, baking on an Equatorial beach somewhere.

Then Garm Braddock's world became white.

———

Natalya Dragunova sagged back into her captain's chair, a dazed look wearying her normally strong features. She, and her equally-stunned primaries, had just been privy to *Gryphon*'s final moments, including those of her captain, and an undetermined number of crew.

She'd seen it all: the bridge crew's valiant-but-futile struggle against an actual Kraken, Garm Braddock's heroic attempt to save as many people as possible, his courageous decision to remain behind aboard his dying submarine, and the apocalyptic outcome.

It was beyond awful. The abuse her lover had suffered at the "hands" of the monstrous cephalopod was beyond belief: being smashed like a pinball, over and over, against *Gryphon*'s steel floors and bulkheads; a brown bear couldn't have survived that kind of punishment. Even *watching* it had been traumatizing. So much so that, several times, Ensign Jackson had to avert her eyes, and Meyers' cheeks were still damp from freshly-wiped tears.

Yet, despite all that, Garm had managed to do what he'd always said he would. He'd gone down like a Spartan. And, to his eternal credit, he'd taken the man-eating monster with him.

But he was dead.

For Natalya, that was the most shocking part. She just couldn't get her head around the notion that he was gone and not coming back. It wasn't like she'd seen a future with the big submariner. Their relationship had been a physical one, and in that arena, she'd had no complaints. As bedmates went, he'd been fantastic, and a fun companion.

Except, of course, when he was being an obnoxious egomaniac whose balls she wanted to cut off.

To be fair, his reaction to her telling him how she'd been raped as a girl *had* been surprisingly touching. She'd warmed up to him then. But, even so, she'd never pictured them being anything more than just paramours. It just wasn't . . . *there.*

Still, regardless of the nature of their relationship, the one thing she'd always thought of Garm as being was indestructible. In her eyes, he was like some invincible cyborg or golem – nothing could kill him.

She'd obviously been wrong.

Of course, the SOB had had the last laugh, outing their relationship like he had in front of her primaries. She wondered if, somehow, he'd known about her ability to spy on *Gryphon*'s bridge and staged that.

Nyet. Impossible, even for Wolfie.

So, now what? Was she supposed to honor a dead man's last request and play custodian to his little brother? *'Look after him . . .'* What did that even *mean*?

Natalya shook her tawny head. A ridiculous thing to ask. Derek was a man, and *as* a man, he needed to stand on his own two feet. A smart, funny guy like that? He should never have become reliant on his twin to fight his battles for him, whether he'd asked him to or not. She snorted irritably, then decided she would deal with the problem at another time.

She glanced at the staticky dead air still occupying their bow viewer. "Communications, end transmeession with *Gryphon* and restore external view to main," she commanded, leaning forward in her seat. She looked around, noting that every one of her primaries – even the redoubtable Gonzalez – made it a point to avoid her gaze.

"Yes, captain," Bender said, sitting rigidly erect.

Natalya decided it was best to ignore the specter of the dead six-foot-four elephant in the room. It was by far the easiest means of dealing with it. And, if any of her crew were brazen enough to bring up her and Wolfie, she would make a quick example of them – one that would ensure no one else followed suit.

She snapped her fingers. "Bender, you're with me."

"Uh, with you?"

"Yes. Commander Gonzalez," Natalya said, rising to her feet. "The ensign and I are en route to the *Remora*. You have the conn."

Gonzalez opened his mouth to say something, but then reconsidered. "Yes, ma'am. Mission proceeding on schedule?"

"Of course," she said matter-of-factly. "Tell Sato and Archer we're on our way."

As she finished prepping *Remora* for launch, Natalya glanced up at the overhead monitor that functioned as her rearview mirror, sizing up the landing team she'd assembled.

Ensign Bart Bender was riding copilot to her right. Judging by the huge grin he wore as his furry fingers tap danced across the mini-sub's keyboards, checking and rechecking their systems, he was in too good of a mood. Especially, when she considered they'd just watched their sister ship incinerated by a nuclear fireball, and were headed past a hostile naval blockade, into a forbidden island that was, reputedly, filled with man-eating, prehistoric monsters.

As he turned and winked at her, Natalya could have vomited. The pint-sized pervert must have subconsciously assumed that her choosing him meant they were on a date or something.

Directly behind Bender sat 40-year-old Petty Officer George Sato, *Antrodemus*'s electronics technician. Sato had a rep for being calm, efficient, and, workwise, an utter perfectionist. His combat skills were only so-so, but with them being forced to traverse waters that might include aggressive *Kronosaurus imperators*, she wanted someone available who could effect required repairs – preferably on the fly.

The last thing she needed was to be stuck with a dead submersible, stranded on an island filled with hungry refugees from the Cretaceous.

I swear, eef there ees a T-rex there I will sheet myself!

"PO Sato, are you prepared?" Natalya asked, studying him via the HD monitor. With his thin frame, bulky armored vest, and red motion-sensing goggles already on, he looked like a little kid playing GI dress-up for Halloween.

"Yes, captain," Sato replied. "I brought my lug wrench, my Swiss army knife, and a roll of duct tape." He reached down between his legs and pulled up a thick hardbound volume of some kind, sealed in a heavy-gauge waterproof envelope. "I even have a hardcopy of the *Remora*'s owner's manual, with full schematics. Just in case . . ."

Natalya grinned and nodded. "Good theenking."

To the engineer's left and occupying two-thirds of the space they shared, sat Independent Duty Corpsman Lieutenant Alger Archer. At a towering six-foot-five and a muscular 250 pounds, the med-school-dropout-turned-corpsman was nine inches taller and ninety pounds heavier than their electronics tech. Even so, mission-wise, he was "worth the weight".

Because of Archer's size and physique, in private, Natalya liked to refer to him as *Antrodemus*'s answer to Garm Braddock. The 33-year-old, brown-eyed, brown-haired New Englander was definitely not the battle-hardened warrior Wolfie was . . . make that *had* been. But, he was strong as an ox, good with guns, and had an impressive knowledge of zoology.

Sometimes, being a failed veterinarian had its benefits. And, with his past training, he was as close to a doctor as they were going to find in these parts.

"How are we doing back there, IDC Archer?" Natalya asked.

The big corpsman adjusted his ceramic-composite combat helmet, then shifted uncomfortably in his seat. "All good, ma'am." He reached down and patted his luggage-sized med kit. "I brought everything I hope we'll never need."

Natalya nodded, then went back to her system's analysis. "Initiating prelaunch warm-up," she said, flipping a switch. Bender nodded and took notes on a digital clipboard.

There was a low purr as the mini-sub's engines powered up. A many-times-modified descendant of the original *Eurypterid* that Dr. Amara Braddock, Garm and Derek's mother, had based her patented submersible designs on, the *Remora* was originally intended for military reconnaissance.

Nowadays, with its high-tech sensors and added armament, it was the bread and butter of JAW Robotics product line. Combined with the profits from their latest series of military robotics systems and civilian bionics, it helped keep parent company GDT solidly in the pink.

Like the first *Eurypterid,* the *Remora* was a sleek and streamlined vessel. Reminiscent of a thick-bodied manta ray, it was larger than its now archaic ancestor, measuring a full thirty-two feet in length and weighing over eight tons. It was designed, as its name implied, to conform and adhere directly to its mother vessel's hull, with access to and from accomplished via floodable airlock.

The original impeller engines had been upgraded, with the current powerplant consisting of a pair of MAKO M33 Magnetohydrodynamic Drive Propulsors. Smaller versions of the MHD powerhouses that propelled the imposing ORION-class, these generated almost 600 HP each, and could push the hydrodynamic mini-sub through the water at a scalding 50 knots – enough to escape a hungry pliosaur, if they saw it coming.

Running was fine, of course, but considering where they were going, Natalya was more concerned with offense and defense. Fortunately, for its size, the *Remora* packed both, and in decent quantity.

Armor-wise, the submersible utilized a downscaled version of the pressure hull that shielded *Antrodemus* and her ilk from harm – four inches of ceramic-steel composite, backed by another four inches of hardened titanium. As a bonus, she had an additional outer layer of reactive armor which, given their destination, might well come in handy.

Embedded in the *Remora*'s skin were hundreds of tiny shaped charges, each of which was topped by a miniature SODOME. Originally designed to deflect torpedoes and cruise missiles, when the sub was subjected to attacks from a large biologic, the smart charges would sense the pending impact and detonate a split-second before: reducing damage, and either killing or driving off the attacker, depending on its size.

Each clustered detonation was a one-off, however, and that particular section of plating could only be replaced in drydock. As a result, Natalya hoped to utilize the system as little as possible.

The *Remora*'s offensive weaponry was a bit more traditional, and far less glamourous. It consisted of a pair of forward-facing 20-mm HYDRA Gatling cannons, one in each nacelle. The HYDRAs were the baby brothers of the formidable LADON gun system and, although their position and immobility required a potential target to be directly in the submersible's sights – like a WW2 Corsair chasing a Zero – at close range, the uranium penetrator rounds that spewed from its seven revolving barrels were wonderfully destructive.

Their only downside was a magazine capacity of 2,000 rounds per nacelle. To a civilian, that might have sounded like a lot. But at 3,000 RPM, shells went fast. In the event HYDRA was brought to bear, the key words were *short bursts*.

"Okay, people," Natalya said, scanning their primary systems one last time. "Every theeng looks good. I hope everyone remembered to take their Dramamine."

Bender turned to her and grinned. "Release umbilical?"

"Da."

There was a loud clunk, followed by the release of pressurized air and a series of low thumps. A moment later, Natalya experienced the unmistakable sensation of free-falling, as the mini-sub dropped away from *Antrodemus*'s protective hull and powered to life.

"We are detached and under way," she announced. On her rear monitor, she saw Sato and Archer reflexively grab their armrests, like they were on a roller coaster. Grinning, she gripped the *Remora*'s circular yoke, engaged thrusters, and started them moving.

Their sonar screens showed no potential threats, and the seas before them were a dazzling mixture of turquoise and blue, with fields of pale green seagrass wafting back and forth with the movement of the waves. Despite the jagged spires of black lava that jutted up like spears – a sobering reminder of the violence of Diablo's ancient eruption – the place was far from devoid of life. In fact, colorful fish and squid, and an assortment of other marine creatures, abounded.

Natalya accelerated forward, reveling in the power and agility of the *Remora*. It felt good to be out of the captain's chair and riding helm. Running *Antrodemus* had its perks, but it got monotonous with her always giving orders and someone else carrying them out. Here, things were hands-on, and she relished the opportunity to be in the driver's seat for a change.

Leaning forward, she tapped the communications switch. "Captain Dragunova to *Antrodemus*, come een, *Antrodemus*."

A foot-wide screen in the center console shimmered to life, and her first mate's image appeared. "Gonzalez here, ma'am."

"Status."

"Not good," he replied. "Those Helix choppers are sweeping the battlefield's debris. They're wiping out any survivors from the rebel fleet, chain-gunning them in their life rafts."

Savages. "You know we cannot intervene."

"Yes, captain. Holding position and cloaked, as ordered," Gonzales replied. "However, the regime destroyers are sniffing around our immediate area. They may have detected your launch."

She exhaled. "You have the conn. Eef you need to take evasive action, do so. I trust your judgment."

"Thank you, captain. Gonzalez out."

With a quick spin of the wheel, Natalya dodged a trio of Caribbean monk seals that had blundered into their path, then said to Bender, "Ensign, you're my eyes and ears out here. I want you on sonar. Any theeng of note, seeng out."

Her freckly co-pilot smirked. "Ah, so, you've heard about my vocal prowess in the shower, eh?"

She resisted the impulse to smack him and redirected by pointing out the gurgling cauldron that awaited them, less than one hundred yards away. "The Mouth of Hell ees open wide, people," she advised. "Make sure safety harnesses are on; we are going een."

Bender cleared his throat. "Wouldn't it be safer to let the computer drive?"

She shot him a look. "Don't be a pussy."

Accelerating like a crimson-hued Eagle ray, riding an underwater current, the *Remora* cruised nimbly toward Diablo Caldera's yawning entrance. Closer and closer they got, and soon the submersible began to be buffeted by the boiling seawater that hurtled out of that lightless hole.

The temperature began to climb, and Natalya flipped a series of switches, before wiping her brow with the back of one hand. Her eyes bounced from their Celazole viewer, over to their sonar map, and back again.

Seconds later, with the *Remora*'s thermal management systems now at maximum, and her passenger climate controls set to compensate for the searing seawater, they slipped soundlessly inside.

SEVENTEEN

If Sam Mot still had knees, he'd have been on them. As it was, he stood shakily at the still-smoldering edge of the debris-strewn drop-off; the same one which, up until a few minutes earlier, had been the giant U-boat U-420's resting place for over a century. Reflecting Sam's mood, the TALOS Mark VII's massive "shoulders" were slumped down, and he stared forlornly down into the abyss, his vision clouded by unshed tears.

More than a mile below the point where he stood – the AWES's optical systems could've told him exactly how far if he'd asked – hung the radioactive cloud marking *Gryphon*'s grave. It gave off an eerie blue glow, just like you saw in the movies, visible to the naked eye and pulsing in the darkness like some cobalt wraith.

No, not a wraith. A ghost. The collective ghosts of all the armored warship's slain crew. It was a roster that included his best friend.

Sam's breath came out a heart-wrenching shudder and, despite its climate-controlled interior, he shivered within the cockpit of the TALOS exoskeleton. He'd had a front row seat to the greatest heavyweight fight in history, but still couldn't come to terms with it. Fighting back a sniffle, he willed the Mark VII's auto-record system to playback *Gryphon*'s final moments.

Sam shook his head as he watched the one-sided battle. There was the initial ambush – something he might have detected with his full-spectrum vision, if he hadn't been hiding in a crevasse – as the *Octopus giganteus*, disguised as a portion of the nearby reef, T-boned the off-guard ORION-class anti-biologic submarine.

The recording went haywire for a moment, as he'd been forced to dive for cover, then refocused, just as the monstrous cephalopod dragged *Gryphon* right over his head. It was aiming for the wreck. There was an incredibly loud impact, as the GDT sub collided with U-420's already mashed conning tower and portside, followed by an ear-splitting groan as the three juggernauts, momentarily conjoined, tumbled over the cliff's edge amid a shower of coral, sand, and shattered pieces of hull and machine parts.

Sam had rushed to the seamount's lip, watching with his infrared vision and near-unlimited zoom, as the enraged mother octopus continued to pull the embattled submarine steadily downward.

Gryphon hadn't gone down without a fight, however, and Sam's chest had swelled with pride as her crew waged a protracted brawl against their cold-blooded opponent. In the end, however, and despite their fanciest maneuvers and advanced weapons, the battle was lost.

The still shaken AWES operator didn't know if Garm had deliberately programmed his vessel's reactor to go critical, in the hopes of taking the giant octopus with him, or if he'd fired one of the nuclear-tipped torpedoes the sub's manifest indicated they had aboard. Whichever it was, the heated blast that scaled the cliff like a white-hot firestorm, burning away all its vegetation and incinerating most of the local marine life, had to have been caused by a fission-type device.

Nothing else could've done it.

Sam stared down at the bluish-white glow and shook his head. He'd been lucky the battlefield-tested TALOS system had auto-safety features to protect its operator's eyes, specifically in the event of a nuclear bomb burst, and was shielded against the resultant EMP as well. As it was, the shockwave that followed the initial explosion had knocked him on his metal ass and overloaded half his systems. Fortunately, the AWES had quickly recalibrated itself, and appeared to be back at 100% capacity.

With the exception of his plasma weapon being nearly exhausted, he was in perfect working order. For a guy with no arms and legs, that is.

Of course, unlike everyone else, he was still alive.

That counted for something, too.

Sam leaned forward and sighed, the suit's huge gray forearms resting on its mechanized thighs, as he gave the abyss a long and sorrowful look.

A _nuke_, you crazy bastard? I can't believe you went and did it! Well, at least you took that mountain of calamari with you. He glanced around, apprehensively. *I just hope you didn't cause a tsunami somewhere with that move!*

Sam straightened up and tried to speak, but his voice came out a dusty squeak. He moistened his throat by swallowing a few times and then tried again.

"Hey, Garm. Thanks for taking my back with "Octzilla," he managed. "You definitely saved my bacon. I-I guess that puts you one up on me. I'm, uh, I'm gonna miss you. Rest easy, old buddy, and . . . give your parents my best."

He allowed himself one manly tear, then turned and began clomping up along the now barren cliff's sloped edge, like some mobile marine monolith. He scanned the surrounding region with every visual spectrum the TALOS suit had but found nothing.

The sample tube he'd stashed, the one that contained the three infant octopi, had vanished. *Swept away, undoubtedly.*

He did, however, see evidence of radiation oozing up with the incoming tide. Accompanying it, and scattered over the surrounding reef like a dismembered rainbow, were numerous brightly-colored scent trails. Each one glowed a different hue, depending on its origin. Some were faded, especially after the recent shockwave, but they were all visible to his eyes.

Noting one azure-colored trace that led straight to the site, moved all over, and then eventually ended up going over the edge, Sam realized it was the heat bloom generated by *Gryphon*'s engines. Which meant, it could be traced all the way back to Tartarus.

Sam sighed. There was nothing to do but go back.

Willing a comm link open, he attempted to phone home. "Attention, Tartarus, this is AWES operator Sam Mot, I repeat, AWES operator Sam Mot. Come in, Tartarus."

He waited a good thirty seconds. When he got no reply, he tried again.

"Attention, Tartarus, this is AWES operator Sam Mot, I repeat, AWES operator Sam Mot on secure channel. Please come in, Tartarus."

His frown deepened, and he willed a system's check. The results were near-instant, and a quick glance at his internal monitors confirmed that his communications emitters and receiver relays were in perfect working order.

The base was hearing him. They just weren't responding. Maybe they were having problems on their end?

He decided to not leave anything to chance.

"Attention, Tartarus, this is Sam Mot," he began, then hesitated. He was a civilian, so he wasn't sure how to put it, and decided to just do the best he could. "I am, I mean I *regret* to report that USS *Gryphon* went down with all hands. The submarine was attacked by a Kraken, an octopus of extraordinary size. I'm transmitting all the footage I have of the incident, in case any of you think I'm suffering from raptures of the deep."

He paused transmission and rolled his eyes. That last part was probably not up to snuff, but whatever.

"Special message to Doctor Dirk Braddock; the samples requested were lost as a result of the shockwave generated when the sub exploded. I have been unable to locate and retrieve. I am . . . very sorry for your loss. Your brother, I mean." He took a breath before signing off. "I am returning to base under my own power. Sam Mot, out."

He took a lengthy look around and marveled at the changes to the once colorful submarine ridge, since he'd first explored it. Scoured clean of its plants and resident sea life, it looked like one of those dead coral reefs you saw in the news – the ones those hordes of crown-of-thorns starfish killed off – skeletal and lifeless.

Sam kicked at a nearby bare patch of sand, one of the few that remained around the pile of shattered rocks and metal fragments, left behind after U-420 tumbled to her permanent grave. He spotted some of those black, radioactive granules, mixed in with the seabed: glowing specks of turquoise pepper on his screens.

He snorted as he turned his back. So much for an historical shipwreck, destined for scientists and dive experts to explore and marvel over.

Suddenly, a glint of silver, far off to the right, drew his gaze, and he willed the TALOS to swivel at the waist. There was something shiny peeking out from underneath a nearby stone outcropping. Was it the cannister with his samples?

Forgetting all else, Sam stomped over a low-lying hill and made for it, eagerness plainly visible on his face. With everything that had happened, if he at least came back with the embryos, maybe his portion of the mission wouldn't be viewed as a complete disaster. And, who knows? Maybe Grayson might consider it a success and consider his contract fulfilled.

It's not like they have anywhere else for me to go.

Sam was fifty feet from the outcropping, with the midday sun's golden beams dancing willy-nilly all around him, when something unusual happened. He felt strangely cold and, on his screens, noticed that the outside temperature was dropping rapidly; already, it was down a good twenty degrees. The sunlight had also vanished, and he found himself in near-dusk conditions.

A sudden chill drag-raced up and down his spine. The inexplicable darkness and temperature dip had to have been caused by more than just a cloud, briefly blotting out the sun. He had to be near something. Either that, or he was in something's--

Shadow.

Wheeling around, Sam's eyes bulged from their sockets. The hillock he'd just crested had vanished, and in its place and rising up behind him like some bark-coated Zeppelin, was the octopus. Towering at least sixty feet in height, it loomed over him, its enormous yellowed eyes radiating ill-contained malice.

Sam's heart skydived into his stomach as he stared up at it. He felt cold fear surfing on waves of adrenaline throughout his bloodstream, and a terrible realization took hold. This was *not* the same one that had attacked *Gryphon.*

This one was bigger.

Much bigger.

Sam's heart was beating so fast he thought it would implode, and his breathing had grown so rapid that, even with the AWES's air circulatory system, he was fogging his clear titanium faceplate. His green eyes widened as he continued to meet the colossal cephalopod's gaze, and he began to feel light-headed.

It was glaring down at him, its mantle pumping untold quantities of seawater through its gills, almost as fast as his lungs were pumping air. Then, its gelatinous body began to tremble.

It looks angry. More than angry, it's . . . enraged! It-it . . .

Then, as he remembered the tube of samples, sequestered in a tiny crack, fifty feet over his shoulder, it hit him like a knee to the nuts.

It <u>knows</u>! It, no, not it, <u>she</u> knows! This one is the—

Sam barely had time to draw a breath to scream, before a tidal wave of steely tentacles, each lined with hundreds of manhole-sized suckers, came flying at him.

In an instant, he was enveloped.

"Co-pilot, geev me a temperature update," Natalya Dragunova said. She'd been piloting the mini-sub *Remora* through the pitch-black lava tube that connected to Diablo Caldera's hidden lake for a nerve-wracking ten minutes now, with the searing current fighting her every step of the way. Knowing one bad slipup could result in a ruptured hull and them being instantly parboiled, she was feeling the heat – both literally and figuratively.

"External temps are at 675 degrees," Ensign Bart Bender said, licking dry lips as he rechecked their instruments. "Just to put that in perspective," he added, twisting in his seat to face IDC Alger Archer and PO George Sato, and winking, "a lit match is around 750."

"Focus," Natalya snapped. Scowling, she eyed their mapped route and reduced speed, before taking the next left. The tunnels they'd chosen varied wildly in diameter, ranging from as much as eighty feet, to as little as forty, and at times gave new meaning to the phrase, 'it feels close in here'. "Thermal shielding status?"

"Currently at 98%. Cabin temp holding steady at a balmy eighty degrees."

Behind them, and weighed down by his armor and gear, Archer shifted in his seat, then wiped away a trickle of sweat that crept down his brow. "Hey, Bender. Have you considered a career change? I think you'd make a talented, albeit sadistic, weatherman."

"Nah, I can take the heat. Can you?"

Archer made a face. "Time will tell . . ."

Bender turned back and threw an exaggerated leer at his commanding officer. "How about you, high-pockets? You like it hot?"

Natalya faked a girly laugh, then leaned in close. "Keep eet up, and I *weel* hurt you," she said softly.

The sonar tech's face fell, and he rebooted his personality back to professional settings. "Better watch that next turn," he warned. "Topography's showing some sort of big rubble pile. We'll have to skirt it."

Natalya cut her speed to five knots, before commencing her turn. It was black as the void in there, but with the superheated water, thermal imaging was useless. She was forced to reply on sonar readings and the *Remora's* powerful floodlights to light their way. Ahead, the obstacle Bender warned of towered above them, a hundred-foot pile of jagged black rocks, with several boulders as big as the mini-sub.

"Over there," he said, indicating the lava tube opening, peeking out to the right of the mound.

"Thees looks less aged than the rest of the tunnel," Natalya said, eyeing the colossal stones to port, as she skirted them at a distance of less than ten feet.

"It is," Bender confirmed. "Active sonar scan indicates the collapse took place in the last few centuries. It, hmm. Now, *that* is interesting."

"What?"

"The computer calculates that, prior to the collapse, which ended up connecting two diverging lava tubes, and increased the amount of geothermal heat substantially, this portion of the original tunnel was much cooler."

"How much cooler?"

"Maybe 200 degrees? A bit less than the temperature of boiling water."

Natalya scoffed. "Hot enough to hard-boil an egg ees steel pretty hot."

Bender nodded. "True, but it's possible that something could've gotten out – if it was heat resistant and fast enough."

"Bah."

The comms tech leaned forward, squinting as he peered through their sloped bow viewer. "Hey, do you see that faint glow up ahead?"

"Da," Natalya said, checking their weapon's status to make sure the system was armed. "Eet cannot be the caldera pool, we steel have a mile to go."

Bender quirked an eyebrow as he studied his readouts. "Active sonar is designating it as a concentration of some sort of biologic. They're an unknown species of . . . tube worm?"

She slowed to a crawl, as they traversed a downward-sloping portion of the tunnel. Everywhere she looked, the irregular surface of the lava tube was coated with a whitish layer of tightly packed structures, reminiscent of yard-high termite mounds. Protruding from the top of each hillock was a large, segmented worm, with cilia-like legs. They had palm-shaped, feathery structures protruding from what appeared to be their heads, which undulated non-stop in the current, like slow-moving butterfly wings.

Lieutenant Archer undid his seat belt and stepped toward the bow, ducking under a support beam to avoid injury. "Fascinating. Hundreds of thousands of them, maybe millions. They must feed on detritus as it's carried in and out with the tide." He rested a big hand atop Bender's seatback. "Kill the lights, will you?"

Natalya threw her copilot a nod of approval.

He hit the switch, but instead of the pitch blackness she'd anticipated, the tunnel around them instantly lit up like a red-light district nightclub. In the distance, the lava tube angled away from them but, due to the crimson glow, she could still see a good five hundred feet.

"Bioluminescence," Archer said, nodding approvingly. "Probably some form of colony communication, like ants do with pheromones." He turned to his captain. "Ma'am, are we documenting this?"

"Of course," she said. She half-smiled, imagining how excited that uber-nerd Derek Braddock would've been if he'd been there, then indicated a pulsing amber light on the *Remora*'s main control panel. "We are keeping detailed records of our course and every theeng we see."

Bender stroked his speckled chin contemplatively, as Archer retook his seat. "So, if we have our course already mapped out, and it's in the computer, why are we using *Gemini*? Isn't that redundant?"

Natalya considered his question. *Gemini* was JAW Robotics version of a last-destination auto-pilot. When activated, it utilized sonar, optical, and satellite data to track and record its parent vessel's current course. Later, it could be reactivated with the push of a button and would implement a precise return. It was fully automated and, even sans pilot, could flawlessly bring the *Remora* from point B, back to point A.

"Eef something happens to me on caldera," she said, speaking loud enough that everyone could hear, "The rest of you are not as proficient weeth piloting the submersible. Eef you breeng system online, eet can at least return you to where we separated from *Antrodemus*."

"Ah," Bender said, nodding and pursing his lips. "And here I thought it was in case those two in the back didn't make it, and--"

"*Antrodemus* to *Remora*," Gonzalez's booming voice almost made Natalya jump. It wasn't just the volume, but the uncharacteristic urgency it contained as it emanated from their speakers. "Come in, please."

She snatched up the radio mike so quickly, her comms tech blinked. "Thees is Dragunova, go."

"We're taking fire from those destroyers!" her first mate radioed back. There was no image to go with the secure acoustic link, but in the background, she heard a muffled thump that could only have been a depth charge. "We're taking evasive and have utilized any and all defensive measures, but somehow they keep finding us. It doesn't make sense. I'm starting to think . . ."

"Theenk what?"

"I-I think they've got our transponder code!"

Natalya's head pulled back sharp on her toned shoulders. It was impossible; only someone high up in the CDF or one of GDT's actual officers would have access to an ORION-class submarine's top-secret security code. And to give it to a foreign entity – a hostile one?

It was treason, pure and simple. No one in their right mind would do that. But still, given the advanced technology *Antrodemus* possessed, versus the antiquated ships that were pursuing her, it was the only thing that made sense.

"Commander Gonzalez, you are to deactivate *Antrodemus*'s transponder, immediately."

"Uh, are you sure?"

"That ees a direct order," Natalya said. Penalties or no, she'd be damned if she would lose her boat and her crew. "Kill the transponder and initiate emergency evasive." She ground her molars, then added, "Eef necessary, use any means necessary to protect my sub."

"*Any* means?"

"You heard me. I don't care eef you have to send all three destroyers to the bottom, and their helicopters, too."

Gonzalez's voice sounded much calmer as he replied. "Yes, captain. What about the landing party?"

"Abandon us," she said, ignoring the sharp inhalations from the three men accompanying her. "We have ample supplies and weapons. We'll be fine. Protect my vessel and people. I weel radio you, once we have completed our survey, and arrange rendezvous."

"Yes, captain," Gonzalez acknowledged. "I'm on it."

Natalya heard the change in the timbre of his voice, felt the rigidity of his posture as he snapped to.

"Disabling transponder as we speak," Gonzalez announced. "Arming NAEGLING torpedoes and bringing LADON Gatling cannon online. If they want a fight, we'll give them one. *Antrodemus* out."

———

Dirk Braddock leaned forward and rubbed his temples, trying to get his head around the ramifications of what he'd just found on his mother's computer.

When he'd first entered her dusty quarters and plopped down behind her monstrosity of a desk, he'd been resolute, yet reserved. He hadn't expected much, and the distracting familiarity of Amara Braddock's personal items: the framed photo of her and Willie Daniels, her and his dad's wedding photo, the video of their father playing with them in their high chairs, and the aged tooth fragment and skin sample from the original Paradise Cove pliosaur, had each seized upon their respective opportunities to deluge him with remembrances.

Some were welcomed with open arms. Others, not so much. But none of the emotions they'd evoked held a candle to what he was feeling now.

The moment he spotted the desktop shortcut titled, "Jake's Dad's 65th Birthday Party", Dirk knew he was onto something. Actually, to anyone who'd known Jake Braddock, it would've stood out like a T-rex stomping down Wall street. The retired lawman had despised his father, John: a violent and abusive man who'd beaten and bullied his only son from the moment he could walk. He was a sadistic drunkard, too, one who would eventually be charged with vehicular manslaughter in the death of his wife.

The last meeting between father and son had ended in a violent altercation, and Jake had, fittingly, left his abusive sire lying face down atop a mound of freshly dug soil, piled beside his mother's waiting grave. They'd never spoken since, and Dirk knew as well as anyone that it would've been a cold day in hell when the family threw John Braddock a party.

Not to mention, he'd died from pancreatic cancer at age 62.

Dirk was intrigued when he opened the file. Or, rather, when he tried to. It was both encrypted and password secured, and he'd wasted two of his three tries trying to guess it. After ten minutes of meditation, it came to him like a smack from his brother Garm.

It was so obvious, he wanted to kick himself. The password was the first word the shortcut's title brought to mind.

Bullshit.

Once he'd gotten in, however, Dirk was unprepared for the full magnitude of what his impromptu investigation had unearthed. In gambling terms, if Amara Braddock's computer had been a one-armed bandit in Las Vegas, he'd just bankrupted the casino.

His mother had been doing clandestine research on Tartarus's former epidemiologist, the much-vaunted Dr. Stanley Wilkins. Wilkins had resigned and dropped off the grid a month ago. But, cyber-sleuth that she was, at least six months earlier, she'd gotten her hands on data his successor had been unable to find – his missing notes and research records.

That reminds me, Dr. Bane is still MIA. And not a word from Smirnov yet.

Dirk reached for his radio.

"Acting Chief Smirnov, this is Dr. Derek Braddock; come in, please."

He waited a full minute, then tried again.

"Attention, security staff, this is Dr. Derek Braddock. Acting Chief Oleg Smirnov, please come in."

When no response was forthcoming, Dirk decided to put the matter on hold and focused on the info laid out before him. What he'd found was unbelievable.

According to the files his mother had accumulated, Kimberly Bane's concerns about Dr. Wilkins' potentially unethical activities had been spot-on. Instead of focusing on a cure for Cretaceous cancer, he'd been deliberately and systematically building up the virulence of the bacterium that caused it. Worse, he'd been strengthening its resistance to the only known antibiotics – the ones cultivated from Jake Braddock's blood.

It was blood Dirk's father had voluntarily offered, whenever a sample was needed. He'd never known what Wilkins was up to.

Besides building up the pathogen's lethality and ease of transmission, Tartarus's very own Dr. Mengele had, for whatever reason, managed to alter it at the molecular level, increasing its mutative effects on a given recipient. In fact, if his notes were legit, he'd gotten to the point that the host experienced a sort of secondary morphogenesis – like a caterpillar transforming into a butterfly.

Based on the included photographic and video documentation, however, the end result was hardly some beauteous, winged wonder.

As he swept his fingers across the yard-wide touchscreen, flipping page after page, Dirk grew more and more astonished. Wilkins had evidently experimented on hundreds of human guinea pigs, all eager "volunteers" for Dr. Grayson's "last chancers" program. The list of degenerates was like a roll call from the cesspools of hell: murderers, arsonists, rapists, child molesters . . . each one worse than the next. But, as it turned out, they'd gotten what was coming to them; they'd died by the scores.

Dirk scrolled down page after page of volunteers, reviewing each patient's status. Most were marked with a large red letter "X", which he assumed indicated a fatality. A few dozen were stamped with a green envelope symbol. Most likely "Return to Sender", he figured. That meant, presumably, that they'd survived the experiment, with little or no symptoms, and had been shipped back to whatever penitentiary they'd come from.

Strange.

Suddenly, Dirk came across a subfolder that contained detailed financial information. Apparently, many of Wilkins' secret experiments had been privately funded, by the military.

He stopped and did a doubletake. The lion's share of disbursements had been personally issued by Admiral Ward Callahan.

Dirk's hand went to his mouth as he stared at the collective statements. That ogre Callahan was mixed up in this? What was he after, some sort of biological weapon to use on enemy troops? Maybe that was the goal; to reduce a foreign army, or even their general population, to a horde of mindless monsters, incapable of using technology, and that fed on one another? A horrifying but potentially effective strategy; it would allow seasoned, well-armed troops to sweep in and slaughter everything that moved, and with impunity. Nobody would question or complain.

No, that couldn't be it. There had to be more than that, Dirk realized, as he further analyzed test results. On the mutagenic side of things, he detected a deliberate focus on the infectees, centered on increasing strength, speed, stamina . . . even cellular regeneration. If you were going to kill something you didn't make it stronger. Was Callahan actually crazy enough to try and go the much-maligned "super soldier" route?

Man, wait until Grayson finds out about this. Military funded and right under our noses? No wonder Wilkins was able to hide his work for so long!

Dirk continued reading, his eyes gradually narrowing into slits. That maniac, Wilkins, had been directly responsible for his father's death. He'd injected him with ever-stronger variants of the Cretaceous Cancer pathogen, until they'd finally overcome his acquired immunity.

The results had been horrific. He'd seen them with his own eyes.

Oh, Wilkins was going to pay for this. And for all the lives he'd destroyed.

Dirk's heart was pounding so hard he started to feel light-headed, and he placed his palms on his mother's desk, drawing in a series of calming, meditational-style breaths. He snorted in disgust as he closed the financials and resumed flipping through the report.

A moment later, he stopped and shook his head in disbelief. In addition to infecting his father, Wilkins had arranged for shipments of over a hundred first-stage infectees to be smuggled into an assortment of foreign locales: England, Taiwan, the Philippines, Okinawa, the Ivory Coast, Cuba . . .

My God, he was deliberately spreading Cretaceous cancer across the globe! What was he trying to do, start his own version of the Black Death? Or was this some sort of bigger, profit-sharing scheme – maybe infect tens of millions, and then sell them all an antidote at a 5,000% markup?

Just when he thought he'd seen everything and was prepared to call Dr. Grayson, Dirk stopped dead.

He'd come to the final section of the report, a folder marked "viable candidates". It was a list of infectees whose condition was considered "stable", and who exhibited only minor detectable symptoms, namely increased aggression and reddening of the whites of the eyes. Each of them had been assigned some sort of undocumented serum: a booster shot that all but eliminated their body's reaction to the pathogen, minimizing its negative and debilitating effects, and amplifying any desired ones.

Dirk gasped as he reviewed the list. There were scores of them, and all were registered as active GDT employees. In fact, most were on Tartarus's payroll.

The guards.

His jaw slowly dropped, millimeter by millimeter, as he reviewed each personnel file. Bryan Wurmer, Jamal White, Kevin Griffith: every one of them had been injected with some version of the modified pathogen and was taking shots to control it. Despite the serum, however, there had been marked side effects. All of them had suffered extreme physiological and psychological changes because of their long-term exposure to the primeval bacteria. Their collective photos looked like a rogue's gallery of before-and-afters from some 1950's monster movie

Take White, for example. His police and arrest records listed him as being six feet tall. Now, he stood six-foot-three. And Griffith, at age twenty-six, had somehow sprouted four inches in twelve months. They were all bigger and heavier and—

Dirk's eyes rounded. He'd found Angus Dwyer's records.

He blinked a few times to make sure, then clicked open the file with an unsteady hand. He was right, it *was* Dwyer's file – the one that was missing from the employee database. Except, his legal name *wasn't* Angus Dwyer. It was Angel Dwyerson, AKA the Angel of Death, AKA the Beast of Bayonne.

AKA the *Bogeyman of Bayonne* . . .

Dirk's mind started moving at Mach speed and he swallowed nervously as he read the file. He remembered the news reports from years prior, how the infamous child rapist, murderer, and cannibal, had cut a bloody swath of terror though even the toughest parts of Bayonne, New Jersey.

Infamous for stalking young boys between the ages of six and ten, Dwyerson, or rather, Dwyer, had proven a stealthy and cunning opponent for the federal task force assigned to bring him to justice. A former cat burglar, he had a penchant for scouting his target's home before striking. He preferred single moms, usually with one child, and would often ingratiate himself to the unwitting woman ahead of time. His usual modus operandi was to pose as a friendly neighbor, social worker, grocery store clerk, or utilities employee, in order to get their guard down.

Once he'd familiarized himself with their routine, he'd break into the house while they were at work and hide under their son's bed. He'd stay there, listening and biding his time. Later, once the whole household was asleep, he'd creep out from under the bed, like the evil spirit he'd been named after, and snatch the helpless youngster, right under his mother's nose.

After that, it was off to whatever temporary kill room he'd prepped: usually a condemned building, abandoned park, or isolated sewer drain. What happened next, Dirk couldn't even contemplate.

That explains that oval-shaped scar the bastard has on his face, the one Garm called him on.

It also explained how, shortly after escaping from the psych ward he was being held in, pending trial, Dwyer managed to vanish without a trace. The nationwide manhunt for him had found nothing. But, how could they? He'd been hiding in Tartarus the entire time.

He glanced at the psychopath's chilling mug shot and blanched. It was no wonder nobody recognized him now. When he'd been processed, Dwyer had been a slim five-foot-ten. Now, he was six-foot-five at least, and built like a mountain gorilla. Even his face had been altered, by what looked like acromegaly.

What the <u>hell</u> is in that pathogen?

Suddenly, a cold anger began to flow through Dirk and he started to shake. He realized he'd uncovered not only the motive for his mother's murder – and a murder it had no doubt been – but also the people responsible.

Amara had discovered all of Wilkins' nasty little secrets: the money, the experiments, the *genocide* . . . even what was going on with the guards. She had undoubtedly planned on exposing all of it to Grayson and the authorities. And the culprits found out about it and killed her.

One of those jack-booted thugs had thrown her to her death, while another watched from shore, making sure she didn't swim to safety.

A particularly unpleasant thought came to Dirk, and he reached for the thumb drive in his pocket. He needed to save this information at once, before anything happened to it. He was certain, once Grayson found out about it, he'd focus on it entirely, but he wanted to have the evidence backed up, just in case. If anything happened to his mother's computer, he—

Dirk jumped at the loud knock on the door.

He licked his lips and opened the monitor window for the peephole camera. That was strange; it showed the hallway outside was empty.

Bam, bam, bam.

Whoever had knocked was back, and more insistent this time. Yet, infuriatingly, the security camera still showed nothing.

Dirk hurriedly inserted his thumb drive, only to discover the system was frozen. He frowned. Well, at least that explained the camera issue. As he got up to answer the door, his eyes flitted to one of his mother's hanging flowerpots, the dried remains of long-dead ivy gardenias, ready to crumble at the slightest touch. Beyond them stood her balcony, and the missing Celazole and steel segment of railing where she'd fallen – make that been pushed – 200 feet to her death.

The banging continued, becoming louder, angrier. Dirk thought it might be Smirnov with an update on Kimberly Bane, but that made no sense. He hadn't told him where he was, so unless he'd used the employee tracking system to find him via his locator implant--

Bam-bam-bam!

Dirk grunted irritably, got up, and stormed toward the door, temper flaring. Whoever the rude SOB was, he was in for a serious chewing out. He gripped the handle with whitened knuckles. A moment later, he yanked the door open, only to have his righteous indignation replaced by shock and panic.

Filling the doorway was a smirking Angus Dwyer.

Dirk barely had time to look up and gasp, before one of the suspended security chief's massive arms lashed out. He had something in his hand, a leather sap, maybe. Whatever it was, it impacted on the astonished scientist's crown with enough force to stun an ox, dropping him.

Now flat on his back, Dirk tried to get up, to fight back, but his limbs refused to respond. He tasted blood and his eyes were unable to focus as he wavered in and out of consciousness. He heard voices, Dwyer's and a few others, but their words were garbled and hard to make out.

Around him, Dirk saw multiple pairs of combat boots. He opened his mouth and tried to shout, tried to warn the rest of them that they had a serial child murderer in their midst. But all that came out was a gurgling sound.

Suddenly, he felt fingers pawing at him, moving him on the floor and tugging at his sleeve. Panic set in, and he began to flail. Powerful hands gripped his shoulders and hips, pushing down and pinning him in place. He felt a sharp, stabbing pain in his right arm and cried out. Whatever they'd stuck him with, it burned like a red-hot needle.

Then, a surprisingly calm voice spoke.

"Fear nothing further, Derek: There is no devil and no hell. Your soul will be dead even sooner than your body."

With his head ready to explode from the pain, Dirk blinked and tried to make sense of what he'd just heard. The quote was familiar – a Nietzsche one, if he wasn't mistaken, but it had been misquoted, rearranged.

He recoiled as Dwyer's evilly grinning face appeared directly above him. Then his teeth clenched and raw anger took over.

"You . . . idiot. That's not even . . . how it goes. Wait until Dr. Grayson--"

Dirk's heart froze in his chest as Dwyer's face inexplicably blurred and someone else's cross-dissolved in its place.

It was Eric Grayson.

"I'm sorry, my dear boy," his silver-haired mentor said, regarding him with those dark, clinical eyes of his. "But, you've made a real mess of things. And now we have to clean it up."

No.

For the first time in his life, Dirk realized how it felt to have the blood drain from his face. It left him cold – cadaver cold – and dead inside. The numbness spread rapidly, and his body twitched as he absorbed the full weight of the astonishing betrayal.

"W-what? You-you're *in* on this?" he stuttered, trying and failing to rise. "You . . . you're *behind* it? W-why? H-how?"

Grayson ignored him and began muttering instructions to Dwyer and the other two guards, discussing how to dispose of his mother's computer. Dirk's vision cleared, and he was able to ID Griffith and a new guard, someone he didn't know.

Then, an adrenaline-buoyed surge of strength came over him and he sat up, forcing the two nearest guards to restrain him. "I don't believe this! Do you know what you've *done*, Grayson?" he shouted. "You're going to *pay* for this, you son of a bitch! Do you hear me? My brother will stop you, you'll see!"

Dwyer leaned forward at the waist, the oval-shaped scar on his upper lip flushing pink as he gave Dirk his most diabolical smile.

"Sounds like you haven't been keeping up on current events, lab rat," he gloated. "Newsflash: Garm 'the Gate' Braddock is dead."

"W-what? That's bullshit!"

Dwyer's snigger chilled him to the core. "His sub exploded. Pity. But in case you don't believe me . . ."

The hulking security chief looked at his employer for approval, then extracted a phone-sized tablet from his rear pocket. He hit a few tabs and shoved it in Dirk's face. He listened amusedly to *Gryphon*'s final moments, relishing the young scientist's horrified expression as he watched his brother die.

Dirk's cry of anguish, backed by the guards' guffawing, echoed throughout his mother's barren quarters. He felt a primal rage well up and welcomed it. With a guttural cry, he threw himself at his assailants, punching, kicking, and even biting so viciously, it took all of them to restrain him.

Then, somewhere in between his yelling and cursing and screams of denial, he heard Eric Grayson say, "Enough of this. It's time for him to meet his maker."

A moment later, with blood seeping steadily from his scalp wound and his arm on fire, Dirk was dragged away. They'd barely traveled fifty feet down one of the complex's dimly-lit concrete corridors before he faded into unconsciousness.

Yet, somehow, he could still hear them laughing.

Eighteen

Sam Mot was fleeing for his life.

With his vision obscured by pinkish drops of sweat, and his heart booming in his chest, the traumatized former LifeGiver scattered a frightened school of amberjack, as he aimed what remained of his TALOS Mark VII combat chassis in a straight line, running fifty feet off the bottom. He exhaled to relieve stress and prayed for more speed, though he knew his surviving pump jet propulsor was already cranking out the max it was capable of – a paltry twenty knots. The MHD had taken quite a beating, but the readings he managed whenever his internal display managed to pop back up told him it still functioned at 81% capacity.

All he could do was keep the hammer down and pray he could made it back. He was fresh out of options.

The ferocity of the mother octopus's attack – and he had no doubt it was the vengeful female that crept up on him – had been astonishing. In the blink of an eye, she snatched up the six-ton AWES like it was made of paper and enveloped it.

He'd fought back, of course, but the superhuman strength TALOS provided proved useless against her. He was pinned almost before he knew it, and helpless. Worse, according to his system's readouts, her truck-tire-sized suction cups secreted some sort of lethal corrosive, strong enough to melt steel.

Sam shuddered at the thought; it had been like swimming in a vat of hydrochloric acid, eating away at his protective exoskeleton, while a hideous beak that looked like it belonged on a kaiju alternated trying to crush and pry open his suit, like a clam in its shell.

He'd been lucky. The Mark VII's enhanced, non-explosive reactive armor had taken most of the initial hits, redirecting the impact of each bite, and keeping the cephalopod from penetrating the most vulnerable portion of the AWES: his mirrored titanium faceplate.

Eventually, however, his outer armor began to fail, section by section, succumbing to the octopus's relentless bludgeoning. Eventually, it gave up the ghost entirely, leaving just four inches of titanium-ceramic composite between him and Death's monstrous maw.

It was then that TALOS's design flaw came to light.

The system's ADCAP reserve armor, unlike the rigid outer layer – designed to shatter as it repelled or redirected impacts – was intended to flex inward under heavy load. It had integrated "crumple zones", designed to increase the pilot's ability to weather prolonged assaults.

Sam licked at the blood dripping from his nose and scoffed. He was fairly certain the mechanical engineers who'd designed the robotic wonder never anticipated a protracted attack of the magnitude he'd endured.

Once the berserk octopus had penetrated his outer defenses, it proceeded with its ultimate goal: tearing him limb from limb. It nearly succeeded, he lamented, sucking in a series of quick breaths to offset the next wave of pain. His taloned right arm – the one he'd used during the initial scuffle, to tear a big chunk out of one of the bitch's tentacles – had been the first to go. Biting into the offending limb at the elbow joint and shaking it, and him, like a pit bull does a sewer rat, she crunched right through it.

Until that moment, Sam hadn't realized how right the pretty ginger back at Tartarus had been about his neural connection to the combat suit. He could feel the AWES' limbs like they were his own, and when he lost the arm, his synapses lit up like a Christmas tree. It was just like when the school of *Xiphactinus* tore him apart, a decade earlier; all he could do was scream.

Encouraged by her victim's agonized shrieks, the octopus went after Sam's right leg next. That one proved more difficult, and required a combination of savage bites, coupled with bridge-cable-thick tentacles twisting him like a pretzel, before it succeeded.

When the leg was wrenched clean from its socket, he nearly blacked out.

As bad as losing two of his mechanical limbs had been, the abdominal bite was the worst by far. With the titanium composite armor designed to flex inward, instead of cracking, it prevented the Mark VII's inner skin from rupturing.

But that didn't make things any better.

Sam glanced down at his midsection and shook his sweat-drenched head. He might've preferred seawater rushing in to end things, as opposed to what happened. The octopus's black, razor-tipped beak had punched deep into the AWES's midsection, deforming it, and driving a pyramid-shaped section of armor, eight inches thick, clean through his stomach. The makeshift spear remained there, and no amount of screaming or crying could dislodge it.

It was at that moment, thank the Universe, that Sam finally broke free. Activating his plasma sword, he'd swung the blazing blue blade with hysterical strength. The creature hadn't been expecting it, and he managed to inflict several deep, cauterized wounds in its pale underside, before it realized what was happening and spat him out.

He'd been near the crumbly edge of the drop-off at that point, with the thing circling him like a colossal wolf, preparing to finish off a surprisingly spunky vole: a vole with a white-hot sword that could cut an anchor chain in two.

Emboldened by the cephalopod's unexpected hesitation, Sam managed to lift off the bottom using his remaining propulsor. His plasma blade flared with the last of its reserves, and he did an aggressive feint. His pseudo-rush worked, and when the surprised colossus sprang backward, displacing enough water to wobble a destroyer, he'd rocketed straight up into the thermocline and hauled ass. The last thing he'd seen was its baleful yellow eyes, watching hatefully as it faded into the murk at his six.

Sam glanced down at the bloodied cone of metal, buried in his intestines, and the torn flesh around it, and fought down the urge to vomit. He wasn't sure if it had hit his spine or not, but it didn't really matter. Only the overdoses of synthetic coagulants he'd willed the Mark VII to inject all around the wound area, combined with enough pain meds and adrenaline to numb an elephant while simultaneously driving it into a frenzy, were keeping him alive and functional.

His only hope was to make it back to the med-techs at Tartarus. That was, assuming the place was still operational.

After the fifth attempt, he'd given up on calling them. His comm system indicated they were receiving his transmissions, so it was a mystery why no one was answering the phone. They had to be aware of Garm's death and the loss of *Gryphon* by now. Maybe the whole place was on lockdown: the crazy SOB *had* set off a nuke, after all.

Sam felt himself starting to get woozy again and willed another shot of epinephrine into his skewered torso, backed by a nice dose of synthetic morphine and some additional stimulants. He snickered as he felt the buoying effect of the powerful meds take effect.

Whoa . . . a guy could get addicted to these, he thought. *Assuming he didn't bleed to death first.*

Checking his course, Sam licked his lips, then cursed as his display sputtered and went out again. As far as he could tell, he was on a straight line run to Rock Key, with a little over sixty miles to go. At his current velocity and, assuming the warning gauge starting to flicker on his reactor readout wasn't a portent of more dire things to come, it would take him a good three hours to get there.

He could do this. He could make it there in one piece. Make that half a piece . . . maybe a third. He activated his rear camera and checked his backdoor, swallowing fearfully.

His dread of a reactor leak was overshadowed – literally – by something far more terrifying. Although he couldn't see it on his screens, his instincts, and the total absence of marine life ahead of him, told him that the octopus was still back there. It was in pursuit, stealthily following him but hanging back, waiting for him to tire.

When he did, and it finally caught up to him, it would finish what it had started.

———

Lurking in Sam's shadow, four hundred yards back, the female *Octopus giganteus* jetted along in stony silence. She stopped, every so often, her gnarled 300-ton body displacing over an acre of sand and silt as she dropped like a deflating zeppelin, down onto the nearby seabed. Each time she did, her color and texture altered, blending in with the nearby coral, and she drew oxygenated water rapidly over her gills, replenishing her strength. She knew the stalk would be a long one, and she was pacing herself for what was to come.

Ahead of her, the female could sense the region's resident marine life vanishing for miles in advance, as they detected her presence. Orca-sized predatory fish, sharks, whales, even a few of the large marine reptiles that appeared to have taken hold of late, all tucked tail and fled.

The beckoning seas before her were a desert, bereft of sustenance.

The female cared not. Although hungry, she made no effort to stalk them. Nor did she expend any energy trying to conceal herself. At least, not from her usual fare. All that mattered to her was the tiny mammal that continued to abscond, terror-stricken, before her.

She could sense the broadband sonar clicks it periodically emitted. Each time she did she ceased her pursuit, merging with the bottom before the sound waves could reach her. The biped's echolocation was sporadic and spotty – undoubtedly, due to its wounds – and of limited range. She made sure to remain well beyond that, keeping at the very edge of its sensory field, and relying on the unique scent trail it exuded to track her prey.

No. It was not her prey.

It was her enemy.

Prey was something to be seized and devoured. The creature she tracked was to be *destroyed*. Utterly. She would devour it, of course, but first she would make it suffer, as slowly and painfully as possible. She had . . . plans for it. Macabre plans, fermenting in the darkest depths of her cold molluscan mind.

Resuming her normal shape, the octopus shot back up off the seabed and jetted forward, her trailing hundred-foot tentacles casting a shadow reminiscent of a colossal Medusa's head, as she crested an approaching underwater peak and swept on. Above her, she spotted one of the floating white constructs she and her mate had recently learned to feed from. This one was small – barely the size of her mantle – hardly worth the effort. It took willpower, but she resisted the urge to surface and tear it and its parasitic inhabitants to pieces.

There would be plenty of time for that, once she had avenged herself.

An hour earlier, when the female arrived at the lair, tense and weary after a frustrating hunt, she was greeted by disaster. The nursery she'd chosen had been destroyed in its entirety, its rusted remnants hurled down into the submarine canyons below. Worse, whatever was responsible for the attack had annihilated not only the midden, but her brood as well.

Her offspring were dead, all of them, and her mate, too. She could still hear his gurgled death knell, echoing throughout the water column, but it was to no avail. There was no body. In fact, she could detect no trace of him whatsoever – his scent trail vanished into the strange sphere of fire that continued to heat the deep, marking the place where he'd fallen.

Reeling from the enormity of her loss, the female had sunk to the bottom and lain there, trembling with rage and grief. She soon found something to vent her fast-growing ire upon, however; a tiny intruder, walking boldly around the rubble-strewn remains of her lair, as if it belonged there.

She began to stalk it. Then, just before she pounced, the tide shifted and she realized that, whatever it was, it smelled like her nursery. In fact, it carried the exact same odor that she, herself, did; the acrid, unpleasant scent of the tiny black granules that littered her former midden's floor. The biped literally reeked of it.

She knew then that it had been inside the nest. *Her* nest.

And that it was *responsible*.

With eyes blazing like twin balls of fire, the astonished female had attacked in a frenzy, rolling over her tiny adversary like an avalanche of sucker-lined tendrils. Shearing jaws snapping wildly, she snatched it up in a windstorm of sand and detritus and quickly overpowered it.

Innate caution kicked in then, and she hesitated, unsure as to what kind of bizarre creature she faced. Although similar in shape to the beak-sized warmbloods that had become her favorite food, it was bigger, heavier, and possibly inedible. Its body was covered with a hardened shell, like some big lobster, but it was a shell that smelled like distasteful iron.

A series of exploratory bites proved her correct. The biped was both resilient and similar in flavor to some of the larger constructs she and her mate had attacked.

Fearing it was some uninhabited construct, the female was on the verge of abandoning her desperately struggling victim, when she managed to sever one of its limbs. The cry of agony it emitted assured her that there was, indeed, a tiny warmblood secreted within that hardened exterior. With cool deliberateness, she went about the process of extracting it.

Before she managed to do so, however, her well-protected adversary surprised her. It possessed a sting of some kind, a bright, impossibly hot weapon that burned like molten lava. She took several agonizing strikes from it, before she flung the vile thing away.

Now, the warmblood was on the run. It was grievously wounded, but the female was in no rush to finish it off. The glittering grains of obsidian, still embedded in her thick skin, had done more than just increase her energy and appetite; they had given her something far more valuable – clarity.

And with that clarity came purpose.

Hard-shelled or no, the biped would die, but it would not die alone. The female knew from experience that, to compensate for their pathetic size and weakness, the air-breathing warmbloods tended to be hive creatures. They congregated in large groups: dozens, sometimes hundreds.

Based on the oily chemicals her enemy exuded, and the ionization trail it left behind – a trail that mimicked a larger one it currently ran parallel to – it was retreating to its lair. And she planned on following it.

She knew in her boneless core that this creature, and others of its kind, had destroyed her precious progeny. They had killed her mate and possibly doomed her species, and she would have her vengeance. Whatever flimsy construct her tiny adversary called home, she would find it. And, once she did, she would invade it as it had invaded hers. She would tear its sheltering walls down around it, destroying and devouring everything it loved, while it watched, cringing.

Then, finally, when all of its brethren had been torn to pieces, the last thing the despicable brood-killer would see was her glistening black beak, as she prized its tiny head off its shoulders and popped it like a ripe piece of roe.

The foreboding depths of Diablo Caldera's saltwater lake, immediately adjacent to the lava tube's ragged opening, were silty and cold: colder than Natalya Dragunova had expected them to be. Despite the annoying sediment, which reduced visibility and wreaked havoc with their sonar systems, it was a welcome change from the gurgling furnace she'd been navigating for the last twenty minutes. She breathed a sigh of relief as the *Remora*'s cabin temperature dropped to endurable levels.

"Whew, that is *much* better," Bender remarked from his copilot's chair. "A few more minutes and I was gonna have to wring out my undies!"

Natalya's brow tightened, and she shot him a baleful look.

"Uh, sorry, ma'am," he mumbled, then turned to Sato and Archer and whispered, "Actually, I go commando."

Archer rolled his eyes. "Captain, all jokes aside, if you decide to shoot him, I'll testify that it was an accidental discharge."

"Me, too," Sato said, his dark eyes dancing. "Probably how he was conceived, anyway . . ."

Natalya caught Bender's chagrined look, then turned toward the two of them, wearing her best deadpan expression. It was useless, and a moment later, she burst out laughing. "Ah, thank you, boys. I needed that." She dabbed at the corners of her eyes, then gave her co-pilot a playful punch to the shoulder that, judging by his wince, might've had a little too much on it. "Okay, playtime's over, ensign. There's going to be more een here than tubeworms. *Focus.*"

"Yes, captain," the redhead said, straightening up. "Water temp is currently 68 degrees, depth just under 3,000 feet." He paused to check his systems. "We're in what appears to be an established thermocline. Temp's a few hundred feet above us climb fast, and the entire phototropic zone hovers at around 82 degrees."

"And the lower regions?" she asked, angling the *Remora* upward, hoping to leave the layer of stained water behind.

Bender indicated their main sonar screen. "As anticipated, the interior of the lake is basically a giant fish bowl. Max depth is just under two miles – around 10,000 feet. It shallows up gradually, eventually sloping upward to dry land." He indicated a few glowing spots on the long-range thermal. "Here and here, you've got some mild geothermal activity. Nothing active, so no worries. In fact, other than those two hot-spots, it's pretty chilly down there. I'm reading temps that match standard ocean bathypelagic ranges: around 40 degrees Fahrenheit."

Natalya inhaled sharply, as the seawater around them unexpectedly cleared. Despite the seemingly endless darkness of the deep, there was no shortage of life. All around them were fast-moving fish of every conceivable color, spiraling around the *Remora* like an iridescent whirlpool, yet never quite touching it. Their movements were so graceful, to her it almost seemed like a ballet. It reminded her of that magical night she'd spent snorkeling in a protected lagoon in the Bahamas, during her honeymoon.

But that was a lifetime ago. Before . . .

Shaking it off, Natalya spotted two huge shoals of fish, directly ahead. They were running parallel to one other and, in the hopes of increasing visibility, she guided the ray-shaped mini-sub directly between them. Their species was an enigma; all she could tell was that they had large scales and were a lustrous copper color. They were small, only a foot or two in length, and each school numbered in the hundreds of thousands. Luckily, they tended to shy away from the *Remora*, scattering the instant its powerful floodlights shone on them.

"Archer," Natalya said over her shoulder, "Anything you recognize?"

The big IDC shook his head. "No, ma'am. Must be a completely undocumented genus."

"I theenk we weel see plenty of those," she said. "And don't worry; auto-record ees activated."

Suddenly, both shoals of fish started to change direction. Separating, each school began swimming in an erratic-yet-organized manner: speeding up, slowing down, shifting left, right, up and down. They moved in unison, in what had to be an orchestrated, instinctive pattern.

"That's murmuration," Archer stated, leaning forward in his seat. "Flock behavior, like swarms of starlings do, all moving as one. There must be – *holy shit!*"

Natalya pulled back hard on the yoke as a pack of six-foot fanged salmonids came rushing in. There were dozens of them, each 200 pounds or more, and moving at incredible speed as they passed the *Remora*'s portside. Like toothy missiles, they powered into the hapless school of baitfish, their open jaws slashing left and right as they did and leaving dead and dying fish spasming in their wake.

"*Enchodus petrosus*," Archer remarked. "Like Goliath tigerfish, only bigger and badder." His eyebrows climbed as the saber-toothed salmon turned on their tails, wheeling back to gorge on their decimated prey.

Natalya eyed the gory spectacle and nodded. "You wouldn't want to go sweeming in thees water, I bet."

Bender swallowed nervously. "Uh, captain?"

Natalya turned to her left to see what he was pointing at and gave a start. A huge squid, as large as the submersible, had pulled up alongside. Its basketball-sized eye appeared to be peering directly at her. It was running parallel to them and, a second later, began to flicker, changing colors rapidly.

She tensed and flipped a switch, checking to make sure the HYDRA cannons were functioning and online. Her eyes narrowed in anticipation of an attack, and her thumbs hovered above the weapon's twin triggers. A notion came to her, and she changed course unexpectedly, heading directly toward the giant cephalopod. Obviously alarmed, it paled and jetted away, leaving a room-sized ink cloud behind, like a truck with a bad exhaust system.

"I forgot our observation portal ees mirrored," she said, chuckling. "Squid must've thought we were potential date. I turned heem down."

All of a sudden, the voracious pack of *Enchodus* ceased their attack. Their rigid fins and humped backs indicated a drastic mood shift. A moment later, they started to disperse. One by one, they abandoned their frenzied feasting, leaving clouds of blood and glittering pennies in their wake.

Still distracted by the limitless bounty, a last *Enchodus* paid a heavy price for its gluttony. In the blink of an eye, five huge forms exploded out of the darkness, and into the illumination provided by the *Remora*'s lights. The startled salmon, spotting the newcomers, turned to flee.

It was a second too late.

In an instant, it was seized by cruel jaws that clamped down on it, driving six-inch ivory spikes deep into its flesh. The terrified *Enchodus* snapped and thrashed with all its might, but it was hopeless. Bit by bit, it was consumed; choked down tail-first by the larger predator.

Sato spoke up. "Wow, I've seen them in the aquarium back home, but never out in the wild and underwater."

At a full twenty feet in length and weighing over 3,000 pounds, the adult *Xiphactinus audax* was a sight to see. Its armored gill plates flared as it finished its meal, then it cast about, looking for more. Not seeing anything of worth, it gave the *Remora* a baleful look from one of its big amber eyes, then jetted away, joining its pod-mates in their pursuit of the retreating *Enchodus* pack.

"Can you imagine seeing one of them on ice?" Bender chirped, "Maybe at the local fish market?"

"Da, ees very beeg... feesh," Natalya said, her words bringing back more unwelcome memories. She shuddered, then glanced around pensively, wondering what else might answer the dinner bell. "We are going shallow," she announced. "Bender, anything beeg on sonar?"

"If you mean any *Imperators*, I don't see anything, at least, not on long range," he advised. He played with the controls, adjusting their emitters and apertures to maximum sensitivity.

"Of course, there are literally millions of life forms in here, and a hatchling or sub-adult could easily be . . . wait, I've got something."

"A pliosaur? Is it inbound?"

"No, it's down deep," Bender said. "Like, abyssal zone deep. There's more than one, they're – what the hell?"

"What ees eet?"

He shook his freckled head. "It's a bunch of fish of some kind. At least, that's what the system says. Species is unknown. Holy crap, they're--"

"They're *what*?" Natalya pressed.

"They're ginormous!" Bender said, his eyes like saucers as he doublechecked his readings. "I'm talking blue whale big!"

Archer leaned into his seatbelt. "Really? How many are there?"

"Dozens," the communications officer replied. He pointed at a series of blips on the scope. "There's a whole school, or pod, down near the bottom. They're just hanging out."

Archer cleared his throat. "Captain, do you think we could--"

He stopped as a dull flash of light appeared on their ventral camera monitor.

"Whoa, did you see that?" he asked, craning his neck and pushing hard on his armrests, fighting his seatbelt.

There was a second flash, and then a third. The momentary bursts of illumination were tiny but intense, like someone dropped a camera overboard on a moonless night and its flash went off, a hundred feet below.

"Copilot, what the hell am I looking at?" Natalya demanded. The light show was alarming, and she experienced a sudden urge to gun it. Instead, she took a calming breath; they were in a primeval world. It could be anything.

Bender looked confused. "It's uh, some kind of electrical discharge."

"Like, from another submarine?"

"I don't think so. It, uh, it looks organic-based."

Archer spoke up. "Captain, maybe we should investigate?"

Natalya threw him a dubious look, then looked at Bender. "How powerful is thees discharge; could it affect us?"

His lips did the fish thing as he puffed a breath. "Hell, yeah. It could fry every circuit we've got."

"There's your answer, Archer," Natalya said, reaching for the throttle. The inertia pressed everyone tightly into their seats, as she kicked the *Remora* into high gear. The feel of the powerful craft was intoxicating, slicing through the water like the flying wing it was.

"Speed is forty knots," Bender observed. When he got no reply, his expression turned edgy and he focused on their sonar screens.

"Relax, ensign," Natalya said, smirking. "Nothing ees chasing us." She gave him an ominous look and added, "At least, not yet."

"We're at 900 feet," he advised, eyeing their depth gauge.

She continued cruising at a steep angle, anxious to get into the sunlit portion of Diablo's lake. Odds were, they were far from the biggest predator in the place, and she preferred to be able to see threats coming with her own two eyes.

"Five hundred, four hundred . . ." Her copilot glanced forward. "Entering phototropic zone."

Natalya could actually feel her pupils contract as she penetrated the dazzling upper depths of the Cretaceous-era reservoir. At three hundred feet, the water transformed from a dark bluish gray to a brilliant blue azure. At one hundred, it was a dazzling turquoise, with gleaming golden spears of sunlight penetrating all around them.

Marine life was so omnipresent, she began to wonder if there were any pliosaurs left. The absence of an established apex predator would throw everything out of whack. It would certainly explain the abundance of giant fish, and why everything seemed to be eating everything else.

"Deestance to beach," she requested, leveling off at the fifty-foot mark and dropping their speed to a more comfortable thirty knots.

"Just over two miles," Bender advised. "At our current velocity, we should make landfall in four minutes."

"Khorosho." Natalya indicated their console's main viewer. "I prefer to not use drone yet. Pull up overview of landing area, based on satellite report."

"You got it," Bender said, typing rapidly. "Keep in mind, it's not textbook perfect, due to the prevailing cloud cover and mist, but it should do the job."

He hit a key, converting the flat screen image to hologram format, and adjusted it into a four-foot-wide projection, sitting on their dash.

"Our chosen landing site is the forest bordering the caldera's southern shore," Bender said. He twisted in his seat to give Sato and Archer a better vantage, then pointed at the multi-colored image. "Evidence suggests that the tsunami that inundated the island during the Chicxulub impact deposited a tremendous amount of soil and substrate into that region. This created an artificial landmass, absent from the initial eruption, millions of years earlier. It borders half the lake and, when viewed from above, gives the island's interior an oval shape." He indicated a heavily wooded region. "Whatever plant life exists seems to have done well and, despite damage from the eruption thirty years ago, the rain forest has rebounded nicely."

I'd like to see them try logging there, Natalya thought darkly.

Archer stroked his chin. "I'm reminded of the Wollemi pine. So, what are the conditions? And how big is the actual forest?"

"Tropical, for sure. We're looking at a crescent-shaped region pushing eight miles from tip to tip, but with a maximal diameter of less than half that." He paused, studying the lieutenant's face. "The first hundred yards or so are beach and a few palms. After that, it gets very dense, so stay on your toes. Anything could be in there."

"He's expecting to see a dinosaur," Natalya remarked, grinning.

Sato warily eyed the pixelated image. "Okay, so my job here is to help take samples, but also to make sure our ride stays in one piece." He tapped his chair arm with his palm. "That said – and I know these bad girls are pretty rugged – I think it's best we avoid as many knocks as possible. So, where and how are we planning on docking?"

Natalya pointed at a section of the hologram, where the lake met the shore. "There ees a nice, sandy spot on thees section. We weel beach the *Remora* there and use her land anchors to hold position."

Sato licked his lips and nodded, then pulled a small tablet from his shirt pocket and did some quick fingering. "Okay, good news is the tide's just starting to turn, so we've got inbound and slack for the next few hours. That should work. I can set the anchors to auto-adjust, so Mother Nature doesn't end up swamping us."

"And the bad news?" Natalya asked.

"Bad news is, if we don't make it back before the next outgoing tide, we'll end up stranded and have to spend the night here."

"Thees is exactly why I brought you," she said, smiling. "To cheer us up and solve problems."

"And me?" Archer asked.

"You, my large friend? You're here for medical skeels, and for ballast."

"Ah . . ." The hulking lieutenant grinned, then indicated Bender. "And what about our gabby communications officer?"

"Heem?" Natalya regarded the diminutive Irishman with appraising eyes. "He's here for added security."

Bender's mouth flew open wide. "W-what? How the hell am I--"

"Eef something beeg tries to eat us, I weel throw you to eet."

He snorted. "And *that's* going to buy you enough time to get away?"

"Absolutely. Do you know how long eet takes to get taste of bullsheet out of mouth?"

Natalya turned and gave them all a look of mock astonishment, then joined them in a hearty round of guffawing. It was good to keep things light. Given the caldera's relatively small forest, she doubted they would run into any large carnivores. But then again, it *was* Diablo.

And the name said it all.

———

Despite the unsteady footing, Natalya moved lithely around the beached *Remora*, avoiding the lapping waves and double-checking its stability. She exhaled hard and shook her maned head. It was hot as hell inside Diablo Caldera, maybe hotter.

She figured that was apropos.

They'd beached themselves on a relatively level stretch – an accomplishment, given the area's innumerable dunes. The sand was pale gray in color, a far cry from what she'd been expecting. She supposed it had something to do with the volcanic soil, ash, or lava, but it was far from her area of expertise.

Satisfied that Petty Officer Sato was correct, and that the mini-sub's automated anchors would keep the eight-ton craft in place, Natalya adjusted her tinted ADCAP combat goggles' fit and went to check on Lieutenant Archer. En route, she took a swig from the insulated canteen she had clipped to her belt and wiped her brow with an equally sweaty forearm. She wore only fatigue trousers and a tank top, having ditched her cumbersome helmet and body armor

Even that did little to offset the oppressive heat and humidity. As she approached Archer, distracted as he surveyed the caldera's towering interior walls though a pair of electronic range finders, she noticed he and the rest of her team still had the bulk of their protective gear on.

Apparently, they didn't share her overly optimistic view of the place being uninhabited. That, or they were masochists who hoped to lose twenty pounds of water weight, before their departure.

"Any theeng of interest?" Natalya asked as she drew near. Even with her boots on, she had to glance upward; at six-foot-five, the heavily muscled corpsman was a full three inches taller than her. She liked that; it made her feel like Garm had, more feminine. When it came to a woman's primal response to a man, size really did matter.

Archer lowered his optics, allowing them to hang suspended from his neck. "You could say that." He took a moment to wipe the sweat from around his eyelids and donned his own goggles. "According to my scans, the caldera's walls were originally much higher." He indicated the huge saltwater lake, stretching farther than the eye could see. "Water levels, on the other hand, have risen and fallen over time, more or less matching sea levels."

Natalya nodded, then looked around for Sato. He was busy lugging a heavy armload of GDT M18-DT carbines and clips from the *Remora*'s onboard armory. He paused as he stepped off the end of the armored hatch that also served as their gangplank. "Computer: close hatch."

The curved door curled smoothly upward in response, closing with a low thud and a hiss. Sato gave the ADCAP submersible a final once-over. Then, satisfied that their ride home was safe and secure, he made his way over to his captain and started handing out weapons.

Impressed with his efficiency, Natalya gave him an approving look.

"Sample gathering packs, survey gear, and supplies are all ready," he said to her, indicating a nearby pile. "Here's your insurance policy."

Natalya accepted one of the weighty double-barreled carbines, inspected it, and then slung it over one shoulder. Personally, she preferred the hard-hitting .454 Casull semi-auto she had strapped to her hip, but the M18 packed even more of a wallop and, with dual 60-round clips, a lot in the reserve department. Better safe than sorry.

She gave the caldera's raggedy slopes a long look, trying to picture the terrifying cataclysm that had taken place sixty-five million years earlier, when a thousand-yard-high wall of water plowed into its exterior and inundated the place.

It was hard to imagine. But then, she mused, apocalypses were like that.

A moment later, she saw Bender, thirty yards away, bend at the waist to examine something at the water's edge. She moved to investigate.

"Hey, Archer," the comms officer called out excitedly. "I've got a weird-looking snake for you to tag and bag!"

Still a few paces back, Natalya saw what he was referring to: a chartreuse-colored sea snake of some kind, exploring the shallows in search of a meal. The smooth-scaled serpent was sluggish in its movements and small, maybe four feet in length, but thick bodied.

"Don't touch it!" she yelled, just as Bender was about to grab. He yanked his hand back and gave her a look.

"What's the problem?" he asked. "We're supposed to bring back samples."

"You know nothing about thees animal," she replied. A second later, Archer came hoofing over, only to stop short.

"She's right," he cautioned. Eyes intense, he took off his oversized backpack and extracted a yard-long set of tongs and a plastic capture case. "Think about it. You've got a slow-moving animal that stands out like a neon bass lure, creeping around a predator-rich environment, without a care in the world. Don't you think that's a bit odd?"

Bender swallowed and stepped back as Archer gently hoisted the serpent with his tongs. It was halfway in the container when it lashed out unexpectedly, biting the grippers with surprising speed. Its fangs did little damage to the carbon fiber and metal, but the steaming venom trails it left made quite the impression.

"Definitely an elapid of some kind," Archer said, sealing the aerated container and observing the now-relaxed snake through its translucent walls. "I'm betting toxicity levels match those of the Australian tiger snake. Congrats, Freckles; the captain just saved your life."

Natalya pretended to be angry at herself, then grinned. "Okay, lieutenant. Stow your new pet and let's get theengs under way." She regarded Bender. "And, ensign, stop screwing weeth the local wildlife and get a drone een the air. I want an aerial survey and mapping of the lake perimeter, ASAP."

"Yes, captain."

While the two of them moved to accomplish their assigned tasks, Natalya turned to find Sato studying his tablet. His brow crinkled up.

"Sometheeng of note?" she asked, moving beside him.

"Very curious, captain," Sato said. "I started reviewing our sonar readings of the lake floor as we approached the shallows. You know, to make sure the anchors would hold." He indicated a stratum scan he'd recorded. "Apparently, the first hundred feet or so of the bottom is largely comprised of decayed animal remains – skeletal, for the most part – deposited over seventy million years."

He zoomed in on one image. "See this section, where the sound waves penetrated a good thirty feet?" He indicated a large bone mass with his index finger. "This is definitely the mandible of a large pliosaur – you can see the mandibular symphysis – and around it are the ribs, teeth, and vertebrae of legions of smaller life forms. Some are literally peeking out of the sediment. It's a treasure trove of information down there: a layer-by-layer time capsule of how evolution took place inside the caldera. And all waiting to be explored."

"Very good," Natalya said. "But we don't have that much time."

Sato shrugged. "Yes, ma'am. I mean . . . if we get to come back."

Natalya stiffened as Archer's voice suddenly emanated from her goggles' integrated earpiece. "Captain," he said softly, "Can you come here, please?"

Glancing around, she spotted him at the crest of a nearby dune. He was in a crouch and focused on something on the other side. She loped up to him, slowing as he signaled for caution, and bent down as she reached the hilltop.

"Why the radio?" she asked.

"Shush. What do you make of those?" Archer asked quietly, pulling her down to his level and gesturing at something below them.

Natalya gasped despite herself. Not fifteen yards away and sunning itself on a sandbar at the lake's edge, lay an enormous crocodilian. Actually, it was the nearest of seven of them, she realized, all basking in the sun. Most ranged from thirty-five to forty feet in length, but the closest one was enormous: sixty feet at least. It was a battle-scarred beast with webbed paws the size of hogsheads, and dark, rugged skin, coated with tightly-packed scutes and scales. Its long and slender snout stretched nine feet in length and was lined with sharp, needle-like teeth, the size of icepicks.

"Bozhe moi!" she sputtered. "It's, I mean, *they* are unbelievable!"

At the sound of her voice, the colossal reptile's green eye opened lazily. It studied her and uttered a loud warning hiss, but seemed disinclined to move.

An apprehensive look came over her. "Are they dangerous?"

"If you're a fish, definitely. They look like giant gharials," Archer said, studying them through his optics, and then activating the device's photo app. "I just don't know what they're doing here."

"Why, they're not Cretaceous animals?"

He scratched his head. "No, at least not that I know of. There was a Miocene genus called *Rhamphosuchus* that lived in India, and another called *Gryposuchus* that lived in South America."

"There you go," Natalya said, her eyes still wide as she took in the colossal piscivores. She turned at the waist and indicated a far-off pile of volcanic stone – rubble that had sealed the colossal cleft in the caldera's towering walls during the last eruption. "Maybe one or two rode een on a piece of driftwood and crawled eenside, back when there was steel access via the beach."

"More likely swam in," he concurred. "I seem to recall them inhabiting coastal regions. But the size? Historically, they might have grown as large as the smallest one down there, but the bigger ones . . . Jesus."

"We never have biggest fossil of any extinct animal. And don't forget Foster's rule of island gigantism," Natalya said quietly. "I read up on eet while preparing for the meeshun."

Archer looked impressed. "I just don't see how they made it."

"What do you mean?"

"Well, judging from those mounds of sand, I'm assuming we're looking at a nesting group of females, and this big one," he indicated the sleeping giant, "Must be the dominant male."

"Da, so?"

"Well, think about it, ma'am," he said, shaking his head slowly. "Those things are fish eaters, but for countless millennia they shared a lake of limited size with a breeding population of hypercarnivorous marine reptiles that could bite any one of them in half."

Natalya nodded, "Da, but look at their armor. Ees very strong, don't you theenk?"

Archer nodded. "Yeah. Heavily ossified, extreme dermal armor, probably as hard as turtle shell. Definitely evolved for protection, but I can't see even that withstanding the jaws of an adult pliosaur." He indicated the stretch of beach surrounding the gharials' nesting spot. "Plus, this is the best place to lay eggs in the entire caldera. I doubt very much that a mother *Kronosaurus imperator* would deign to share."

Natalya pointed at the big male gharial. "Look, thees one has old bite scars on hees side and tail. Maybe there ees confrontation between them, after all."

Archer's sharp eyes intensified as he studied the yard-wide, oval-shaped indentations she'd pointed out. He grabbed his optics and swept the group. "Those aren't pliosaur bites," he announced. "They're the wrong shape." He pointed at a far-off gharial. "See that small one on the left? She has a fresh bite on her shoulder region. It's bloody, but her dermal scutes prevented the attacker from causing serious harm."

"So, eef not pliosaur, what ees bite from, an X-feesh?"

Archer clicked his tongue. "I think it's a shark bite."

"Really? Must be beeg shark."

Bender's chortled cry of triumph, coupled with the sound of high-speed rotors, told Natalya her copilot had finished prepping one of their military-issue surveillance drones. Her hair wafted in the breeze as she turned her back on Diablo's windswept waters and gestured for Archer to join her.

"Ees she all set?" she asked the jubilant ensign, as he kept the yard-wide drone hovering at eye level.

"You bet, captain," Bender replied. He eyed the monitor in the center of his remote, as he sent the expensive device hurtling straight up. At the hundred-foot mark, he guided it toward the water. "Commencing sweep and scan of the shoreline, as ordered. I . . . holy shit!" He spun toward her, eyes popping. "Right on the other side of those dunes is a--"

"Sleeping group of giant crocodiles?" Natalya threw Archer a wink. "Da, we already stopped by and said hello. You can skeep them."

Bender shook his head in disbelief and began muttering to himself, before retreating to the *Remora*'s shaded side to focus on his assignment.

She signaled to Sato, who had taken up position atop a grass-dotted hillock, in the sheltering shade of a towering palm tree. He was distracted by something he was studying through his binoculars, to the point she was forced to call him on the comm link.

"On my way, captain," he responded. He was practically panting from the heat and paused to chug water from his canteen, before jogging over to her and Archer.

Sato stood there, eyeing the heavy backpack at Natalya's feet with little enthusiasm. His brow crinkled up and, after a moment's deliberation, he removed his weighty helmet, body armor, and vest, just like his captain had. His white undershirt was practically soaked, and he sighed pleasurably as he felt a cooling breeze's caress.

"Your choice," Natalya stated. "But you are breenging your carbine."

"Absolutely. Better to have and not need, right?"

"Da." She gave Archer an inquiring look.

"I'm fine, ma'am," the big corpsman replied. He tapped his helmet with his knuckles, then picked up his weighty gear bag and shouldered it like it was nothing. "When you work a job that requires you to carry bodies around, you get used to toting a load."

Natalya nodded approvingly. Meanwhile, Sato finished struggling into his pack and donned his combat goggles. "Okay, you two," she began. "I weel conduct a survey of the immediate shoreline and make sure Bender doesn't leave us behind." She indicated the nearby rain forest. "Your job ees to explore the woods. I suggest you cut straight through until you see the caldera wall, then do a zeeg-zag as you work your way back."

"Yes, ma'am," Archer said, gripping his M18.

"Try not to deesturb any theeng. Remember, we are first humans to set foot in caldera. No littering."

Sato held up a finger. "Actually, I don't think we are."

Natalya gave him a look.

"I mean, we're not the first humans." He turned and started trudging back up the hill he'd just come down. "Come on, I'll show you."

Intrigued, she bounded after him, with Archer running a close second, doing the pack mule thing. At the top, her curiosity cross-dissolved into disbelief as she saw what he was pointing at.

Two hundred yards away, and protruding out from the shoreline, were a series of rotted tree stumps. There were two rows of them, and they ran parallel in a straight line, extending perhaps a hundred feet from shore, before disappearing beneath the surface of the lake.

"Are those . . . pilings?" she asked, already knowing the answer.

"Absolutely," Sato said. "You can still see the cut marks." He handed her his optics, so she could take a closer look.

Archer peered through his own binoculars. "Judging by the degree of decay, I'd say whatever structure that was, it was maintained until the last eruption."

"So, there were *people* here?" Natalya breathed.

"Yes, and there may *still* be some," Sato advised.

"That ees impossible. Nothing could survive the gas and heat een thees enclosed place."

"Why not?" Archer said. "The gharials did."

"Da, but thees structure has not been worked on een decades."

Sato cleared his throat and grinned. "Hey, if you guys liked the old pier, you're gonna love this!"

He pointed to a region to their left, some fifty yards closer. In the shade of an invading palm grove, lay a series of irregular mounds of sand and vegetation. There was nothing definable about them, however, until she zoomed in.

In the center of the mounds, Natalya saw what resembled the surviving framework of a burned-down home. Except, the beams that remained upright like blackened sentinels, bared to the sky, appeared to have been made from huge animal bones. Some had a decided reptilian look to them, others didn't.

"You've got to be sheeting me," she muttered.

"Not my thing," Archer said, grinning. "But, Sato's right. That certainly looks like a big, burned-out hut of some kind." He exhaled heavily, inserting his fingertips beneath his helmet's thick overhang to wipe his brow. "There's way too much to see here in the brief time we have. We need to come back with a full team, including a few anthropologists I know."

Natalya thought it over and shrugged. "We make the most of the time we have. I weel use long-range cameras, or maybe second drone, and gather documentation of old village. You two explore the rain forest and breeng back samples of unknown plants and animals, as planned. We need to make Grayson and Doctor Derek happy."

"So, no digging for human remains . . ." Sato said.

"Nyet, but be careful," she warned. "Eef there are people steel here, they may not like us dropping een."

Sato adjusted his rifle's position. "Yes, ma'am. If they are, they must be in the woods. We'll be careful."

"Keep een touch regularly on the multiband and use your bodycams and goggles' motion sensors." She held up a warning finger. "Remember, *Remora*'s sonar ees useless een here."

"Don't worry, captain," Archer said good-naturedly. "I'll take care of him."

Natalya half-smiled. "I deed not theenk eet would be other way around."

"Oh, so *that's* how it is?" Sato chuckled as he turned and took the lead. "Believe me, if you get hurt, I am *so* leaving your overgrown ass in the bush!"

Archer fell in after him. "You mean, you wouldn't drag me to safety?"

"And ruin my back? Are you nuts?"

"Oh, c'mon, man. I had a light lunch!"

Natalya snickered as she started back toward the mini-sub, intent on hauling out the other drone. Behind her, she could still hear Archer and Sato yakking away, with the latter asking his cohort what kind of imaginative tale he'd like him to concoct, in the event he was forced to abandon him to an untimely demise.

"Make my death glorious . . ."

Garm would have approved.

NINETEEN

There's nothing like the wet, crunchy sound of ridged fangs punching right through bones and shearing flesh. Maybe some people find it horrifying, but to me, it's exhilarating. I love it, because it means I'm a good "mom".

Dr. Stacy Daniels smiled, as she watched *Gretchen* finish scarfing down the nearly 2,000 pound. Atlantic bluefin she'd just lowered into her paddock. After an initial exploration of the still-twitching fish, the cow pliosaur had taken to rubbing her muzzle back and forth on its warm flesh, overloading the sensitive pores on her muzzle with its scent and flavor, before finally striking.

In human terms, it was like a child relishing a giant cupcake, prior to diving in; the juvenile *Kronosaurus imperator* had been in her glory.

It wasn't just the size of the unexpected treat, but the uncommon flavor. Thirty years ago, bluefin tuna had teetered on the brink of extinction: a sad testimony to mankind's relentless slaughter of the species. Surprisingly, and unlike many fish stocks, the pliosaur "invasion" had proven beneficial to the fast-swimming *Thunnus thynnus*. With recreational fishing all but eliminated by the threat the aggressive marine reptiles posed, bluefin numbers had begun to rebound.

But it wasn't enough. Stacy was hoping a full-scale restocking program, one that incorporated their larger, genetically enhanced fish, would turn the tide. GDT certainly had the resources. All she had to do was convince Grayson of the public relations benefits such a program could provide, and it was a done deal.

Finally convinced of *Gretchen*'s ability to swallow her enormous meal without complications, Stacy gave the fifty-foot Thalassophonean an affectionate pat on the snout and stepped back to enter the details of her latest meal in the log. High above and in the distance, she saw the hydraulic lift that had delivered the fish scooting smoothly back along its web-like track, returning to one of Tartarus's suspended docking stations until its services were once again needed.

She glanced up, eyeing the far-off row of pliosaur tanks, lined up like watery monoliths along the facility's southern wall. With their midday exercise interval completed, the captive saurians were hungry and eager for their next feeding. Which was in . . . ninety minutes, she observed, checking her watch. It was live bison today, if memory served.

Stacy looked around, noting that the facility's sprawling concrete docks were practically deserted. That was odd, considering the hour. But, then again, most of the technicians and engineers tended to make themselves scarce whenever one of her programmed workout sessions started. She might've loved the rhythm and beat that 80's pop classics like Scandal's *"The Warrior"* provided her saurians, but not everyone's tastes mirrored her own.

Stacy pursed her lips, wondering how their latest sale, the wild-caught Gen-1 cow now designated *Goliath*, was doing. In her opinion, Rear Admiral Ward Callahan was a loose cannon, and she was legitimately worried that he might do something reckless with the newly implanted beast he had in thrall.

Which reminded her, she needed to schedule *Polyphemus* and *Charybdis* for their cortical implant upgrades. Callahan had already issued a check to cover their purchase, and he wanted his next two bioweapons prepped and delivered, ASAP.

Personally, Stacy thought Grayson was making a mistake, selling the two pliosaurs. The huge, one-eyed bull maybe, but not *Charybdis*. The scarred cow's unique approach to avoiding aerial attacks was an adaptation no other *Kronosaurus impera-tor* exhibited. From a behavioral perspective alone, she was a study specimen worth holding onto.

Or, she grudgingly admitted, it was possible she had a habit of becoming too attached to some of her charges.

She sighed as she finished her log entry, then made a face as she reached down and tugged at the crotch of her admittedly snug neoprene wetsuit. She smirked, knowing if Dirk had been there he'd have made one of his typical, "too much junk in the trunk" jokes, while unabashedly ogling her backside. And she would have gotten even with him, later that night, by sitting on his face until he almost suffocated.

Her eyes lit up. *Maybe I'll just pretend he said it and teach him a lesson.*

Grinning ear-to-ear now, Stacy walked away from *Gretchen*'s pool. She used her wristband to buzz open the sole egress in the chain link fence that kept passersby from straying into the plio-saur's domain. With the gate still open, she looked back at the watchful marine reptile and smiled, albeit fretfully.

She was worried about *Gretchen*. Especially, now that Dirk knew she'd been faking the captive *Kronosaurus*'s implant all these months. It wasn't that she expected him to act on this newfound knowledge. In fact, after his experience in the water with the cow, the scientist in him had to be fascinated.

That was, if he'd gotten over his near-death experience.

Stacy's hand crept to her heart. She could feel it, pounding like a marching band's drum section in her chest. God, it had been *so* close. She'd nearly lost Dirk. Just a few more seconds and--

Tears came unbidden to her eyes and she blinked repeat-edly, trying to clear her vision. If the man she loved had been bitten apart by the animal she'd taken in and raised, ostensibly because she'd refused to do the implant, it would've destroyed her. There was no coming back from something like that.

The man I love. Wow.

It was hard to admit, but it was time she fessed up. She was in love with Dr. Derek J. Braddock, lock, stock, and barrel. Whenever she wasn't occupied, he was all she thought about. His keen intellect and crooked smile, his mischievous sense of humor . . . he could be a real charmer, too. That is, when he wasn't being an intellectual jerk or obsessing over that over-grown she-wolf, Natalya Dragunova.

And, of course, there was the physical aspect of their bonding, feelings of passion she'd never experienced with anyone else.

Stacy sighed. If only they could have a future together. If only she could give him what he truly needed, if she could only *be* what he needed.

But, she couldn't; it was as simple as that. She'd kept something from him, and when he found out – and he would – it would be over. It was inevitable. She'd thought about telling him many times, had even *tried* to, once or twice, but the timing never seemed right. Or, if it had been, her cowardice won out.

She sighed. Nobody knew the terrible secret she carried.

Actually, that wasn't entirely true. His mother had known it, but she--

God, what would Amara have done if he'd died?

Stacy started crying at that point, but then shook her head spasmodically, forcing herself to stop. She scrubbed away the tears with her palms, chiding herself for being an emotional fool. Yes, it *could've* happened, but it *didn't*, she reminded herself. Dirk had emerged unscathed, because Karma had decreed he wasn't meant to die like that. Everything was fine.

But was it? Eric Grayson had eyes and ears everywhere. What if the CEO found out? Would he order her do *Gretchen*'s procedure: install the cybernetic implant, and turn her beloved pet into a mindless automaton? And, if he tried, could she possibly go through with it? She'd be fired and replaced if she refused, and if she *did* go through with it, it would be such a betrayal. How could she live with herself?

Stacy gave the big pliosaur a distraught look, while her surgeon's mind speed-dissected possible options. Suddenly, a wanton, rebellious look came over her and her amber eyes began to gleam from within.

She had a solution. She could set *Gretchen* free.

Yes, it was possible. Every one of the saurian paddocks – even *Tiamat*'s – had a reinforced gate at one end, a portal that opened into a series of water-filled submarine tunnels that connected to a main conduit, leading out to sea. During Tartarus's initial construction, they'd been intended as a means of conveyance for captured specimens. But, now, with the advent of the ORION-class, they were primarily relegated to providing access to clean seawater and microorganisms for each paddock's impeller-driven filtration system.

The gates could be opened individually or, in the event of a disaster, like an earthquake or reactor leak, simultaneously. Unlocking *Gretchen*'s paddock doors wouldn't raise any alarms. But deactivating the canal locks that would allow the huge predator to escape into the Atlantic, would be like setting off the 4th of July.

If she were caught, it would mean termination, the mother of all lawsuits, and probably some jailtime. But who said she'd be caught?

She'd rigged the system before – incapacitated an entire floor of security cameras and motion detectors. She could do it again; it was simply a matter of outwitting the system's designers and keeping the gatekeepers distracted.

A look into *Gretchen*'s worshipful eyes was all it took to steel Stacy to start preparing for the task ahead. The decision was made. She would begin researching tonight. Hopefully, she would not have to move past the preparatory stage, and her plan would end up being something she kept in reserve, a worst-case scenario type option.

Still, it *was* appealing. The thought of the captive-raised pliosaur roaming free for the first time in her life brought a huge smile to her face. How *Gretchen*'s senses would soar!

She could even picture herself accompanying her pet: donning one of their high-tech rebreathers and riding the whale-sized saurian into the sunset, like some colossal, armor-plated seahorse. The thought of flipping Grayson the bird as they made their escape made her giggle.

What a pair they'd be. She visualized them snacking on fresh fish and porpoising through the waves at breathtaking speed, with the seven seas as their playground. Ironically, many times she'd considered broaching the topic of taking *Gretchen* out through the Vault doors. It would have been an experimental outing, maybe an extended workout.

In the end, she'd never brought it up. It wasn't fear of being told no, it was what might happen if the answer was yes. Although the adolescent *Kronosaurus* cow was docile and even playful in the confines of her paddock, Stacy had no idea what a taste of freedom might do to her. She probably wouldn't turn on her "mother", but she might prove difficult to entice back into the dark and dismal prison she'd grown up in.

Freedom, once given, was a gift that came with "no returns" stamped on it in very big, very bold letters.

Stacy sighed. Maybe she was getting worked up over nothing. Everything would probably be fine. But, just in case, a little research into Tartarus's tunnel schematics, and the security systems that warded them, wouldn't hurt.

She was just reaching for the gate, with the intent of swinging it closed, when she heard something. It was a dull crashing sound, like something heavy had fallen. It came from a nearby tool shed, the one where she and Dirk had made love, just a few days ago.

It was the one where she kept the adhesive she used to fake *Gretchen*'s scar.

Was someone in there?

Stacy thought she saw a light flicker inside the darkened shed and started toward it. She was halfway there, when a hulking shadow detached itself from the surrounding darkness and started in her direction. Startled, she cried out.

"Doc Daniels," a baritone voice said. "I've been looking for you."

Stacy's chest began to tighten, but she breathed a sigh of relief as one of Tartarus's black-clad security guards stepped into the light and walked toward her.

She faked a smile and did her best to hide the instinctive revulsion she felt. It was Kevin Griffith, the 27-year-old former farmhand who, according to his records, had been given a life sentence after he skewered his former employer with a pitch fork.

Apparently, as Dirk had put it, he didn't appreciate his honeymoon with one of his boss's prize Holsteins being interrupted.

"Hello, Officer Griffith," Stacy intoned. Her nose crinkled up involuntarily as he drew close. *Jesus, he stinks like fresh manure. Did he just come from the lower levels, where we store the livestock?*

"I need you to come with me, ma'am," Griffith said, his eyes shifting from her partially-exposed breasts back to her face, as he noticed her catching him ogling.

Stacy felt the hairs on the back of her neck prick up. "Come with you where?" she asked, guardedly.

"Doctor Braddock asked me to bring you to him, immediately," Griffith replied, now boldly looking her up and down. "It's an emergency."

"An 'emergency'? Really . . . Is that why you're checking me out, so *inappropriately*?"

The freckle-faced zoosexual tried to appear disarming, but between his brutish physique and the gap-toothed leer he attempted to pass off as a smile, he failed miserably.

"Uh, sorry, ma'am," he replied, obviously annoyed. Suddenly, a 'fuck it' look came over him and he stepped intimidatingly close. His hand shot out, encompassing Stacy's upper arm hard enough to leave a bruise. "Look, let's not make this unpleasant. Just come with me, okay?"

"Get your fucking hands off me!" she snapped, trying and failing to yank her arm away. As Griffith looked around to see if anyone was watching, alarm bells started going off in Stacy's head. She decided to hang tough. "What the hell do you want?" she demanded.

"You," he said creepily.

As his other hand reached for her breasts, she freaked. She extended her free arm and shoved hard at the pervert's collarbone region, trying to exert enough pressure to break away.

It was useless. At six-foot-three and an easy 230, her opponent was five inches taller and eighty pounds heavier. A one-sided wrestling match ensued, with Griffith smiling sinisterly as he pulled her pelvis roughly against him and started groping her ass.

"Man, that shit is *tight*," he said huskily. "You're black and Chinese, right? Nice! I've never fucked a *chigger* before. This should be *sweet*."

Stacy's blood pressure spiked, but the sheer incredulousness of the situation momentarily froze her into immobility. She couldn't believe it; this creep, this "last chancer", was willing to throw away his freedom and rape her, then and there, on the concrete floor of Tartarus!

Icy anger took over then and she decided to fight.

She could tell Griffith was expecting a struggle and, from the way his eyes kept glancing down, an attempt on her part to knee him in the groin. She fed off that, faking it, and when his free hand dropped to protect his crotch, she hit him with an open-hand throat strike as hard as she could.

The brutish guard's eyes nearly spilled from his skull, and he made a loud, choking sound as Stacy's unexpected blow nearly ruptured his trachea. Struggling to breathe, he staggered back. She wasted no time and followed up with a stiff roundhouse kick, snapping it off the outside of his left knee, and then gave him what he'd been expecting, a hard snap-kick, right to the testicles.

As she heard him groan, she smiled mirthlessly, then started bouncing up and down on her toes, waiting for him to drop.

"You . . . stupid bitch!" Griffith snarled from a hunched-over position.

To her astonishment, not only didn't the raw-boned guard go down, he started to chuckle. Fear began to build, and she wallowed in adrenaline-laced indecision. Then, her pride took over, and she started looked for another opening, a way to finish things.

She paid a heavy price for her brash decision. Out of no-where, a surprise backhand caught her across the mouth, knocking her clean off her feet and sending her crashing to the ground with a badly split lip.

Stacy tasted blood and saw stars. Despite her disorientation, however, she could feel terror tap dancing up and down her spine as Griffith shook off the effects of her blows. Frantic, she tried to rise, only to discover her legs wouldn't respond. Teeth gritted, she resorted to using her forearms to crawl backwards, with her butt dragging on the floor. She had no choice; she had to put some distance between them – to buy herself time.

"That was a one elephant-sized fuckwad of a mistake," the ex-con said coldly, straightening up and checking his throat.

He glared ominously in her direction, watching her crawl, and smiled. Was she imagining it, or were his eyes an unnaturally red color?

"You know, they told me to bring you in alive," he mentioned. "But they didn't say anything about condition . . ."

Smirking, he crept toward her like a stalking tarantula: patient, taunting, taking his time closing the distance, so that he could relish her fear. Stacy felt cold, damp concrete under her elbows and rump and looked around, despairingly. There was no one for her to call out to.

Why is nobody around?

Griffith was only ten feet away now, his toothy smile reminiscent of a cat stalking a crippled mouse. He reached down with an exaggerated smirk and made a show of pulling down his zipper.

"You know, me and the boys always wondered what you saw in that dickless wonder, Derek Braddock," he remarked, his thick eyebrows rising. "Personally, I think you need a bigger cock stuffed in those tight holes. You know, to keep you in line."

Stacy smelled fish and scoffed at him as she continued her retreat. "Oh, please. He's packing more than you ever will, you inbred hillbilly!"

"Is that right?" Griffith said, his feral eyes oozing a combination of lust and insanity. He whipped out his uncircumcised member and shook it at her.

Stacy's eyes peeled wide and she burst out laughing. "Hell, yes," she said scornfully. She knew mocking the ex-con was stupid, but she couldn't help herself. "And, you molest *cows* with that baby aardvark? Boy, you better stick to chickens!"

"Oh, you won't think it's so small as it's bloodying your ass, bitch!"

"Go fuck your mother."

"Meh, maybe next time." With an inhuman snarl, Griffith came for her.

Stacy braced herself. He was three paces away and coming fast.

Suddenly, a dark shadow fell over the guard and he came to a screeching halt. His bloodshot eyes expanded to the size of saucers and he gazed upward, slack jawed.

"G-g-g--"

"Her name is *Gretchen*, you stuttering fool," Stacy seethed, propping herself up on her elbows as cold seawater streamed on and around her.

Then she glanced up and smiled.

Grrraaaaaaarrrrr!

With her ten-foot, crocodile-like jaws, lined with needle-sharp teeth the size of railroad spikes, and supported by a similar sized neck, extended up and out of her pool, *Gretchen* loomed over Stacy's attacker. Her normally-quiet breath came in raspy hisses as she drew in Griffith's scent, and her bus-sized body trembled with pent-up fury.

"I'm sorry," Stacy said, sitting in the shelter of the big pliosaur's shadow. She licked her torn lip, tasted the blood. "We were, uh, comparing dick sizes, right?" She gestured up at the infuriated marine reptile, then threw him a disdainful look. "Well, you see mine. Now, let's see that little worm of yours again."

Paralyzed with fear, Griffith's whole body shook as he stared into *Gretchen*'s ruby-red orbs. A dark spot began to form around the head of his now-shriveled organ, spreading rapidly across his crotch region, and he struggled to swallow the enormous lump in his throat.

His gaze fell, and he glanced at Stacy with fear-filled eyes.

Coolly, she met his stare. Then, she raised her right hand like it was a snake's head and pulled it back into an obviously cocked position. Above her, the seething *Kronosaurus* mirrored her movements like a gigantic shadow puppet. Its slavering jaws pulled back several feet, and the steely muscles of its nape flexed.

"Well, come on!" Stacy taunted. "Show me what you've got!"

Pale and trembling, Griffith began to back away. He took one hesitant step, and then another, each time leaving a foot-shaped puddle of urine in his wake. A moment later, he uttered a cry of unadulterated terror and broke into a run.

"I guess not!" Stacy shouted after him.

An intense rumble of annoyance reverberated from *Gretchen*'s throat, and Stacy's body shook from it.

As she let out the breath she'd been holding, she felt all the life drain from her. She sagged back, her torso propped against the pliosaur's throat like it was a scale-coated tree trunk. Her vision swam from the blow she'd taken, and she blinked repeatedly. She decided to close her eyes for a moment, focusing on breathing and calming herself.

A minute later, she felt warm breath on her face and opened her eyes to find *Gretchen* staring at her from less than three feet away. She stared back in surprise, realizing she could see genuine concern radiating from the huge saurian's gleaming eyes.

"Hey, fish breath," she muttered, smiling weakly. She reached up and gave the pliosaur a scratch under its rock-hard battering-ram chin. "Thanks, I owe you one."

Gretchen uttered a deep, rumbling sound – the pliosaur's equivalent of a purr – and came closer, gently nudging Stacy's shoulders. Her thick-scaled throat pulsated as she scanned her guardian with powerful echolocation clicks. A moment later, her wedge-shaped head swung back in the direction Griffith had gone, and her thick lips snarled slowly back, revealing spiky rows of sharp-ridged teeth.

"Easy, girl," Stacy said, sitting upright. Although she had one hell of a headache, she was starting to feel like herself again. She made it to her feet, one hand resting atop the pliosaur's broad crown. "Don't worry, that swizzle dick's going to get what's coming to him when he goes back to prison. *Trust* me."

She took another minute to get her bearings, then reached for her radio. She pressed the talk button, but then released it and frowned. Although protocol and her position required her to call Tartarus's head of security and request an arrest, something told her doing so would be a bad move.

Griffith had said "they" sent him to get her. She had no idea who "they" were, but she didn't like the sound of it. Were other guards involved, maybe in some sort of conspiracy? Did they know that Dirk had discovered their involvement in Amara's death? If so, were they trying to eliminate any witnesses, before Grayson's return?

Dirk!

Stacy's heart started thumping so hard it hurt. If she was right, and they knew about his discovery, he was in terrible danger!

She switched to her cell phone and dialed his, pacing back and forth as she waited for the call to go through.

Damn it, voicemail.

She tried again and again, and each time the call went straight to his outgoing announcement. What the hell? Was his phone off?

Stacy's jaw muscles grew taut. She had to get to him before the guards did. She had to warn him about Griffith, and the danger they were in.

Despite a wave of dizziness, she pulled away from *Gretchen's* comforting presence and started to step. The adolescent cow uttered a grunt of concern, and she turned back to her. "It's okay, girl. I'm going to find Dirk and we're calling Dr. Grayson. We'll get this mess sorted out quickly, don't worry!"

With that, Stacy turned on her heel and headed toward the distant elevators. Her vision was much better now, but she still felt dazed. She rubbed the growing lump on the back of her head, worried that she had a concussion.

She decided to try jogging, but two wobbly steps quickly cured her of that notion. Her mind churned, and she glanced around the sprawling dock floor, past the fenced-off regions, hoping to spot a discarded MarshCat.

Naturally, there was none to be found.

She passed the surgical center, with its newly-cleaned and sterilized healing pool, and the replacement spotlight tower, already welded in place. Her head started pounding, but she continued doing the only thing she could: walk. The exertion was doing her well, she decided, helping to clear her head and improve focus, so that she could better address the nightmarish scenario she'd been thrust into.

I can't believe that filthy pig tried to force himself on me!

Stacy started to shiver inside her soggy wetsuit and hugged herself for warmth. She wished Garm was there. Garm, and that Amazon Dragunova. They were a formidable team, those two, and with them by her side she'd have felt much better.

Stacy exhaled heavily, then paused for a moment. She felt light-headed and leaned forward with her hands atop her thighs, fighting to catch her breath. She was only one hundred feet from the nearest lift. Once safely inside, she would take it straight to the top, to Amara's old quarters.

Dirk had said he'd be there, and she was sure he would. There was no need to keep calling. Better to keep things on the downlow.

As she passed beneath the shadows of the suspended Gen-1 pliosaur skeleton and the last utility room, Stacy eyed the elevator's beckoning doors. They were open and waiting for her, only fifty feet away.

All of a sudden, Stacy heard a strange rustling sound. She thought she saw movement out of the corner of her eye and started to turn.

"Gotcha!" a gruff voice said.

Out of nowhere, something dropped over her head and her world turned dark and smelly. She heard voices and felt a suffocating pressure around her throat. Panic set in and she fought: elbowing, punching, and kicking. Thudding footsteps followed, and she felt strong hands gripping her, pinning her arms and legs.

Though overwhelmed, Stacy continued to struggle; but her strength faded fast. Inexorably, she felt herself being bound. From the tiny bits of light that she could see, she deduced that her head was in a dark sack and, judging by the painful pressure on her ribs, she had been slung over someone's shoulder like a sack of grain.

The gruff voice said, "Couldn't catch a little girl by yourself, loser?"

There was a muttered, whiny response that she couldn't quite make out. Then, whoever was carrying her said, "Just shut your fucking face, pissant, before I drag your pimply ass down to the corral and let one of those bulls fuck *you* for a change!"

Stacy heard loud, raucous laughter then, coming from multiple individuals. Her dizziness grew from being jostled so hard, and the pain in her head increased to agonizing levels.

She felt unconsciousness coming at her in a wave, and her body drooped in response. A final thought came to her, just before the curtain fell, one that made her feel strangely proud.

At least I wasn't raped.

The desolate remains of Diablo Caldera's long-dead village – a depressing collection of crushed huts, buried beneath towering mounds of petrified ash – had an almost otherworldly feel emanating from it. There was no avoiding the ghostly vibe the place gave off; it leached into the bones of any who saw it, and Natalya could feel it even through the surveillance drone's insulating lens system. Every so often, she had to stop and look away, to distance herself.

She'd been recording the dwellings of the dead for the last twenty minutes. Fortunately, apart from one partially buried skull, she'd come across no significant human remains. At least, on the surface. The military drone's ground penetrating radar scans, however, were another story. Those results, and they were substantial, would require intensive analysis from the lab rats back in Tartarus. For her team, identifying whatever subspecies of humanity once called the caldera home was impossible. They lacked the equipment, the personnel, and, most importantly, the time.

Still, the evidence of their existence and the lives they'd lived was there, and in abundance. The shattered remnants of a miscellany of thick-hulled ceramic vessels could be seen, here and there, peeking up like dilapidated grave markers, amongst rotting piles of fallen palm fronds. And the burnt-out hull of what had to be an ancient dugout canoe was plainly visible, not ten paces from the rows of rotting pilings that extended out from the beach.

Natalya imagined the pilings had once supported a pier of sorts, used by the peaceful villagers to catch fish, no doubt. It would certainly have been safer than taking a tiny boat like that onto a lake that was populated by monsters. More likely, the dugout was carried outside, to reap the bounties of the surrounding sea.

They would never know.

"Hey, captain, how you doing?" Bender prodded from fifteen yards away. He was still wearing his tinted goggles, even though he'd been lurking in the shade of the *Remora* since Archer and Sato left. His eyes were supposed to be on the screen of his drone's remote module, overseeing its efforts to map Diablo's saltwater lake, but the tilt of his head betrayed where they really were.

"Ees fine," Natalya intoned. "People are all dead, burned to death thirty years ago. Definitely a great vacation spot."

"A shame," Bender offered, licking his lips as he scoped out her curves. "Can you imagine an entire race, living in this place and surviving for tens of thousands of years, and then one day, BOOM! The place does a Pompeii on you? Nobody would see that coming."

Annoyed by his continued scrutiny, Natalya said nothing. She just nodded and arced the surveillance drone around for one final pass, before programming it to return.

Bender cleared his throat. "Trivia fact for you: dolphins sleep with one eye open. Did you know that?"

She whipped her head around unexpectedly, catching him in mid-ogle. "Ensign, I know all the sweat ees making eet look like I'm contestant in, how you say, 'wet t-shirt contest'?" She indicated her cantaloupe-sized breasts, starkly outlined by her clinging tank-top. "But, eef you don't stop staring at my boobs, *you* are going to be one who sleeps weeth one eye open." She raised her own goggles and gave him her most lethal stare. "Last warning. Do I make myself clear?"

"Yes, ma'am," Bender said, flushing a deep scarlet. His involuntary headshake spoke volumes, and he touched a control on the drone remote before setting it down at his feet. "I'm, uh, I'm gonna go take a leak. It's on autopilot for now."

Natalya drew a breath and held it, the same way she held her temper. Now was hardly the time or place to deal with the horny Irishman, but enough was enough. He needed to be taught a lesson. It was hardly her style, but if Garm was still alive, she'd be sorely tempted to ask him to—

She stopped and sighed. *Poor Wolfie* . . .

A minute later, with the blazing sun beginning to get to her, she programmed her own drone to return to base and stepped down from the low dune she'd chosen as her vantage point. As she paused to take and relish a much-needed drink, she heard a splash and spun, just in time to see a geyser-like explosion erupt from the lake, fifty yards out. A moment later, the heady smell of fish oil wafted in on the breeze.

Looks like something just had lunch.

It wasn't a *Kronosaurus imperator*, of course. Maybe a *Xiphactinus* or one of their mystery sharks. She hadn't seen a pliosaur since they got there, and Bender hadn't been able to locate one, either, even using their drones' long-range thermals to penetrate the water. She began to wonder if the adult female that escaped into the Atlantic during the previous eruption – the one that started it all – had been the last of her kind.

She shook her head. It was a marvel, that a single animal could reproduce so efficiently that its descendants had all but taken over the world's oceans. Then again, the prevailing theory was that all extant cheetahs were descended from a single pregnant female that crossed over from North America before the last Ice Age. Anything was possible.

Distracted by her ponderings, Natalya ended up getting her bootheel caught up as she stepped back. She uttered a grunt of surprise as her feet went out from under her. A split-second later, she landed with a painful thud, right on her broad backside. She uttered a vile curse in Russian and regained her feet, praying that Bender hadn't seen.

Relieved that he hadn't, she glanced down to see what she'd tripped over.

It was a dirty white cord of some kind, protruding from the sand like a foot-long tripwire. Curious, she pulled on it, only to discover it was far lengthier than she'd expected. It was connected to a partly-decayed, once-white fabric of some kind, buried beneath hundreds of gallons of sand.

She began to tug on the trapped cloth, gritting her teeth as the slippery material resisted her efforts. She managed to get a yard or so free, only to discover that it was very large and had many other cords connected to it. She snapped her fingers as realization set in.

It was a parachute.

Natalya looked around to see if Bender was back yet, then snorted annoyedly and moved to investigate on her own. Gauging the buried chute's position underneath the sand, she started working her way down along its projected length, looking to see what it was connected to.

She expected it to be some sort of harness, and was surprised to find a hard piece of metal protruding from the ground. Her eyes shone with inquisitiveness, and she started digging with her hands.

Whatever was buried there was large and definitely man-made. It was smooth to the touch, a dull gray in color, and had rounded edges, like a desk or table. She grasped the object by its nearest corner and pulled.

It wouldn't budge. Determined, she spread her feet wide and dropped down into a Sumo stance, trying to deadlift it free. Her jaw tightened, and her powerful back and thigh muscles flexed, as she heaved with every ounce of her considerable strength.

Damn. It's bigger than I thought and too deeply buried.

Pausing to catch her breath and wipe away the sweat that streamed down her face and chest, Natalya sat back on her haunches and mulled over her discovery. What could it possibly be? And how the hell did it get there? Was it trash, jettisoned from a passing plane? Maybe it was a piece of space debris, like one of the old command modules they used, during the early days of the Space Race?

She dismissed that last possibility. Whatever she'd found, the materials and technology used in its construction were modern. Her lips crinkled up in the quirky way they did when she grew frustrated, and she shook her head.

She was about to give up and settle for a few pictures, when she noticed a second, similar object.

This one was protruding from the base of a nearby dune. It reminded her of a truck's bumper, poking out after the rest of the vehicle had been buried in a sandstorm. Intrigued, Natalya loped over and dropped down to examine it. Using her palms, she swept away the sand that covered the exposed corner.

It was definitely the same as the last one – same metal, same construction. Encouraged, she began to dig. Using her callused hands like scoops, she pulled away big armfuls of sand, exposing more and more.

Suddenly, Natalya stopped and stared. She'd managed to exhume a good third of the mysterious object. Any more, and the dune above it began to cascade down, negating further progress. She'd uncovered what appeared to be the top; she could see the connection points for the chute cords.

She estimated the object's total length to be about eight feet. It appeared to be a coffin of some kind. No, not a coffin. There was a heavily tinted window of some kind toward the top, at what would've been eye level.

Natalya scratched her head. It was a capsule of some kind. But what kind? She checked to see if it was a freezer pod, like the kind used to cryogenically preserve specimens, but discerned that it lacked the appropriate tech. It was more like a sealed container of some kind, and yet, it was not airtight. There were gill-like vents on the sides, to allow whatever was inside to breathe.

She stood up and stared down at the capsule, her hands on her hips. How did this thing – make that these *things* – get there? She looked around, trying to see if there were more of them.

There were.

Now that she knew what to look for, she saw telltale signs indicating many more. An exposed piece of chute cord here, a piece of fabric or a telltale mound there . . . She calculated there were at least a dozen of the containers within forty yards of her position, all concealed beneath Diablo's windswept sands.

Natalya snorted irritably. "Who the hell ees dumping these--"

Her gray eyes widened as she noticed something on the side of the one she'd partly unearthed. It was a laser-etched insignia of some kind. She dropped down on one knee to take a closer look.

The disc-shaped crest was faded yet familiar.

She raised her tinted goggles and shielded her eyes, trying to make sure. A moment later, her head pulled back on her shoulders and she let out a tiny gasp. The familiar trademarked logo, with its characteristic Greek-styled lettering, was unmistakable.

It was GDT: Grayson Defense Technologies.

Natalya stood up and dusted the sand off her pants, trying to make sense of her find. Why was GDT tech being dumped inside Diablo Caldera? It couldn't be to get rid of obsolete hardware. That could be done anywhere, not to mention, flying covert missions to parachute the pods inside the volcanic island – a huge violation of Cuban airspace – was risky and must have cost a fortune. So, why do it?

She was in the midst of reaching for the mike button on her goggles' polycarbonate temple, when she heard a twig snap behind her.

"Bender," she breathed, whirling around. "You won't *believe* what I--"

Natalya's heart pole-vaulted into her throat and stayed there. Not ten yards away, and standing by the water's edge, was a pair of reptiles.

Make that *dinosaurs*.

They were theropods of some kind, tall and bipedal, with strong forelimbs and powerful hind legs, balanced by a long

and muscular tail. They reminded her of the pack-hunting raptors from the old dinosaur movies she used to watch as a child.
Except, these looked different.

They were big, over four feet at the hip, and nearly fourteen feet in length. She estimated each weighed a good 400
pounds but, judging by the way their padded feet adapted to
the unstable sand, they appeared quite nimble. Their arms
were muscular and long and ended in thick-based, hooked
claws a good five inches in length, designed to impale and
slash. Their hind legs were far larger and incredibly muscular,
especially the thigh portions. The feet were disproportionately large, with long, broad toes. Three of the toes supported
the animal's weight, but there was an innermost toe – like the
dew claw on a dog – that ended in a curved black talon. It was
carried off the ground like a cat's claw, presumably to ensure
it stayed sharp. The talons looked like sickles and were nearly
twice the size of the other toe claws, a good nine inches in
length.

The skin of the two dromaeosaurs – and Natalya had no
doubt that she was looking at some sort of Cretaceous hold-
overs – was not wrinkled and knobby, like she would've expected. There were finely-scaled, smooth sections on the flanks
and upper thighs, but much of the animals' hides were coated
with long, flat scales that stood up and out like hairs. The scales
were so long in places that they seemed almost like feathers,
but not quite. On the back of the neck, and along the spine, they
were at their longest, forming an elongated crest that reminded
her of the mane of a horse.

Their extended tails were completely coated with a fine layer
of these protofeathers, and had an extra-long ridge of them on
either side that flared outward, protruding for a foot or more.
The elongated scales gave the tail the appearance of a long, flat
blade or spatula. Natalya imagined they were used for balance,
like a cheetah's tail. The raptors' huge feet had long, thick scales
on them as well, particularly the outer edges of each toe, but

these were carried erect and angled inward, towards one another, giving the feet a bizarre, crested look.

Although similar in terms of size and build, when it came to
pigmentation, there were marked differences between the two
animals. The one with the feathery "mane", which she deemed
to be the male, was a bright teal or turquoise in color, with pale
undersides and striking cobalt highlights that formed a zebra-
like pattern. Beneath his chin he had a bright red wattle, that
expanded and contracted as he breathed.

The female had no lion's mane or wattle and was a less au-
dacious bluish-gray in color, with pale undersides and whitish
bands that broke up her pattern, like sunlight when it dapples
the surface of the water, especially when seen from below.

Both animals had large, wedge-shaped heads, a solid two
feet in length, and strong jaws, lined with rows of two-inch serrated fangs. Their eyes were a bright orange with vertical pupils, and those eyes zeroed Natalya.

She saw hunger there, and a cold, calculating intelligence as well.

The two raptors shifted from side to side as they studied her,
and she felt goosebumps break out all over her body. The male
uttered a loud hiss, then they both started making a series of
low, chittering sounds, almost like a language. She got the distinct impression they were communicating.

The realization that she'd discovered what was in the capsules came to her, and she cast about, desperately looking for
her M18. To her disgust, she spotted it, twenty feet away and
leaning against the *Remora*'s hull. She wouldn't make it three
steps before the pair of dromaeosaurs were on her. In fact, any
sudden movement might be taken as an act of aggression.

Or an invitation.

As the male raptor took a step, Natalya's hand crept toward
the .454 Casull she had holstered on her hip. She considered
trying to reach Bender on the comm, but then realized the
fool wasn't even armed. Apart from using him as bait, her best
chance was to try and double tap both reptiles in mid-charge.

The problem was, she wasn't confident her pistol rounds would stop them. Kill, yes, especially over time. But *stop* was another matter. And, there were two of them. If either was able to close the distance before it was lights out, well, she had no desire to find out what those lethal-looking foot-claws were capable of.

Natalya's heart kicked into high gear as the raptors continued to edge closer. Their mouths were open now and they were making loud, raspy noises as they inhaled. She realized it was a Flehmen response, like a lion does; they were smelling her, trying to make up their minds about attacking.

Something about her scent seemed to be holding them back, and each time the male – obviously, the more eager of the two – was about to pounce, the female issued some sort of warbling sound, restraining him.

Finally, the pair seemed to agree that Natalya was, indeed, a potential meal, and they began to separate. Soon, they were at her ten and two, their glistening eyes locked onto hers like orange-hued rifle scopes and backed with murderous design. She gripped her pistol and tensed, waiting to see which one would make the first move.

Suddenly, the breeze shifted and the two theropods stopped cold. Their heads popped up and they began to scent the wind, simultaneously vocalizing back and forth.

Then, the impossible happened.

Without warning, they spun on their tails and ran off – *right across the surface of the lake.*

As near as Natalya could figure from the wide footprints they'd left behind, the long scales on their toes could flex downward, turning their feet into scaly snowshoes, and enabling them to literally run on water. She could see their powerful thigh muscles pumping as they moved, each step a watery explosion. Their speed was astonishing, at least sixty miles an hour, and they raced across the caldera pool in a zigzag pattern, before vanishing in the distance.

Natalya stood where she was, hand still on her rubberized gun butt and heart pounding, but this time from amazement instead of fear. She wouldn't have believed it if she hadn't seen it. A living theropod was incredible to begin with, but one that could *run on water*?

Her mind swirled at the possibilities. They were undoubtedly the top terrestrial predators on the island, and fed on an assortment of life: fish, smaller reptiles, birds: basically, anything they wanted. They could roam the entire caldera, not just the wooded portions, and their speed allowed them to do so with relative impunity. Even the most athletic fish or pliosaur would have found them difficult, if not impossible to catch.

Archer was going to go nuts when she told him. She could hear him now, trying to come up with names for them. As if he deserved the credit . . .

Then, another thought came to her. Why was she still alive? The raptors had had her dead to rights. Why did they run away?

Her brow crinkling up, Natalya reached for her goggle's comm link, to call in her discovery. She had just tapped the mike tab when she heard it.

It was a long, eerie cry, like some primeval wolf's howl, only higher-pitched. It had a bizarre, ratcheting quality to it, one that made it linger in the air.

She heard it again. It was far off and coming from the rain forest.

Then, another yowl came. And another, and another. Soon, there was a chorus of them, growing louder and louder and echoing off the caldera's stony slopes.

Natalya felt a sudden chill and the hairs on her nape pricked up like porcupine quills. There was something out there. And whatever it was, it just sent two flesh-eating theropods that could've given a pride of lions a run for their money, running for their lives.

And it was on the hunt.

TWENTY

"Dirk! Dirk, can you hear me?"

I hurt. Go away, let me sleep . . .

"Dirk, it's me! Open your eyes, please!"

That same voice, over and over. So tired . . . please, let me rest.

"Baby? Please wake up. Please! I *need* you!"

So familiar, and damnably persistent. Okay, just for a minute, maybe . . .

As Dirk Braddock cranked his eyelids to half-mast, he instantly regretted it. His world became a heavy metal band of pain, with a stroke-level headache as its front man and backup vocals consisting of dizziness and nausea. He had no idea where he was – barely knew *who* he was. All he knew was that he wanted to die.

Or was he already dead?

"Oh, my God, you're alive!" an obviously distraught-yet-relieved voice said.

Dirk heard a combination of nervous laughter and sobbing and fought to bring his eyes into focus.

Jesus, that was a bad idea; even his eyeballs hurt.

"W-where . . . w-what?" he finally managed through cracked lips. He felt like he was in a delirium. Everything started spinning, like that time he and his brother had gotten shit-faced in college and the room turned into a merry-go-round, even thought they were both flat on their backs on the carpet.

He started taking quick, shallow breaths, trying to focus, trying to master the waves of discomfort that shot up and down his limbs like jolts of electricity. After what seemed an eternity of blinking, his eyeballs at last started to obey him and he was able to make them do what he wanted. He bore down, trying with all his might to bring the blurred image above him into focus.

Finally, he succeeded. He breathed a pain-filled sigh of relief. It was Stacy.

"Omigod, Dirk, you're awake, you're alive!" she cried out. She leaned over and hugged him desperately, her normally-welcome embrace causing him to hiss in pain and recoil.

"S-sorry," he managed, blinking non-stop. "M-my body hurts."

"I know," she sobbed, her eyes welling with tears. She reached up, gently pushed a stray lock of hair away from his face. It was sticky with blood. "They beat you up pretty bad."

"W-where are we?" Dirk said. He realized he was once again on his back, but this time on a cold and uncomfortable surface. He tried shifting, but movement was apparently not on the menu. He looked up at Stace, his dark eyes concerned as he took in the damage to her face. "What happened to your lip? Did someone--"

She shook her head. "The guards know what you discovered about your mother's death. They've turned on us, taken over Tartarus."

He shook his head weakly and winced. "No . . . not just them. It's Grayson."

"Dr. Grayson? Wait, he's involved in this, too?"

Dirk tried to nod, then cried out as a fiery explosion of pain in his throat made everything he saw turn red.

"Easy, baby," Stacy cooed. "Your glands are badly swollen."

"G-Grayson is . . . behind it all," he said through his teeth. "He's the puppet master. He betrayed you, me, my family . . . all of us."

Despite the waves of agony that wracked his battered body, Dirk's fury got the better of him. He tried and failed to sit up, then attempted to use his elbows to prop himself upright. His right arm felt like it was filled with white phosphorus, and he screamed as he collapsed back down.

"Baby, please!" Stacy begged. "Lie still, you're making it worse!"

"M-my arm . . . it's--"

"Swollen to twice normal size and hot enough to fry eggs." She touched her hand to his forehead – her palm was delightfully cold – then pulled away and shook her head. "You're experiencing hyperpyrexia," she said, the surgeon in her suddenly asserting itself. "I'm guessing your overall body temperature is around 107 degrees, but your arm . . ."

Dirk studied her face, impressed with the level of concern. "See," he deadpanned. "And you once told me I wasn't . . . as hot as I thought I was."

Somehow, Stacy managed to laugh and cry at the same time. She wiped away a fresh river of tears and shook her head. "Seriously, I don't know what's going on with your arm. I don't think there's anything broken, but there's a nasty section where--"

"He injected me."

"Who did?"

"Grayson," Dirk said, grinding his molars to let off steam. "I suspect with their latest super pathogen. A fatal dose, I'm . . . sure."

"What are you talking about?" Stacy asked.

"He's been making *monsters*, Stace. Some sort of super soldier program using strengthened pliosaur bacteria to stimulate mutations, and I think Admiral Callahan is in on it, too."

"Holy fuck. Have they had any success?"

Dirk nodded warily. "The guards. His so-called 'last chancers.' They're guinea pigs, every one of them."

"Well, that explains Griffith," Stacy said, sitting down next to him and shaking her head. When Dirk stared at her, she said,

"He sexually assaulted me in the middle of the docking bay, in broad daylight!"

"Son of a . . ." a dreadful thought came to him. "Did he, I mean, are you--"

"I'm okay," she said, her scoff converting into a nasal chuckle. "I managed to crawl away from him, right to the edge of *Gretchen*'s pool. She saved me."

Dirk's eyes widened despite the resultant hurt. "Did she . . ."

"Eat him?" Stacy shook her head. "No, I don't allow my baby-girl to ingest sewage." She nodded her head and sniggered. "But, I do believe the little-dicked bastard left some behind as he hauled ass."

"Dwyer's here, too."

"I know. You saw him?"

Dirk nodded, then used his left arm to indicate the blood-caked gash on his head. "Yeah, bastard gave me this." He thought for a moment. "You know, I don't think he ever actually left. I think his 'suspension' was all smoke and mirrors."

Stacy's expression turned dark and ugly. "He and a few of his goons grabbed me after I fought off Griffith, dragged me here. They had you trussed up and lying on the floor, waiting. When I saw all the blood, I thought you were dead. He's such an asshole."

"Why, did he hurt you?"

"No, not much." She gazed up at the cobweb-coated stone walls surrounding them and hugged herself. "They tossed us both in here, all the while yucking it up." One of them, that other creep, you know, the one with the salt-and-pepper hair?"

"Wurmer."

"Yeah, he was blabbing non-stop, said, 'When your boy-friend comes to, tell him the guard he's been looking for is in-side. Should be some reunion. I wish I could stick around to see you guys meet up!'"

"Really?" he said, looking around and seeing nothing.

Stacy nodded, her amber eyes flashing angrily. "Last thing I heard was them muttering, 'So much for the Golden boy!', or something to that effect."

Dirk swallowed, then grimaced from the burning in his throat. "So, where exactly are we?"

He took in their surroundings. They appeared to be in some sort of subterranean cave. From the gouged-out granite that made up the walls and floor, it must've been carved from Tartarus's core, he deduced. Visibility was minimal; the single LED bulb that shone down from above amounted to little more than candlelight. He could just make out a dark metal door, some twenty feet to his right, and a scattering of debris on the floor nearby. But beyond that, he could see little. There was lots of moisture in the place: a light sheen, that made even the walls slippery to the touch.

"I hate to say it, but I think it's some sort of dungeon," Stacy hazarded. She looked around glumly, then indicated a faint glow about sixty feet away. "I did a little exploring while you were unconscious. There's some sort of manmade grotto at the far end. It's saltwater and, judging by the daylight that filters in, must connect to the sea, somehow. It's creepy looking; I wasn't about to dive in."

Dirk nodded weakly, suddenly feeling drained. "We must be in the lower regions, at or near sea level." He tried to say something else, but his mouth went completely dry and all that came out were smacking sounds.

"Oh, Jesus, I'm so sorry, honey," Stacy blurted out.

As she got up, Dirk couldn't help but notice she was wearing his favorite, curve-hugging bodysuit. Despite all his misery, he grinned.

Boys will be boys.

"There's nothing to eat," Stacy said. "But, for some reason, there *is* a drinking fountain of sorts." She leaned over the water source, protruding from a nearby wall, and filled a container.

"I had to come up with a makeshift cup," she said apologetically. "I used it to pour water over your arm and brow while you were out."

Unable to speak, Dirk could only nod his gratitude. Eyes half-closed, he carefully sipped the welcome liquid as she held the container to his lips. The water was a bit silty and had a metallic aftertaste to it, but it was cold and wet.

Frankly, he thought he'd never tasted anything so delicious in his life.

"Th-thanks, Stace," he managed, after a few painful swallows. He glanced down at the cup she held under his chin and blinked a few times, to make sure he wasn't seeing things. "Is that a . . . section of someone's *cranium*?"

"Yes," she confessed from beneath raised eyebrows. She smacked her lips as she turned toward the nearby pile of refuse. "I'm afraid we're not the first poor bastards to end up here."

Dirk's eyes popped as he took in what, in the poor lighting, he'd assumed to be a collection of refuse. He'd been wrong. What he thought were broken branches and pieces of fence, was actually a collection of bones.

Human bones.

And there were a lot of them.

The Kraken was in dogged pursuit. It was on a blood trail, and it was *his* blood that it wanted.

Sam Mot swallowed nervously, then checked the battered TALOS Mark VII AWES's staticky rearview monitor, hoping to catch another glimpse of it. *Nothing.* He shook his head, growing even more frustrated and tense. He'd spotted it fleetingly maybe twenty minutes back, as it crested an underwater ridge, but nothing since then. For some strange reason, it appeared unable to close the distance between them.

Sam licked his lips, then ground the skin on the inside of his cheek between his molars, grateful for the pain. Besides being a much-needed pick-me-up, it reminded him that he wasn't dead yet.

He was befuddled, however, as to why the revenge-driven monstrosity hadn't come for him in a rush. He'd seen the smaller one jet away from *Gryphon*, during their protracted showdown. It was unbelievably fast. Maybe this one's mass slowed it down, he considered. Or, perhaps the species wasn't built for endurance and, luckily, it was moving as fast as it could.

Regardless, and as terrifying as it had been to see its mammoth silhouette rise in the distance, he was grateful for the brief sighting. The adrenaline rush it precipitated was pretty much the only thing keeping him going.

Sam winced, as he willed the Mark VII to start him on another round of plasma, then took stock of his situation. He was still a good forty miles from Rock Key: two more hours, at his current velocity.

That was, assuming TALOS held together long enough for him to get there. For all its high-tech sensors, superhuman strength, and tank-like armor, the ADCAP weapon's system had proven far from indestructible.

Something wet struck his eye, causing Sam to look up. What he saw made him feel like vomiting. There was a trickle of seawater, dripping down the inside of his clear titanium faceplate.

And . . . it looks like the seal on my ride's going. Well, that's fucking great.

He sighed, wondered which of them was in worse shape, him or the machine. Both had been smashed, bashed, bitten, and broken. Of course, the Mark VII was only missing one arm and leg, so he supposed he had the advantage there.

Sucking in a few Lamaze-style breaths, Sam pondered whether it was worth hitting himself with another round of stimulants. He decided to try to hold out; he was jittery enough as it was.

On a whim, he checked the suit's medical stores, then snorted in disgust. He was running low on the synthetic coagulant that was not only keeping his horrific abdominal wound sealed, but his internal bleeding to a minimum. Of course, if it hadn't been life or death, he'd have passed on the potent drug altogether. He knew its unpleasant side effects, including the gastrointestinal ones; based on what he'd already taken, he'd be constipated for a month at least.

That was, assuming he lived that long.

Truth was, he had no idea how the doctors in Tartarus were going to keep him from bleeding out like a geyser, once they peeled TALOS's smashed shell off. He imagined it would not be pretty.

Sam checked his course and speed. He had the pedal to the metal, but with only one boot propulsor, he was pretty much maxed out at twenty knots.

According to his built-in GPS, his current location put him along the outermost edges of Cay Sal Bank. He'd diverted to the huge atoll, once he confirmed the octopus was tracking him. His hope had been to lose it by weaving around the myriad islets that bordered the bank's expansive lagoon. Or, that failing, perhaps the bank's 50-foot maximum depth might discourage the huge beast, and it would return to the deep.

It hadn't. A quick trip to the surface on Sam's part had confirmed things. Courtesy of cryptozoology groups like *Into the Fray* and *Undiscovered Beasts and Strange Phenomena*, social media was ablaze with sightings of a gigantic "Lusca" from the Bahamas, swamping pleasure boats and terrifying anglers. He'd seen some of the footage himself; the telltale wake caused as the amorphous horror swept along was unmistakable. At times, its slimy body even broke the surface, so tenacious was it in its pursuit.

Yeah, it was back there. Hot on his trail and coming on strong.

If only he had some way to call for help. He'd tried Tartarus and got nothing, and the Coast Guard operator thought he was on drugs which, technically, was true. He'd even tried reaching out to the two Bearcats that had been working the area, during Garm's hunt for the man-eating behemoth. Or rather, behemoths.

It was to no avail. By the time he'd managed to get through, he discovered someone had already ordered the attack choppers back to base.

Sam was on his own.

Suddenly, colored motes began to swirl before his eyes and he felt himself getting light-headed again. He gave a snort of repugnance, then injected himself with yet another cocktail of anesthetics and amphetamines. His limbless torso shuddered as the potent meds kicked in. Green eyes now wide and staring, he steeled himself for the task ahead.

Barring any unexpected change, he would soon be down to the home stretch. The only question that remained was, would he make it to the safety of Rock Key before the monster caught up with him? Or, would it close the distance and bite his remaining mechanical limbs off, before it ended up shucking him, like an oyster from its shell?

The exploration of Diablo Caldera's mysterious rain forest was giving Ensign George Sato the willies. It wasn't the oppressive heat and humidity – although he was sure he'd eventually end up bribing Lieutenant Alger Archer for a share of his canteen – it was the uneasiness brought on by traversing a primeval landscape. The feeling that you were being watched, and knowing that, when it came to the position of top predator, you were low on the totem pole. And, of course, there was the incessant worrying and wondering as to when the real apex would show itself.

His partner Archer, on the other hand, seemed to have no such reservations. In fact, judging by his carefree whistling, the big galoot was in his glory.

"Hey, Sato, check out the size of these prehistoric angiosperms," the IDC said, indicating the group of towering trees they'd been working toward.

Sato shrugged. Despite their height and long, nearly branch-free trunks, which reminded him of African acacias, the trees in question seemed remarkably ordinary. To a non-naturalist such as himself, they were just big, exotic-looking pines.

"Very impressive," he said, as Archer snapped photos of the soaring plants from assorted angles, then switched to digital footage.

"They must be 150 feet," the corpsman said, craning his neck back and smiling. "It's fascinating. Those proto-palms we documented during the first few hundred yards have become less and less prevalent toward the interior." He pointed skyward, the sunlight barely visible through the thickly interwoven tree tops. "And look at how dense the canopy is! The conifers definitely hold sway here."

"Yeah, they're great," Sato commented, looking around apprehensively. The deeper portions of the rainforest were shrouded in perpetual mist, and he was unenthused about going in there. He caught a sudden movement, high up in one of the trees, and tensed. Donning his ADCAP combat goggles, he switched their motion detector function on and zoomed in, scanning the trunk. For a moment, he thought he had something on infrared, but it was nothing. "This place really creeps me out," he confessed, shaking his head. "Come on, let's keep moving. We're looking for specimens, right?"

Archer threw him an amused look and grinned. "Relax, my Nipponese friend. Odds are, we're the biggest things in this forest." He dropped to one knee. "And examples of flora work fine." He reached down and gently prized a small plant from the roots of a black-barked forest giant. "Man, check out all the epiphytic ferns; these are Cretaceous era, no doubt, and they're everywhere. I haven't seen a bit of grass, except for that scraggly stuff on the beach!"

"That's terrific," Sato said, scanning their six as his comrade gingerly inserted the little plant, complete with a tiny root ball, into one of their sample cases, and then placed it in his rapidly-filling pack. "I'm glad to see you're enjoying yourself."

"I like this place," Archer said, cinching his pack closed and glancing around. He breathed deeply through his nostrils, reveling in the highly oxygenated air. "And not just because we're not out risking our necks, gunning down sea monsters. I mean, yeah, it's hot and muggy," he noted, swiping at a trickle of sweat on his temple, "But it's so . . . natural. You hear those birds calling? I've never heard anything like that before."

"Yeah, quite the racket," Sato observed. "Of course, you're assuming those *are* birds."

"Mostly. Maybe a few amphibians mixed in."

"Hopefully, small ones."

"Hey, watch your step," Archer said, indicating the ground at Sato's feet.

His eyes rounded as he noticed the huge pile of dried feces and took a step back. "Yuck, thanks, man."

"No problem."

Sato arched an eyebrow as he saw the contemplative look on his comrade's face. "Wait, you're not thinking of taking a sample of this shit, are you?"

"Why not. You can learn all sorts of things from scat."

"Yeah, but it's all dried out."

Archer winked. "Hey, no stool like the old stool."

Sato grinned and shook his head. "Whatever. If you want some of that, you can scoop it up yourself."

"Meh, maybe on the way back."

"That's what I thought." He looked around. "So, uh, how far in are we?"

Archer shrugged inside his khaki-colored body armor. "I don't know, maybe two hundred yards, give or take." He stopped to insert his fingers underneath the shoulder portion of his graphene vest and scratched.

Sato cleared his throat. "So, if you're so sure there are no mons . . . large predators in here, why are you still wearing that vest? Isn't it hot as balls?"

"Interesting analogy," Archer said, chuckling. "I think your temperature estimate is spot-on." He stood up straight and patted the armored vest. "Yeah, it's toasty in this thing. But, it's pretty light to begin with, at least compared to the older vests. And, since the odds of us taking fire here are slim, I took the liberty of removing the ceramic chest and spinal plates, so it's barely ten pounds."

"I see."

Reaching down to touch the mesh-like leaves of a large fern at his feet, a smiling Archer took the lead, stepping carefully over fallen branches, and avoiding treading on any of the myriad flowering plants they encountered. Sato followed suit and trailed after him, all the while hawking his goggles' motion detectors for any sign of potential trouble.

He'd wisely adjusted the frequency to ignore anything smaller than a dog. Otherwise, the damn thing would be pinging in his ear every time a bird flapped its wings or a dragonfly took flight.

Suddenly, Archer froze and extended his arm like the letter "L", his fist pointed toward the sky. Sato recognized the military signal to freeze instantly, and crouched down, before easing closer.

"What is it?" he asked, eyeing what little he could see of the surrounding terrain through the mist and endless tree trunks. On his goggles' inside screen, he saw nothing.

"I think we've got a potential specimen," Archer said, indicating a five-foot hunk of rotting tree bark, directly at his feet.

He unshouldered his carbine and oversized pack, placing them carefully on the ground behind them. Then, he opened the pack and extracted a foot-long plastic capture case and the tongs he'd used at the beach. He signaled Sato to grab the piece of bark and raise it carefully.

"Whatever you say . . ." the electronics tech said, looking around warily, before gripping the rotted section where he was instructed. The underside of the wood was mushy to the touch and he smelled leaf litter and decay.

"Ready . . . set . . . now!"

Sato flipped the piece of bark over and stepped back in one smooth motion. He caught a glimpse of something worming its way through the loamy soil underneath: a coppery-brown blur that undulated as it traveled.

Archer's tongs shot out like a boxer's jab. "Gotcha!" he exulted. He pulled his hand back and held his prize out triumphantly, like a father showing off his newborn son. "Well, what do you think?"

The two-foot-long centipede that writhed like an angry serpent at the end of the carbon fiber tongs was something to see. *Actually, forget serpent*, Sato thought. It was more like a demon, he noted with more than a little trepidation, as the overgrown myriapod tore at the tongs with three-inch, sickle-shaped fangs.

"Wow, that's, um . . . charming."

"Be careful," Archer cautioned, as he gestured for him to bring the capture case closer. "They're highly venomous."

Sato hesitated. "Wait, how venomous? Is this a known species?"

"No, but it's probably related to—what the hell?"

Suddenly, the leaf-strewn soil at Archer's feet split apart and a broad, tubercle-dotted head the size of a dinner plate emerged. With lighting speed, it lunged upward, powerful jaws clamping down on the flailing centipede.

There was a low crunch, coupled with a spurting sound reminiscent of a rotten cucumber being stepped on. Then, before either of them could react, the hapless arthropod was torn from the big corpsman's grasp and swallowed.

"Holy shit! Did you see that?" Sato sputtered, pointing at the ground. The head began to retract, sinking back down into its leafy lair like a doodlebug, preparing for its next ambush. "What the hell is that?"

"It's a frog of some kind," Archer noted, leaning forward and studying the big amphibian from a few feet away.

Sato blinked a few times to make sure he hadn't imagined things. The "frog" his friend was referring to was about the size of a throw pillow and must've weighed fifteen pounds. Its head was gigantic – fully half its total length – and it had horn-like mounds of tissue over its blazing, bronze-colored eyes. Around those eyes was damp, lumpy skin that matched the color and pattern of the leaf litter it used for concealment.

"A 'frog?' You've gotta be shitting me."

"It's a Beelzebufo, if I'm not mistaken," Archer said, fascinated with the bulbous creature. "It means 'Frog from Hell', or something like that."

Sato nodded. "Well, he's in the right place. Is this a known species?"

"An 'extinct' genus from the Cretaceous. They were, make that *are*, like the horned frogs from South America, only bigger."

"Shit. You have that 'Dad, can I keep him' look in your eye," Sato observed. "Does this mean he's coming with us?"

"Hell, yeah," Archer affirmed. "In fact, we should curtail our exploration for now and bring him straight back. He could be incredibly valuable for GDT's pharma division, and we want him healthy and in once piece."

"You're the ranking officer . . ." Sato drawled. In truth, the words "curtail our expedition" were music to his ears. He couldn't wait to get Diablo's bigmouth version of "Kermit" tagged and bagged so they could get the hell out of there.

"Okay, so here's the plan--"

Archer's words were cut short by a sudden cacophony of bird shrieks, rising like a maniacal orchestra in the distance. A moment later, the birdcalls went silent.

And the forest with them.

"Did you hear that?" Sato asked, feeling like an idiot.

Archer stood up, obviously worried about losing his soon-to-be-pet, but curious as to the cause of the sudden ruckus. "Just a bunch of birds," he offered, his big head swiveling mechanically from side to side as he swept the surrounding rain forest. "It's stopped."

"Yeah, but *everything's* stopped," Sato whispered.

Archer's lips tightened, and he slipped on his combat goggles, keying them to his bodycam. "Bring your motion detectors online."

"Way ahead of you, friend."

"Are you reading anything?"

Sato's heartrate spiked as a signal popped up at the far edge of his optics' sensory field. "I've got a reading, sixty yards . . . *that* way," he said, pointing into the mist. "Man-sized and moving fast. Wait, there are--"

"More," Archer interjected. His jaw muscles began to bulge as he tapped his goggles' temple repeatedly. "I'm showing six, seven, no . . . twelve readings, all similar size and inbound. ETA, twenty seconds."

Sato's mouth went dry, and it wasn't from thirst. "There's more!" He spun around, scanning the area behind them. "I've got at least ten more at our seven, and even more at our three!"

"Time to go," Archer said, shouldering his pack and gripping his M18. He checked the weapon's settings and magazine and pulled its charging handle back. "Leave the frog."

Sato unshouldered his own rifle and followed suit. He felt better holding the weighty carbine, but not much. "What are they, animals?"

"If they are, they're smart, well organized, and proficient at driving game."

"So, what do we do?"

"We haul ass back to camp," Archer replied. He retreated back over a batch of fallen logs, his expression serious. "I'll take point. Stay on my six and keep up." He started to stride, then paused and looked back. "Keep your eyes peeled, and your muzzle pointed either left or right. Last, but not least, if we have to defend ourselves, please, try not to shoot me."

"Roger that," Sato said.

They began to move, quickly and quietly, with Archer's considerable stride eating up the yards as they worked their way back. Any fear of getting lost evaporated; their ADCAP goggles were already locked onto the *Remora*'s position and would lead them unfailingly home.

Around them, Sato noted, the three groups of signals were on the move. They'd bunched up tighter and were closing faster now, especially the ones behind them.

They must know we're on the run. What the hell are *they?*

They'd traveled only a hundred yards and Sato's breath was already coming in pants. He shook his head, jealous of Archer's impressive physique and seeming tirelessness. His jealousy quickly evaporated, however, when he noticed his superior deliberately slow so that he could keep pace, and looking back often, to ensure they weren't separated.

Everything will be fine, Sato told himself. They'd be back in minutes and would deliver their samples and give a full report. He was sure Captain Dragunova would—

Sato froze as an eerie sound echoed throughout the surrounding woods. It was something he'd never heard before, an otherworldly howl, like the cry of some huge hyena, but shakier and longer in duration. All around them, terrified birds burst out of the surrounding trees in a colorful explosion.

He checked his optic's motion detector overlay and gasped.

"Archer! They're closing in!"

"I know," the IDC said quietly. Dripping sweat, he continued to lope along, his rifle held in one hand, its double barrel pointed ahead like a two-pronged pike.

"We've got a score of them behind us now, and dozens more spreading out to cut off our retreat!"

"They're trying to drive us away from the lake," Archer observed. He stopped for a moment, breathing hard and eying the dense foliage.

The frightening call they'd heard repeated, first to their left, and then to their right. It began to multiply in number. Soon, it was coming from all over, its echoes so raucous and penetrating, it was impossible to think.

"What do we do?"

The big man's jaw was set. "We go straight through them," he growled. He removed his pack and signaled for Sato to do the same. "We can come back for these," he said, then indicated a dense field of low palm plants, the height of corn stalks. "The *Remora* is seventy yards, straight that way. We make a beeline for it and cut down anything in our path."

Sato nodded and continued sucking as much air as would fit into his burning lungs. "But, what if they're *people*?"

"Whatever's coming has non-mammalian body temps. They're not people, and they're planning to kill us." He checked the .45 on his hip, then hoisted his M18. "I say we return the favor."

Sato nodded. The calls of the hunters were growing louder, and his motion detector was going crazy; there were readings all around them.

"Come on," Archer said. "I'll ride point, you guard our flanks."

Grateful for the brief respite, Sato fell in behind him, his ragged breathing competing with his heartbeat to see which one was louder. Soon, they were deep in the palm field and moving fast. He was less than five yards behind, listening as his comrade opened a comm link to update Dragunova, when something stepped out of the grove, right in front of him.

He stopped short and stared.

The creature was naked and stank like an ill-kept zoo. It was olive-green in color and big, as big as Archer, and bipedal. At first glance, it looked like a man, but it wasn't. It was a reptile of some kind. It had a thick neck and enormous trapezius muscles, affixed to low slung shoulders from which drooped long, rangy arms. Its hands were five-fingered and huge, with knotted tendons and long, filthy nails. Its skin was relatively thin and covered with the tiniest of scales and, on its arms and throat, thick veins bulged, just beneath the surface.

The head was hairless, with a domed forehead, a projecting brow, and a small brain pan. The jaw was large and unslung, like a bulldog's, and a string of drool ran down its broad chin. The mouth, itself, seemed somehow disjointed and gaped wide as Sato stared up at it. Then, to his horror, the thing met his gaze and smiled. The insides of its mouth were red, and its teeth were numerous and small, about the size of his thumbnail, but sharp and pointed, designed to tear flesh.

The creature's eyes were, by far, the most disquieting part of it. They were an intense scarlet, like a red snapper's eyes, with large, black pupils. As it studied him, he saw madness in those eyes, fueled by a ravening hunger.

As the creature stepped toward him, Sato froze. He had his hands wrapped around his rifle, his finger on the trigger, but he was too terrified to move.

A gunshot snapped him back to reality, as Archer fired into the air.

"Sato, get down!" he cried.

An adrenaline rush brought on by sheer terror coursed through him and he dove to the side. He heard the M18's powerful report again, and this time the hulking creature shuddered. A confused look came over it and it turned around, facing Archer as if noticing him for the first time.

Sato gaped in disbelief. There was a pair of spurting, inch-wide wounds where the carbine's two expanding copper slugs had punched through the thing's shoulder blade, before burying themselves inside its barrel-shaped chest. Incredibly, it didn't go down. Instead, it uttered that same, shrieking cry that filled the air all around them and then charged.

"Fuck this!" Archer bellowed. He flipped a switch, then fired full-auto at the approaching monster, putting two dozen rounds into its chest at point blank range. It staggered back under the thunderous barrage, then fell sideways to the ground with a hiss, blood and spittle spewing from its lifeless mouth.

"Definitely *not* people!" he yelled, rushing over and hoisting Sato to his feet. "Let's go!"

Sato's mind was gone, and his body on autopilot at that point. He followed along, running as fast as his legs could carry him, and opened up on anything that moved. Soon, his M18's barrel was smoking, but he continued cutting down one attacker after another.

Five paces ahead, Archer was fighting like Arnold Schwarzenegger in one of his old cyborg movies. Jogging calmly along, he fired short bursts left and right, at one point blowing the face off one of the things as it sprang at him from behind a nearby palm. He kicked it in the chest as it dropped to its knees and ran right over it.

Sato smiled grimly from beneath a sheen of sweat and reptilian blood. Things were going better than he expected.

Suddenly, one of the creatures leapt at him from out of nowhere. He aimed and fired, only to feel his heart drop into his balls as he heard the nagging click that reminded him he'd forgotten to reload.

"Archer!" he screamed as the towering reptile seized him in its powerful, clawed hands. It hoisted him off the ground like he was a rag doll and brought him to eye level. Its breath smelled like rot and, as it licked its scaly lips, he got the distinct impression it was going to bite his face off and eat it, then and there.

Suddenly, the entire top of the creature's head exploded in a crimson cloud of bone and brains, and Sato fell to the ground atop its spasming corpse.

He wiped the gore from his eyes and turned to say "thanks", only to scream a warning as a trio of the things took advantage of Archer's distracted state and pounced. There was a protracted struggle as they tried to drag him to the ground. His M18 spat fire, cutting the middle one practically in half, but then he, too, ran out of ammunition.

Sato shot up like he had springs under him and reached for another ammo clip. To his horror, he realized he had none. He'd brought only one spare to save on weight and had already exhausted it.

Desperate to help, he flew forward and used his gun butt as a club, bashing the nearest creature over the head as Archer rolled around on the ground with them. The blow did absolutely nothing and the two reptiles ignored him, obviously having decided their larger, armored opponent was the more dangerous one by far.

"Get out of here!" Archer bellowed as he headbutted one of his opponents. "That's an order!" He had the bigger of the two in a desperate headlock, and was kicking frantically at the other, trying to keep it from sinking its fangs into his thigh.

"Are you crazy?" Sato cried, casting about for a weapon. The thought of abandoning a comrade on the battlefield was a shame he could not endure.

"Run and call it in! Bring the captain and Bender back here with everything they've got. Hurry!"

Sato realized Archer was right. They needed reinforcements and firepower.

"Hang on!" he yelled, rushing past the frenzied combatants and making for the end of the grove. The palms flew past him in a blur, and he could just about see the beach through the last of them, only fifteen yards away.

Tapping his goggles, he opened a comm link.

"Captain, it's Sato! We--"

He hesitated as he realized a score of motion detector readings were converging on Archer's position. He heard the muffled sound of gunshots – not an M18, judging by the sound, but the IDC's .45 – followed by a bloodcurdling scream.

Sato's mind reeled at the awful realization.

Archer was gone.

TWENTY-ONE

"*A*rcher's dead! He's dead! Jesus Christ, I think they're eating *him!*"

Ensign Sato's horror-filled words continued to ricochet around inside Natalya's head as she readied herself. She had her M18-DT carbine at her feet, locked and loaded with a topped off pair of sixty-round magazines, and propped up against the *Remora*'s suitcase-sized medical kit. There were two backup mags sitting next to it, and an extra ten-rounder for her .454 Casull semi-auto, tucked inside her belt. Last, but not least, for close quarters, she had her *Spetsnaz* elite forces combat knife, strapped to her left thigh.

"Computer, emergency deployment power-up," she commanded. "Breeng all systems online, open hatch, and prepare for emergency evac."

Ten feet to her left, the *Remora* submersible thrummed to life. The heavy armored hatch popped and lowered with a pressurized hiss, and a series of LED navigation lights lit up along its exterior. Out of the corner of her eye, she saw the interior lights go on, and heard the reassuring purr of its MHD thrusters, as they powered up.

Natalya's lips pursed, and she hefted the weighty GDT CAWS she held in both hands, mulling over her options. The imposing select-fire, gas operated 12-gauge shotgun was one of Grayson Defense Technologies latest developments. "CAWS" was an acronym for Close Assault Weapons System and, with its 20-round drum magazine, motion-sensing targeting sensors, and ADCAP recoil system, the fifteen-pound beast was the ultimate street howitzer.

She nodded decisively and walked over to the *Remora*'s open hatch, laying the CAWS just inside, then sprang back and snatched up her M18. She preferred to keep the sinister-looking 12-gauge waiting in reserve, should she be forced to retreat inside the mini-sub. Triple-ought buckshot was at its most lethal at close range and, given the hatch's narrow opening, would be even deadlier there, should the shit hit the fan.

From the look of things, her "fan" was expecting one hell of a dump.

The bizarre animal cries she'd heard were the first sign that something had gone awry, with the bursts of full-auto weapons' fire that followed eliminating any guesswork on her part. The team she'd sent into the rain forest was under attack. She wasn't sure if it was a hunting pack of the water-walking raptors she'd encountered – she'd already started calling them *Messiya yashcheritsa*, meaning "Messiah lizard" – or if there was a human element involved.

From Sato's frantic radio call, just before his comm link was cut off, she was betting on the former. Or something worse.

"Archer, this is Dragunova, come in," she said, tapping her goggles' temple secure-channel mike. Tense and frustrated, she shook her head. Six times was enough. "Ensign Sato, come in. I repeat, Sato, this is Captain Dragunova, come in."

Her lips curled back inside her mouth and she shook her head, ruefully. Then she checked her own goggles' motion sensors, cued in the links to the other landing team members, and uttered a curse.

Archer's comm link was down and dead: most likely the unit, itself, destroyed. Sato's, however, was functioning, or at least his locator was. His body cam wasn't transmitting. According to the readout, he was just over the nearest rise, past a few towering patches of beach grass, and hauling ass. The signal showed him barely fifty yards away.

He had company.

There were scores of other life readings pursuing him, like an angry mob of bees on the inside of her lenses, and closing fast. With Sato leading the way, they were all headed straight for the *Remora*. The only question was, who would get there first?

Natalya tapped the multiband mike again. "Bender, come een. Bender! Where the hell are you?"

Where the hell is that Irish-cursed bastard? she thought. She'd called him five times on the comm link and gotten nothing. His life-signs showed him just twenty-five yards to her left, right over the next dune. How long could it take the imbecile to take a piss? And hadn't he heard the gunshots?

Maybe he's dead, she mused. She scolded herself for being a bitch, as the temptation to smile flirted with her better than the obnoxious communications officer ever had.

Natalya exhaled through her nares, then made her decision. She grabbed the medical kit and, in two quick strides, deposited it back inside the *Remora*, right beside her CAWS. Next, she took up position beside the submersible's armored prow, her carbine at the ready. She figured some cover would be a good idea, in the off chance that Sato's pursuers happened to be humans. Humans with guns.

"*Kakogo cherta?*"

She realized the moment Sato burst through the beach grass, thirty yards away and running for his life, that they weren't.

Behind him charged four huge bipeds. They weren't theropods, however, like the pair of raptors. These were built like large men, but they were *not* men.

They were monsters.

Scale-covered and gnarled, with long, ape-like arms and huge hands, they reminded her of the legendary extraterrestrials that people from her homeland sometimes claimed they encountered: *Reptilians*.

"Sato, run!" Natalya yelled. Behind him, his pursuers uttered a collective cry of anticipation. It was the same gleeful howl she'd heard earlier. It was even creepier, hearing it at close range, and worse seeing where it was coming from.

She gave a headshake of consternation. She could see Sato was on the verge of collapse. Even with all the adrenaline his body could muster, the sedentary technician was simply out of steam. The nearest of the reptilians was only five yards behind him and accelerating, intent on taking him down.

In one smooth motion, Natalya shouldered her M18-DT, took aim through its 2X reticle, and fired. She felt the impressive recoil as it distributed throughout the rifle's shoulder pad, saw the bright white flash erupt from its dual muzzles.

A split-second later, two tungsten-cored, expanding copper slugs smashed into the towering creature's hip with over three thousand foot-pounds of force. It staggered back, obviously surprised, and looked down, touching the gaping wounds. A look of anger came over it. Then, unbelievably, it stayed on its feet and resumed the chase.

"Chto, chert voz'mi?" Natalya couldn't believe it. *What the fuck?* The leader, and she assumed that was exactly what the now-limping frontrunner was, was closing again on poor Sato. She gritted her teeth and fired again, double-tapping this time, and put four slugs into its chest.

This time the reptilian went down, convulsing.

It was dead. But it had friends. Lots of them.

Natalya's heart tightened in her chest as she stepped away from the *Remora*, and toward Sato and his pursuers. She started resolutely firing full-auto bursts. Despite their leader's death, a dozen more of the monsters had burst through the grass directly behind the terrified ensign and, along with the remaining three, were hard on his heels.

"Come on, Sato!" she pleaded, her weapon blazing away as she fired again and again. *Don't do this to me!*

Natalya's eyes began to grow wild. In seconds, she'd managed to kill or cripple at least five more of the reptilians, but hesitated as a fresh horde came over the rise. There were almost too many to count. Refusing to give up, she dumped her spent clip and reached for the next one. Just as she slapped it in hard and chambered the first rounds, Sato tripped and fell.

"NO!"

The creatures were on him before he hit the sand, at least eight strong, snarling, biting, and tearing. She saw the unfortunate tech's legs kicking and he screamed hysterically. A moment later, Natalya slapped her hand over her mouth; it was the only way she could keep from crying out.

They'd ripped open Sato's stomach with their claws and were greedily stuffing his intestines into their mouths. *They were eating him alive.*

"Bastards!"

Simultaneously fighting back tears and the wave of nausea that threatened to incapacitate her, Natalya did the only thing she could. She switched back to semi-auto, took aim, and put a pair of mercy rounds into Sato's sweat-and-gore-soaked head.

Only after the light had faded from his eyes did she allow the breath she'd been holding to escape. It came out a shuddering exhalation that shook her to her very soul. She blinked to clear her rapidly-swirling vision. Then, as her eyes came back into focus, she retargeted the frenzied mob of monsters. Her expression turned cold and mechanical and she began firing again, still on semi-auto, but this time with calmness and precision.

The reptilians were resilient, but headshots worked just fine. One by one they fell to her sniping, until soon, they were dropping like flies. Finally, after she'd killed at least ten of them or, perhaps, simply because they'd finished tearing the majority of the meat off poor Sato's bones, they took notice of her.

They turned as one and stared, their blood-caked muzzles twitching as they drew in her scent. Their muscles tensed and the blinking garnets that were their eyes began to narrow. A moment later, with their ranks continuing to swell, they reared up off the gore-spattered sand like a cresting wave and, with a collective hiss, charged.

There must have been a hundred of them at this point, and, as she noticed the sand atop her boot dancing from their collective weight, Natalya realized it was time to go.

She switched her fire selector back to auto and, with a defiant snarl, emptied her remaining eighty-plus rounds into the reptilians' front ranks. It was a withering blast that sent spent brass flying around her in a huge arc. Four of the creatures dropped, with three more reduced to crawling, yet still, their numbers continued to rise.

Natalya stared in incredulity. They reminded her of the American cockroaches she'd heard about; they were literally "coming out of the woodwork".

She turned, tossing the spent M18-D2 into the *Remora*'s open hatch, then snatched up the GDT-CAWS she had waiting just inside. Behind her, the thunderous footfalls of the enraged horde of reptilians shook the ground like a stampeding herd of bison.

Cold realization hit her in the stomach like a frozen fist. Once they reached the mini-stub, she'd never be able to launch. They'd swarm all over it like locusts, weighing it down and tearing away at its exterior. Even if they couldn't get inside, they could damage the sonar arrays and guidance systems beyond repair – and Sato was dead and gone.

That left only one option.

"Computer, voice command override!" Natalya yelled, simultaneously checking the safety and targeting sensors of her select-fire shotgun. "Prime HYDRA cannons and prepare to fire 500-round bursts. On my command *only*."

She heard the thrum of the twin 20mm Gatling guns' covers sliding open, and the loud whirring sound and click, as the seven-barreled weapons chambered their first shells and then converted to standby mode. Now forty yards away and funneled between the tall dunes on her left and right, the screaming horde of rapacious reptiles couldn't have given her a more concentrated target if they'd tried.

Natalya's eyes were as dark and narrowed as the slits of a knight's helmet, and she licked her lips in anticipation. She wanted to inflict the maximum carnage possible on her attackers and planned on waiting until she saw the reds of their murderous eyes before she delivered her "surprise".

Thirty yards. Twenty.

"Computer, fire HYDRA cannons!"

To her utter disbelief, just then, Ensign Bart Bender, her MIA comms officer, appeared as if by magic. She'd assumed he was dead and had forgotten all about him. He had his headphones on and was adjusting his belt as he walked – right into her weapons system's field of fire.

"Jesus, what's all the racket?" Bender spouted. He looked over at his sweating, weapons-toting captain in growing confusion. "Can't a guy take a shit in--"

As the ginger's eyes swung about and he caught sight of the raging tsunami heading right for him, his jaw dropped. Then, to Natalya's dismay, he did the deer-in-headlights thing and just stood there.

"Bender, get down!" she bellowed. She heard a turbine-like whirring sound, as the HYDRA cannons' collective barrels began to spin, and knew it was too late.

Cursing, Natalya sprang forward with pantherish speed. She saw the comm tech's horror-stricken eyes pop, his lips moving in seeming slow motion. A moment later, she tackled him like a defensive linebacker. He let out a loud "oof" and went down like a bunch of daisies, with her on top of him.

Their gazes met, and a split-second later, a storm of hellfire ripped through the air, less than a foot above their conjoined bodies.

BRAAAAAAAAAAAAAAT!

Natalya covered her ears; the Gatling cannons were deafening at this range – non-stop thunder, combined with an earsplitting, metallic whistling sound. It was even louder than Bender's screaming.

Still draped over him, her tawny head whipped left. The *Remora*'s twin bursts of 20mm shells, any one of which could have dropped a charging rhino, lasered through the onrushing army of reptiles like a Browning machine gun chewing up a field of watermelons.

Chunks of green and red flew in every direction, and the air was thick with shrill screeching and a reddish haze that had to be their blood.

Natalya's goggled eyes swept the impact site, assessing damage. Dozens of the misshapen creatures had fallen, many cut in two, and an equal number were maimed beyond recognition. They began to bunch up, their advance faltering, as they processed the shock of what just happened. The effect was short-lived, however. Already, they were surging forward again, and there were many of them.

She thought about that saying Garm liked to use in bed: *There's plenty more where that came from!*

She smirked evilly. Well, she had plenty more, too.

"Computer, fire again!" she barked.

BRAAAAAAAAAAAAAT!

Another five hundred rounds of armor-piercing, super-cavitating slugs tore into the ravenous throng with devastating results. Designed for underwater use, the depleted uranium rounds were even more effective above the waterline, and she saw shells bore through five of the creatures and keep going.

Again, dozens of them dropped: a mammoth pile of shredded muscles and tendons. The clawed limbs of the dead and dying poked up from beneath glistening mounds of ruptured organs, grasping impotently at the air.

"Fire again!"

BRAAAAAAAAAAAAAT!

"Again!"

BRAAAAAAAAAAAAAT!

Finally, with their dead piled so high that they practically choked the eighty-foot valley between the dunes, the reptilians decided they'd had enough. Barely forty in number now, the survivors staggered to their feet, their ruby eyes wide with fright, and plowed through a wall of gunsmoke, vanishing into the nearby brush.

What wounded were able, crawled off on their own. Those that weren't, remained where they fell. Natalya reasoned their comrades might come back for them, but she doubted it. From what she'd seen, the creatures were a savage mob, driven by primal needs and attacking without organization. She couldn't picture them tending to those unable to fend for themselves.

More likely, they'll come back later and eat them.

Suppressing a shudder, she suddenly felt what she thought was a roll of nickels, poking her in her pubic bone. She glanced down, and a look of revulsion came over her. She was still straddling Bender and the little bastard was getting aroused!

"You disgusting peeg!" Natalya growled as she rolled off him. She sprang to her feet, a field of spent shells crunching under her boots, and grappled with the overpowering urge to draw her pistol and shoot the pervert on the spot.

"S-sorry, I . . ." Bender looked around, obviously having a tough time comprehending what just happened. "Th-those things! What the hell is going on?"

"The rest of the team ees dead, you idiot," she snapped. "And we need to leave, *now*, before--"

If it wasn't for the motion sensors on her goggles, Natalya would've died, then and there. The only warning she had was a tiny blip, coming from above and behind her. The creature had slunk in along the far side of the *Remora* and, unnoticed, scaled its armored hull. As she turned and looked up, it pounced.

She reacted out of pure instinct. Spinning on her heel, she kicked out hard and threw herself backwards. She landed on her backside, the big CAWS 12-gauge raised like a pike as she hit the ground.

Highlighted by her goggles in gleaming shades of crimson, black, and white, the reptilian sprang at her like a pouncing jaguar – a steely mass of sinews, teeth, and talons, with blood-lust in its eyes.

Just as it enveloped her, the shotgun went off.

With over 4,000 foot-pounds of pressure at the muzzle, the three-inch magnum shell smashed into the creature's solar plexus, killing it instantly, and bouncing it nearly five feet back up into the air. Natalya met it as it dropped again, her booted feet catching it at the waist and depositing it in a spasming heap over her head.

She spun sideways and ended up in a catlike crouch, her weapon at the ready. Then her eyes yawned wide in horror. Two more of the creatures had rushed in while she'd been occupied.

They had Bender on the ground and were all over him.

He was kicking and cursing and, for such a small and un-athletic man, putting up one hell of a struggle. Lucklessly for him, to his powerfully built opponents, he was an antelope battling lions. Before she could react, they had pinned his arms and legs to the brass-and-blood-littered sand and were licking their crusty lips.

"H-help!"

The reptilian on the right was literally on top of Bender and, with the CAWS loaded with buckshot, Natalya couldn't risk firing. The one on all fours, gnawing on his shoulder, however, wasn't so fortunate.

Boom.

The buckshot caught the creature right in its scaly ass, the combined power of what was, effectively, a handful of 9mm slugs all striking at the same time, tore it far more than just a "new one". It uttered a high-pitched squeal of agony and fell sideways, then twisted around and glared at her, hissing and spitting.

With murder in its eyes, it struggled to its feet and started forward.

Its advance ended as Natalya coolly blew its head off.

Writhing in agony, Bender uttered a piteous shriek. The remaining creature had buried its tiger-shark-like maw in his exposed stomach. Its sharp teeth went deep, tearing through cloth and the soft flesh below, and it began to shake its head savagely, tearing out a chunk.

Natalya swore under her breath, dropped the CAWS, and sprang forward. She was already in the air, as her combat knife flew from its well-worn sheath. She brought it down with all her might, its eight-inch, spearhead-shaped blade punching through the reptile's thick skull like a spike and burying itself to the hilt in whatever passed for its brain.

The creature froze, its gore-filled mouth gaping wide. Its twisted limbs began to twitch in an unnatural manner, as its nerve endings gradually got word that it was dead.

Looking down, Natalya's face contorted in disgust. She seized the knife's handle with both hands and twisted hard, counter-clockwise. There was a nasty, squelching sound, as the blade enlarged the hole, deep inside the reptile's brain pan, and she pulled it free with a vicious yank.

Blood and clear fluid sprayed, and the creature fell sideways, stone dead.

She gave it a powerful heel kick to speed it on its way, clearing it from Bender. She looked down. Her face became ashen, but her gray eyes were cool and appraising.

The terrified comm tech had a huge tear in his shirt, and a matching rent in his abdominal wall. It was bad; between his trembling fingers, she could see his guts peeking through and blood was everywhere. If she didn't do something quickly, he'd be dead in minutes.

"S-sorry, captain," Bender said, trying to look down, but his muscles not allowing it. He shivered, coughed, and spat up blood – the dark-colored kind. "G-guess I f-fucked up, huh?"

Natalya shook her head as she mulled over her options. Her best bet was to treat him where he lay, but there was no guarantee that the—

The ping of her goggles' motion sensors going off, yet again, and an accompanying, chittering hiss, told her triage would have to wait. There were three more of the creatures creeping over the dune to her left, and two more to the right.

Apparently, they'd missed the carnage from a few moments earlier. They didn't know how dangerous she was.

They were about to find out.

Natalya's gray eyes flared like lighting bolts punching through storm clouds, and she scooped up the CAWS at her feet. She checked to make sure it was still on semi-auto, then turned to greet the charging reptiles, a welcoming smile on her face.

"Come on, you fucks!" she snarled as she pulled the trigger. She caught the lead reptilian on the left in the leg, amputating it at the knee, and causing it to trip up its brethren as it fell. Before they could recover, she spun toward the duo on the right, her weapon bucking as she fired from the hip. She caught the fore-runner in the groin and sent it tumbling to the ground, its scaly body flailing like it was on fire.

"How about you?" she bellowed, shouldering the big 12-gauge and spewing blasts of fire and death at anything still standing. "Schas po poluchish, suka!"

With the last of the reptiles either dead or sprawled in a twitching heap, Natalya spat on the ground and shouldered the smoking CAWS. She flinched and cursed as its overheated barrel singed her exposed shoulder. Ignoring the pain, she reached down and grabbed Bender under one arm. With a strength that surprised them both, she hauled him to his feet.

"Come on!" she yelled, indicating the *Remora*'s beckoning ramp. "Eet ees time to get the fuck out of here!"

Bender grimaced from the pain of his wounds, but nodded and hobbled along as quickly as he could. Once they were inside, Natalya sat the bulky 12-guage down on the rubberized floor of the mini-sib and helped him lay back, propped up against the nearest bulkhead.

Outside, the chittering, cackling calls of more of the creatures increased in both volume and frequency. She didn't know if the survivors of the maelstrom she'd unleashed had decided to come back, or if the place was simply so infested with them that the newcomers were ignorant of the damage the *Remora*'s cannons could do.

Either way, it was time to go.

Natalya sighed as she thought of poor Archer and Sato, torn to pieces by the horde of monstrosities that ruled the island, and fought down the urge to cross herself. She and religion had parted ways ages ago, but old habits died harder than the hardiest pliosaur.

She glanced at Bender as she began departure preparations. He was pasty and his breath was coming in pants. "Computer, prepare for departure," she commanded. With the system occupied, she turned toward the open hatch, reaching for the wall release to close it manually.

As she did, one of the creatures popped up from behind a bush, twenty feet away, and charged the opening on all-fours like a rushing Rottweiler. It was the survivor from the first group, she realized, the one whose leg she'd blown off. It was pissed and, despite its missing lower limb, moving surprisingly fast.

"Computer, emergency hatch close!"

Natalya figured the door wouldn't close in time, at least not fully, and she was right. The six-foot-four reptilian was already a third of the way in, when the heavy hatch rose up under it and attempted to slam shut. The power and speed of the pneumatics caught it off guard, practically catapulting it into the air, but it twisted its body and, with a frantic grab, latched onto the doorway's thick frame. Pulling itself forward, it hissed and snarled as it fought to squirm its way inside, while the hatch's complaining actuators tried to stop it.

Natalya moved closer and stared at the creature, fascinated. Then she turned her attention to the besieged door.

They were at a standstill. The reptilian had its head, left shoulder, and arm wedged inside the partly-closed hatch, and was struggling like a madman. Its baleful eyes bulged, and it began making guttural sounds, deep in its throat. Then, with a surprisingly hateful expression, it lashed out, it claws aiming for Natalya's face.

She didn't flinch, even though its filth-encrusted nails came within inches of her nose. Instead, she yanked her Spetsnaz knife from its sheath and whipped it through the space between them in a blur. The double-edged blade, as sharp as a katana, sliced clean through the creature's thickly muscled arm, severing it mid-point between wrist and elbow. It let out an ear-splitting scream and reddish blood spewed all over the floor of the submersible, spattering its nearby bulkheads.

Despite the severity of its injuries, the squirming reptile refused to give up. Worse, through the open space at the top of the hatch, Natalya could hear more of its kind closing in. She began to worry that, together, a bunch of them might have the strength to force their way inside.

Enough is enough.

She reached down for the heavy CAWS, hoisting it with one hand. Then, weaving around a stream of arterial blood that sprayed from the creature's stump, she walked up and shoved the barrel deep in its mouth.

"Dasvidaniya, *mudak*," she snarled.

Then she pulled the trigger.

The reptilian's head exploded like a rotten pumpkin, leaving a mangled, spurting torso behind. Not satisfied, Natalya rushed forward and struck it ferociously in the shoulder region with the gun butt, once, twice . . . after the third blow its body slipped out enough that only part of its forearm and elbow remained lodged between the hatch and frame.

That would do.

"Computer, emergency breach closure, full power . . . initiate now!"

There was a loud humming noise, as the massive hydraulics that powered the hatch upped their ante. The emergency setting was designed to be used if the hatch failed while submerged and increased its power output from 2,000 to an astounding 10,000 pounds.

Natalya watched from beneath raised eyebrows, as the vault-like door moved, then smirked in satisfaction at the moist crunching that followed. There was a low clunk, and the sound of pressurized air escaping. A moment later, the lights above the hatch switched from red to orange to green.

Finally, they were safe.

Or as safe as could be, she surmised, until more company arrived. Already, more of the bipedal reptiles were beginning to gather at the top of the dunes, their curiosity piqued.

Natalya hopped into the pilot's chair and grabbed the controls, but then hesitated as Bender uttered a pain-filled moan. She swiveled around and considered him, propped against the bulkhead behind the submersible's passenger seats, like a bleeding bag of meat. She shook her head. He was white as a piece of paper and beginning to hyperventilate. She knew in her bones, if she didn't act soon, he'd be dead before they cleared the caldera.

"Computer," she said, rising and grabbing the team's bulky medical kit. "Prepare to initiate launch sequence."

As she unzipped the heavy case, she heard the familiar pinging that indicated the *Remora*'s autopilot feature had taken over. It was followed by a low rumble, as the vessel's MHDs flared to life, and the floor began to tremble as the twin powerplants built up the necessary thrust to back them away from shore. The water beneath their keel was shallow – even at high tide it had barely lapped the sand beneath the open hatch – but once the anchors were retracted, she calculated they would be able to push off with no problem.

Or, rather, she hoped.

Natalya was bent over Bender's prostrate form, when a scuttling noise caused her maned head to turn towards the bow. One of the creatures was scaling the *Remora*'s curved nose, clambering up and over it like a big, olive-colored spider. She could hear its claws, scraping along the exterior, as it disappeared onto the roof. Twenty yards away, a dozen of its more cautious brethren were in the process of screwing up their courage and would soon join it.

"W-we've g-got company . . ." Bender said breathlessly.

"Shush," Natalya reassured. "Eet ees fine." She glanced down at his ghastly abdominal wound and forced herself to remain expressionless. It was worse than she'd thought. Determinedly, she rummaged through the overloaded med kit, digging for the only thing that could stop the hemorrhaging. She breathed a sigh of relief when she found it: a can of synthetic dermal foam that, once sprayed into the wound, would permeate it and expand, before solidifying. It would seal torn blood vessels as it went, and disinfect the area. It even had topical anesthetic qualities.

A loud bang from above caused Natalya to jump. She ground her molars in frustration. She was tired of being hunted. "Computer, retract anchors and launch, now!"

She had to grab onto a nearby handhold, as the *Remora* dropped with a thunderous splash. She heard a dull squeal and smirked with satisfaction, as their visitor slid loudly back down the prow, its jagged nails scratching ineffectually against the mini-sub's near-frictionless hull.

Tenacious to the end, the creature's misshapen head popped eagerly back up, but a moment later the propulsor engines fired in full reverse. Twin jets of seawater and sand slammed into the surprised reptilian, pummeling it with the force of a dozen firehoses. The impact sent it flying head over heels, with the engines' deafening roar causing its companions to dive for the dunes.

For a few seconds, the *Remora* shook and shivered, but then the water beneath it deepened and it began its retreat. Within seconds, it was past the waves and backing down purposefully across the caldera's windswept waters. When it was two hundred feet from shore, in fifty feet of water, the 32-foot vessel did a perfect one-eighty and began to sink.

Natalya looked up momentarily, checking their bow window. In the distance, the corpse-strewn beach where their camp had been was wiped from view, replaced by a fast-rising layer of greenish water that scaled the durable Celazole barrier, until they were completely submerged.

"Hold steel and move your hands," Natalya said, shaking the can of artificial dermis vigorously.

"Is it g-going to hurt?" Bender asked with big eyes.

Her cocked eyebrow and mouthing the word "seriously?" was all it took for the traumatized communications officer to man up. His hands moved shakily away from his ravaged midsection and he looked away, biting his lip.

Natalya had been through only basic emergency first aid and lifesaving, but she was intuitive and had seen a fair share of combat injuries. Following the spray's instructions, she swept it back and forth across the wound, hosing it down and repeating as needed. The pink-colored foam was a true medical miracle, and within less than thirty seconds the fleshy crater was completely filled. Once it stiffened, the stuff would even keep his torn intestines from shifting around, until he could get proper medical care.

"Th-that feels a bit better," Bender said. He tried to shift, but then cried out from the pain and nearly fainted.

"Hold on, I geev you some theeng," she said. She extracted a pair of Decamorph ampoules and injected one at the top of his hip. The second, she shot deep into the left pectoral, near his heart. She held her breath, waiting for the powerful opioids to kick in. With Archer gone, she couldn't administer any much-needed plasma or even an IV. The best she could do was what she had – minimize any additional bleeding and keep him as comfortable as possible. Based on the severity of the wound, and the likelihood he'd been infected with the pathogens Diablo was infamous for, Bender's best, and possibly *only* chance for survival, was to get back to *Antrodemus* ASAP.

That was, assuming her boat was still in one piece.

Natalya's eyes swung forward, gauging their depth. "Computer, activate Gemini program and initiate," she commanded. She turned back to her patient. "How's that?" she asked, trying her best to be maternal.

Eyes half-closed, Bender's sweaty head wobbled slowly from side to side. "I d-don't feel any . . . w-wait, I-I feel . . ." His glazed-over eyes cranked opened. "Wow, I feel *good*."

"I thought you might."

"Thanks."

"Anytime."

Outside, the waters of Diablo Caldera began to churn, as the *Remora* accelerated, fifty feet down and auto-powering its way back the way they'd come. Natalya could feel Bender looked at her with appraising eyes, and prayed he wasn't strong enough to crack jokes about picturing her in a slutty nurse's outfit.

"Da, what ees it?"

"You know, you were a real badass out there," Bender said, gazing at her with worshipful eyes. "I've never seen anything like it. Garm, I mean Captain Braddock, would've been impressed."

"Spasiba."

"You're welcome. I don't speak Russian, but I'm curious. I know what *mudak* means; I looked it up after you called me that once or twice . . ."

"Asshole. Da, and?"

"Well, what was that stuff you were screaming at those things as they came charging at us?"

Natalya stopped to think. A moment later, her full lips curled up into a grin. "Ah, you mean, schas po poluchish, suka?"

"Yeah, that was it."

She chuckled. "Een English, eet means, 'Come and get eet, beech.' Or some theeng like that."

Bender smiled weakly and nodded. "Fucking cool, man."

She smiled genuinely back at him, for what might have been the first time ever. "You know, I like you better when you are high on drugs."

He smiled sleepily and started to close his eyes. Natalya tensed, however, when she saw how ragged his breathing had become. She began to wonder if she'd applied the medical foam in time, or if the damage was simply so severe there was internal hemorrhaging it couldn't reach.

"Hey, Bender, don't you fucking die on me," she said, tapping him gently on the cheek.

He opened his eyes and stared at her. "Die my dear? Why, that's the last thing I'll do!"

When she stared at him, uncomprehendingly, he said, "Supposedly, those were Groucho Marx's last words. Get it, 'the *last* thing I'll do?'"

"Ah, I get eet," she said, forcing a grin.

"I, um, I want you to promise me something, captain."

"Da, what ees eet?"

"If I don't make it, please don't let me come back as one of those things."

Her expression turned morose, and her gaze shifted to the scale-coated forearm, still laying on the deck beside them. "I don't theenk it works like that."

Bender nodded.

Out of nowhere, a high-pitched warning claxon drew Natalya's attention back to the helm. *Now what?* Her lips curled back from her teeth as she saw the red lights flashing on their main sonar screen.

She knew right away what it was.

They had a proximity alert; something was coming for them.

Something big.

She was almost to the helm when there was a thunderous impact. The *Remora* tilted hard to port, like it had been struck by a giant fist, and a collision alarm began to sound.

"Computer, I have the conn!" Natalya shouted, strapping herself into the pilot's chair and seizing the steering yoke. She checked her instruments and saw their reactive armor had gone off, reducing the force of the blow they'd received. "Assume co-pilot's position and utilize auditory responses."

"Working," the system's synthetic voice replied.

"Damage report!"

"There is no significant damage to the vessel at this time."

Good. With one eye on the blip that now moved rapidly away from them, Natalya torqued the *Remora* hard to starboard, matching its speed and plotting an intercept course. "Computer, identify attacker."

"Working. Attacker is a large biologic, size estimate nine meters. Mass est--"

"Fuck the mass!" Natalya snapped. She could see a shadowy form, just beyond visual range. "What *ees* eet?"

"Biologic's designate is an elasmobranch. A shark."

She breathed through her teeth as she brought their HYDRA cannons back online, the system's virtual crosshairs appearing on the bow window.

"Computer, what *kind* of shark?"

"Working. No exact match. Based on fossil record, the closest possible match is *Otodus obliquus*, an extinct species of lamniform shark from the--"

"Computer, enough," Natalya said. "Track incoming biologic and transfer all unnecessary power to maneuvering thrusters."

"Thrusters are now at maximum power."

With her timber wolf's eyes narrowed, Natalya accelerated to a crisp forty knots and aimed directly for the fast-moving shadow. Given their limited armament, she was relieved their attacker wasn't an adult *Kronosaurus imperator*. But that didn't make the situation any less perilous. Any shark that could survive alongside the deadliest predators on the planet had to be formidable.

She spotted it finally, fifty yards ahead and cruising around them in a wide arc. Its eight-foot caudal fin was whipping back and forth to increase thrust, and its wedge-shaped fins were extended for maximum maneuverability.

It was a big bastard, all right, Natalya thought. Just like the computer said. It reminded her of a Shortfin Mako, albeit an eight-ton one. It had the same dark-bluish color above, with white below, but its now-burned snout was blunter, and the four-inch teeth that lined its yard-wide jaws had triple tips, like a drawerful of steak knives, robbed from Hell's kitchen.

The *Otodus*, sensing that its prey had somehow survived its ambush, appeared confused. It accelerated and started moving in a descending spiral, trying to get underneath the mini-sub, to target its underbelly.

Natalya was no fool and cut it off. She could see its softball-sized black eye, staring back at her as she closed in. "That's right, mudak. I'm planning to keel *you*, just like *you're* planning to keel *us*."

At around twenty-five knots, the shark reached its maximum speed. Natalya was befuddled. How its kind had managed to survive for countless millennia around bigger, faster marine reptiles was beyond her. She scoffed. It was irrelevant. She couldn't chance the thing coming after them again; they needed to get home.

She went into a steep dive, outpacing the now-confused shark, until she had the big Gatling cannons' sonar-based targeting system locked onto its gills.

BRAAAAAT!

From less than thirty yards away, a 100-round burst was all it took. The depleted uranium shells, with their bright orange tracers, slammed into the prehistoric predator. Its neck region literally exploded on impact, a horrific plume of red and white chunks of flesh, and its forward momentum ceased. Practically decapitated, it began to sink, its huge head hanging limply by scraps of skin, and the waters above and around it turning a bright crimson.

With a snort of satisfaction, Natalya angled them back on course. As she did, she saw numerous blips appear on the sonar screen. A minute later, a dozen big silver flashes blew past the submersible. A horde of Bulldog fish had arrived, eager to feast on the bloody remains of what must have been their sole remaining predator.

"Computer, resume autopilot function and reactivate Gemini."

"Working."

"Additional command: activate auto-sentry mode. Maneuver as needed, and fire 50-round bursts at any perceived threat that comes within forty yards."

"Acknowledged."

Natalya got up, stretched her arms out to the side, and rounded her lips as she blew out a breath. All the killing and combat was starting to wear on her, and she needed a break. She headed back to check on Bender, to see if he needed anything.

"Well, that was fun," she said. "Deed you see the size of that . . ."

She stopped in mid-step and stood there. Her communications officer's lolling head and unblinking stare transmitted a louder message than he ever had.

He was dead.

She folded her arms across her chest and sagged against a nearby bulkhead, her brow furrowed and jaw set. She couldn't believe it. She'd lost everyone, her entire team. They were dead, all of them.

Dropping down on one knee, Natalya reached out and softly closed Bender's eyes. Then she got up and stormed back to her chair. She reached for the *Remora*'s radio mike and flipped a switch, then changed her mind and put it on speaker.

"Attention, Tartarus, thees is priority one call from Captain Natalya Dragunova, commander of USS *Antrodemus*. Come een, Tartarus."

She waited thirty seconds for a reply, then tried again. Nothing.

What was the problem? Was it her current position? Perhaps the secure acoustic link couldn't function within the caldera? The depth shouldn't have been an issue, but could the walls of the volcanic island be somehow interfering with her transmission?

The memory of how *Antrodemus* had been unable to reach the CDF base earlier came back to her, and she became suspicious. She decided to try a different tack and pulled up Derek Braddock's personal cell phone number. She assumed he already knew about Garm's death, but he didn't know about what they'd found on Diablo. He needed to, especially the creatures.

She hit "send" and waited for the call to go through. To her surprise, someone answered on the second ring. But, whoever it was, had a deep, gruff voice, and was decidedly *not* Derek.

"Hello?"

"Da, thees ees Captain Dra--"

Natalya's head snapped back on her neck as the recipient hung up on her.

Son of a . . .

She called back. This time, the phone went straight to voicemail.

Natalya's nostrils flared, and she snorted irritably. Something was definitely amiss. She didn't know what, but her instincts told her she needed get back to Tartarus at once. And she would. She would find *Antrodemus* and she would set sail for home. And when she got there, someone was going to have a lot of explaining to do.

TWENTY-TWO

The air was clear and bright, high above the Florida Keys, and the sun's brilliance reflecting off the water so blinding, the ocean's surface looked like a sea of flame. Yep, definitely, a great day to be alive. But, for independent news chopper pilot and cameraman, Leon "Eagle Eye" Evans, it was looking like another miserable, unproductive workday.

As Leon swung the vintage Bell Model 707 helicopter back around and hovered at 500 feet, he mentally weighed his choices. A sigh slipped out. An hour earlier, he'd flown all around Marathon, chasing tides and burning a ton of gas, in the hope of finding and filming some debris from that lost schooner – the one with all the kids on it. He'd come up empty. Undaunted, he'd rushed off to film that supposed "Arabian Sheikh's yacht", a few miles from there. As fortune would have it, by the time he'd gotten there, the wreck had already been towed.

There was a lot going on, between all the disappearing fishing boats and the derelict pleasure craft the Coast Guard kept finding, yet nobody had anything definitive. From Leon's decidedly story-driven perspective, there *had* to be some sort of "sea monster" at work. If not, he could certainly invent one. Yet, so far, and despite a considerable investment of time and resources on his part, he'd found diddly squat.

He reached down, grabbed his barely cool can of cola, and finished it in one long draught. Since his wife wasn't there to chide him, he belched loudly. Then he squeezed the aluminum can into an unrecognizable mass and tossed it over his shoulder into the backseat, so it could hang out with its tinny friends.

With a shrug of ineffectuality, Leon checked his radar, adjusted his headset, and, with a roar of his rotors, dropped to 400 feet. He was down to his last option, following the safety nets, in and around the Keys, in the hope of seeing something. It was a longshot; years back, when the titanium towers, complete with their near-indestructible mesh, had first been installed, it seemed like something big got tangled up in them every other day.

Usually, it was a giant sea lizard of some kind, those plesiosaurs, or whatever they called them. Leon had gotten some great clips of some of them over the years, and each one had ended up being a nice payday with the local networks. In fact, one segment, in which a military chopper had come down and chaingunned the thing to death, as it flailed around like a beached whale, had even been snatched up by the big boys. He'd seen part of it on TV, just the other day, in the title sequence for that reality show, *Pliosaur Wars*.

But that was back before the Coastal Defense Force got involved. It seemed like those trigger-happy squid-types had pretty much killed off any lizard that couldn't fit between the openings in the net. That, or the survivors were too cagey to come near it anymore.

Leon spotted the net immediately; the colorful marker buoys that helped boats avoid its submerged towers popped like a flock of cardinals, perched on a snowdrift. He checked his screen, did a manual safety check, then angled forward and began the monotonous task of following the line.

It would take the rest of the day, and more fuel than he had, but if he was lucky, he'd get something. Or, if not, God forbid, maybe some poor bastard, crazy enough to try surfing, might get himself chewed up by one of those giant fish that cruised right through the net. It was sad to say, but footage of those balls-to-the-wall LifeGivers, on their big Jet Skis, pulling some limbless bastard out of the surf, always made for a nice, fat check.

Whatever happened to the good old days, when the only thing beach lovers had to worry about was sharks?

Leon looked around, found a half-eaten box of chocolate-covered mints, and popped one in his mouth. He was borderline diabetic, and if his old lady found out, she'd give him a fat lip for sure. But, hey, what mama don't know . . .

Grinning, he checked his look in a flip-down mirror, only to have his grin become a grimace. He was lucky he'd married young. He might've been "only" fifty-eight, but with all the sun and wind damage he'd suffered, between his aged convertible and hanging by the chopper's window, his crinkled brown face looked more like seventy. He flipped the mirror back up in disgust, slapped on his trusty polarized sunglasses, and grabbed another mint.

Yep, life was tough, Leon thought, and it would never let you live it down. He had one kid in college, another in rehab, and . . . hell, he didn't want to even *think* about what the other one was up to these days. He guided the 707 with one hand and gave his pot belly a quick pat with the other. He obviously wasn't starving, not by any means, but the bills *were* piling up.

He needed a break.

Leon slid his door's plexiglass partition open, stuck his head out of the old Bell's window, and glanced up at the sun, squinting from behind his shades. "Come on, Lord, show me something, brother! Something, big!"

And just like that, he got his wish.

He blinked to make sure he wasn't imagining things, then blinked again. Still not convinced, he rubbed his eyes, checked his sunglasses lenses for a smudge and, finally, even changed his angle of approach, to make sure it wasn't a mirage.

It wasn't. There was something down there. Something big, hugging the seafloor as it swam along, not one hundred feet from the nets. Leon had logged so many hours flying that, as long as he had something to compare it to, he could accurately gauge the size of something on the ground from almost any altitude.

And whatever was down there was *huge*.

He dropped down to 300 feet and leveled off, satisfied with his chosen vantage point. It would allow him to frame his shots and zoom in easily enough, yet the noise of his rotors wouldn't spook whatever it was he was looking at. But what in tarnation was it?

Leon could see its basic shape: an enormous, shadowy form, running parallel to the towers. It wasn't a whale. He'd seen hundreds of grays and humpbacks; it was far too big. It had to be something else.

He felt a jolt of excitement.

It was one of those giant plesiosaur lizards. It had to be.

"Woo-mama, it is *on*, baby!"

Activating his chopper's underbelly camera, Leon zeroed the creature and started filming. HD footage was a must: none of that low-res crap. He dropped back, slowed his roll, and hung tight at a forty-five-degree angle. The creature was staying down and, judging by its size, had to be practically rubbing the reefs. He knew the depth charts for this section of the Keys; the water was eighty feet at most.

He checked his shot on the chopper's dash screen, then decided to do some narration. Talking up footage was always a good idea. It got his name out there, and the networks had to pay more.

He cleared his throat and incorporated his deep "news anchor" voice.

"This is INC cameraman Leon Evans and I am airborne, five miles from Marathon. What you're looking at, directly below us, is an unidentified sea creature which, shortly before filming commenced, attempted to break through the titanium-steel barrier that protects the Florida Keys."

Leon hit the pause button and grinned. He thought that last, "ad-libbed", part added a nice fear factor to what was already shaping up to be some amazing footage. Money in the bank. He thought for a moment, then hit resume.

"Whatever this mysterious creature is, you can tell by comparing it to the outlines of the submerged towers that it is enormous. Conservative estimates put it at blue-whale-size, if not larger." He zoomed in for effect, then pulled back to his original frame. "The consensus is that it is a giant plesiosaur, possibly the largest ever recorded, and maybe even the one responsible for all the boat disappearances that have been reported in the last few days."

Leon hit selfie mode and cut to himself. "We're running low on gas, but will continue to track this thing for as long as we can, in the interest of saving lives."

He switched back to the creature. "Judging by its behavior, and having failed to smash past the net, the plesiosaur appears to be following it along, perhaps looking for an opening." He paused for inspiration, then resumed. "If it continues with its current course and speed, in less than two hours it will arrive at the location of those two recently downed towers, and the breach in the net – a breach it may well have caused. I think someone needs to call the CDF."

Leon stopped filming and smiled hugely. Peddling paranoia was always good for business. And, a little sensationalism never hurt, right?

He continued tailing the slow-swimming behemoth and, as he did, rewound his footage to check for problems. There were none; it was perfect. All he needed to do now was keep tabs on "Godzilla", in case it surfaced or did something exciting; in either case, his fee would go up dramatically.

Just then, something odd caught Leon's eye. There was a tiny burst of light on his footage. He reversed it, checked it, then checked it again, this time frame by frame. Yep, it was definitely there: a little blip of some kind.

He reached underneath his ratty old Yankees cap and scratched his head. What in tarnation *was* that? Was it a problem with the lens or recorder? He didn't need anything odd on this sequence. Besides the fact it might damage his chances of getting a sale, it could hurt his rep. Nothing worse than trying to pass off CGI-augmented crap as something legit.

All hoaxers must hang.

Leon shook his head emphatically. He had to make sure. He switched back to the camera's live feed and checked his dash screen. Yep, there it was again. Some weird flash of light, almost like a strobe or something. It appeared in regular intervals, but it wasn't coming from the equipment. Which meant it was *there*, underwater.

Was it coming from the . . . creature?

Leon pulled his salt-stained partition window open again and poked his head out. He was too high up and had to drop to 200 feet, before he could be sure. When he saw it, his heart sank.

Yep. There it was, a dull red flash of light. It was deep down, coming from what looked to be the head or neck of his so-called "lizard".

Leon's face scrunched up like he'd just chewed a lemon and he started to curse. It *wasn't* an animal that he'd been filming. It was a goddamn submarine! Probably one of those CDF patrol boats you saw periodically, lurking off the coast.

"Fuck!"

He shoved the partition closed so hard, he almost broke it. He couldn't believe it. He'd wasted time and gas on what – some useless stock footage that you could license online for twenty bucks? Who the hell would want *that*?

Leon got so worked up, he felt nauseous. Then, a light bulb went off, and a surge of relief swept through him. He'd been real lucky; with his aging eyes, he might not have noticed the sub's running light. What if he'd ignorantly tried passing it off to the networks as the real McCoy?

Wow, now *that* would've been something. His career as a videographer would've ended, then and there. Nobody would've hired him; he'd have ended up flipping burgers at the local diner, no doubt.

Leon shrugged and started whistling a tune to cheer himself up. With steady hands, he turned his chopper away from the CDF sub, climbed back to 500 feet, and laid in a flight path for home. It had been a long day. He was low on gas, hungry, and looking forward to a homecooked meal. It was meatloaf night, right?

Yep, it sure was. His Melodee always made the best meat loaf. And that gravy of hers? Lord have mercy. A heaping plate or two, a thick slice of pecan pie, and a nice, cold beer (when she wasn't looking) and he'd feel much better.

Oh, yeah. Definitely.

A half-mile behind him, a smiling Leon never saw the huge fin that broke the surface, oh-so-fleetingly, and then submerged again.

———

As she took in the miles-long debris field that littered the sea-floor surrounding Diablo Caldera, Natalya Dragunova realized things weren't looking very good for *Antrodemus*.

Then again, she conceded, things weren't looking very good for her, either. Her taxed mind did a quick accounting, trying to tally the day's events. So far, her paramour had been incinerated in a nuclear fireball, her besieged vessel was MIA and likely destroyed, and she was the sole survivor of the four-person landing party that had – in retrospect, foolishly – attempted to explore the Cretaceous-era island. On top of that, she was cut off from her base and alone, in a tiny, poorly-armed craft, hugging the seafloor, in the middle of hostile seas.

Natalya glanced back over her shoulder at the tagged and bagged body of her communications officer and her demeanor momentarily softened.

Granted, Bender had it worse.

To reduce the risk of being picked up by active enemy sonar buoys, Natalya had set the *Remora* on autopilot twenty minutes earlier, and had the sleek, 32-foot vessel suspended less than a boat-length from the craggy bottom. Her attempts to reach *Antrodemus* on the sub's secure acoustic link had been futile. Either they were ignoring her calls, or they'd been destroyed.

While she'd considering her remaining options, Natalya had busied herself putting Ensign Bartholomew "Bart" Bender into a body bag. As unpleasant as the task had been, at a mere 150 pounds, picking up the comm tech's still-warm remains had been relatively easy. Doing the same for Garm, she imagined, would've been far more difficult. But then, the big submariner had left nothing behind to bury.

She sighed. At least he'd died in a manner he would have approved of: "with his boots on", as the saying went.

Natalya shrugged off her morose ponderings, chiding herself for being sentimental. There was simply no point. She'd always known Wolfie was not "Mr. Right". Even he had joked that he was more like "Mr. Right Now".

She allowed herself a brief smile, before tackling the disagreeable task of cleaning up after Bender. As when most people passed, he'd lost control of his bodily functions, baptizing the submersible's middeck with a foul-smelling stew of urine and feces.

Natalya had never been more grateful in her life for the vessel's standard-issue filtered surgical masks, not to mention a box of thick latex gloves that went halfway up her biceps.

I'd always known you were full of shit, Bender, she'd joked to herself as she scooped, scrubbed, and wiped, all the while trying hard to not look at what she was doing. *But this? Bozhe moi!*

Her warped sense of humor had helped. Considering all the times the lecherous comms officer had pissed her off, this was the first time he'd actually pissed *on* her . . .

Once Bender had been secured away, and she'd said a quick prayer over him, Natalya began a sonar sweep, trying to get a lead on her missing boat. She found nothing. Not for ten miles in any direction. In fact, there were no ships of any kind, rebel or otherwise. No planes, either. There was, however, wreckage as far as human eyes could see.

She'd detected the blown-out remains of at least a dozen warships of assorted classes, all seeping oil and worse into the surrounding sea as they littered the bottom. Most were easily identifiable, especially the large cruiser and destroyers; some were not.

The thought that one of those smaller exploded hulls might be *Antrodemus*, crept up on her like a Siberian wolf, stalking its prey. She refused to believe it. Javier Gonzalez was a top-notch officer. If anyone could've have gotten the crimson-hued ORION-class submarine away safely, it was him.

Unless he'd refused to run, or was cornered and forced to fight.

The discovery of several yard-long fragments of ceramic-composite armor, littering a nearby reef, however, began to gnaw at her already-eroding hopes. The gnawing worsened, when she zoomed in on one and saw a familiar shade of crimson.

A sickly feeling came over Natalya then, one that only worsened as she took the helm and guided the *Remora* soundlessly upward. At periscope depth, she extended her optronics mast and scanned the surface. Here and there, burning hunks of wreckage dotted the seascape, like bonfires on a beach, and there were bodies everywhere. She could see their bright orange life vests, bobbing up and down amid the whitecaps.

Natalya drew a breath through flared nostrils and held it. Seconds later, her acceptance of *Antrodemus*'s fate came out as a drawn-out sigh. Just then, a sudden movement on the dash monitor caught her eye. It was a small helicopter of some kind, not military, either a private bird or a news chopper; there was no way of telling which.

Whatever it was, whoever was controlling it wasn't interested in the marine graveyard beneath their rotors. They flew in a straight line and vanished over the horizon in minutes.

Natalya's shoulder muscles tensed as she made her decision. She had no choice; she had to drive the *Remora* back to Tartarus.

It wouldn't be hard. At top speed, the journey would be less than two hours, possibly only ninety minutes. She turned in her seat and checked the mini-sub's fuel reserves. There was plenty; she could make it there and back with fuel to spare.

She was just laying in her course, when a nasty smell invaded her nostrils. She looked back at the faded stain on the deck next to Bender's body bag. Was it coming from there? She didn't think so. She'd been quite thorough in her efforts and had literally bleached the shit out of the spot, along with much of the surrounding floor.

Was it coming from the body?

Natalya tried to ignore it, but the unfamiliar odor kept getting worse. Finally, with her face so scrunched up she was practically unrecognizable, she went over to the bagged corpse. After a moment's hesitation, she took hold of the body bag's zipper and, holding her breath, yanked it down.

The steamy blast of foulness that hit her between the eyes was so powerful, she literally recoiled. Even worse was the sight that greeted her from within; Bender's entire body was in an impossibly advanced state of decomposition.

The cause was immediately obvious. An army of writhing worm-like creatures, like whitish maggots, but smaller and thinner, had completely infested and encapsulated the comm tech's remains. There were literally millions of them, squirming like a sentient second skin as they feasted and multiplied. The stench the corpse gave off was so putrid, Natalya had to swallow her own vomit.

O moy Bog!

Half-choking, she pulled the zipper back up as fast as her trembling hands could manage and snatched up a nearby bottle of disinfectant. Pumping hard, she sprayed her hands, forearms, and feet, and then hosed down the surrounding deck. The bottle was nearly empty before she stopped and sat back on her haunches, staring at the body bag in disbelief.

God had nothing to do with this. It must've been something from the caldera, she surmised. Or maybe something from the saliva of the creatures that had bitten Bender. That made more sense. It couldn't be Cretaceous cancer, per se; every member of her crew had been fully inoculated before they'd left port.

No, this was something else, she realized, something horrible. It was either a parasitic organism that devoured dead things at an accelerated rate, or an outsized, primeval bacterium they had yet to discover. Whatever it was, the pharma geeks back in Tartarus would be thrilled to examine it. They'd want samples, of course. Or, more likely, the entire corpse.

Fuck that!

Natalya shook her head like she'd touched a live wire. Science or no, there was no way in hell she was helming it all the way back to Tartarus, with Bender decomposing into a vile pile of putrescence, right behind her.

Fat chance. They can kiss my fat Russian ass.

Suddenly, the bag moved – the corpse settling as it was eaten away from the inside, no doubt – but regardless, it made her jump. She shook it off and sprang to her feet. With impressive speed, she donned two surgical masks, one over the other, her combat goggles, and then double-bagged her arms.

Her expression resolute and suppressing an anticipatory shiver, she opened a second body bag and lay it next to Bender's corpse. Then, as quickly as she could, she hoisted his remains (was it just her, or did he weigh less now?) and slid the first bag inside the second. Once the latter was zipped up, she felt a tad better.

At least the stench was reduced.

Tossing her protective gear and reclaiming her seat, Natalya swiveled the mini-sub's photonics mast 360 degrees, scanning the sea and air for any signs of life. She saw nothing but birds and, other than an assortment of small-to-medium sized biologics, there was nothing on sonar, either. She knew there was a chance that, when she surfaced, the *Remora* would be spotted via satellite overview, but she had to chance it. She couldn't bear the smell, let alone the visual of what was going on in that bag, crawling through her head.

With a sudden burst of daylight, so bright it made her squint as it sliced through the sub's mirrored window, Natalya surfaced. Wave action began to cause them to sway from side to side, and she engaged the auto-thrusters.

Once they were stable, she hit the lever to pop the top hatch and scaled its three-rung ladder, poking her head out. The smell of fresh sea air was invigorating, as was the splash of cold brine that sprayed her face, as a wave dashed against the mini-sub's sturdy hull. She drew in a few more welcome breaths, then steeled herself for her pending task.

Sliding back down, she put on a fresh pair of gloves and a clean surgical mask, then picked up Bender's bagged body and slung it over one shoulder. She tried to mentally disconnect herself from her ears, doing her best to pretend that the sloshing sounds she heard coming from inside the layered bag didn't exist.

As she reached the hatch, Natalya rested the corpse atop the hull. Nearby, she could see a distorted, yard-wide section, where the mini-sub's reactive armor had gone off, earlier. A glint of white caught her eye and she reached down, pulling a nearly five-inch shark's tooth free from a rubberized seam. She put the dagger-like tooth in her pocket, to save for later. Then, with a heavy exhalation and an even heavier heart, she began to speak.

"I am . . . sorry eet has to end like thees, Bender," she said. "Although you were a pain een the butt, you were a good worker. You deserve better." She paused as a breeze kicked up and the rank smell of the body momentarily enveloped her. "Unfortunately, I can't breeng you back. As much as you were a steenker on the bridge, you steenk much more now. Forgeev me. Amen."

Crossing herself, Natalya gave the body a quick shove. It slid down the *Remora*'s slick hull and was quickly taken by the current. She watched it, bobbing at the surface, and tensed as a mound of additional regret piled on. She'd considered weighing the body down with one of their reserve ammunition cans but couldn't risk it; she had no idea what was waiting for her back in Tartarus. She might need the ammo.

The body was fifty yards away, with Natalya praying it would become waterlogged and sink, when the predator struck. It was a sub-adult *Kronosaurus imperator*, judging by the fanged jaws, maybe thirty feet in length. Rising like a breaching Orca, it latched onto the body and vanished in a watery detonation.

She blanched. A pliosaur would have to be desperate or starving to eat something like that.

Shaking her head to dislodge some of the horror, Natalya closed the hatch and headed back below. It was time to re-disinfect both herself and the *Remora*.

And then to lay in a course for home.

———

A decade after witnessing his father's horrifying demise, Dirk Braddock finally understood what it would take to make someone pray for death.

He had reached that point. He was borderline delirious from the fever, couldn't move without crying out, and his blood felt like it was boiling. It burned like battery acid as it coursed through his body, eating away at his veins and arteries. Even worse were the waves of agony that repeatedly wracked his sweat-drenched frame. They reminded him of the growing pains he'd experienced as a teenager, except they were a hundred times worse.

Make that a thousand, Dirk thought, as the next wave hit. His whole body locked up and he gritted his teeth, trying with all his might to keep from screaming.

He failed. Miserably.

When he reopened his eyes, Stacy was leaning over him, as distraught as he'd ever seen her. She was sniffling and wiping at her nose, but she wasn't crying; she'd run out of tears an hour ago.

"Easy, baby," she comforted, leaning down and blowing a cooling breath across his burning brow. "I'm here. Don't worry, I'm here."

Dirk didn't know how much of a difference that made, especially when his eyes unexpectedly filled with fluid and he could barely see. He blinked hard, trying to clear his vision. He felt hot tears begin to run unchecked and, through a haze, saw Stacy's already worried expression convert to one of alarm. She swallowed her fear, then reached up with the damp piece of cloth she'd been pressing to his forehead and dabbed around his eyes and cheeks.

When he noticed her trying to secret the rag away, Dirk said, "Let me see."

"Baby, I . . ."

Their eyes met. Then, reluctantly, she showed him the cloth. Even in the dim lighting of their stony prison, he could see it was streaked with red.

Great, I'm shedding tears of blood. Wasn't that how it started with Dad?

Stacy reached out to run her fingertips gently down his arm – the one where the guards had injected him with the pathogen. The bloat had gone down significantly, but he cringed on contact; her lightest touch felt like a firebrand.

"Geez, I'm sorry, hon," she said, her eyes wide. "Your skin, it's . . ."

"It's what?"

"It's starting to crack." She shook her head slowly. "It, uh, it must be a localized side effect, caused by the fever and swelling."

Dirk drew a breath, then clamped his jaw tight as he fought to raise his other arm high enough that he could see it. "You're an even worse liar than I am," he said, forcing a grin as he held up a craggy forearm for her to see.

"I-I'm sorry, I--"

Stacy stopped talking when the music started.

It was loud yet muffled – a byproduct of being funneled through the air vents – and it took a moment for Dirk to realize it was the next scheduled workout interval for Tartarus's captive pliosaurs. He eased his aching head back on the stone floor and relaxed, waiting for the familiar Cranberries song Stacy always used as an opener.

Something was off. The music was different, some sort of orchestra. It sounded familiar, however. Wait, was that—

"What the *hell* is that?" Stacy blurted out. "Is that from '*West Side Story*'?"

Dirk nodded feebly. "It's 'I Feel Pretty', by Leonard Bernstein and Stephen Sondheim."

"Fucking Dwyer!" Stacy snarled. "That cankerous cunt biscuit switched my music!" She listened in fast-growing disbelief, as the song continued jauntily along. "He-he's got the world's greatest predators exercising to Natalie Wood?"

Apparently, the facility's test subjects felt similarly about the unexpected changeup. Their thunderous grunts, growls, and grumbles began to resonate from the air vents, nearly drowning out the music, and even vibrated the dungeon's rough-hewn walls.

"Actually, it's Marni Nixon singing. She did the vocals for both Maria and Rita Moreno's character. The studio never--"

"You know, I don't know what's more disturbing," Stacy cut in, angrily shaking her mane of tight dyed-blonde curls, "The fact that that slut bagel screwed with my lineup, or that you know all that."

Dirk's jaw muscles bunched into knots, and he closed his eyes and rode out the next series of agonizing spasms, before he could even think of answering. "M-my mom, it was her favorite soundtrack. She had an old LP her mom gave her and played it all the t-time . . . even made my brother and I dance with her when my dad wouldn't." He paused, grinning despite the extreme discomfort. "It was the only time I was glad Garm was bigger than me. She'd usually choose him."

He sighed heavily, realizing he and his fraternal twin would never get to laugh about things like that anymore.

"Are you sure he's dead?" Stacy asked. "I mean, this is *Garm* we're talking about. It would take a lot to--"

Dirk shook his head. "I saw the footage. He was locked in a losing battle with a cephalopod big enough to challenge *Tiamat*. He detonated *Gryphon*'s nuclear torpedoes, right in the tubes."

"Jesus, I-I'm so sorry."

"Me too. I-ah-ah-aaarrrgh!" Dirk sensed a far more powerful seizure coming and braced himself. It was no good. He may as well have tried holding back an avalanche with his bare hands. His body bucked and flailed, and his vision went dark as his eyes rolled up inside his head. He was dimly aware of foam spewing from his mouth, and Stacy crying out as she fought to hold him down, trying to keep him from injuring himself.

When the seizure finally abated, Dirk felt like he'd been run over by a New York City subway train – every single car. His muscles hurt so much, he was sure every one of them had torn, and his vision was growing more and more hazy. He hoped the end was near; he couldn't take much more of this.

"That's it, I'm getting us out of here," Stacy stated.

Ignoring his breathy protestations, she rose and raced to the nearby door. Starting with a running sidekick, she bashed and banged on it like a madwoman, cursing all the while.

It was useless.

The riveted steel barrier was strong enough to stop an elephant.

With her fury finally spent, Stacy paused to chase her breath and studied the portal's riveted edges and frame. She grabbed hold of the thick welded handle that functioned as its doorknob, tugging with all her might.

Dirk shook his head. Even with his compromised vision, he could see the steel of the sturdy handle was already deformed. Someone had wedged a heavy piece of wood or metal in it at some point and used it as a fulcrum, trying and failing to leverage the door open.

Like Stacy said, he thought dejectedly, his worn-out eyes falling on the nearby pile of bones; they weren't the first ones to be imprisoned there.

"St-Stace, give it up," he said exhaustedly, swallowing hard and finding his voice. "You couldn't b-break that door in a million years."

"I just need a lever of some kind," she said, stubbornly. She started looking around, then headed for the bone pile. "Maybe a femur or something?"

"Stace . . ."

"Shush, I can *do* this!" Stacy dropped down on one knee and eyed the moist mound of skeletal remains apprehensively, obviously afraid to dig in. "Yuck." With a visible shudder, she began extracting pieces from the pile. A tibia here, a fibula there. She finally found what she was looking for: a long, heavy thigh bone.

Suddenly, she stopped. Her amber eyes narrowed as she focused on something small and shiny, sequestered within a remarkably intact rib cage. With a grimace of disgust, she slid her hand along the slimy, black vertebral column and extracted what looked like a filthy necklace. Her eyebrows rose.

"What the hell?"

"What is it?" Dirk asked.

"Dog tags," Stacy said, making a face as she scraped the mildew off one with her thumbnail and held it to the light. Her jaw dropped. "Holy fuckwad."

He chuckled. "You know, you've been doing a lot of hardcore cursing, lately. What did you find?"

"Dirk, what was the name of that guard from the security footage? The one you said was involved in your mom's death?"

"McHale, why?"

"I think this was him," she said, her lips quirking. She walked over and handed him the filthy dog tags. He licked his lips and raised his head, studying them in the crappy lighting. His vision began to clear, and he suddenly found he could read the name clearly.

Stacy was right.

The son of a bitch was dead. Which meant any info he had, any proof of that bastard Grayson's involvement, died with him.

"We may have bigger problems," she advised, clocking his exasperation.

"Like what?"

She held up the big femur she'd pulled from the bone pile and indicated its abnormally rough surface. "You see these marks? This was gnawed on, and not by rats."

Dirk felt a cold chill creep over him. It started at his feet and ran roughshod up his spine. "By . . . what?"

Stacy shook her head. "I don't know. I've never seen marks like--"

A sudden splash waylaid her contemplating.

The two of them turned as one toward the sound. There was something moving, back toward the very end of their enclosure, by the eerily-lit grotto.

It was in the water.

Buoyed by a few quick breaths, Dirk braced himself for the pain and forced himself up on one elbow. Although his vision began to swim again, he saw something pop up out of the water and start to flop around.

It was just a fish of some kind, a large Jack Crevalle, from the looks of it.

He started to sigh in relief, but then a creepy feeling came over him. His instincts shrieked an alarm, warning him that there was more to come, and he raised trembling fingers to Stacy's lips, silencing her.

A moment later, another fish followed the first. This one was bigger – a good-sized cobia, judging by its silhouette – but it was dead already. It hit the cement floor outside the manmade grotto and lay there, inert. Beside it, the jack continued its slapping dance of death.

Then, the thing Dirk dreaded would happen, did. The waters of the grotto began to churn. His vison cleared completely and he could see it plainly, illuminated by the indirect sunlight coming off the water.

It was a hand.

A monstrous, dark-colored hand, that reared up and out of the water like the Loch Ness monster, before slapping down hard on the cold, wet stone. It was manlike in shape, but it was no man's. It was as big as a catcher's mitt and scaly, with translucent webbing that stretched between each of its misshapen fingers.

A massively-muscled forearm followed, and then a dome-shaped brow. The creature exhaled noisily, taking deep, rasping breaths as it prepared to heave itself up and out of the water.

Dirk's fear-widened eyes darted to the chewed-up leg bone in Stacy's hand, and he shivered. He knew now what had befallen McHale, and a host of other people, from the looks of the grisly bone pile.

They'd been killed and eaten by this . . . this *thing*, this guard-turned-nightmare, that Eric Grayson kept secreted in his private dungeon. He must've been using the thing for years, and under everyone's nose – disposing of problem employees by putting them on the menu for his very own pet monster.

And Dirk and Stacy were today's special.

TWENTY-THREE

Natalya Dragunova was still over an hour from Rock Key, and growing ever more impatient, when *Leonardo* finally announced it had finished its analysis. She'd been cruising along in silence for thirty minutes, holding steady at a depth of 200 feet, and maintaining a respectable forty knots. Twenty minutes earlier, in an attempt to distract herself, she'd decided to initiate an impromptu study of the severed saurian forearm she'd scooped up off the deck.

It sat next to her now, riding shotgun in Bender's vacated copilot's seat, a crooked mass of blood-flecked, greenish-gray tissue, secured within a clear vacuum bag. As she glanced over at it, Natalya pursed her lips and shrugged noncommittally. She'd had less talkative traveling companions. Certainly, more annoying ones.

Although the *Remora* was far from a floating laboratory, and Lieutenant Archer would have done a more capable job, she'd managed to get things started. She submitted a quick video of the surprisingly heavy specimen – complete with a volumetric scan, courtesy of her combat goggles – via secure acoustic link, directly to *Leonardo*, her vessel's analytical archive system.

The system was a derivative of the original *Archimedes* program, designed and developed by the late Dr. Amara Takagi, before she became a Braddock; a multi-million-dollar database that contained bio-schematics on every documented life form on the planet. Standard issue on all GDT vessels, the program could ID a given genus or species within minutes, purely based on fragmentary remains.

Judging by how long it was taking *Leonardo* to complete its assigned task, however, Natalya had no doubts it would come up empty. It had to, she realized; they were dealing with an undocumented life form. Her only hope was that the system's findings would give her some insight as to the incredibly aggressive reptiles' origin. Including whether they were Terran.

"Analysis complete," *Leonardo* said in its decidedly mannish voice.

"Diagnosis?"

"Specimen is of reptilian origin, although the presence of a five-millimeter-thick subcutaneous layer of brown adipose tissue is a strong indicator of possible endothermic activity."

At least partly warm-blooded? Interesting.

"Continue," Natalya commanded.

"Extrapolation based on sample, as well as video footage submitted that confirms proportions and bipedalism, indicates the original specimen stood approximately 195 centimeters in height and weighed 140 kilograms."

"Agreed, but where deed they come from? Ees origin Diablo?"

There was a brief delay as the system worked furiously. Then, "Unable to comply without additional data, including DNA analysis. If--"

"Stop," Natalya said irritably, holding up a hand. She thought for a moment, then decided to try a different tack. "Ees there any theeng een the fossil records that accounts for these creatures?"

"Working. In the past, paleontologists have expressed theories that, were non-avian dinosaurs to have survived past the Cretaceous-Paleogene extinction event, certain species of theropod dinosauria might have evolved into more advanced bipeds."

"Which species?"

"Primarily troodontids, based on their brain size, anatomy, keen senses, and advanced behaviors."

"Show me one."

A picture of what looked, vaguely, like one of the big raptors she'd encountered appeared on the monitor.

She shook her head. That didn't make sense. Those animals were still there.

They've just gotten bigger and smarter, and learned how to walk on water.

"Computer, what other changes would have taken place?"

"Increased intelligence, improved social skills, tool use, and--"

"Stop."

Strikes one, two, and three, there.

Natalya reached over and hefted the weighty forearm, holding it up and studying its cruel talons. "Computer, ees there any theeng that would explain thees?"

"Specify."

"The development of opposable thumbs."

"Working. Based on limited data, and, in the absence of DNA analysis, the only other possibility is parallel evolution."

She sighed. "Thank you, *Leonardo*."

"You are welcome."

Natalya sat there brooding, her left hand still gripping the *Remora*'s steering wheel. She held the severed forelimb in her right and angled it beneath the mini-sub's bright overheads, studying it. The structure of the hand was decidedly man-like, only disproportionately large. The skin was thin but leathery and coated with minute scales.

She looked over the stump portion and took a moment to admire her handiwork. She'd relished cutting the bastard's arm off as it tried to slash her face. A nice cut, too, she noticed, grinning. There was nothing like a quality piece of steel.

What the . . .?

Natalya spotted something unusual through the vacuum bag's clear material and pressed it tightly against the stump's gushy redness and protruding arm bones, to get a clearer look.

There was something embedded in the flesh, something . . . metallic?

Her gut reaction was that it was a bullet, but the shape and color were off.

Nyet. This looked to be something else.

"Computer," Natalya said, rising. "Activate auto-pilot and continue current course and heading. Also, activate obstacle avoidance system and implement sentry mode, weeth previous settings."

"Acknowledged."

Although she preferred to do the driving herself, she felt confident knowing that, with its current settings, the *Remora* was not only capable of dodging anything that got in its way, it could defend itself as well. At forty knots, the only predator big and fast enough to take a shot at them would be a bull pliosaur, and even then, she was sure their HYDRA cannons could discourage one with little problem.

Even *Typhon* would have a hard time surviving a point-blank burst from a pair of 20mm Gatling cannons spitting depleted uranium penetrator rounds at 3,000 RPM.

Moving around the submersible's empty passenger seats, Natalya headed to the medical supply cabinet and grabbed a large forceps and a pair of latex gloves. She hesitated, then reached for her goggles and a surgical mask as well.

After seeing the squirming sea of larvae that had ravaged Bender's corpse, she was taking no chances. She'd rather eat a bullet than go out like that.

Protective garb in place, Natalya flipped the vacuum bag's release lever and peeled open the end that exposed the amputated portion of the ablated limb. Using the stainless-steel forceps, she reached inside the bag and gripped the exposed piece of metal. It was small, less than half-an-inch wide, and only a millimeter thick. It was well-embedded, however, and she had to exert careful pressure while coaxing it backward. Finally, with a faint, gushy sound, it popped free.

Natalya held the tiny, blood-streaked device up to her protected eyes and gaped. She knew instantly what she was holding, she just couldn't believe it.

It's a fucking locator.

Suddenly, her eyes peeled wide and a slide-show of images flashed rapid-fire through her head. The sand-covered pods on the beach, the parachutes, the hordes of ravenous reptilians, the two raptors fleeing . . .

She pictured the hateful expression on the disfigured face of the creature whose arm she'd taken, and the murderous look in its eyes as it lashed out at her. She'd seen that same red-eyed fury before. It was back at Tartarus, during her confrontation in the gym with--

Dwyer.

Natalya's head recoiled hard on well-toned shoulders. "Parallel evolution, my ass!"

Her face contorted angrily, and she resealed the vacuum bag and tossed it back in the copilot's chair. Stripping off and discarding her gloves and mask, she removed her goggles and hopped back into her seat.

"Computer, I have the conn," she said, seizing the yoke.

Grabbing the accelerator lever, she pushed it smoothly forward, all the way into the red. She felt the sudden inertia increase pushing back at her and absorbed it, before leaning forward and gripping the steering wheel tight.

Their speed began to increase. 42 . . . 46 . . . 50 . . . At just over fifty knots, the *Remora* hit its maximum. Like a giant, blood-bellied manta ray, it sliced through the azure seas before it, its twin cannons armed and primed and ready to deal death to anything that dared approach.

Natalya breathed in deep through her nostrils, then shook her head angrily as it came out her mouth. She'd been wrong. The pods she found on Diablo weren't where the "Messiah lizards" had come from. The *Messiya yashcheritsa* were indigenous to the caldera; they'd been there since the Cretaceous.

The *reptilians* were the invaders. Someone had flown them there and dumped them. Someone who liked to play around with people's lives, not to mention technology and weapons, including, apparently, the biological kind. Someone looking to hide their dirty little secret – make that secrets. The same someone whose insignia she'd found on one of the capsules.

Natalya growled through her teeth and pushed harder on the accelerator, trying to go faster. When that failed, she double-checked her course, to make sure she was on the most direct route.

There was no doubt in her mind that CEO Eric Grayson was the progenitor of the reptilian horde.

He had created those monsters and left them there for someone to stumble on. *He* was responsible for the landing party deaths, and the loss of her crew, and *Antrodemus* as well.

Garm had been right all along about that *mudak*. He'd said . . . *shit!*

Natalya swore vilely. Wolfie had asked her to take care of his little brother, but he had no idea just what it was he was requesting. Dr. Derek Braddock didn't know it yet, but he was in serious trouble. He was surrounded by a nest of vipers, all coiled and waiting to strike. Worse, if her experiences over the last few hours were any kind of indicator, they may well have already done so.

She glanced over at the reptilian's severed limb and sneered.

"I don't know who you were," she said, "And, I don't fucking care. You are my evidence, and when we get there, you and I are going to show them the truth. Even eef I must shove you up Grayson's saggy, old ass." She smiled mirthlessly as she reached over and patted the cold piece of corpse through its protective plastic coating. "Oh, and thank you, for geeving me a hand."

With her eyes facing front and glacier cold, Natalya raced silently on.

Dirk Braddock felt the blood chill in his veins as, with a prodigious splash, Grayson's pet monster heaved itself up and out of the grotto's swirling waters. He was dimly aware of the old Bee Gees song "Stayin' Alive" resounding through the walls, as Tartarus's captive pliosaurs continued their bastardized exercise interval.

Despite his collective misery, the irony of the song's title was not lost on him, and he realized that living up to it was likely to become a major challenge.

He and Stacy were huddled together against the far wall of the dungeon, like fear-paralyzed fawns in a fox-infested field. She was literally shaking with fright, and had her lithe arms wrapped around him in a tight hug, one that bespoke of both protectiveness and a need for comfort.

Dirk could see the thing clearly, its monstrous form silhouetted by the eerie light that reflected off the grotto's surface in greenish-gold ripples. It was huge – he estimated a full seven feet in height – and must have weighed close to four hundred pounds. It had a hyper-muscular physique, almost like a bodybuilder's, but with longer arms and incredibly wide shoulders. He couldn't see its face yet, but it had a large, domed head, topped with what looked like a mane of matted hair or, perhaps, scaly strands hanging down. It was hard to say.

If asked to describe it succinctly, he'd have said it reminded him of a smoother-skinned version of the "Gillman" from the old classic 50's movies, only a lot more human-looking, and far more massive.

Dirk felt Stacy tense, as the dripping monster lowered itself into a crouch and considered the fish it had caught. The Jack Crevalle's incessant flapping drew its eye, and it snatched it up in one webbed hand, holding it tightly as it continued to wriggle. The Crevalle's persistence appeared to anger it after a while and, with a quick snap and a crackling crunch, it bit the fish's head clean off and spat it back into the water, watching unfeelingly as it was carried off by the current.

Dropping the decapitated Jack, the monster sat back on its haunches and glanced at the far larger cobia. It scratched itself, then picked up the Jack, bit and pulled, stripping off a thick strip of skin and fillet. In between chews, it started making batches of low, grumbling sounds, as if it was muttering to itself. Although Dirk could barely hear it over the music, he was certain it wasn't any language he'd ever heard.

Stacy turned toward him, her amber eyes the size of saucers, and her bronze skin paler than he'd ever seen. As she mouthed the words, 'What do we do?', he pressed his index finger to her lips, cautioning her. Although his vison had cleared, and the adrenaline rush brought on by extreme fear appeared to have, at least for the moment, applied the brakes to his debilitating muscle spasms, he was still burning up and could barely stand. There was no way they could fight this thing. The only reason it hadn't spotted them yet was its eyes were adapted to the filtered sunlight coming off the water, leaving them effectively hidden in the shadows.

But that was temporary, at best.

Their only chance was to lay still and hope it went back into the water. Once it did, they could try to figure out a way to escape or, perhaps, a means of summoning help.

Finally finished with the Jack, the monster stopped feeding and tossed the stripped carcass into the water. It landed with a slapping sound and drifted away, following its head.

Dirk had to admit, he was impressed. With the exception of its collection of human bones, the creature appeared to be smart enough to toss its garbage into the water, to be carried off. He began to wonder why it hadn't done the same with the bone pile, but then decided he didn't want to know.

Moving past its appetizer now, the monster rose, bent at the waist, and seized the big cobia by its lower jaw. With impressive strength, it hoisted the six-foot fish with one clawed hand and held it at arm's length, like it was admiring it. Then, with cat-like speed, it ripped open the cobia's belly. Reaching inside the spurting opening, it grabbed a huge handful of gushy entrails and wrenched them free with a horrid splurching sound.

The glistening mass of offal hit the water with a smack, punctuated by the sound of the thing burying its gore-coated muzzle in the dead fish's gaping abdominal cavity. With violent snaps, it began to gorge on huge mouthfuls of flesh, chewing loudly and swallowing them in loud gulps. Blood streamed down its anvil-like chin in red rivulets, pooling on the wet concrete all around it.

The sight and sounds proved too much for Stacy, and Dirk felt her start to shake all over. He could tell the scream was coming, and managed to slap a hand over her mouth, just in time.

Or, rather, *almost* in time.

Instantly, the monster's disfigured head snapped up and it stopped in mid-chew. Eyes squinting against the glare, it rose to its full height, the ravaged cobia still gripped in one taloned hand.

Its head pulled back on massive shoulders and it began making what sounded like a low-pitched purr. The sound spread rapidly, and began to reverberate back and forth, bouncing off the walls, floor, and ceiling, all around him and Stacy. Dirk felt himself begin to itch, and the tiny hairs on his arm stood on end. He swore silently to himself.

Does this thing have echolocation?

The creature's repulsive grimace, as its lips snarled slowly back, answered his question. It dropped the remains of its meal and let loose a thunderous roar. An eyeblink later, it charged unerringly in their direction.

And it meant business.

Dirk's heart leapfrogged into his throat, then plummeted back down into his bowels, as Stacy shook off her fear and moved to intercept it. Like a lioness protecting its cub, she placed herself defiantly in its path, feet spread apart and ready to fight.

"Oh, no, you *don't*, you disgusting piece of shit!" she snarled back at it. Scooping up chunks of vertebrae, ribs – even a skull

– she started pelting the behemoth, fastball-style, as it stormed toward them.

Dirk couldn't believe it. Obviously, not accustomed to such reactions, the monster slowed its roll; it looked even more astonished than he was, if that was possible. It stopped twenty feet away, blinking confusedly as Stacy's hurled missiles continued to ricochet off its tough hide.

Its tentativeness faded a moment later.

A cranium hit it hard, right in the groin, and the thing let out another ear-splitting bellow. In an instant, it was in motion again. It closed the distance between it and Stacy in less than a second and smacked a partial pelvis out of her hand in a shower of bony fragments. Seizing her in its mammoth paws, it pinned her arms to her sides and picked her up like she was made of paper.

Undeterred by her feet hanging a foot from the ground, Stacy started kicking, striking the monster repeatedly in the knees and shins. Her blows failed to faze it, however, and she screamed in horror and averted her eyes, as it began to pull her, face-first, toward its waiting maw.

"Hey, gruesome!"

As the monster spun toward the sound of his voice, Dirk hit it in the nose with everything he had. The notion of Stacy being mutilated in front of him was more than he could bear, and with so much adrenaline pumping through his veins, he discovered he could not only stand, he could fight.

The dog tags helped, of course, wrapped around his hand like brass knuckles. The monster's head snapped back from the force of his punch and it stared at him. It licked its upper lip, tasting its own blood, then shook its head chidingly from side to side.

A moment later, it hurled Stacy at him like a throw pillow. Her 150 pounds felt like a linebacker as she slammed into him, and they both ended up sprawled flat on their backs.

As Dirk struggled to right himself, a wave of pain and disorientation surged up within him. He could tell his epinephrine rush was beginning to fade, and the fever was starting to re-assert itself. He saw the monster coming and cast desperately about for a weapon.

There was none.

Before he could react, it seized him by the throat with one huge hand and lifted him right off the floor. His teeth rattled as his upper back slammed against the wall's rough-hewn stone, and he uttered a pain-filled gasp.

The thing had him by the neck and was holding him, pinned like a mounted butterfly. It started eyeing his exposed trapezius muscle, streaked with the blood that had run down from his scalp wound, and he paled as he saw the tip of its pinkish tongue lick its scaled lips.

Oh, God. It-it's going to eat me!

"Get away from him, you slavering son of a bitch!" Stacy shrieked.

Dirk heard a low thud, then another, and both saw and felt the monster's body quiver. With him still pinned to the wall, it turned confusedly and glanced over one heavily-muscled shoulder, back at Stacy.

He saw its red-rimmed eyes blink in disbelief as she swung for the fences yet again, using the femur she'd found like a make-shift baseball bat. The blow caught it right where a man's kid-ney would be and, judging by its expression, really pissed it off.

It uttered a menacing hiss and lashed out with unbelievable speed. A clawed hand the size of a Virginia ham caught Stacy square across the chest and sent her flying. She landed atop the bone pile, spitting blood and struggling to breathe.

Dirk realized what was next and fought like a madman to free himself, but it was hopeless. Even at his full strength, he couldn't have escaped the behemoth's iron grip. It felt like a rubber-coated statue; even Garm would have been outmatched.

Suddenly, a bizarre feeling of detachment began to top off all the pain and suffering he'd been going through, and Dirk re-alized his brain was pumping hormones throughout his body, enticing him to relax and accept his fate. His struggles lessened, and he felt what little strength he had left begin to fade.

The creature seemed to notice his pending submission. It's tooth-lined jaws broke into a smile and it drew steadily closer, its eyes widening in anticipation as it tried to decide where it would take its first bite.

This is the end, he thought. *This—*

"Dirk, no!" Stacy screamed. She was fighting to stand, her neoprene bodysuit ripped and torn as she scraped and scrabbled over a moist minefield of blackened bones. "Please! Not Dirk! Take me, not Dirk!"

The creature's vaguely man-like ears twitched at the sound of her voice, and it stopped. Its head whipped around toward Stacy, studying her tear-streaked face, and then back to Dirk. Its demeanor seemed to change, and it reached forward, replacing its grip around his neck with one under his armpit, but keeping him pinned in place.

It leaned closer, its nasal flaps flaring as it sniffed deeply. It recoiled and shook its head, like a dog that smells something disagreeable. Apparently not satisfied, it reached up with its free hand, gripping him roughly by the chin. It proceeded to push his head left and right, its now-slitted eyes studying his brow, cheekbones, and jawline. Half-paralyzed with fear, he stayed stock-still, knowing he was powerless to stop it.

Suddenly, the creature stiffened, and its head recoiled on its thick neck. Its gaze fell, focusing on the filth-encrusted floor, and it started making deep coughing sounds, like it was trying to clear its throat. Then, it raised its free hand and extended a knotted index finger the size of a banana.

Terrified beyond the point of reason now, Dirk fought down the instinctive urge to flail like the Jack Crevalle had. He hung frozen, watching with dread-filled eyes, as the filthy digit came closer and closer to his face.

It was less than six inches away and hovering there, when these bizarre stuttering noises started coming from the thing's misshapen mouth.

"Duh . . . duh . . . duh . . ."

The finger started forward again and then stopped, just as its padded phalange touched the tip of his nose.

"Doink!"

As the creature's deep voice filled his ears, Dirk felt himself go limp. He couldn't move, couldn't breathe; all he could hear was that one word and the booming of his heart, beating with machine-gun rapidity beneath his sternum. In a daze, he craned his neck forward, his disbelieving eyes seeking and finding the creature's, concealed beneath its beetling brow. There, amid a swirling sea of red, he saw two familiar islands of cobalt blue staring back at him.

N-no! It-it can't be . . . it can't!

But it was.

The monster was his father.

The Adventure Continues In
KRONOS RISING: KRAKEN (Volume 3)
Coming Soon!

Also, by Max Hawthorne
KRONOS RISING
KRONOS RISING: KRAKEN (Volume 1)
KRONOS RISING: DIABLO
KRONOS RISING: PLAGUE
MEMOIRS OF A GYM RAT

ABOUT THE AUTHOR

Heralded as the *"Prince of Paleo-fiction"* by *Fangoria Magazine*, Max Hawthorne was born in Brooklyn and grew up in Philadelphia, where he graduated with a BA from Central High School and a BFA from the University of the Arts. He is the author of MEMOIRS OF A GYM RAT, an outrageous exposé of the health club industry, as well as the award-winning KRONOS RISING marine terror novel series. In addition to hosting the acclaimed ICRA Blog Talk Radio show "Max Hawthorne's Marine Mysteries", Max is a bestselling indie novelist, a voting member of the Author's Guild, an IGFA world-record-holding angler, and an avid sportsman and conservationist. His hobbies include archery, fishing, boating, boxing, and collecting fossils and antiquities. He lives with his wife, daughter, and an impossibly large rabbit in the Greater Northeast.

GLOSSARY OF UNIQUE/ SCIENTIFIC/NAUTICAL/ MARINE TERMS

Abyssal Plains: The vast underwater plains at the bottom of the ocean, with water depths averaging between 10,000-20,000 feet. Largely unexplored, they represent more than 50% of the Earth's surface.

Acoustics: The science and study of mechanical *waves* in liquids, solids, and gases. This includes vibrations, as well as sound, ultrasound, and infrasound waves.

ADCAP: Military Acronym for *Advanced Capability*.

Aft: Naval terminology indicating the stern or rear of a ship. *"Aft section"* indicates the rear portion of a ship.

Amidships: The center/middle portion of a vessel.

ANCILE: Advanced Obstacle Avoidance sonar system with acoustic intercept. ANCILE's active sonar pings target incoming signals and can be fed directly into a vessel's fire control (weapons) systems.

Anti-Biologic: Designed to kill biologics, i.e. living organisms.

Archelon: The largest known sea turtle, with a flipper span of over sixteen feet. Archelon went extinct at the end of the Cretaceous.

Argentinosaurus: An enormous titanosaur sauropod dinosaur, and one of the largest living land animals of all time. Argentinosaurus is estimated at well over 100 feet in length, with a body mass exceeding 90 tons.

ATV: All-Terrain Vehicle.

Autonomous: Independent and self-governing, i.e. freethinking surveillance drones.

Autotomic Response: Self amputation, a defensive response in certain animals wherein a portion of the body (tail, tentacle) is shed to distract a predator. The shed portion continues to writhe on its own to keep the attacker interested while the host animal escapes.

Autotomous: Separate parts of an organism that are free thinking and independent of the originating organism's control or influence, i.e. the tentacles of an octopus performing complex tasks while the host animal's attention is focused elsewhere.

AWES Suits: Acronym for *Armored Weaponized Exoskeleton System*. Manufactured by GDT through its subsidiary, JAW Robotics, the AWES Talos Mark VII and VIII are heavily armored, nuclear-powered combat chassis. Both suits are designed to be worn by quadruple amputees. The six-ton Mark VII is designed for undersea exploration/combat, whereas the larger, more heavily armed Mark VIII is a land-based anti-materiel/anti-personnel weapons platform.

Ballast: In submarine terms, a compartment (ballast tank) that holds water of varied quantities to balance the vessel underway and help control its depth. Pumping water out of the ballast tank ("blow ballast") increases a submarine's buoyancy and can be used for an emergency rise.

Barotrauma: Physical trauma to body tissues due to a sudden and dramatic change in ambient pressure, AKA *"The Bends."*

Barrett XM500: A .50 caliber sniper rifle, circa 2006, developed by the *Barrett Firearms Company*. The XM500 fires the powerful .50 caliber BMG round and is equipped with a detachable 10-round magazine.

Bathymetric Gigantism: A tendency for certain deep-dwelling marine animals, particularly invertebrates, to grow to colossal size in a dark, cold, high-pressure environment. Comparable to *Abyssal gigantism*.

Beam: A ship's width at its widest point.

Bearcat: Also known as the GDT (Grayson Defense Technologies) Bearcat: an ultra-quiet, heavily armed and armored anti-materiel helicopter, known for its stealthy approach.

Bearing: Navigation term as relates to course changes.

Berth: A designated location where a boat or ship is *moored* (attached), usually for purposes of loading and unloading passengers or cargo.

Beta-Endorphin: A neuropeptide found in the neurons of the central nervous system that functions as a natural analgesic. Endorphins dull or numb the pain from trauma-based injuries.

Bezumnyy: Russian word meaning "mad" or "insane".

Bioluminescence: The manufacturing and emission of light by an organism.

Blake Plateau: A submarine plateau off the southeastern coast of the United States. The plateau borders North and South Carolina, Georgia and Florida, and stretches between the Continental Shelf and the Deep Ocean basin. It measures approximately 90 by 106 miles and ranges in depth from approximately 500 to 1,000 yards.

BMG 50: The powerful .50 caliber Browning machine gun round.

Bow: The foremost point of the hull of a boat or ship.

Bozhe Moi/ Bozhe moy: Russian phrase meaning *"Oh my God."*

Bridge: The room or point on a boat or ship from which it is commanded.

Broadband Clicks: High frequency sonar clicks used in *echolocation.*

Brumation: The reptilian equivalent of hibernation. During the winter, brumating marine reptiles sleep on the seabed for extended periods, breathing entirely through their skins and waking only to drink water.

Bulkhead: A wall within the hull of a boat or ship.

Cachalot: Archaic term for the Sperm whale, from the French word *cachalot*, meaning "tooth."

Caldera: A bowl-like geological formation, usually formed by the partial collapse of a volcano, following an eruption.

Carcharodon megalodon: Binomial nomenclature for a species of giant shark that lived during the Cenozoic Era and fed on sea turtles and marine mammals, including cetaceans. Megalodon had teeth over seven inches in slant height and exceeded 50 feet in length.

Caudal Fin: The tail fin of a fish.

Celazole: (see polybenzimidazole/PBI)

Cenomanian-Turonian Extinction Event: An extinction event during the early Cretaceous Period (approx. 91.5mya) that resulted in the extinction of the pliosaurs and ichthyosaurs.

Center Console: A single-decked, open hull boat with all the controls (console) located in the center of the vessel.

Cephalopod: Marine animals such as the octopus, squid, and cuttlefish, wherein limbs or tentacles extend from a prominent head. Cephalopods are also *mollusks*.

Cetacean: Marine mammals, including whales, dolphins and porpoises.

Cetaceanist: A marine biologist who specializes in cetaceans – whales, dolphins, and porpoises.

Charybdis: A mythological sea monster from Greek mythology. Charybdis lived under a rock in a narrow strait and, when ships approached, would suck in huge quantities of water, creating a giant whirlpool that dragged hapless sailors to their deaths.

Chelonian: Turtles and tortoises.

Chemoreceptors: A sensory receptor that detects chemical stimuli in an environment, i.e. taste.

Chromatophores: Cells or groups of cells containing various types of pigmentation or with light reflective qualities. Typically found in animals.

Chronospecies: A species that evolves in sequences over time from an extinct ancestral form.

Circle Hook: A fishing hook with a point that curves sharply inward. Circle hooks are designed to catch a fish in the corner of the jaw and are rarely swallowed.

Claxon: A low-frequency horn used by ships to signal one another.

Cleat: A nautical term for a narrow, anvil-shaped device used to secure a rope or line. Cleats are often used to tie boats to docks.

Clew: On a sailboat, the lower aft corner of a sail.

Cloaca: A posterior orifice found in reptiles, birds, amphibians and a few mammals that serves as a combined opening for both the reproductive, digestive, and urinary tracts.

Coastal Defense Force (CDF): A sub-branch of the military (formally part of the US Coast Guard, now overseen by GDT). The CDF has bases off the coast of Maine, Florida, Washington, and Hawaii, and utilizes Anti-Biologic submarines, such as the ORION Class, to seek out and destroy rogue pliosaurs that threaten America's waterways.

Conning Tower: An elevated platform on a ship or submarine, from which an officer can command (*"con"*) the vessel.

Continental Shelf: The extended (and submerged) border of any given continent and its associated *coastal plain*.

Counter-shading: Evolution-induced color patterns in marine organisms designed to make the organism difficult to spot by both predator and prey. Typical counter-shading patterns are dark above and light below.

Convergent Evolution: The evolution of analogous structures with similar design in different species, i.e. the body design share by both dolphins and ichthyosaurs.

Cretaceous: A period of geologic time from 145 to 65 million years ago. The end of the Cretaceous Period was marked by the sudden extinction of all non-avian dinosaurs.

Crevalle Jack: A species of large saltwater fish, common throughout the Atlantic Ocean.

Cronavrol: A powerful and fast-acting sedative designed to be used against pliosaurs. When injected directly into the spine, Cronavrol instantly forces the recipient into deep *brumation*.

Crustacean: Crustaceans are members of a large group of *arthropods* and include such creatures as lobsters, crabs, and shrimp.

Cryogenics: The study of freezing materials at extremely low temperatures (-238 F or lower)

Cybernetics: Using advanced technology to control a given system.

Dakuwaqa: A shark god from Fijian mythology.

Deinosuchus: An extinct, Cretaceous Era crocodile that once hunted dinosaurs. Deinosuchus reached at least 40 feet in length and weighed 10+ tons.

Detritus: Referred to as *marine snow*, detritus is non-living particles of organic material suspended in water.

Diablo Caldera: A dormant volcano whose upper portion was blown off during a violent eruption during the early *Cretaceous Period*. When the KT asteroid struck, Diablo was flooded by a mega-tsunami and became an eight-mile-wide saltwater lake that imprisoned an assortment of prehistoric marine life. Diablo has a network of superheated lava tubes running underneath it, some of which connect its lake to the sea. In recent years, a portion of the caldera collapsed, allowing some of its inhabitants to escape.

Dinghy: A small boat, often towed behind a larger vessel for use as a ship-to-ship or ship-to-shore boat.

Djöfullinn: Icelandic for demon or devil.

Dopamine: A neurotransmitter in the brain whose neural pathways govern both reward-based behavior and motor control.

Dorsal: The upper side of an animal that swims in a horizontal position. The dorsal *region* refers to that general area on the animal. Dorsal *fin* refers to one or more fins that protrude from that region, i.e. a shark's distinctive, curved fin.

Draft (or Draught): The measurement from a vessel's waterline to the bottom of its hull. Draft determines the minimum water depth a ship or boat requires in order to navigate safely.

Dromaeosaurs: An extinct group of small to medium-sized carnivorous dinosaurs, popularly known as raptors.

Echolocation: In marine animals, the emission of sonar sound waves and the absorption of their echoes to "see" underwater.

Economic Exclusive Zone: An *EEZ* is a sea zone over which a country has specific rights relating to the exploration and exploitation of its natural resources. It stretches from the end of said country's territorial waters (the *12-mile limit*) an additional 200 nautical miles.

Electronic Iridophore: An artificial type of chromatophore with reflective/iridescent properties.

Electroreceptor: One of a group of organs on mainly marine organisms that allow them to perceive and detect electrical stimuli.

Enchodus petrosus: Binomial nomenclature for a Cretaceous-era, predatory salmonid that escaped Diablo Caldera. *Enchodus* are known as the "Sabretooth salmon" or "Sabretooth herring" and have large eyes and long fangs. Maximum length: six feet.

Ensign: Naval rank, equivalent to a second lieutenant in the U.S. Army.

Epidemiology: The study of infectious diseases in defined populations.

ESA: The Endangered Species Act.

Eschrichtius robustus: Binomial nomenclature for the Gray whale. Gray whales can reach 50 feet in length and weigh more than 40 tons.

Fafnir: A powerful dragon from Norse mythology, eventually slain by Sigurd.

Fathometer: Passive sonar system that substitutes ambient sounds generated by surface waves and biologics to create a 3-D map of the seabed and surrounding water. Instead of using an active sonar projector, the fathometer utilizes beam-forming and a vertical array of hydrophones to cross-correlate noise from the surface with its echoes from the seabed, thereby reducing interference from horizontally propagating noise.

Fenris: A monstrous wolf from Norse mythology that bit of the hand of Tyr, god of war. During the battle of Ragnarok, Fenris kills Odin, the ruler of the gods.

Flagorneur: French for a groveling toady or sycophant.

Flats Boat: A small draft boat designed to safely run and operate in extremely shallow bodies of water, such as the Florida Keys.

Flying Gaff: A specialized gaff designed to land very large fish. The hook portion of the gaff detaches when embedded in a fish and remains secured to the boat by a strong cable or rope.

Fore: The front or *bow* of a ship or boat.

Foredeck: The bow portion of a ship's deck.

Forecastle: The foremost portion of a ship's upper deck. In medieval ships it served as a defensive stronghold where archers could rain fire down upon opposing vessels.

Galley: The kitchen on a ship or boat.

Gangplank: A moveable construct, often formed of strong planks, which bridges the distance between a ship and its mooring station. It enables the loading and offloading of goods and personnel.

GDT: Acronym for Grayson Defense Technologies, one of the largest manufacturers of military weapons, pharmaceuticals, and robotics on the planet. GDT both bankrolls and directs the newly formed Coastal Defense Force (CDF).

Gen-1: A member of a first or initial generation.

Gimbal: The receiving point (socket) of a big-game fishing fighting belt or chair. The butt of the fishing rod inserts into this point and can swivel up and down to exert pressure on fish.

Gin Pole: A strong, vertical pole or tower, equipped with an extending arm and pulley system. Gin poles are used on fishing vessels to hoist very large fish onboard.

Gladius: Also called cuttlebone. A hard internal shell found in cuttlefish and squid that gives the body rigidity.

Glycoproteins: Integral cellular membrane proteins that play a role in cell-to-cell interactions.

Gunnels/Gunwales: The uppermost/top edges of a ship or boat's hull.

Gryphon: A powerful mythical creature in Greek mythology, said to have the head and wings (and sometimes forelimbs) of an eagle and the body of a lion. Alternative spelling: *Griffin*.

Harbormaster: The official that enforces the regulations of a port or harbor.

Hazmat: Short for hazardous materials.

Helm: A ship's wheel or other steering mechanism (tiller, steering wheel, etc.).

Helmsman: The individual that steers a ship or boat.

Hvalur: Icelandic for *whale*.

Hydrophone: An underwater microphone.

Hydrostatic Pressure: The pressure exerted by water, due to the effects of gravity.

Hyperion: one of the monstrous Titans from Greek mythology.

Idling: When a boat sits *idle* with its engine running (in neutral). Idle boats tend to drift because of wind and tide.

Intermittent Transients: Hard to track and sporadic radar or sonar readings, usually indicative of a shielded (military) craft.

Isopod: A group of oval-shaped, segmented crustaceans that inhabit land, fresh and saltwater environments. Scavenging abyssal isopods can exceed 20 inches in length.

Kaiju: Japanese for *strange beast*.

Kauhuhu: The ancient Hawaiian's shark god of Molokai.

Kakogo cherta: Russian phrase meaning, "What the hell?"

Khorosho: Russian word meaning "good".

Knot: A nautical unit of speed equivalent to one *nautical* mile per hour, or about 1.151 mph.

Koshka: Russian word for a female *cat*.

Kraken: A mythological marine monster said to feed on whales and drag ships to their destruction. The Kraken is believed to be based on early sailors' encounters with the *giant squid*.

Kronosaurus imperator: Binomial nomenclature ("Ruler of God of Time Reptiles") for a giant species of pliosaur imprisoned in Diablo Caldera during the KT/Yucatan impact. Males can exceed 60 feet in length, females 80. The species is based on fragmentary fossil remains, including tooth marks on the Mexican pliosaur known as the "Monster of Aramberri," which indicate a creature with a potential tooth crown length of twelve inches.

Kronosaurus queenslandicus: Binomial nomenclature for a mid-sized species of pliosaur from the Cretaceous Period. K. Queenslandicus had rounded fangs, as opposed to the ridged teeth of Pliosaurus, and fed upon plesiosaurs, sea turtles, fish and squid. Size estimate is 33 feet with a weight of 12 tons.

Landing: A designated docking location for vessels at a marina.

Lanyard: A length or cord used to carry something and worn around the neck or wrist. Safety lanyards on boats and Jet Skis function as kill switches and shut down the vessel's engine in the event the pilot falls overboard.

Lazarus Taxon: A species that vanishes from the fossil record, only to reappear later.

Lexan: A clear thermoplastic/polycarbonate, known for its strength and durability.

Livyatan melvillei: An extinct raptorial sperm whale that lived during the Miocene Epoch. One of the largest marine predators of all time.

LRIT: Long Range Intelligence and Tracking. An international system of tracking ships using shipborne satellite communications equipment.

Macropliosaur: One of the giant species of pliosaur.

Macropredator: A large predator.

Malacologist: One who studies mollusks.

Mandible: One of a pair (mandibles) of bones in the mouth that comprise the lower jaw.

Mandibular Symphysis: Where the two lower jaw bones (mandibles) fuse together.

Manifest: A document listing the passengers, crew, and cargo of a vessel for official purposes.

Marguerite Formation: A defensive formation utilized by sperm whales and other cetaceans to defend their young. The adults encircle the vulnerable calves, typically with either their flukes or jaws pointed outward, to ward off attackers.

MarshCat: A six-wheeled, amphibious ATV developed by GDT and used in the CDF's top-secret Tartarus research facility. MarshCats have sturdy roll bars, front row bucket seats, a rear bench seat that accommodates three, and are powered by a 90 HP diesel engine.

Maxilla: One of a pair (maxillae) of bones in the mouth that comprise the upper jaw and palate.

Messiya yashcheritsa: Russian term, first credited to Captain Natalya Dragunova, for the large, water-running raptors found on Diablo Caldera. Translation: "Messiah lizard"

MHD Propulsors: Magnetohydrodynamic Drive Propulsors are marine-based thrust generators typically used in submarines that utilize electrified water as a propellant to drive a vessel in the opposite direction. MHD Drives are powerful and silent and have few moving parts.

Midgard Serpent: Also known as *Jörmungandr* and the *World Serpent*, a gigantic sea serpent from Norse mythology, said to be so huge it could encircle the earth and could bite its own tail. It was Thor's nemesis and during the final battle of Ragnarok was killed by the Thunder God. Thor then perished in the resultant flood of venom that spewed from the dying beast's mouth.

Minke Whale: A lesser Rorqual and the second smallest baleen whale, averaging 23-26 feet in length and weighing 4-5 tons.

Mollusk: A large phylum of invertebrate animals, including gastropods (snails and slugs) and cephalopods (octopus and squid).

Mizzen: A mast on a sailing ship; the Mizzen-mast is the mast immediately aft (behind) the main mast. It is typically shorter.

Mooring: A permanent structure where a boat or ship may be *moored* (attached) such as a dock or jetty.

Mooring Line: Line of rope used to tie off or affix a boat or ship.

Mooring Station: An assigned location where a boat or ship is to be attached or tied off.

Mosasaur: A group of extinct marine lizards that died out at the end of the Cretaceous. The largest mosasaurs reached 60 feet in length and weighed 30 tons.

Mudak: Russian word meaning "asshole".

Nares: Nostrils.

Nematodes: Roundworms.

Neveroyatno: Russian word for *unbelievable.*

NOAA: The National Oceanic and Atmospheric Administration.

Norepinephrine: A chemical in the brain that functions as a hormone and neurotransmitter.

Notothenioid Fish: A group of Antarctic icefishes, known for antifreeze proteins in their blood. They have no red blood cells; hence their blood appears as a clear, viscous liquid.

O moy Bog: Russian phrase/exclamation, meaning, "Oh my God!"

Oceanus: A fictional Florida marine park, named after *Oceanus,* the Greek god of the sea.

***Octopus giganteus*:** A species of gigantic cephalopod, believed to inhabit the ocean's extreme depths. The remains of one reported specimen were calculated to have had a tentacular span of 200 feet.

OMNI ADCAP Sonar: A hull/bow mounted (spherical) ADCAP (Advanced Capabilities) active sonar system using medium frequency broadband clicks to provide all-around coverage. Almost impossible to detect and includes active search and attack capabilities.

Ophion's Deep: A Cretaceous-era submarine canyon named after the Greek God *Ophion*. It starts in the *Straits of Florida* and carves its way 125 miles along Florida's *Continental Rise*.

Outboard: A non-integral and removable propulsion system for boats. Outboard motors attach directly to the transom. Multiple motors can be used for larger boats, with horsepower typically ranging from single digits all the way to three hundred or more.

Papillae (singular Papilla): A nipple or cuticle-like structure.

Pectoral Fin(s): Paired fins in fish that provide dynamic lifting force, enabling some fish to maintain depth.

Peduncle: In fish and cetaceans, the narrow portion of the body where the tail (caudal fin or flukes) attaches to the body.

Pelagic: The portion of the ocean that is neither near the bottom nor close to shore.

Phalanx Anti-Missile Battery: A shipboard anti-aircraft/anti-missile Gatling gun system.

Pheromones: An excreted or secreted chemical that triggers a response in members of the same species.

Phototropic Zone: Also known as the *Photic Zone*, the upper portion of a body of water where sunlight is the primary stimulus for growth and nourishment – typically from the surface down to around 600 feet. 90% of all marine life lives in the Phototropic Zone.

Physeter macrocephalus: Binomial nomenclature (Latin) for the sperm whale.

Pinnipeds: Seals, sea lions, and walruses.

Pixilated: An image breaking up into visible pixels, typically a distortion when enlarged.

Plankton: Tiny organisms that live in the water column. Plankton are incapable of swimming against either tide or current. They are an important food source for many marine organisms.

Plastron: The almost flat underbelly/ventral portion of a turtle's shell.

Pliosaur: A group of plesiosaurs characterized by short necks and large skulls, armed with sharp teeth. Pliosaurs were fast and maneuverable swimmers and the apex predators of their day.

Pod: A group of whales. Unlike a school of fish, pod members are often related individuals.

Polybenzimidazole (PBI): Also known as *"Celazole,"* it is a space-age polymer/polycarbonate thermoplastic, reported to have the highest compressive strength of any unfilled plastic material.

Polycarbonate: A group of thermoplastic polymers known for their toughness and durability. Some polycarbonates are engineered to be optically transparent.

Port: Direction-wise, turning a boat or ship to the left. *Portside* = the left side of a boat or ship.

Portcullis: A sturdy steel or iron gate with a row of sharpened spikes at the bottom that is lowered to protect or reinforce a castle's gates or drawbridge.

Porthole: A round window on a boat or ship.

POSEIDON M45: Advanced passive fathometer sonar system (see *Fathometer*) using wide aperture arrays and hydrophone complexes set on submarine hulls. Arrays are set both port and starboard. The Poseidon relays readings into a detailed 3D image on the bridge. The system has no sonar projector or active emissions and is impossible to detect. Its only weakness is its limitations in shallow water (waves bounce too repeatedly, reducing range) and under silty conditions (i.e. excessive detritus) which can "blind" it.

Poulpe Colossal: French for Colossal Octopus.

Proboscideans: Modern day elephants and their extinct relatives.

Prop: A boat or ship's propeller.

Proteus: A shape-shifting sea beast from Greek mythology. Proteus could foretell the future, but the creature answered only to someone capable of overpowering it.

Prow: The foremost portion of a ship's bow. The prow cuts through the water and is the portion of the bow above the waterline.

Ragnarok: Translated as the "Twilight of the Gods," Ragnarok represents an apocalyptic battle between the Norse gods and the forces of evil, including the Frost giants and an assortment of inhuman monsters. All major figures perish in the battle, with mankind rising from the ashes.

REAPER: Acronym for: Rail Energized Armor Piercing Electromagnetic Repulsion gun: a close-range submarine-based weapon that fires kinetic energy projectiles using electricity instead of chemical propellants. Powerful electrical currents generated by the sub's reactor create magnetic fields that accelerate a sliding metal conductor between rails lining the barrel. When fired, the conductor launches a projectile at over 5,000 mph. To power the weapon, electricity is allowed to build over several seconds in the pulsed power system. It is then sent through the rail gun as a powerful surge of energy, creating an electromagnetic force accelerating a 2,000 lb. tungsten projectile to nearly Mach 8. The kinetic energy generated exceeds 600 megajoules: equivalent to a 100-ton locomotive striking a target at 250 mph. To protect both the weapon and its host vessel during sustained firing, a thermal management system is required for both the launcher and the pulsed power system.

Remora Mini-Sub: A sleek, 4-person submersible designed and manufactured by Grayson Defense Technologies. The Remora is a fast and highly maneuverable vessel powered by pump-jet propulsors. Based on original designs by JAW Robotics, it attaches directly to the outside of an ORION-class submarine via its airlock and remains flush to the hull until detached.

Roman Gladius: The standard-issue sword of Roman foot soldiers. Length: 24-33 inches.

Romulus and Remus: Twin brothers and the mythological founders of Rome, they were purportedly suckled by a she-wolf.

Rorqual: The largest group of baleen whales, including the blue and fin whales.

Rostrum: The crocodile-like muzzle of a pliosaur.

Runabout: A small boat, often used in the service of a larger vessel.

Rusticle: Icicle-like formations of rust that form on the edges of shipwrecks as saltwater acts upon the wrought iron in their hulls.

Saepia inferni: Literal translation: "Cuttlefish from Hell." Binomial nomenclature for a Cretaceous species of heavy-bodied squid that inhabited Diablo Caldera. Inferni are very aggressive. They can grow to thirty feet in length and weigh several tons.

Salmonid: One of a family of ray-finned fish, collectively known as *Salmonidae*. The family includes salmon, trout, char, whitefish and graylings.

Saurian War: Formally labeled a "suppression exercise" – an ongoing attempt by the nations of the world's militaries to exterminate aggressive pliosaurs (*Kronosaurus imperators*).

Sauropterygians: An extinct group of marine reptiles including plesiosaurs and pliosaurs.

Schooner: A sailing vessel characterized by fore and aft sails on two or more masts.

Sclerotic Ring: A ring of small bones encircling the eye that support it. Tiny muscles connect to the sclerotic ring and aid in focusing by helping the eye to compress inward. Found in many prehistoric marine reptiles, including mosasaurs and ichthyosaurs.

Sea Crusade: A fictional animal rights/conservation group, specializing in protecting the oceans and marine life.

Shastasaurus sikanniensis: An extinct species of Triassic Ichthyosaur similar to *Shonisaurus* and one of the largest marine reptiles of all time. Adults were estimated to reach 70 feet in length.

Shoal: A group of fish that stay together for social reasons.

Singulare Monstrum: Individual (unique) monster.

Slip: A reserved docking space for a boat, like a rented parking spot.

Sloop: A sailboat with a fore and aft rig and a single mast.

SODOME: Sonar Dome (military designate).

SOP: Acronym for Standard Operating Procedure.

Sound: Also known as a seaway, a sound is a large inlet between two bodies of land.

Spasiba: Russian for *thank you*.

Starboard: Direction-wise, turning a boat or ship to the right. Also, a term for the right side of a boat or ship.

Stern: The rear portion of a boat or ship.

Sub-Aqueous: Beneath the surface of the water.

Supercavitating: A moving submarine object that generates a bubble of gas in its wake to eliminate water friction/resistance and increase speed. Supercavitating ammunition and torpedoes travel many times faster than their non-cavitating counterparts.

Surtur: A fire giant from Norse mythology. During the battle of Ragnarok his flaming sword sets the Earth ablaze.

SVALINN: A submarine-based, active sonar suppression system that targets incoming sonar with out-of-phase emissions. SVALINN can effectively cancel enemy pinging if the sonar is not too powerful or sophisticated. A ship cloaked with SVALINN becomes all but invisible as long as it remains motionless. Moving toward or away from active pinging would still register in an enemy's sonar's signal processors, giving away the sub's position.

Swells: Ocean surface waves moving in long-wave formation.

Temporal Openings/Temporal Fenestrae: Bilaterally symmetrical holes in the temporal bone of the skull through which the mandibular (jaw) muscles travel and attach to the mandible (jaw bone). The connection point at the mandible is called the *Mandibular Fenestrae*. Some animals (including most reptiles) have two pairs of *Temporal Fenestrae*, the upper (*Supratemporal Fenestrae*) and lower (*Infratemporal Fenestrae*)

Thalassophonean: Literally translated as "Sea Slayer," a group of macropredatory pliosaurs including *Liopleurodon, Pliosaurus* and *Kronosaurus*.

Thanatos: In Greek mythology, the demonic personification of *death*.

Thermocline: A distinctive layer in a body of water where temperature changes more rapidly than in the layers above and below it. Thermoclines can be either permanent or transitory, depending on prevailing climate conditions. They separate surface water from the calmer, often colder, deep water below.

Thermoplastic: A polymer that becomes moldable when heated to a certain temperature and solidifies upon being cooled.

Tiamat: A sea goddess from Babylonian, Assyrian, and Sumerian mythology, known as "The Glistening One." Although feminine and a creator goddess, Tiamat appears as a monstrous dragon or sea serpent and is considered the embodiment of primordial chaos.

Titanoboa: An enormous constrictor snake that lived during the Paleocene, 60-58mya. The snake was estimated to reach around 50 feet in length.

Transom: The flat, back panel that comprises the stern of a boat or ship. Outboard motors are affixed directly to the transom.

Triassic: A geological time period ranging from approximately 250 to 200 million years ago.

Typhon: In Greek mythology, the titanic son of *Tartarus* and Earth and the most fearsome of all monsters. Typhon was a deadly enemy of the gods of Olympus and fathered many horrifying creatures, including *Cerberus*, the *Chimera*, and the multi-headed *Hydra*.

Vermitus gigas: Binomial nomenclature for the giant parasitic worms found in the digestive tracts of extant pliosauridae. In appearance, Vermitus look like a mixture betw\een a sandworm and a lamprey. The worms typically grow to 20 feet, but if able to penetrate the host's abdominal wall can continue to grow, reaching colossal size and eventually killing the host animal.

Watch Commander: Nautical term for a shift supervisor on a marine vessel.

Water Column: A theoretical column of water that ranges from the ocean's surface, all the way to the seafloor. The water column consists of thermal or chemically stratified layers, the mixing of which is brought on by wind and current.

Waterfront: A group of manmade structures designed to handle boats and ships.

Whale Killer: Also known as a *Whale Catcher*, a high-speed surface ship designed to hunt and kill whales, then hand the carcasses over to a larger *Factory Ship* for processing. Whale killers typically use grenade-tipped harpoon cannons to disable and kill their prey.

Wharf: A structure built along the shore of a harbor where boats and ships may dock while loading or unloading passengers or cargo.

Windward Passage: A strait in the Caribbean Sea between Cuba and Hispaniola. The passage is 50 miles wide and averages 5,600 feet in depth.

Zodiac: A rubber inflatable boat, equipped with an outboard motor. Used as a dinghy or runabout.

Zooplankton: Drifting clouds of marine and freshwater organisms that range in size. Some are microscopic. Some, such as copepods and jellyfish, are visible to the naked eye.

Zoosexual: A human being who engages in *Bestiality*, i.e. sex with non-human animals.

Made in the USA
Middletown, DE
13 November 2023

42621450R10308